"Until the sea runs dry."
-Merfolk oath

TO BRAVE THE DEEP

KINGSPORT CHRONICLES BOOK 2

C.H. CARTER

C.H. CARTER BOOKS

Paperback ISBN: 979-8-9888820-3-9

eBook ISBN: 979-8-9888820-2-2

Book Cover & Chapter Graphics by Maldo Designs – https://maldodesigns.com

Map Design by Cartographybird – https://www.cartographybird.com

Edited by Rowe Carenen – https://www.thebookconcierge.com/

First edition 2024

To everyone who read and loved *To Kiss the Sea*.

To everyone who couldn't wait for the story to continue.

This one's for you.

Notes & Content Warnings

Notes:

The full cast of characters, including name and birthplace pronunciations, can be found in the Index at the back of the book. (Seriously though, I'm not a stickler for name pronunciation, this is just how they sound in my head!)

The Kingsport Chronicles is a high **romantic fantasy** series, meaning it is a fantasy epic first and foremost with romantic subplots that develop over time for various characters. If you are looking for **fantasy romance**, or "romantasy", where the plot centers around the romance between characters set in a fantasy world, I understand this may not be the book for you.

The central romance of the series is most definitely a slow burn, but hopefully the romance fans will enjoy the dash of spice in book 2!

Content Warnings:

To Brave the Deep contains themes that may be distressing to some readers including serious injury, physical violence and bloodshed, character death (on and off page), child abandonment, drowning or near-drowning, mention of aquaphobia (fear of water), panic attacks (on page), parental manipulation, implied assault (off page), mention of coerced sex work (off page), consensual sex work (off page), and consensual sexual relationships (off page).

As much as I hope everyone who picks up this book will be able to read and enjoy the whole story, please be kind to yourselves.

CONTENTS

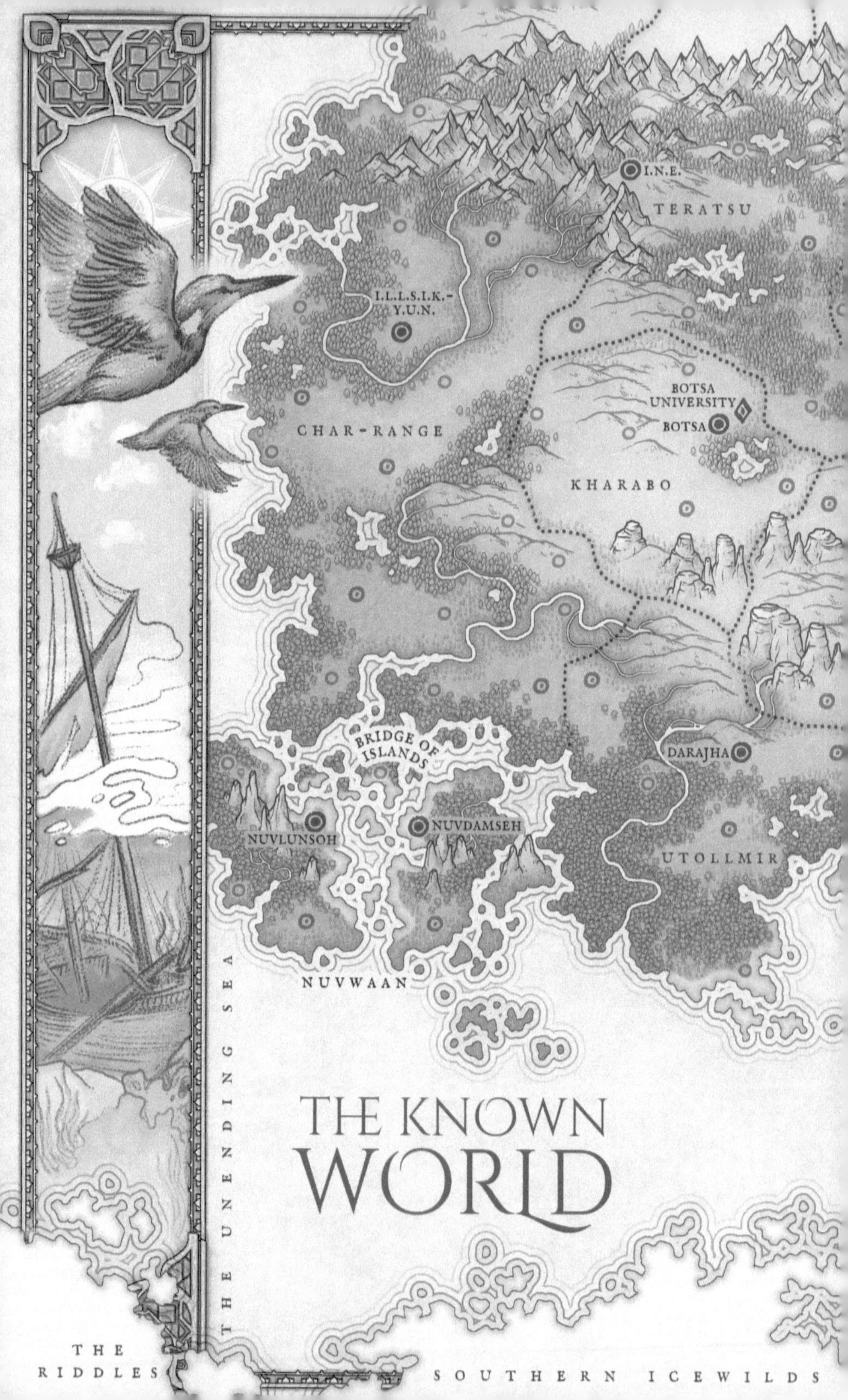

THE UNENDING SEA
I.N.E.
TERATSU
I.L.L.S.I.K.-Y.U.N.
BOTSA UNIVERSITY
BOTSA
CHAR-RANGE
KHARABO
BRIDGE OF ISLANDS
DARAJHA
NUVDAMSEH
NUVLUNSOH
UTOLLMIR
NUVWAAN
THE KNOWN WORLD
THE RIDDLES
SOUTHERN ICEWILDS

FRAOLLKIN FLEET
THE PASTURES
STRAIHORN
ZAVATLEO
FRAOLLAND
LAIVASTHO
FRAOLLISH TERRITORY
THE SPLIT SEA
LALESEIR
TJORDUN
MIDTHE
EHLAFI
SAPREA
BALAH
MUEVAT
AGRIYA
MEREDIA
PRAVIL
MYRRE
SAN AVETH
EAST TO THE BIRDE ISLES
THE SOUTHERN STRAIT

THE EASTERN SEA
THE BIRDE
ISLES
SWAN ISLAND
STONE QUARRY
SWANSPORT
INLAND FARMS
THE LIGHTHOUSE
TRADER'S BAY
GULL ISLAND
GULLSPORT
KINGSPORT HARBOR
KINGSPORT
SNAKE ISLAND
THE OLD SEAWALL
KINGFISHER MANOR
TEMPLE OF THE SEA
KINGFISHER ISLAND
TO THE CONTINENT
LEGEND
MAJOR SETTLEMENTS
MINOR SETTLEMENTS
LIGHTHOUSES
PIRATE CORRIDOR

ALLY

CHAPTER ONE

Time moved differently underwater.

Ally Kingfisher clung to that thought, even as she rode on the back of a sea creature that was not supposed to exist. A sailor's yarn come to life. A creature so old, or so forgotten, Ally had no name to call it by.

Whenever her mind wandered back to the places she wasn't ready to revisit, Ally would latch onto the riddle of time again and again. She imagined they were swimming through time itself, going backward. Before her mother was ransomed by pirates. Before Mama even left the Birde Isles. Ally would stop her from going, keep her safely on land.

Back before the threads of her friendship with Maher were stretched and frayed. Before he put himself in harm's way just to help her, and then their ship went down... She never could let herself finish that last part. Maher was waiting for her, somewhere; that was all she needed to know.

And what about Pasha? The trouble with going backward was knowing it would take Ally to a place where the mermaid was merely a character in Priestess Esa's stories. A mosaic in the Kingsport marketplace. A breath of sea air, and nothing more. Undoing it all would mean losing the time they'd had together. Ally wouldn't pretend they had a peaceful beginning, but something *had* shifted once she looked past Pasha the sharp-toothed and sharp-tongued mermaid, and saw Pasha the sensitive, lonely soul who wanted nothing more than a friend.

And for a brief moment, they *were* friends. It came on so gradually; Ally was so focused on her mother, she didn't realize what she had in Pasha until she'd pushed her away. Even as the mermaid was trying to make up for the century-long bargain that began their reluctant alliance, Ally had dismissed her out of hand. She'd hurt Pasha. Guilt burrowed under her skin and took root. When they found her, if they found her, it didn't matter if the mermaid agreed to help her again or not. Ally wasn't expecting anything from her. The chance to apologize would be enough. Almost enough.

There was no going backward, no matter what she imagined.

Ally's eyelids grew heavy, when had she last slept? Again she thought about time, or the lack thereof, beneath the sea.

It was the endless stretch of mottled blue on all sides. The constant brushing sensation of the current against her skin. The way the light never seemed to change at this depth. They were deep enough to blot out the sun yet contained in a bubble of light from the glowing orb attached to the creature's head by a long, flexible appendage.

Even the way the creature moved, steady and sure with no sign of fatigue, defied the laws of time as she knew them to be. They could have been traveling an hour, a day, or an entire year and still feel as if they hadn't moved at all.

Ally's face brushed the long, spiny fin in front of her and she jerked her head up. However long they'd been moving, she guessed the sea monster wouldn't be stopping to rest anytime soon. In her inside coat pocket, Ally felt the bulge of the jeweled necklace Pasha had brought to add to her mother's ransom, right before Ally turned on her. The mermaid's scent on the brocade pouch holding the priceless ornament was Ally's only hope the creature could locate Pasha. How far could she have gone in the days since Ally last saw her?

Working the drawstring from the pouch, Ally looped one end around the sharp end of one of the spines in the creature's fin and tied the other to her wrist. She stuffed the pouch and necklace back inside her coat. Giving the silken lifeline an experimental tug to ensure it wouldn't come undone, Ally wedged herself tighter into her place on the creature's back. At least if she slid off, the string might catch long enough for either of them to notice.

Pasha, can you hear me? Ally sent the tentative thought out into the sea as her eyes finally closed. She pressed a hand against the shark tooth hanging beneath her shirt. Warmth seeped into her chest and the tides rolled on.

Pasha?

CHAPTER TWO

*C*an you hear me?

Pasha woke with a gasp, her tail flinging up a thick cloud of sand into the water. It stung her eyes and nose, crunched between her sharp teeth. A small collection of fish bones swirled around her head like insects over a corpse; she batted them away.

She might as well have been dead, for all that she'd moved since finding the abandoned mermaid trove that became her hiding place. Each morning Pasha woke, thinking this would be the day she'd make the rest of the journey back to the islands. And each morning, the thought of returning to those empty caverns without Ally made her stomach twist until she gave up and stayed.

How many days had it been since they'd parted? Since Pasha had tossed a damned necklace at her and jumped from the ship like a coward? Ally was hurting. She was frightened for her mother. She'd just fought with her closest friend. And what had Pasha done?

You abandoned her.

Pasha sagged against the cave wall.

Left her alone, calling after you while you ran away.

"Swam away…"

A long-buried memory broke through the surface of Pasha's mind. Two centuries ago, when her own family left a confused, terrified child by herself to guard their home. She'd called after them too, at first, but one by one they swam through the tunnel leading out of the great cavern, until Pasha was alone.

And you're alone again, aren't you? The nasty voice, the one that had gone quiet the day Pasha and Ally began forming a kind of friendship, sneered at her.

"What took you so long?" she grumbled.

Pasha couldn't stay in the trove forever, she knew that. It was hardly large enough to fit two mermaids, assuming neither had a particularly long fluke. She was barely eating, only venturing far enough into the kelp forest outside to catch a few fish. And sleep? Sleep only came when she was too exhausted to fight it off. Every time she closed her eyes, the same nightmare played out. The cliff. Ally covered in blood and frost. The great-jawed shark tooth drained of the energy that had been sustaining Ally for years without her knowledge. Each time, Pasha tried to reach Ally on legs that wouldn't cooperate, over grass that sliced her feet like a thousand blades. And each time, Pasha was too late, too slow, too weak to stop Ally from falling backward over the cliff and into the sea.

Was this her life now? Her long, long, lonely life? Only seeing Ally in this one horrible dream?

Selfish, the voice chimed in. *Thinking only of yourself, as always. No regard for where Ally is now or what she's doing. Has she saved her mother? Are they safely home? Did the pirates slit her throat?*

"Stop!" Pasha curled inward, shaking her head so hard that a muscle in her neck pulled.

Don't worry. Surely she's home and well. Maybe she'll consider marrying her friend after all. Or find someone new.

"No no no!" Pasha's tail jerked, electric arcs raced across her skin. The sand around her trembled as more long-buried bones fought their way out. This had happened so many times, Pasha almost couldn't believe there were any bones left in the small cave to heed her call. They whirled and bounced around the trove, clanging against the moldering treasures left centuries ago by other mermaids.

You don't care. If you cared, you wouldn't have abandoned her. You broke the bargain.

"I *do* care. I broke the bargain *for* her. Everyone else in Ally's life took her choices away from her, I couldn't do that. I –"

You what? The voice prompted, speaking more softly than it ever had before. *Say it.*

"I... I care for her."

Care for her? Is that all?

"It's the truth."

Not entirely. Say it.

Pasha rubbed her palm over a sudden ache in her chest. "I *care* for her."

Coward.

Sitting up was difficult, her muscles ached and she needed a proper meal. It was time to leave the trove and go home, but she couldn't stay at home forever either. Not while knowing Ally was walking the land somewhere above her, never to see each other again.

Pasha needed to see home one more time, then she would leave. She'd leave Ally to live her life however she chose, because that's what Ally deserved. It didn't matter what Pasha wanted.

Building up her strength to leave would take some time. More importantly, Pasha still hadn't found something to trade for the mermaid spear she'd discovered that first night in the trove. It would be wrong to take it without leaving another treasure in return. After eating more fish in one sitting than she had in days, Pasha spent the remainder of the day tidying the small cave. The next morning Pasha began slowly circling the perimeter of the trove, her eyes and senses searching for something of value. She wasn't strong enough yet to send tendrils of energy out to search farther, and that's what it might take to make the trade happen.

After a fruitless search, Pasha went back to the trove around midday. Rest was what she really needed, but even her new sense of resolve couldn't chase away the nightmares. She'd settled down to attempt a nap, when a low humming sound thrummed through the rock around her. Pasha's ears perked up and she listened for it again. Only silence followed, maybe she'd imagined it. Her eyes slipped closed and Pasha tried to concentrate on the gentle sway of the kelp forest, the slow unending roll of the tides, the –

The entire rock formation shuddered around her as something large struck it from the outside. Bits of loose stone broke from the cave walls and skittered across the floor. Pasha clapped her hands over her ears as a bone-rattling growl rolled through the trove. Without thinking twice, Pasha grabbed the spear lying by her side. Whatever was out there, it was big and it wanted her attention.

Gripping the carved green stone of the spear with both hands, feeling the energy of its former owner pulsing from within, Pasha braced herself and swam out to face her visitor.

Chapter Three

Somehow, Ally managed to fall asleep and stay on the creature's back. When her eyes blinked open some time later, Ally found herself hunched over, cheek pressed into the webbing of the creature's spine. The pliant skin cradling Ally's head, rocking back and forth, was oddly comforting. As if sensing she was awake, its eel-like body gave a sharp flick, and they picked up speed. Ally sat up as the water rushed by, whipping her hair back and blurring everything around them. Maybe the creature had picked up Pasha's scent?

"Are we nearly there?" Ally thought the question might have been carried off with the current, but the creature gradually slowed until it was swimming at a more leisurely pace. They were in a deep part of the sea, most of their light coming from the orb attached to the creature's grayish-blue head. Ally tried to not look down too often into the ravines and crevices spread out beneath them, places that reached down farther than she could see. Maybe they went on forever, endless pits of nothingness.

Instead, Ally made a mental list of everything she needed. She needed to find Pasha. She needed food. Though she was hungry, *ravenous* even, she wasn't thirsty. Maybe the invisible gills Pasha gave her were keeping her thirst at bay? She needed a bandage for the cut on her hand, though the salt in the seawater had eased some of the discomfort in her palm.

The shark tooth around Ally's neck was heavy against her skin, it had kept her warm enough while the creature took them through the chilled water. Ally felt for the jeweled necklace and its pouch, both were still inside her coat. If they couldn't find Pasha, which was a possibility Ally forced herself to acknowledge, she could pry the jewels from their settings and use them to purchase necessities from the closest port. And food. So much food. Why had Ally never asked Pasha to point out some things that were safe to eat down here?

Before too long, the creature changed direction and swam out of the fissure they'd been traveling through since Ally woke. Shafts of light blazed through the sea from somewhere above, the water sparkled and fractured into a dozen shades of blue. They crested a ridge, and Ally blinked as a shimmering, teeming kelp forest stretched out before them.

Are we close to land? Ally's hold on the creature's fin loosened, her fingers stiff from clinging to its back for so long. They might be at the far end of the kelp forest, but they tended to grow in shallower water. Something to do with how deep the stalks could take root and still trap sunlight from the surface. Tilting her head back, Ally could just make out where the tops of the giant algae touched the place where the water met the air. They were swimming low, through the forest floor. Schools of fish changed direction and other, more solitary, sea creatures darted out of their path. None wanted to be caught in the monster's shadow, let alone within reach of her overlapped jaws. Even the prickly sea urchins clinging to the kelp holdfasts seemed to strain their spines in the opposite direction. Ally had a feeling her new companion didn't travel into the shallows very often.

They dipped down into a gently sloping valley, where the kelp stalks cleared out a bit and a crop of rock spires rose up from a deeper drop beyond the forest. Stopping in front of the spires, the creature's nostrils flared and a low, grating sound vibrated from beneath Ally's legs. Was that a growl?

When nothing happened, the creature whipped around and Ally seized a fin to keep from losing her seat.

"A little warning would be nice," she muttered.

Bringing its narrowed tail around, the creature banged twice against the rock and growled again, louder and more insistent this time. Ally winced as the sound reverberated through the forest, scattering the fish who'd grown brave enough to creep up behind them.

They circled around and were facing the rocks again when Pasha appeared from a narrow opening in the widest point of a spire, a black-bladed spear at the ready.

Ally's heart all but leapt into her throat, every muscle in her body tensed. Her vision narrowed until the mermaid was all she could see. She was afraid to blink, lest this turn out to be nothing but a hallucination from lack of food and sleep. They'd really found her, they'd found Pasha. Ally wanted to kiss the sea monster, giant teeth and all.

When Pasha spoke her voice was lower, huskier than Ally'd heard before. "Why are you here?"

The blunt question stung, but Ally worked up the courage to reply anyway. Before she could, the sea monster rumbled deep in its rib cage and Ally realized Pasha wasn't speaking to her. Could she even see Ally from her place between the creature's back fins? Gently, she nudged its side with her heel. Taking the hint, the creature swerved its massive head to the side so the mermaid could see her.

"Why are you here?" she said again. "This isn't your territory..." Pasha trailed off as she finally spotted Ally latched onto the creature's back. The mermaid's mouth dropped open and her arms went lax.

Ally's grip tightened on the spiny fin in front of her. "Hello Pasha."

CHAPTER FOUR

Esa looked up from the leatherbound text she'd been reading aloud to find herself alone. Again.

The little lady of the house had slipped away in the middle of her lessons. And Esa knew exactly where she'd toddled off to: the statuary hall just off from the manor library. With a heavy sigh, Esa closed the history tome and stretched, then made her way to a back corner door hidden behind a freestanding bookshelf.

Perhaps three years old was too young for the girl to begin her lessons; her brothers didn't start until they were five or six, but Lady Kingfisher had insisted. As Esa suspected, the door to the statuary hall was propped open with one of the books from the bottom shelf. Smart girl.

"Where are you, child?" Esa's voice echoed down the corridor lined with metal and marble sentries.

Candlelight flickered off their faces, making them almost look alive. The tapers in this hall were always lit in case any of the family chose to pay their respects. The other Kingfisher children avoided the place entirely. Esa couldn't decide if it frightened them or they simply weren't interested. She passed smaller statues of sea turtles, eels, and swirling schools of fish. Gradually, the creatures grew larger – sharks, dolphins, baby whales –

then they became things of legend, great serpents, and giant squid, sea monsters whose names had been long forgotten but whose stone teeth were still as sharp as the day they were carved. Finally, there were two stoic figures flanking the end of the hall. Merfolk. The early people of these islands were said to be descended from those powerful half-human creatures. They were fixed with thick spears in their hands, guarding the oldest statue in Kingsport: The Goddess of the Sea.

She was carved by the first people who settled in the Birde Isles. Her face had long been worn away by time and the elements, but the rest of her body was remarkably well-preserved once she was moved inside.

The goddess' left hand was open, palm up, as if she were offering a blessing to those who stood before her. It was her right hand, indeed her entire right arm, which spoke of the power she possessed. In place of that arm was a powerful tentacle, curled at the end to draw the attention of all the sea creatures that gathered at her feet.

Carved into the base of the statue, beneath the captivated creatures, were the words the priestesses recited every day: **You cannot take what the sea is not willing to give.**

A tiny face peeked out at her from behind the base of the statue. Round cheeks flushed and wide eyes bright with the excitement of evading her tutor once again.

"Alphonsine, you know you mustn't run off like this," the priestess scolded gently.

The child giggled at her from beneath a mop of brown curls. Her maids had given up on weaving through many of the ribbons and charms most girls her age wore in their hair. Alphonsine was constantly touching and tugging them out to wrap the ribbons around her fingers. At the moment, a silver seahorse attached to a cornflower blue ribbon was dangling precariously next to her face.

Alphonsine looked more and more like her mother every day. She'd have the same sun-kissed complexion and Bahlan aquiline nose. Even the Kingfisher moss green eyes she was born with had steadily darkened to a burnt hazel.

Sitting down on the floor, Esa arranged her pale blue robes around her crossed legs. "Would you like to continue our lesson here?"

"Yes, Esa! Yes!" Alphonsine tumbled out from behind the statue and threw herself into Esa's lap.

Esa smiled and situated the child so she was facing the goddess. Something about this statue had drawn Alphonsine to it nearly every day since she'd learned to walk on her own. The elder priestesses believed the child was perhaps meant to serve the goddess in some way, but Esa doubted whether the Kingfishers would wish for their only daughter to follow that path.

For now, Esa had two tasks before her. The first: teach the child all that she could. The second: keep her away from the sea. A child born on an island, and she wasn't allowed to even set foot on the shore. Head Priestess Aithne had been so sure, so adamant the vision she received during the month of Alphonsine's birth was true, that the child would only know misery if she went near the sea before she came of age, Lord and Lady Kingfisher eventually agreed to keep their daughter on land for the time being. That seemed to placate Aithne for now, though the elder priestess still reminded Esa constantly of their charge from the goddess.

"Now, where were we?" Esa pushed another of Alphonsine's loose ribbons out from under her nose. "The first people of the Birde Isles, yes?"

Alphonsine nodded, her eyes locked on the faded face of the goddess.

Esa's hold around the child tightened. Something told her it was going to be difficult to keep the youngest Kingfisher away from the sea.

PASHA

CHAPTER FIVE

Ally was here, really here. Somehow, in the vastness of the sea, Ally had found Pasha and was riding on the back of a...

"Hello, Pasha," Ally said softly.

"Hello," Pasha rasped, worried she was dreaming again, that this wasn't real and the moment she tried to get close, it would all disappear. She wanted to embrace her, to hold Ally and convince herself that this was real. Even just touching her hand would be enough, but Pasha kept her fingers locked around the spear.

"I'm... I'm glad we found you."

"I see you've made a new friend," Pasha's brow ridges rose. "Though I must admit, I'm surprised she came to you. She can be... mercurial in nature. A bit testy, even."

"She?" Ally slid off the creature's back, face scrunching as she stretched out her legs. "I'm not entirely sure I want to know how you can tell."

"It's the light. The males of her kind don't have them." Pasha nodded at the orb hanging on its lever, now barely glowing in the sunlight streaming through the water. "She doesn't come out of the deep often. We were always told to leave plenty of space if we ever encountered her."

"Because she might hurt you?" Ally glanced back at the rows of teeth that hovered by her head.

"Out of respect," Pasha bowed to the creature who regarded the mermaid carefully with one opaque eye, as if Ally were under her charge and Pasha might still prove to be a threat. "She's very old. She was old when the elders in my community were hatchlings."

"That's good to know." Ally looked as if she were about to swim closer but stopped herself.

The hope that had begun to lift in Pasha's chest dropped. "Why are you here, Ally? Why aren't you with your friend and your mother?"

"I know I have no right to ask for it but," Ally's face paled and she wrapped one hand over her stomach, using the other to brace herself against the creature's side. "Pasha, I need your help."

CHAPTER SIX

"Mama is still with the pirates and Maher..." Ally choked back the sob that had lodged in her throat from the moment she saw the *Pike* go down with Maher on board. "I'm sure he's dead. Everyone from the ship is probably dead, and if I'd listened to you, they might still be alive. It was a trap, just like you said it could be. Dare ambushed us." Ally swam as close as she dared, keenly aware of the strange spear Pasha held. "I've been angrier this summer than I've been in my entire life. Angry with my family for hiding Gaius I's bargain and doing nothing to bring me out of my fear of the sea; that I'd been too afraid to go with Mama on that voyage and wasn't with her when the pirates attacked; even with Maher because, for the first time, it felt like our friendship was fracturing and I couldn't stop it." She breathed deep, willing the cool rush over her neck to slow her down.

But the words had tumbled out as if she were afraid she wouldn't get to the most important part before she ran out of time and Pasha sent her away. The apology. "The night you caught up to the ship, I took all of that out on you and I'm so sorry. You didn't deserve that, and I should have trusted you, Pasha. I'm sorry, you have no idea how much."

Several heartbeats passed between them, then Pasha said, "Tell me what happened."

Treading water between the mermaid and the sea monster, Ally told her. She told Pasha everything that took place from the time of their argument to finding her here. Even the bizarre reaction from the shark tooth, burning an imprint into her skin after Pasha left the *Pike*.

Ally rubbed her chest, where the mark from the tooth no longer pained her but was still etched into her skin. "I thought it meant you'd taken back your gift, that I wouldn't be able to breathe underwater anymore."

She drew back slightly, hurt flashing through her dark eyes. "I wouldn't have done that to you."

"I know that, now."

When Ally recounted the ambush by the pirate fleet and the weapon hidden inside the *Maiden's Revenge*, Pasha hissed. "The charges that thing creates must have been what confused the whales. Even when not in use, it must send small pulses around the ship."

Ally described every detail of the sinking of the *Pike* but found herself skipping over Captain Dare's real identity and the threats she'd made against Pasha. It somehow felt that admitting the connection would make everything so much worse, that Pasha would turn her away the moment she revealed that part of the tale. The mermaid's expression darkened when Ally mentioned her attempted attack on the captain and being thrown overboard. Then her face smoothed out and Pasha said nothing.

"This is all my fault. I thought I could do this all on my own, and I can't." Ally swallowed thickly as she finished her story, unable to look at Pasha any longer. She stared at the places where the nearest kelp stalks rooted into the sand instead. Tiny cramps pinched at the muscles of her legs and hips, she needed to stop, to rest.

Maybe Pasha would forgive her. Maybe she'd even understand why Ally'd behaved the way she did on the *Pike*. But why would Pasha want to involve herself again? There was nothing tying them together any longer, no reason for Pasha to put herself back in harm's way. Ally screwed her eyes shut, blocking out the horrible images of whatever Dare had planned if she caught Pasha. She had to tell Pasha the truth. By some miracle, if she agreed to help Ally again, it couldn't be without the whole story.

"You're swimming on your own," said Pasha, slowly drifting closer. "You survived out in the open ocean on your own. You even called one of the mightiest creatures from the darkest depths of the sea and *rode* her here, to find me. It's not your fault that captain is a liar. Nothing she does is your fault, Ally."

Ally's head shot up. "You... you're not angry with me?" Her legs and arms stilled, and she started to sink. Pasha used her tail fins to pop the bottoms of Ally's feet and push her back into motion.

"You were clearly upset and I left without giving you the chance to tell me what you really wanted." Her hands flexed around the spear, the green stone sparked beneath her fingers.

"So, you forgive me?" Ally asked, voice small and hating that she still felt so unsure.

"Of course," Pasha's dark eyes held hers and warmth that had nothing to do with the shark tooth bloomed in Ally's chest, "and I hope you can forgive me."

"Pasha, I –" Ally's stomach growled, loud enough that even the sea monster tilted her head and made an answering rumble. Her face warmed, but Pasha only gave a half-smile and shook her head.

"When was the last time you had something to eat?"

"I'm not sure," Ally admitted. "I'm not even sure how long I've been down here."

Pasha glanced at the ancient creature, then back to Ally. "Come inside. You can rest while I find you some food."

Ally ate so much kelp Pasha eventually made her stop before she became sick. The slippery, chewy leaves didn't taste like much, not with the seawater going into her mouth with them, but her stomach recognized them as food easily enough. While Ally waited in the trove, sitting on her hands to keep herself from picking up any of the ancient contents and breaking some kind of mermaid etiquette, Pasha went out and hunted for something more filling than seaweed. She returned sometime later with an armful of various shellfish, including some Ally had never seen before.

"I thought this might be easier for you than raw fish." Pasha located a knife in the trove, a once-beautiful thing with a gilt handle that had flaked and peeled over time, and used it to crack the shells open. Ally tried to convince herself this would be just like the oysters Maher bought in the Kingsport market. It wasn't, not quite. The first mollusk didn't go down easily, and Ally had to hold her mouth shut until it did. Pasha offered to find something else, but Ally shook her head. There wasn't much time, and she needed all the strength she could get. Ally ate every one of the shellfish, grit and all.

They were cleaning up when Ally forced the words out, "There's something else I need to tell you."

"What's that?" Pasha swept the last of the empty shells out of the cave. Daylight was fading, but the spear leaning against the rock wall behind Pasha had gradually taken on a soft glow, not unlike the corals living beneath Kingfisher Island.

"It's about Captain Dare," Ally shuddered, seeing that scornful green gaze in her mind's eye. Pasha still hadn't said whether she'd help or not and deserved to know exactly who they were dealing with. "I don't know how, but she knows about you, who you are, and…"

"And?" Pasha prompted.

Ally braced herself, ready for Pasha to refuse her once the whole story was out. "She's my aunt."

CHAPTER SEVEN

Pasha's head tilted. "Your aunt? Your mother was kidnapped by her own sister?"

"Not my mother's sister. My father's."

Pasha's dark eyes widened as the meaning of Ally's words sank in. "She was one of the baby girls your great-grandfather sent away because of the bargain he made with me."

Ally nodded quickly. "I don't know where she's been all this time or what brought her to this, but yes."

"I did," the mermaid whispered. "I brought her to this. If it weren't for me, she'd never have been sent away in the first place. None of them would have been sent away." Tiny arcs of energy skipped down Pasha's arms. "I started this."

Ally pushed off the cave floor and nearly collided with her. "That's not what I was saying at all."

Pasha looked up; this was the closest Ally had gotten since she arrived with the creature still waiting out in the kelp forest. The glow from the spear brought out the flecks of green in Ally's eyes. "Your mother is in danger because of me, Ally."

"You might have made that deal with Gaius, but he's the one who decided to send his own family away, you didn't do that. And you didn't make Captain Dare take Mama or hurt Maher. You told me nothing Dare does is my fault, and you were right. But it's not your fault either."

Sharp nails dug into Pasha's palms, close to drawing blood. Ally's hands covered hers and a stray arc leapt between them.

"Ah! That stings," Ally took one hand back and Pasha saw a fresh cut running across her palm.

"How did this happen?" Pasha took Ally's wrist. The wound itself had clotted, but the skin around the cut was swollen and hot to the touch.

"It, uh, happened when I was thrown off the ship," Ally's breath hitched as Pasha probed the inflamed skin. The second pass of Pasha's thumb over her palm was gentler. "I felt my necklace slip off and grabbed the sharp end of the tooth."

"I wish you'd mentioned it sooner," she huffed out a small laugh. "No wonder that creature waiting outside heard your call. You gave her a blood signal to follow."

"Blood signal?"

"It's supposed to be a distress call, the elders in my shoal taught it to the humans back when they were playing goddess." Pasha glanced at the cave opening. "She must have thought you were a mermaid calling for help."

Ally flexed her fingers. "It's healing faster than I expected."

"The saltwater helps," Pasha sighed, her chest constricting. "I felt it, I think, when you hit the water. Maybe I even felt the call you sent out but was too far away to recognize it for what it was. I had this dream, this nightmare, you were..." She blinked hard, and a silvery tear welled up in the corner of her eye.

"Don't cry, please, there's no need." Ally tried to wipe it away.

"Let me," Pasha gently pushed her uninjured hand down. The tear slipped free, a liquid pearl rolling down her face, and she felt Ally's pulse quicken beneath her fingers. Mermaids didn't cry easily. When the heavy tear reached the middle of her cheek, Pasha drew closer, pressing her face into Ally's palm. She heard the fizzle as it soaked into the wound.

Reluctant to let go, Pasha let Ally pull her hand back. A trail of foaming bubbles hung between them as the cut healed completely.

Ally gawked at the thin scar. Pasha couldn't help remembering the young priestess who'd worn a similar expression so many years ago. The night the humans woke her from a long sleep and Pasha pretended to be their sea goddess. "I think we should stay here tonight and gather what we can in the morning. I have to find something to trade for the spear." She'd briefly explained the trove rules before going to find Ally something edible.

"Hmm?" Ally was still looking at her hand. "Oh, I have something you can leave." Fishing around inside her coat, she handed Pasha a familiar brocade pouch. The top gaped open, but the necklace she'd taken from the ship was still inside.

"Are you sure?"

"Absolutely, Dare isn't even interested in the ransom. It was just another detail in her plan to hurt the Isles," Ally trailed off. "Did you say we?"

"Yes, *we* are going to get your mother back."

Ally threw her arms around Pasha's neck. The pouch went flying and Pasha braced a hand on the cave wall to stop them from tumbling over. Her other arm flailed until she wrapped it around Ally's waist.

"Thank you, Pasha. Thank you, thank you." She drew back only far enough to take Pasha's face in her hands. Those beautiful, not-quite-green eyes shining at her.

Then, Ally's lips were on hers. It lasted only a moment, not even a full breath passed before Ally released her and went to retrieve the jeweled necklace from wherever it had landed. Pasha couldn't have cared less about the wayward jewels.

When Ally returned, she put the pouch with the rest of the treasures and resumed her seat across the cave. They might as well have been on opposite ends of the great cavern in Pasha's home.

"So, mermaids and sea monsters are real," Ally's smile was tentative, but she said nothing about the kiss. "Anyone else I should know about?"

Pasha blinked slowly, coming out of the daze the kiss had sent her to. "Oh, I'd say there are quite a few someones you should know about." She let go of the wall and sank to the floor. "In fact, I have an idea. You've given us a good start, but if we're going to take on a pirate fleet, we're going to need more help."

FORAOISE

Chapter Eight

Captain Foraoise Dare stood on the deck of the *Maiden's Revenge*, green eyes trained on the empty horizon.

A casual observer might assume she was seasick with how tightly she gripped the railing, knuckles blanched white and fingernails digging into the worn wood.

Foraoise snorted, she hadn't been seasick since the day Jon brought her onto the ship. It wouldn't have done for the captain's betrothed to be green around the gills. Even less so when he made her third in command under Swain, shortly after they were wed. Foraoise had *willed* herself not to be sick. Willed herself to learn every task on board, the name and purpose of every last piece of the ship, faster than any other member of the crew expected of a girl who'd spent the first nineteen years of her life on land.

Had she done it to please Jon? At first, maybe. Soon after, she'd realized it was really to earn the respect of the crew. A captain or officer wouldn't keep their posts long without the crew's backing. Swain took her under his wing, as it were, as Jon became more occupied with his dealings with the Meredians. And even Captain Jon Dare was impressed with how quickly Foraoise infixed herself into life on the ship, the daily operations of the vessel. Her adopted mother's training in the running of a household had proven useful after all. To no one's surprise more than Foraoise.

A sailor hauling a line of rope took pains to give the captain a wide berth as he passed. Trotting by as quickly as he could with such a cumbersome burden.

Foraoise took a deep pull of sea air, let the salt and spray sting her nose and leave the familiar bitter taste at the back of her throat. It was good to have the crew's respect, sure enough. But as time went by, she'd learned it was even better to earn their fear.

Three days.

It had been three days since she'd sent that little chit into the depths. Three days they'd idled and waited for some sign her gamble would pay its dues. The machine below decks needed repair; that last demonstration had blown one of the cables clean out of its mooring. But the materials they needed were all on land. So said the sailors they'd pressed into service from the machine's first transport.

The scar wrapping around one side of her skull itched, the phantom blow of Jon's blade rising to the surface like it always did when she was agitated. Though Foraoise wouldn't allow herself to touch the shaved side of her head. She wouldn't give Jon the satisfaction.

Three days of waiting and still nothing out of the ordinary had presented itself.

Wrenching her hands from the rail, the captain stalked the length of the deck. Sailors scurried out of her path, none daring to make eye contact. They'd watched their captain's mood darken with each passing day. She reached the hatch leading belowdecks and practically leapt down the short stack of steps.

If I've killed my niece ahead of schedule for nothing, Foraoise thought grimly, *my dear letter-writing friend will be losing a few fingers once we meet face to face. Maybe then they'll think twice about spinning stories of mermaids and sea goddesses.*

The sailor guarding the section of the ship that housed the brig snapped to attention when she saw the captain.

"Do all of the prisoners still live?"

"Aye Captain," she tapped the key ring on her belt. "Just checked them two bells ago."

Foraoise held out a hand, and the keys were hastily placed in her palm. "Stay here."

Moving into the near-lightless hold, Foraoise took up a lantern and picked her way to the iron cage built against one wall. A dozen or so bodies were packed inside. All survivors of the *Pike* plucked from the sea. Only one appeared to be of much value as a hostage and was the worst injured by far. Stepping close to the gate, Foraoise held the lantern high and rapped the key ring against the bars.

"Show a leg, sailor," she barked.

Shoulders tensed and shadows flinched. The former first mate of the sunken ship stood slowly, towering over the captain. A barrel-chested Char-range man stood next to her, the rest watched warily.

"Is he awake?"

The tall woman pushed a handful of disheveled, blood-caked braids off one shoulder. "No, the fever still has him. If you would only give us medical supplies –"

"So you can share them among the rest? Hardly."

"What would you have us do, then?" the man growled.

Foraoise looked past them at the lanky figure slumped against the hull of the ship. Coal black hair fell limply across his forehead, a makeshift bandage was wrapped around his left shoulder. Despite the cool dampness of the hold, she could make out the sheen of sweat on his brow, the gray pallor creeping over the dark brown skin of his face.

"I expect you to keep him alive," the captain sneered. "If you can't, I'll put the rest of what remains of your crew back where I found them."

PASHA

Chapter Nine

*P*asha had only been close to land a few times, had only been allowed to split her tail and walk on the sand once. And now the elders had forbidden any mermaid from their shoal to leave the sea at all.

Yet, here she was, cautiously making her way through the shallows, following the faint trail of energy Pallagia had left in her wake. She'd been in such a hurry, she hadn't bothered to mask the unique signature they all carried. Pasha couldn't imagine what her older sister was up to, but this was the third time in as many days that Pallagia had sneaked out of their home in broad daylight.

Pausing, Pasha carefully flexed her tail until just the top of her head cleared the surface. The afternoon sun glanced off the water; Pasha blinked hard to clear her vision. The trail had led her to the side of the big island where gray cliffs rose out of the water, the sandy shore narrowing until it disappeared altogether.

Sitting on a low rock jutting up from the last strip of beach, was a young human woman. The sea breeze lifted her long golden hair and plucked at the cloak wrapped around her shoulders. In her lap she held something too small for Pasha to make out what it was. Pallagia's trail had faded here. Where was she?

Pasha's fingers twitched, erratic sparks of energy pulled from the water around her to dance across her skin.

"Ealasaid." Pallagia's husky voice bounded off the cliffs and Pasha skittered back deeper into the waves. She scanned the water but couldn't find her sister anywhere. The human on the rock turned, obviously she'd heard it too, and Pasha followed her gaze down to the point where the beach blended into the cliffside.

Pallagia stood there, tail nowhere in sight, knee-deep in the surf. Her fern green hair was pulled over one shoulder, silvery skin and emerald scales glistened in the sunlight.

Move! *Pasha wanted to scream at her.* What was she thinking, letting that human see her?

"Ealasaid," Pallagia said again, bracing one hand on the stone and raising the other in greeting.

What was that? Eal-ah-saych? What did that mean? Pasha's eyes darted back to the human, expecting her to already be running back up the beach in fright. But instead, she was... smiling? Pallagia started towards her and Pasha held her breath as the woman slid off the rock and waited on the sand. Next thing Pasha knew, they were locked in a tight embrace. No hesitation or fear, as if they'd done it a thousand times before.

Breathing in too fast, Pasha sputtered and choked when too much water went down her throat. She ducked beneath the waves so they wouldn't hear her coughing it back up.

What's happening? How does Pallagia even know a human?

Finally back under control, Pasha slowly lifted her head to the surface again. They were still holding each other, though they'd moved into the shade of the cliff. She couldn't hear what was being said, but Pallagia clearly knew this woman very well. Their hands were constantly moving, touching each other's face, hair, and arms as they talked.

Pasha suddenly felt like she shouldn't be there, she was obviously intruding on a private moment. The woman gave the small bundle she'd brought to Pallagia. Even from a distance, Pasha could see the joy on her sister's face when she unwrapped the cloth. Then Pallagia was kissing the woman, and Pasha quickly retreated farther out to sea.

Some of this made sense now. Pallagia was in love. In all of Pasha's life, she'd never seen her sister form a romantic attachment to anyone. It wasn't that unusual; mermaids lived for so long many chose not to pursue serious partnerships. Still, there were plenty of mermaids who'd tried to woo her, but Pallagia had never shown any interest. Even Pasha could see this human had to be special, but none of that explained how they could have met in the first place.

Pasha gnawed the inside of her cheek hard enough to draw a drop of blood. She wished now she hadn't followed Pallagia. One look at Pasha's face later and her sister would know something was bothering her.

And what would the elders do if they found out? Pasha wouldn't say anything, but how long could Pallagia keep this a secret? Someone else from the shoal was bound to notice how often she left the caves alone.

Swimming faster, Pasha headed for the nearest tunnel leading into the caverns beneath the island. Maybe there was something she could do to help. Pallagia had always been there for her, even when many of the others began avoiding Pasha after learning she could speak to bones. Even when they warned visitors from other shoals to steer clear, Pallagia would ensure they greeted Pasha just like everyone else. When Pallagia was old enough to move out into her own chamber, she'd gladly stayed in the one they shared, so Pasha wouldn't be alone.

Pasha loved her sister, and Pallagia deserved happiness outside of the little world they shared.

Corals lit up to greet her as she reached the mouth of the tunnel.

"Hello," Pasha whispered to the glowing creatures. "Would you like to help me with something?"

Chapter Ten

"Are you certain this is the right place?"

Pasha nodded slowly; eyes trained on the jagged cave mouth in front of them.

They'd come down into one of the deep-sea trenches Ally passed in her search for Pasha. The walls of these crevices were riddled with hiding places, small and large, secret openings, and lairs. Pasha wasn't positive which deep-sea predators lived in this particular den, but they'd soon find out. And it was indeed a predator's den. The smell hit her long before the opening was visible. Death. Decay. Despair. The hint of blood seemed to linger in the water around the edges of the cave, seeping out from inside. They could only see it now thanks to the light from Ally's creature – Pasha still couldn't think of what her kind was once called, she could very well be the last one. But she'd clearly adopted the young human woman who'd managed to call her up from a place far deeper than this.

That thought both intrigued and worried Pasha. How attached would the creature become? Enough to follow Ally home and hunt in the waters around the islands? The humans would surely panic. Ally'd explained when they first met, it seemed so long ago now, that humans didn't really believe in any of the old, mythical creatures anymore. Why would they, when those that were left had gone into hiding long before Pasha was born? As a youngling, Pasha had asked each elder in her shoal the same question: Why? Why tuck themselves away when they once ruled entire seas? Most told her it was simply the way things were, that their day was over. She needed to know what to do in case she ever met one of the old ones, which to greet and which to avoid if she valued her life. But it was unlikely she'd ever come across any of them.

If only the elders could see where Pasha was now.

A sensation not unlike a crab grabbing onto her insides with its claws had settled into the pit of Pasha's stomach. It told her this was probably the home of a creature she was meant to avoid. In fact, she was certain of it. But they had no time to search for friendlier predators. Ally's new friend could guide them back to where she found Ally, but where to go from there? The sea was vast. The farther that pirate ship sailed, the harder they'd be to track down, even with help. This place was the first response she'd gotten after sending tendrils of energy out to search for energies close to her own.

At the very least, Pasha knew Ally would be protected from whatever came out of that cave. The opal-eyed creature had already tucked her behind one wide side fin.

Quit stalling. Pasha adjusted her grip on the spear, flexed her pelvic fins. Energy pulsed through the green stone; the former owner of the spear would probably not approve of what Pasha was about to do with it.

"Pasha," Ally murmured. "Be careful."

The massive creature shielding her rumbled in what might have been agreement. Or perhaps she didn't care if Pasha acted rashly, as long as nothing happened to Ally.

Drawing in a charge from the water around them, Pasha focused until the arcs gathered over her fingers and climbed up to the point of the spear's black blade. When she had a ball of white energy the size of her fist, Pasha used the spear to send it floating into the cave.

The ball met a brief force of resistance, then stilled in place. Puzzled, she scanned the rock for some kind of barrier but saw nothing. With a grunt, Pasha thrust the spear again, pushing even more energy behind it. Whatever had blocked her the first time stretched, and stretched, and then Pasha broke through. The ball sailed into the darkness, a signal that they meant the occupants no harm.

Hopefully, the occupants were feeling equally as cordial.

Several long moments went by before Ally peeked over the top of the fin, "Maybe no one is home. Let's try another..." she trailed off when a pair of dark red eyes appeared in the shadows of the cave. They slowly blinked once, twice, as if their owner had just woken from a deep slumber. They lazily scanned the massive creature behind her, before settling on Pasha.

"Hmmm," the rasping, rattling voice turned Pasha's insides to ice. "What brings you here, little mermaid?"

"We..." every instinct was screaming at Pasha to get away, to take Ally and never return to this place again. Instead, she gave a stilted bow, hugging the spear close. "We've come to you in need of a favor, ancient one."

"A favor?" The creature lingered on the word as if savoring the taste. "It's been several lifetimes since one of your kin came asking for favors. That bargain did not end so well for those involved."

My kin? Pasha pushed the question away, along with the creeping sensation that she'd said something similar once.

Pasha kept her voice steady, even as her heart pounded in her chest. "We are short on time, ancient one. There is a group of humans that threaten land and sea alike, we want to stop them. Will you help us?"

"Would this help you seek require leaving this place?"

What other kind of help did the den dweller think she was asking for? There was nothing blocking it in here, no stones or bars or spaces too small to pass through.

It made no sense.

Then a long-forgotten lesson leapt to the front of her mind: Many of the ancient sea creatures thrived on making deals, intentionally seeking them out even when they needed nothing. Maybe that was why the offer of a bargain had come so easily to her the night she met Gaius I. If this creature needed her confirmation to continue, that was easy enough to give.

Pasha nodded.

The eyes closed, blotting out any hint of the location of the creature. Even Pasha's sharp eyesight was useless at this depth. Unable to control her tail any longer, Pasha's fluke flipped hard enough to back her farther away from the cave.

When the eyes returned, a second pair opened alongside them. Then a third. And a fourth. Soon, Pasha was faced with no less than ten sets of shrewd, blood-red eyes. And the feeling that she'd just made a very big mistake.

A deep, tooth-grinding growl echoed out from the lair. With it came a fresh wave of death, clouding the water and making Pasha feel sick. Ally gasped sharply from her hiding place.

"We accept."

CHAPTER ELEVEN

"What *were* those things?" Ally asked the moment they were clear of the trench.

"I'm not sure what it would be in any human language; they could have been snapjaws. That's what my sister called them. But I've never seen one before."

That explanation brought Ally no comfort.

Pasha was swimming high enough to see her on the sea monster's back. Although, Ally was coming to think of the creature less and less as a monster. Especially after encountering those things, the snapjaws.

"She needs a name," Ally said, mostly to herself.

"Who does?"

Patting the smooth, thick skin of the creature's side, Ally shrugged. "I'm tired of calling her a creature and calling her a monster feels insulting."

The mermaid glanced back at the long, eel-like body weaving behind them. "I've tried to remember, but I still don't know the name of her kind, it's lost."

"Then we'll have to think of something." Ally worried her bottom lip as she turned several names over in her head, none seemed right. They needed something musical, something that matched the creature's gentle nature, in such stark contrast to her appearance. Looking up, she caught Pasha's black eyes focused on the place where her teeth met flesh. Slowly, she let go of her lip. "Where are we going now?"

"What?" Pasha said, blinking rapidly. "I mean, I need to send out another signal to know that. I wanted to put some distance between us and that lair first."

"I see." She knew the mermaid wouldn't bring it up, not when so much was at stake and they only had so much time to catch up to Dare's ship.

But Ally thought about it, the kiss. It wasn't planned, and she wasn't the type of person to kiss someone else without asking their permission first. Yet Ally'd been so overcome – being thrown overboard, thinking she was going to die. The deaths of every soul on her brother's ship, losing Maher, losing Mama all over again. Accidentally calling the sea creature and managing to find Pasha again. And the tear. Like a drop of pure magic on Pasha's cheek. It was cool and silky against Ally's palm; the bubbles tickled her skin as the cut healed before her eyes. All the time they'd spent together, and Ally still knew so little about Pasha. How magical she truly was.

At that moment, in that tiny cave, kissing Pasha felt like the most natural thing in the world. The moment their lips touched, Ally came back to herself and gave Pasha space. Hoping she hadn't just squandered the newfound peace between them. Pasha didn't seem angry. She was stunned, spectacularly so, but not angry or even upset. Just stunned.

It didn't occur to Ally until later, while they tried to catch a few hours of sleep before departing the trove, that it might've been Pasha's first kiss.

She was so young when the other mermaids left her alone beneath the Isles. And Ally was the only human Pasha'd gotten to know, she'd said so herself. There was no one else. For all of Pasha's teasing when she revealed it would take a kiss to bestow the gift of breathing underwater, this was very different. Ally had a chance to refuse. Those three slight kisses were placed on her neck for a purpose.

The realization hit so hard that Ally's cheeks flamed and she sat up to check if Pasha was truly asleep, or if she too was worrying over what Ally had done. But the mermaid was dead to the world. She'd mentioned something about having nightmares before Ally found her but wouldn't elaborate beyond that. The guilt Ally felt over stealing that moment, then pulling away before Pasha had a chance to react, was burning a hole through her chest. Ally had to apologize, and the longer they went without talking about it, the harder it would become.

"What about Euphonia?" Pasha startled Ally out of her thoughts.

"Pardon?"

"Euphonia. For a name."

"Euphonia." Ally leaned around to glimpse the side of the creature's head. "Do you like that?"

A low croon was her answer and, despite the daunting tasks still on the horizon, Ally smiled.

ALLY

CHAPTER TWELVE

"Goddess save me!" Ally balked and grabbed Pasha's arm when she saw the next creature turned up by the mermaid's searching tendrils.

"What's wrong?"

"I thought after the snapjaws, we agreed to find allies less likely to turn around and gobble us up when this is all over."

Chuckling, Pasha shifted the spear to her other side and took Ally's hand. "And that's what I've done, I promise."

Ally wanted to believe Pasha, and yet they were looking down into the nesting place of yet another creature Ally had thought only existed in Priestess Esa's stories.

A squid. A *giant* squid.

No, that wasn't right. Actual giant squid were large, true enough. The few she'd heard of being accidentally caught by fishing crews all took at least three sailors to hold the strong creatures steady enough to toss them back. They were always thrown back into the sea. Giant squid were once thought to be messengers of the goddess, not to be captured or eaten lest a missive go undelivered.

The more likely reason they weren't fit for food, according to her brother Cal, was that they tasted terrible.

This creature was something else altogether. The sort of fantastical animal sailors often bragged about seeing out in the open ocean, though no one really believed them.

"How can you be so sure?" The squid's rust-colored body alone was three times the size of Euphonia. One of those never-ending tentacles could easily wrap around a ship's hull and crack it like a walnut. Only a few of its appendages were even visible, the rest were hidden in the shadows beneath it.

"His kind have always been friendly towards merfolk," Pasha said simply. As if that should explain away all of Ally's worries.

Ally looked back at Euphonia. She too seemed unbothered, perfectly content to let Ally approach the monstrous squid. That had to be some kind of endorsement, didn't it?

A small tug from Pasha and they swam to the edge of the ravine. It took a moment for Ally to locate the squid's front. Eyes as wide and round as a ship's helm were set at a forward angle and covered with thin lids that blended with the expanse of dusky skin.

"He's asleep," she whispered. "Shared history or not, I don't know how friendly he'll be if we wake him."

"We don't have time to wait for him to wake on his own," Pasha reminded her. "That could take days, even a whole season if he's fed recently."

Ally reined in the stream of new questions that revelation invited. The least of which being what could possibly be big enough to feed a squid this size, let alone fill it up.

She's right. Help Mama now, ask questions about the ridiculously massive squid later.

Giving Pasha's hand one last squeeze, she let go and nodded for the mermaid to send the signal.

Pasha was getting more adept at using the spear to channel her energy charges. Within a few minutes, she sent a melon-sized ball of light floating down to where the squid slept. For a brief moment, the ball hovered over the squid's head. It melted against his skin, soaking in and sending a current of electricity through the water around it.

Ally shifted closer to Pasha. A tremor rippled through the squid's oblong body, each tentacle rolled and stretched. The two longest tentacles, the ones it would use to grab and pull in its prey, were tipped by wide, fleshy clubs. Dozens of white suction cups flashed from underneath the appendages. Finally, his eyes peeled open, circling until he found the pair looking down at him from the top of the ravine. Ally expected to feel the same bitter spike of fear that hit her when the snapjaws first appeared. Instead, she was struck by the calm intelligence behind the squid's gaze.

"Greetings friend," Pasha called down. She gave a low bow and Ally copied her. "My apologies for waking you like this. We need your help, if you'll give it."

Nightfall found Ally and Pasha back at the mermaid trove, tucked away in the kelp forest. Euphonia was somewhere outside, perhaps hunting for her evening meal. They'd done as much as they could in the day they'd agreed to take to find extra help. The creatures they'd gathered were waiting for Pasha's signal to follow them back to the *Maiden's Revenge*. If they'd had more time to search maybe they could have left the snapjaws alone, but...

Ally shook her head, there was no point in second-guessing the plan now. It was far too late. They were sitting on opposite ends of the small cave. Ally was weaving thick strands of kelp into small nets, each with four long ends to tie them onto whatever could be found on the seafloor. Pasha leaned on her hip with her tail curved around to one side, silvery blue fluke splayed against the wall behind her. All the mermaid's concentration was focused on the space between her palms, as she pulled in charge after charge from the salt water around them to form solid, shining spheres of light. They littered the sand around Pasha, lighting the cave up brighter and brighter as the pile grew. Each sphere would be secured inside one of Ally's nets and placed along their path back to the pirates' ship, a trail for their new allies to follow.

The words Ally had left unsaid since her first night here still weighed heavily on her mind. Things would move quickly once they set out in the morning. Even more so once they caught up to Dare and found where on that ship she was keeping Mama. Neither of them had said it, but there was no guarantee this would work. Or that they would all make it out unharmed.

A hunk of slippery kelp twisted out of her hands and the net she'd nearly finished unraveled. Ally huffed at her traitorous fingers and started over. Now was the time to say something, in this last bit of calm before they swam head-first into the fight ahead.

Ally cleared her throat. "Pasha?"

"Hmm?" She didn't look up from the new charges gathering between her hands.

"I need to apologize to you... again."

Pasha's smooth brow creased as she formed the next beacon. "For what?"

"For before, in the trove, when I first arrived. I was so grateful we were friends again and you were willing to help me rescue Mama that I… reacted inappropriately. I should have asked you before getting so close."

The ball of light fizzled out and Pasha turned wide eyes to focus on Ally's face. Ally tasted the sharp tang of unspent electricity and her scalp tingled. If they were on land, her curls would probably have puffed out to twice their size.

"You," Pasha's tongue paused against the points of her upper teeth, she was searching for the right words. "you think it was inappropriate? Because it's not something *friends* would do?"

The inflection she put on the word 'friends' puzzled Ally. Was Pasha this uncomfortable talking about the fact they'd shared a kiss, however brief it was? "I'm sorry, I didn't mean to make you uncomfortable. I won't bring it up again." Ally looked down at the net in her lap, taking up the loose strands again.

Pasha's sharp, obsidian nails came into view as her hands covered Ally's. "I'm not *uncomfortable*, Ally. I was surprised, but not uncomfortable. Not upset."

Ally glanced up at the mermaid from beneath her lashes, "Still, I shouldn't have…"

"Listen, I don't know much about human relationships. Mermaids, from what I can remember, are tactile. Affectionate. Always living in close-knit groups. I'd actually get upset if my sister didn't hug me goodbye for long enough –" Pasha huffed and gave a quick shake of her head. "Maybe humans aren't like that," she finished with a shrug.

"It depends on the humans in question, really." Ally almost couldn't believe they were having this conversation.

"Well, what I'm saying is, I don't want you to feel badly about it because I didn't mind. I've missed this," she squeezed Ally's fingers.

"Being close to someone. Even just being comfortable around someone again. I don't care how we define it, I'm just grateful you're here."

Blinking back tears, Ally turned her palms up and intertwined their fingers. She'd never get used to how soft Pasha's skin was, like running her hands over a bolt of satin.

"I'm grateful you're here too."

MAHER

CHAPTER THIRTEEN

Maher Villaon couldn't decide if he was dead or not.

Flashes and scraps of memories that may or may not have happened flitted through his mind. Screams, blood, dragging his spent body across the deck of a ship to lift injured and dying sailors into a longboat. Feeling like his skull would split from the inside. Lightning from the sea. Someone yelling his name. And then... being surrounded by blissful quiet, nothing but the roll of the water and the ease of letting it all slip away.

It was a nice distraction from the fire raging beneath his skin. From the feeling that he'd been run clean through by a bowsprit. From the moans of pain and the stench hanging in the stale air. Surely if he was dead, something else would be happening. There'd be some sense of peace, or at least a lack of pain. Death couldn't possibly be just the reliving of whatever happened in the moments before your life ended.

Maybe it was all a dream. Maybe he was still in that box in the cargo hold of the *Pike*, caught in a fitful sleep. Maybe he'd accidentally picked a bouquet of foxglove and the sprites had whisked him away to their faraway lands, where he'd be trapped for a hundred years.

None of that sounded right either.

There was also a nagging sense that he'd forgotten something important. Something Maher knew he was supposed to remember, but for the life of him he couldn't grasp it. What was it? He should ask Ally, she would know.

Ally! Maher's breath hitched. It was like a thousand tiny insects were crawling over the skin of his left shoulder and down his front, at least Maher thought it was his left. Fuck, they were crawling *underneath* his skin.

"He's getting worse." A soft voice reached him through the haze.

Who? Maher tried to ask. They didn't hear him.

"I know, but what else can we do?" a second voice growled.

Whoever they're talking about must be in pretty bad shape.

"Unless we move to land soon, unless *she* deigns to give us something - *anything* - to help him, Maher is not going to last much longer."

"And neither will we." The deeper voice sounded closer this time. A faint pressure was placed on Maher's shoulder, the fire licked up the side of his neck and down his arm.

Oh. Maher blinked and the world came briefly into focus. Watery light filtered through the gaps in the boards behind his back and around the porthole seams. The damp floor beneath him lurched with the roll of the sea. At least Maher thought it was from the sea. Faces swam around him, most he didn't recognize, until the speakers came into view. The solemn set of their faces did not lift his spirits.

Kamharida shifted closer as Ga-Seung lifted the material wrapped around Maher's shoulder. He grunted, "He's got a few more days before this goes beyond repair."

Maher wanted to know what exactly had happened, but for the first time in his life his mouth just wouldn't work. His head lolled to the side and Kamharida gently righted it as Ga-Seung rewrapped his shoulder.

"Do you think he could lose the arm?" she whispered.

Dear gods, I hope not. Maher blinked sluggishly. The lines of their faces blurred.

"Too soon to tell. But, without treatment?" Ga-Seung left the rest unsaid.

I suppose I'm not dead. His eyes slid closed; the lids too heavy to do much else. *Not yet, anyway.*

Chapter Fourteen

"*Alphonsine, please come back inside.*"

Ally glanced back at her mother, sitting in the lavishly decorated parlor of an ambassador's home. They'd been invited for tea, but all she cared about was the spectacular view of the harbor from the parlor's terrace. From this place built high above the street below and the docks just ahead, Ally could see past the crowded forest of ship masts to the glittering stretch of water beyond.

More importantly, she could see the small group of women preparing to dive from the edge of the nearest dock. If Ally stood on her toes and propped her forearms on the polished stone railing, she could watch them unobstructed. One tall woman with a shaved head was passing nets and knives to the rest.

The selkies.

"Alphonsine?" Rochelle called again.

"Just a little longer, please, Mama?"

"What is so fascinating out there that you're ignoring our host?"

"I can see the selkies from here!" Ally bounced on her toes. A hair ribbon attached to a tiny silver kingfisher bird fell into her face and she pushed it back.

"It's quite alright, my lady," the ambassador's wife offered, blonde hair falling around her shoulders as she poured the tea. Ally'd already forgotten her name. "She'll have someone her own age to talk to once Thara arrives with the children."

Ally gnawed on her bottom lip. There was no use pointing out that she'd met the woman's children before, and they already thought Ally was odd. She'd take the time alone to watch the selkies while she could.

They were already slipping into the water, ready to dive for the oysters clinging to the beams and rocks beneath the dock. Ally longed to get closer, but this was as near to the sea as she was allowed. It wasn't fair. Her brothers could swim and sail to their hearts' content. Luthais was always ducking his comportment tutor to go out on some boat or another. All three of them were planning a trip around the harbor to Snake Island, they were discussing it at breakfast that morning. When Ally asked if she could join them, just this once, their father said the same thing as always, "It's not safe for you right now, Ally. You'll stay on land a while longer."

The last selkie to dive in stretched her arms overhead and twisted around to look over each shoulder. A braid of long, pitch-black hair hung down her back. She caught Ally staring from the terrace and raised a hand in greeting. Ally froze for a moment, then lifted one hand from the railing and gave a small wave back. Smiling, the selkie grabbed her knife and net, then plunged into the deep water lapping against the docks.

"Ah, Thara, there you are!"

The door to the parlor swung open. In walked the ambassador whose house they were visiting, a bronze-skinned woman dressed head-to-toe in orange. Three children, all around Ally's age, trailed behind her. Ally took a minute to recall the brief history she'd been given during the carriage ride into town. Originally from Agriya, which explained her clothing, the ambassador had come into much success lately garnering deals between the Birde Isles and her home country. Thanks, in large part, to her wife's family connections on the Isles. Their children were all adopted in Agriya, though only one was sporting clothes in varying shades of orange.

Ally tore herself away from the terrace, slowly crossing back into the house and to her mother's side.

"Apologies for the delay, Etty darling." Thara kissed her wife's cheek, then gave them a short bow. "Lady Kingfisher, you honor us with your company today. And you as well, of course, Lady Alphonsine."

"Children," their other mother, Etty, prompted. "Say hello to her ladyship and Lady Alphonsine."

There was a flurry of hasty bows and curtsies. Rochelle then stood and clasped the ambassador's wrist rather than her hand. A greeting that showed respect in Agriya, she'd told Ally before they arrived. Ally greeted everyone as she was taught to do, but the moment the adults resumed their conversation, she couldn't help but notice the looks the other children were giving her over their teacups. Maybe if Ally told her parents how strange others found it, her not being allowed even on the shore, they'd finally let her free from this rule that seemed to apply to her alone in all of the Isles.

Ally suddenly wished she'd brought her needlework practice hoop, something to distract her and keep her hands busy. But Mama would have said it was rude to do something like that as a guest in someone else's house.

"By the way, my lady," Etty slipped an opened letter from the pocket of her gown. "I've had a letter from my brother, on Gull Island. You might remember him, August Tapper? His wife died two seasons ago, you see,"

Mama gave a hum of sympathy, "I am sorry to hear that."

"Thank you, it was quite sudden. He's written he will be moving to Kingsport with his daughter, Beitris, and will conduct his business here. She's closer to his lordship's youngest son in age, but no doubt she'd love to meet Lady Alphonsine as well."

"That sounds lovely," Rochelle set her own cup down and ran a hand gently over Ally's curls. "You'll have to introduce us when they are settled in town."

"Of course, I'm sure the girls will be like sisters before you know it."

FORAOISE

Chapter Fifteen

"We must move, Captain. The ship's been dragging anchor for nigh on a week now."

"Your point, Swain?"

The long, graying mustache hanging down either side of the older man's face twitched. "The rest of the fleet's been waiting on the open sea, we were meant to have left by now."

"Just a little longer." Foraoise leaned over the map table, staring at the same hand-inked lines until everything around the Birde Isles blurred together. Her gaze cut to the woman bound in the corner of the cabin. The restraints became necessary again after her daughter went overboard. "Anything to share, Rochelle?"

Bloodshot eyes glared at her from beneath a curtain of dark, matted hair. With each passing day she looked less like the regal lady they'd brought aboard and more like a feral animal caught in a trap. The younger woman croaked out something in Balahn.

"What was that?" The captain arched a red-stained brow.

"May your body be struck down and your soul trapped in the In-Between for all eternity."

Beside her Swain hissed out a breath. It was an impressive malediction, but Foraoise only sneered. "That curse only works on those who believe in your trio of gods, *sister* dear."

Rochelle spat onto the cabin floor and turned away.

"Don't worry, you'll be home soon enough. All the sooner if you'll only confirm what I already have here." Foraoise's fist landed on the map hard enough to make Rochelle jump. Her so-called *friend* had sent a sketch of all the weak points around the Isles, but now the captain wasn't so sure of this information. No amount of threatening or cajoling so far had persuaded the lady of the Birde Isles to even glance at the map. Yet another reason she should have held onto the girl longer.

"Are we to sail soon, Captain?" Swain waved a hand over the map. "We have more than enough to get us there and let's not forget..." he paused, glancing at the corner.

"Say whatever it is you need to; she won't have the chance to repeat anything."

"Let's not forget the repairs the machine needs before we set off for the Isles. The damned thing's gone wayward since it was used last, setting off sparks out of nowhere. We've had to lower the cables to hang out the portholes to keep the crew from being shocked at random."

"And we wouldn't want that, would we?"

"Captain," Swain's brows knit together. "The crew has to believe you'll not lead them astray, trust your judgement's not clouded."

"You think I'm not in my right mind, Swain?" Her already hoarse voice cracked. "You think I'm going the same way as Jon?"

"No, lass," he said softly, turning so his back was to Lady Kingfisher. He hadn't called Foraoise that since she joined the crew herself, so many years ago. "I don't believe you've got the same affliction as Jon, but I am worried about you. Give me that at least."

"*Affliction*? He was off his head, or have you forgotten?"

"I've not forgotten. Never could." His eyes flicked up to the scar curving around her head. "You did what needed done. Don't let some fishwives' tale about a mermaid keep you from what we've been working towards all this time."

Something nasty twisted in Foraoise's chest, the old wound. Not a physical injury, a healed over scar, that she could have dealt with. This went deeper.

"We'll stay put the rest of the day and leave tomorrow."

"Aye, Captain." Swain lifted a hand, as if to rest it on her shoulder, and she turned away. Soon she heard the cabin door shut behind him.

Foraoise braced her hands on the table, breathed slowly in and out. Swain was right, they had no proof the mermaid even existed. None was offered in the letter, only the anonymous writer's word. Better to cut their losses and move forward.

From the corner, Rochelle snorted. "Jon again? I always knew your quarrel was with a dead man, just not the one I was imagining."

Slowly, as if her movements weren't her own, Foraoise turned, one hand coming to rest on the hilt of the dagger hanging at her hip.

Rochelle's eyes darted around the cabin, her back pressed against the wall. Without a second thought, the captain strode across the cabin and yanked the other woman up by her hair.

Crouching until they were nose-to-nose, Foraoise hissed through clenched teeth, "What did I tell you, about speaking his name?"

Grunting, Rochelle twisted and tried to swing her bound hands, sagging under the rope's weight. Her pretty face twisted in agony, mouth falling open in a silent scream.

"You will never say that name again." Spittle flew with each clipped word. Using one leg to pin her down by her skirts, Foraoise jerked Rochelle's head back and raised the dagger.

PASHA

CHAPTER SIXTEEN

Something wasn't right.

Ally and Pasha floated beneath the hulking shadow of the *Maiden's Revenge*. Night had fallen and their only light came from the beacon they were attaching to the ship's rudder. The soft, white glow illuminated the concern etched onto Ally's face, no doubt it matched her own. This ship had been entirely too easy to find again.

"They've hardly moved at all," Ally voiced Pasha's thoughts. "I thought they'd be halfway to the Isles by now."

"They have not," she peered down at the anchor firmly planted on the seafloor. "And there's something strange about the water here. Can you feel it?"

"Now that you mention it," Ally's nose wrinkled as if she were about to sneeze. "The water smells bitter. Like when you pull charges out of the sea, only stronger."

"You can *smell* the charges?"

"That's the best way I can describe it." Her lips pursed. "What if it's that weapon on board, the one they used on the *Pike*?"

Pasha considered that. To her, this feeling was like an invisible net dragging through the water. Another repellent layer hit them, making her skin crawl and temples throb. "Whatever this is, it's giving me a headache."

"Could this be the reason the whales couldn't get a clear impression of the ship or where it was located?"

"I wouldn't be surprised if that's exactly what happened, they were all so muddled."

"What about our... allies? Will this prevent them from finding us?"

"Not with the beacons in place. Besides, they're all so ancient they may not notice until they get close. Do you think there's any way to stop it? Who knows how many other creatures are being affected, how many schools and pods have been thrown off course."

"I'm not sure," Ally readjusted her grip on the rudder, using the ship to hold herself steady instead of treading water. Conserving her energy for the next step in their plan. "We don't even know how it works, and out here on the open ocean as well?"

Pasha's jaw tightened; her tail snapped angrily from side to side. A hand slid gently into hers.

"Listen, we'll get Mama out of harm's way and then I swear we'll find out what this thing is and how to destroy it. Even if we have to come back out here, track Dare's ship down all over again, and take it apart one board at a time."

"Thank you, Ally." Pasha swam out far enough to check the sky hanging above the surface, then returned to her side. "It's nearly time, are you ready?"

"I think so, as ready as I can be." She pressed her palm to the shark tooth hanging beneath her shirt. "At least I have my lucky charm."

"I'm not sure how lucky it's been," The guilt of unwittingly making Ally dependent on the energy housed inside that fossil was still alive and well. Made that much stronger by the nightmares born from the dread of what might happen if Ally removed it. "I meant what I said, I'm going to fix it."

A strange, resigned look passed over Ally's face. It reminded Pasha too much of how she looked in the dream. "It's been more helpful than I've let on. In fact, I don't know that I'd have made it this far without it."

"What?" A cold trickle of panic started at the back of Pasha's neck.

"It's a long story, I'll explain better after this is over. When all's said and done, and despite the strange circumstances, receiving this gift was one of the most fortunate things to happen to me."

Shaking her head, Pasha told herself to let that go for now. It seemed to her she'd brought nothing but grief to Ally since they met. Since before they met, really. There would be time later to hear the whole story, Pasha would make sure of it.

"Are *you* ready?" asked Ally. She let go of the rudder, hands and arms slowly circling like Pasha had taught her. "I know this was your idea, Pasha, but you know you can change your mind, right?"

"No need, it's our best option and, what's more, something they'll not suspect." Pasha reached for Ally, then stopped herself, hands dropping to her sides.

After a moment's thought, Ally nodded and opened her arms. "Would it help if I hugged you?"

Hesitation gripped Pasha yet again. She'd told Ally mermaids were tactile creatures... When Ally started to sink, unable to keep herself up with only her legs, Pasha slid into her embrace. Using her tail to keep them both afloat. Heat bloomed from the shark tooth pressed between them and Pasha sank into the sensation.

"You tell me how long you want to stay here," Ally murmured, her lips close to Pasha's fanned ear.

Always.

"We don't have long,"

"You're right," Ally's hold loosened.

"One more thing."

"What's that?"

Before she could change her mind, Pasha grazed her lips over Ally's cheek. "For extra luck."

Ally smiled softly as they separated.

"I'll find you when this is over."

"Promise?" Pasha's cheeks warmed with how small and fragile that one word made her feel.

Ally placed a hand over her heart. "Until the sea runs dry."

There were suddenly so many things Pasha wanted to say, words she feared would be left unspoken forever. Instead she repeated, "Until the sea runs dry."

CHAPTER SEVENTEEN

Squeezing through the porthole of a pirate ship in the dead of night was not something Ally ever envisioned herself doing. She counted herself lucky this particular porthole was built to house a cannon. Otherwise her hips might have been a hindrance.

Once Pasha wrenched the wooden cover from the opening and gave her a boost until her top half was hanging through, Ally had to move quickly. She knew Pasha would leave as soon as she made it inside, to check the beacons that would lead their new allies to the *Maiden's Revenge* and the handful of other vessels under Dare's flag that floated nearby. It still didn't sit right with either of them that the ships were still so close to the place where Ally was thrown overboard. Did Captain Dare believe they were safe in this part of the sea, with no one to tell where the fleet was waiting?

It turned out the porthole Pasha chose was also an extra opening used if the bilge pump was overburdened. Ally wriggled through, wet clothes scrunching around her, until she tumbled down into the hold and startled an unsuspecting family of rats. The smell in this part of the ship was enough to make her gag, the bilge pump was definitely close by. Since the ship was sitting in a calm sea, there would be no one running the pump this late at night. She'd check the brig first, if Mama was being held there all they'd have to do was make their way back to the porthole and wait for Pasha. If she was on a higher deck or worse, in the captain's cabin, Ally would have to get creative.

There was a stack of old hogshead barrels lined up against one side of the narrow space, cracked or lids missing, no longer in use. Ally pressed between the barrels and the hull, inching forward. Every few breaths, she would pause and look over the nearest barrel, checking for any wandering pirates. There wasn't much light, so Ally moved as quickly as she could without knocking anything over.

"My lady!" A high voice hissed from the gloom and Ally ducked down. "My lady, over here!"

Ally kept her back to the hull of the ship, moving as soundlessly as possible towards the voice. As she peeked around one of the barrels she was using for cover, Ally saw a pair of wide eyes and a slender hand waving at her.

It was the barrelman from the *Pike*, miraculously unharmed beyond a few cuts and bruises, and supporting Grant, the helmsman, against her wiry frame. There were more shadowy figures behind them. The girl's face pressed close to the bars around the brig. "My lady!"

"You're alive! Thank the goddess," Ally whispered. "What's your name?"

"Anya, my lady."

"Just Ally, please, Anya. Wait while I get a light." She retrieved the lone lantern hanging nearby, taking the same path around the barrels. When she returned, Ally could scarcely believe what she saw. Roughly a dozen people were crammed into the brig, all survivors from the *Pike*. Much more than Ally was planning to get off the ship, but she'd worry about that later.

Anya had leaned Grant against the bars and was shaking the others awake, urging them to keep quiet if they questioned what she was doing. As the realization of what was happening spread, some of the sailors stared at Ally as if she were a ghost or made their signs against evil. Ally supposed she probably was a ghost at this point.

"Lady Alphonsine!" Kamharida surged forward, gripping the edges of the locked gate. The first mate was covered in dried blood and grime, but she too appeared to be in one piece. Ally brought the light closer and clasped the older woman's hand. "How are you here? The quartermaster claimed Dare threw you overboard after she turned on us."

"I'll explain everything later," Ally searched the group, hoping to find a pair of chestnut eyes and a cocky smile waiting for her. But she didn't see him. Of course she didn't. Steeling herself against the sorrow that twisted in her chest, Ally turned watery eyes to the lock keeping them inside. "We need to get you all out of here. How many are wounded?"

"Not too many, but Maher is going to need help."

"Maher…" Ally's heart seized and she nearly dropped the lantern. It couldn't be, she didn't see him. Maher was gone. Kamharida was still speaking, but Ally heard nothing over the roar in her ears. "*Where is he? I don't see him. Where…*"

Several of the crewmates shuffled out of the way. An unconscious Maher leaned against the back wall, where the bars connected to the hull. His coat and suit jacket had been removed; his shirt bunched down around his waist. The bosun from the *Pike*, Ga-Seung, knelt next to him, mopping a sheen of sweat from Maher's brow, then holding an ear to his reedy chest.

"What happened?" Ally breathed. Her heart couldn't take it, she wanted to rush to his side, to hold him and convince herself he was truly alive. Only the blasted bars kept her from pushing past the others.

Kamharida looked back at them. "Maher and I tried to get as many wounded sailors off the ship as we could, when that *noise* happened."

Ally nodded, there was only one noise the first mate could mean. The others visibly shuddered and twitched at the mention of it.

"Without warning, he knocked us both overboard. I thought he'd lost his mind, but then that wave, that lightning, or whatever it was, hit the ship and I realized he'd saved my life."

Another sailor spoke up, "Aye, and when the rest of us that was on deck saw Mister Villaon and our first mate go over," he shrugged, "we thought it best to follow 'em."

"When I found Maher, after the ship went down, he'd taken a hunk of shrapnel through the shoulder. We got the metal out, it went clean through in one piece, but we had nothing to properly dress the wound," said Kamharida.

They'd made a crude bandage from someone's shirt and wrapped it around Maher's shoulder, but a bloom of red had already soaked through.

"I'm amazed he's even alive, the metal must have pulled some of the lightning from the ship." The bosun lifted the bandage and Ally caught a glimpse of charred flesh around the edges of a gaping hole in the front of his shoulder, just to the inside of the main joint. A spiderweb of angry, raised lines spread out from the center-point of the wound, running nearly down to his elbow.

"Oh, Maher," she gasped, a hand pressed to her throat.

"I've seen another barrelman who was struck by lightning in the crow's nest," said Anya. "The place where it hit looked very much the same."

"Alright, alright," Ally steadied herself. They only had so much time before a pirate on the watch came by, and Pasha hadn't been sure how long it would take for the rest of their help to arrive. "We've got to get you all out of here, find my mother, and get Maher to the nearest physician."

Ga-Seung said, "And how do you propose to do that? With pirates swarming the decks above us?"

"I have help coming," said Ally. "Did you happen to see where they keep the keys to this gate?"

"There might be a hook closer to the steps that lead into the cargo deck." Kamharida pursed her lips, "But if they're not there, the quartermaster could very well have them on his belt."

"Fantastic," Ally passed the lamp to her. "Try to stay quiet, I'm going to check by the steps."

There wasn't much to hide behind once she exited the blocked-off area that held the brig and bilge pump and reached the short set of stairs leading to the mid-ship cargo deck. Nailed into one of the posts on either side of the hatchway was a large iron nail, but no keys hung from it. Taking a deep breath of slightly fresher air, Ally made her way back to the brig.

"No keys," she whispered when Kamharida spotted her.

"What if we find something to pick it with?" said Anya.

Ally frowned. "Do I look like I know how to pick a lock?"

The young barrelman gave her a lopsided grin. "Not really, but I can."

Ally hunted around the barrels and came back with a collection of old nails, broken hoop bits, and anything else that might be useful. While Anya worked on the lock, Ally went back to the open porthole. No sign of Pasha yet. The waning half-moon was lower in the sky than when she climbed onto the ship. A sense of apprehension settled over her when she realized some of the *Pike* sailors would be too large to fit through the porthole. Ally mulled over her options as she returned once again to the brig.

Anya had squished one thin shoulder between the bars, her other arm was wrapped over the top of the lock. A bead of sweat trickled down her face. "I'm not used to doing this with one hand upside down." She caught her tongue between her teeth and leaned an ear closer, as if she could discern the random series of clicks her tools made.

Leaving her to it, Ally found Kamharida nearby. Keeping her voice low, she shared her concerns with the first mate. "Not everyone is going to fit through the porthole I used to get in, we need another way to get off the ship."

Kamharida's brow pinched. "Our only hope is to get to a longboat, without any of the pirate crew spotting us."

"And we have to find where they're keeping my mother."

"She'll be in the captain's cabin." Ga-Seung ripped another strip from Maher's tattered shirt. "That's where they've been keeping her the whole time."

"How do you know?" Ally tried to imagine where the cabin was housed above them.

"Heard one of the crew complaining about it. Apparently, Lady Kingfisher's been giving them a lot of trouble, said he'd be glad not to have to go into the captain's quarters and risk having something chucked at his head."

Ally couldn't help but smile, glad to know Mama hadn't gone easy on them. There was a loud series of clinks that had Ally ducking out of the way, then the brig gate swung open on rusted hinges.

The barrelman held up her makeshift lock picks, she'd nicked several of her fingers in the process. "Everyone must learn a useful skill."

"You can brag about that later. We have to move." Kamharida squeezed past them and dug through a pile of old fishing nets left on the floor.

In a blink, Ally was kneeling by Maher's side. He looked even sicker up close. She took his clammy hand in hers. "Maher, can you hear me darling?"

With a groan that ripped through Ally's heart, Maher's head lolled to one side. His chestnut eyes looked at her without seeing, but the limp hand in hers flexed.

He pulled in a shuddery breath. "Al... Are we dead now?"

"No, no of course not." She smoothed his hair back.

"Are you sure?" Maher winced, his eyes closing. "Sure feels like we ought to be."

Having found a suitable hunk of netting, Kamharida came back into the brig as everyone else crept out. Ga-Seung helped her fashion the net into a sling, and they strapped Maher to her back. His arms hung limply around her neck, head resting on her shoulder. "The night watch could be here any minute. My lady, how big of a boat is waiting at the porthole you came through? Those who will fit can go out that way."

Anya supported Grant as he limped. Upon closer inspection, they looked enough alike to be related. "I'm sure we can fit through."

"Boat?" Ally hedged. "I, that is, there's not one."

The more superstitious sailors, who'd become somewhat relaxed in her presence while Anya got them free, all backed away again. Closing the gate to the brig, the bosun moved next to Kamharida. "How did you get back to this part of the sea if there's no boat?"

"That's what I was going to explain once we have Lady Kingfisher," Ally spoke quickly. Kamharida's reminder about the watch made her uneasy. Even on a calm night, didn't the crew assigned to patrol the ship do so at regular intervals? She hadn't seen anyone else but the survivors from the *Pike* this whole time. "I've got someone coming to help us, even if we can't get the longboat, we'll be alright if we can make it into the sea."

"Are you mad?" a sailor in the back piped up.

Ally recognized the woman who'd tried to lead Luthais' crew into a mutiny only a handful of days ago. "Glad to know you won't be haunting me just yet."

"Enough!" Kamharida hoisted Maher higher and gripped the ropes crossed over her chest. "Some of us are too weak or injured to swim for long, when will this help arrive?"

"I'm not sure," Ally could feel the distrust building in most of them. As glad as she was that they were alive, she'd only been prepared to get one person off the *Maiden's Revenge*. "Listen, why don't I sneak up and see if I can find Lady Kingfisher? The rest of you wait here. You can pretend to still be locked up when the watch comes by."

"That would be clever," the harsh voice was like a set of claws running down Ally's back. "If I didn't already know someone had opened the brig."

Lamplight flooded the hold and Captain Dare stood in the entryway. More than two dozen pirates swarmed in from the bow and upper decks, many brandishing blades and hatchets.

Ally backed up until she was between Kamharida and Anya. The knife Pasha had given her from the trove was tucked inside Ally's boot. Pasha'd insisted the necklace and pouch counted as two things instead of one. Mermaid logic. Ally didn't reach for it yet, better for them to think the naive lord's daughter hadn't thought to bring a weapon.

Now that the hold was well lit, they could see what had been missed before. A thin, wire-wrapped rod was attached to the top hinge of the gate. It disappeared through a hole in the deck above. Whatever lay on the other end must have alerted the pirates as soon as the door opened.

Ga-Seung crossed thick forearms over his bloodstained jacket. "I've seen a trick like that before, used by the Char-range navy to guard prisoners taken during battle. I knew you weren't stupid enough to just be a pirate, Dare."

The captain's razor-thin smile made the *Pike* sailors shift uneasily. "Since you've taken the liberty of letting yourselves out, why don't you join us on the main deck? I'm eager to hear Lady Alphonsine's brilliant rescue plan."

CHAPTER EIGHTEEN

Night had passed by the time they were ushered into the open air above decks. The pirates hadn't bothered to restrain them, they were far outnumbered. Kamharida was breathing hard, an unconscious Maher still strapped to her back, but she refused to put him down. Foraoise lined them up against the portside rail. Ally found herself between Kamharida and Ga-Seung. The bosun had hooked an arm through hers on the way up, only letting go when it appeared they weren't being taken further.

Ally shivered in the crisp breeze, her damp clothes stiffened and stuck to her skin. Only the shark tooth's warmth kept her teeth from chattering. Could Pasha sense Ally's anxiety surging through whatever connection the tooth offered? She wanted to hold it, to press some of that urgency in Pasha's direction. But if Dare saw, and took it from her? Maher whimpered and Ally cast a quick look in his direction. His eyes shifted beneath their lids, but his body stayed limp.

The sky was just turning pink when Foraoise strode in front of them, hands clasped behind her back. Her wide-brimmed hat was gone, the scar that cleaved into one side of her skull on full display. Many of the *Maiden's Revenge* crew had gathered to watch.

"I have a simple question. Once it's answered, we can all go about our day." She stopped and faced them. "How did Lady Alphonsine get back onto my ship?"

No one so much as breathed too loudly. Next to her, Maher's hands spasmed once and went still.

"I'll ask again: how did Lady Alphonsine get back onto my ship? Indeed, how did she survive being tossed overboard for nearly a week, with no land in sight? I suppose that's two questions." When she got no answer a second time, Captain Dare drew her sword. "Let's try an easier question. Who picked the lock to the brig?"

Ally felt Ga-Seung tense up. From the corner of his mouth, he ordered, "Eyes straight ahead."

She couldn't have looked at Anya without turning her body, but Ally understood what the bosun meant. It probably wouldn't matter if it was the truth, whoever flinched first would get the blame.

Stalking to the end of the line, where Anya still supported Grant, the captain pointed to the fresh scratches on the girl's fingers. "Why don't you tell me, girl. Who picked the lock?"

Ally's eyes watered with the effort it took not to look at them. Several of the pirates muttered angrily, shifting restlessly from their posts across the deck. They must have expected more of a show for the early hour. Ally bit the inside of her cheek to stop herself from snapping at them.

Where are you? She tried to push the words to Pasha. Damned if she knew if it would work, she hadn't been able to communicate that way even with Pasha right in front of her.

"I did it."

Ally blinked rapidly. It wasn't Anya who said that.

"I did it," Grant said again, limping out of the line. "I picked the lock."

"Thank you," Dare turned. In one short thrust, her sword pierced through Grant's stomach and out his back.

"GRANT!" Anya wailed, catching his body as the sword pulled free. Blood coated her hands and spread across the deck. None of the watching pirates even blinked.

Another sailor from the *Pike* rushed at the captain from the side. She turned on her heel and drove the blade beneath the man's chin. More blood sprayed across Captain Dare's face, splashing her smiling teeth with streaks of red.

Ally couldn't take it. She couldn't stand there and watch more innocent people die.

"That's *enough*!" She shook Ga-Seung off when he tried to stop her. "That's enough, Dare!"

The captain was in front of her in three strides. "Something to say?"

"That. Is. Enough." Ally's skin crawled when Foraoise smirked and looped their elbows together as if they were taking a garden stroll. The captain took them a few paces away and turned until Ally was looking at what remained of the survivors she'd both found and failed. Anya was still on the deck, holding Grant's lifeless body and sobbing into his hair. The other sailor lay where Dare had dropped him, her sword stuck in his neck.

Dare doesn't have her sword. Ally tried to think quickly. That didn't mean there weren't other weapons on her, but if Ally could free the knife in her boot...

"Swain?" That hoarse voice burrowed into Ally's ear. "Fetch Rochelle while I have a talk with my niece."

"Aye Captain." The mustached man, the one who'd already stopped Ally from killing the captain once, headed for the cabins at the back of the ship.

"Now, Ally – I can call you Ally, can't I? We are related, after all."

Saying nothing, Ally's teeth ground together. Finally, they were bringing Mama where she could see her.

"Tell me Ally, how did you do it? How did you survive for so long in the sea and find my ship again? Quickly, before I get cross."

Ally held her gaze. "Why does it matter? It won't help you with whatever you're trying to prove. It won't change how your life could have turned out if Gaius hadn't sent you away."

Foraoise's expression hardened; Ally'd struck that same nerve. Then the captain smiled, her teeth still slick with blood. "Who I might have been is of no consequence. It's who I *will* be that matters."

Swain returned with Rochelle in tow. She stumbled behind him, one arm locked in the quartermaster's grip, but her hands were unbound. All of her beautiful, dark brown hair had been hacked off. Patches of red, irritated scalp showed through. When she saw Ally standing next to the captain, Rochelle screamed.

"Ally! My Ally, You're alive!" She tried to run for her daughter, and Swain yanked her back. Rochelle's free hand pressed over her belly. "How is this possible?"

"We were just coming to that." Foraoise released Ally's arm and got very close to her face, blocking out everyone else. She spoke softly, her eyes promising more bloodshed if Ally didn't answer truthfully. "I know you have a mermaid, Ally, or perhaps the mermaid has you. I don't care either way."

"And how do you know that?"

"I have a friend who keeps me informed."

A friend? She wracked her brain, tried to dredge up everything she'd overheard in her father's meetings, everything Maher had been trying to tell her on the *Pike*.

My lord, how could they possibly have known about Lady Alphonsine's fear of the sea?

Word travels beyond these islands,

I think one of your brothers may be involved...

Why not let her go?

All of the air whooshed out of Ally's chest. It couldn't be.

"Who," she rasped, "who is this friend?"

The captain's head tilted. "Even if I knew, why would I reveal that?"

"Answer my question, and I'll answer yours."

"We're not making deals here, niece, and I'm done waiting. Either tell me what I need to know, or we'll see how well your mother does when she's cast into the sea. I'd wager it wouldn't work out as well for her as it did for you. Especially as I plan to tie her hands and feet before she goes over."

Ally's mouth went dry and a cold sweat broke across her brow. If she knew for sure that Pasha was down there, she'd take that chance. Pasha would save Mama; Ally knew she would. Why couldn't the godsbedamned shark tooth work the other way around and tell Ally where the mermaid was?

"Swain, get a rope!"

"Stop! I'll tell you," Ally grabbed Dare's arm. "I'll tell you."

The captain glanced at Ally's hands but didn't shake her off. "I'm listening."

"Come this way," she backed away from Mama and the others. "You don't want your whole crew to know, they'll try to take the gift for themselves."

Foraoise allowed her to pull them across the ship, nearly to the opposite rail, shaking Ally off when they arrived. "Start talking."

"It's true, there is a mermaid. She saved me the day you pushed me overboard."

"How? What's this gift you're hiding?"

Ally licked her lips. "The gift of breathing underwater. Only a woman truly called by the sea can claim it, though. I stayed under with her the whole time, without the need to come up for air, and she brought me back here when I asked."

The captain's face showed no reaction, but a muscle in her jaw ticked. "Where is she now?"

"I don't know," Ally lifted a shoulder. "She said I was on my own with this. It wasn't her concern."

Dare frowned, "And what of this help you promised the rest of them?"

She glanced at the last of the *Pike* crew and snorted. "I wasn't expecting to find anyone else alive after you attacked their ship. What else was I going to say to keep them quiet while I found my mother?"

Green eyes roved over her before Foraoise's scarred face cracked into a smile. "Perhaps we're more alike than I gave you credit for. Now," she spoke low, implying Ally should do the same, "tell me how you convinced the mermaid to give you her power."

Ally pushed her salt-crusted hair over her shoulder and did her best impression of Beitris Tapper's haughty tone. "Easy. You take a handful of her scales, grind them up, and drink them in a cup of wine."

The captain jerked back. "You're sure about that."

"Of course," Ally raised her voice. "Honestly, I wouldn't go through all the trouble of trying to catch a mermaid. There's a market vendor in Kingsport who sells genuine mermaid scales at a fair price. I don't know if you share a bed with any of your crew, but he says they're also good for stamina –"

The back of Captain Dare's hand connected with Ally's face, and she went down. Stars exploded in her vision and, for a brief moment, the woman had four feet instead of two.

"You think you're clever, do you? Who do you think you're talking to?" Foraoise was screaming over her. "Kill two more of her friends."

Ally made it to her hands and knees as shouts and cries rang out across the ship. Unable to look as their bodies landed on the deck, she reached into her boot. Ally had never wanted to harm another person in her life, but for a second time the captain brought something dark to life in her. She'd gladly drive that knife into...

Ally's boot was empty. The knife from the trove wasn't where it should have been. It was gone.

"Get up!"

Staring at the point of another dagger, still not her own, Ally's gaze sharpened as it traveled up the blade and the arm holding it. The skin around the captain's many scars and freckles was as red as her hair.

"I said, get up!"

Ally pushed onto one knee and tried to stand without the world spinning too much. Apparently, that wasn't fast enough. Foraoise grabbed Ally by the hair and yanked hard enough to bring tears to her eyes. She finally found her footing, but the captain didn't let go.

"Do you know what I think? I think you started to tell me the truth, then decided to play your little game. How do you like the results?" She turned Ally's head until she saw the two new bodies bleeding out on the deck. A young man whose name she hadn't caught, and her would-be mutineer.

I suppose I have a ghost now. Ally couldn't tell if she'd said the words aloud or in her head, but a few of the nearer pirates looked at her strangely.

Dare was speaking again, "This could have been over so quickly. I might even have let you stay in the cabin with your precious mother." The edge of the dagger pressed against Ally's neck. "Now they're all going to die anyway, because of you."

"Let her go."

Foraoise whipped around, taking Ally with her. She flipped them so Ally's back was against her chest. Ally felt the captain's sudden intake of breath when she saw Pasha standing on the rail of the ship.

Ally was sorely tempted to yell at Pasha for taking so long to get there (and making her stall longer than planned), but the blade still resting against her throat kept her from doing anything too rash.

"I knew it," the captain rasped into Ally's ear. "I knew it was true."

"Let her go," Pasha repeated, using that part of her voice that sounded like waves rolling onto the shore. Rivulets of water ran through her long, blue hair and dripped onto the deck. Her silvery gray skin and scattered scales gleamed in the morning sun. She was also completely naked and holding the spear from the trove, looking for all the world like a wrathful goddess summoned up from the sea. Ally had gotten used to Pasha's natural state, but it was causing a stir among the pirates. Pasha bared her sharp teeth. "Let them all go, and I'll spare your ship."

"Spare us? You may have given yourself legs, but I know what you are. Take her!" Dare barked. Her crew were rooted where they stood, none dared approach. She raised the dagger beneath Ally's chin. "She isn't a goddess, you fucking idiots! And she won't harm anyone, not while I have her pet. Take her, now!"

When two pirates approached her, Pasha lifted the spear. They halted, wary of the black metal blade, but she merely dropped it into the sea before stepping down onto the deck. The pirates grabbed the mermaid's arms, visibly recoiling at the feel of her shark-like skin.

Foraoise spun Ally around again and laid the blade against her cheek. "Tell me how to really take the gift, and I'll let the rest of your friends join my crew instead of feeding them to the sharks."

"Ally, don't!" Pasha growled.

She looked to Pasha, voice cracking, "I'm sorry."

"Ally!"

The edge of the dagger nicked her cheek and Ally flinched. "I kissed her."

"Say that again." Captain Dare sheathed her weapon, Ally breathed a little easier.

"I kissed her. If a woman called by the sea can kiss a mermaid, she'll receive the power to breathe underwater."

Foraoise tossed her head back, laughing. "How poetic."

"You ungrateful, little traitor!" Pasha thrashed against the pirates holding her. They kept their heads turned, far out of range of her teeth.

Foraoise pushed Ally aside, she stumbled and fought to stay standing. Without another moment's hesitation, the captain grabbed Pasha's twisting head and kissed her hard on the mouth.

FORAOISE

CHAPTER NINETEEN

The Captain Who Could Not Drown

The title swam through her mind as she held the mermaid's head, lips mashed together in some semblance of a kiss. One of the creature's sharkish teeth pricked Foraoise's lower lip, but she paid it no mind. Her little bitch of a niece hadn't said how long to hold the kiss, so Foraoise kept her mouth against the mermaid's for five ragged breaths, tasting salt and her own blood before letting go.

Black eyes glittering with rage, those teeth snapped at the air in front of Foraoise's face, like the girl had done before the captain tossed her overboard. Ally must have picked up on some of the mermaid's habits. Foraoise wouldn't have thought one of the most vicious, most legendary creatures of the deep would be so slight. Then again, what did size matter when you possessed such gifts? The ransom on the Kingfisher ship had been a pittance compared to the riches the mermaid would bring up for her from the seafloor. What price would other pirate captains pay for a chance to see the creature, maybe even take a scale back with them as proof of Captain Dare's wealth? Surely it would shed scales occasionally, and if not, a few could always be harvested here and there. And wouldn't her mysterious friend be surprised when Foraoise sailed into Kingsport with a fleet, a ship equipped with the greatest weapon on the sea, and a mermaid?

Stepping back, Foraoise contemplated the best way to contain the creature. With more time to plan, she could have already built some kind of tank... Foraoise doubled over. Her chest contracted, ribs squeezing inward and locking tight over her lungs. It was happening. Her body was changing, adapting into whatever form would enable her to breathe underwater like a fish. The pain would be worth it to become the one captain on the sea who could never drown.

As quickly as it began, the pressure released, bones expanded into place. Standing straight, Foraoise locked eyes with Ally and smiled, "Swain? Cut my dear niece's throat."

"No, no!" Rochelle struggled against the sailors that took her from the quartermaster. "You got what you wanted! You got everything you wanted!"

"Have I?" She eyed her handiwork. Swain had heard Lady Kingfisher's screams and curses when Foraoise took her blade to the other woman's hair. He'd come barreling into the cabin and stopped Foraoise from removing anything that wouldn't grow back. They still needed Rochelle for leverage, after all.

Foraoise passed her own dagger to Swain, he wrapped an arm around the girl's neck from behind. "I'll have everything when I see the look on my dear brother's face, as he learns his only daughter is dead. I think I'll wait until we're in front of him to kill you, Rochelle, just to hear him beg as – Ugh!" A spike of throbbing pain shot through her chest. The space between her eyes burned and she coughed hard against a sudden, sharp rattle in her lungs. "What..." Foraoise tried to get a new breath in through her nose and choked. Clear liquid trickled from her nostrils. More fluid sloshed through her sinuses and dripped down the back of her throat. She gagged, tasted salt.

Her crew were all backing away, their captives forgotten. Swain's hold on Ally's shoulders slackened until he was barely touching her, the dagger slipped from his hand and landed on the deck.

"What is this?" Foraoise rounded on the mermaid. The men who'd been guarding her had already taken off for the other side of the deck. "What have you done to me?" She spat out a mouthful of water, a hunk of green seaweed came with it.

"I didn't do anything." The mermaid's face split into a wide, shark-toothed grin, "You tried to steal it."

"You missed out on an important lesson, *Aunt* Foraoise. Our priestesses recite it every day." Ally pulled away from Swain, "You cannot take what the sea is not willing to give."

The captain's head wrenched to the side as more water poured from her nose and ears. Her vision blurred, eyes filling to the brim. Fingers curling into claws, she threw herself at Ally, grabbing for any part of the girl she could get. An arm like an iron band wrapped around Foraoise's neck and yanked her back before letting go. Seawater surged up the captain's throat and spilled out of her mouth.

The mermaid released Foraoise's neck and circled her, a predator watching its prey. "How are you feeling, Captain?"

"Kill them!" Foraoise shrieked, the words coming out gargled. No one moved. The crew had backed up against the railings and onto the quarterdeck. They stared at her as if she were some disgusting creature that had climbed on board from the deepest pits of the sea. Only the prisoners from the *Pike* drew closer, picking up discarded weapons along the way.

Air. She needed air. Her lungs couldn't pull any in, they were already full to bursting. Pressure squeezed all around her skull, the pounding in her head drowned out everything else. Foraoise lurched forward, the mermaid's grinning face swam in front of her. Grasping for the pistol in her belt, she struggled to wrap rapidly swelling fingers around the stock. She wasn't going to just lay the fuck down and die while they watched. She was Foraoise Dare, captain of the *Maiden's Revenge* and the largest pirate fleet in the history of the Eastern Sea. The woman who cheated death and slew the mad Captain Jon Dare on his own ship. Her story would *not* end this way.

The pistol swung into the air, wavered, then settled on Ally Kingfisher.

"Ally! Move!"

Foraoise closed her swimming eyes and squeezed the trigger.

CHAPTER TWENTY

Everything else faded away as Ally looked down the barrel of Captain Dare's pistol. It was uncannily like one of her panic attacks but, instead of the world around her going gray, all her senses narrowed in on this single thing.

"Ally! Move!"

She had just enough time to recognize that Maher was awake and yelling at her before the words registered. Throwing her arms over her head, Ally's knees hit the deck as the pistol went off. The sharp odor of black powder filled her nose.

There was no pain. No sear of a metal ball tearing through flesh. Slowly, Ally lifted her head.

Foraoise's arm, the one holding the pistol, was pointed up into the air. Wrapped around her wrist was a thick tentacle that connected back into Pasha's forearm. It pulsed, the color shifting from mottled maroon to a bruised purple and back again, like an octopus warding off a threat.

Ally's hands fell to her sides. All those weeks spent with Pasha, and she'd never once let on that anything was hidden beneath the scar on her arm. *This* was the reminder Pasha's family had given her before they left?

The pirates and crew from the *Pike* scrambled back from where Ally, Pasha, and Captain Dare stood.

"Dear gods..." Maher sagged against Kamharida's shoulder.

Pasha's jaw was clenched tight. Dark, carmine blood trickled from the open wound as the tentacle writhed and clutched at the captain's wrist. The pistol slipped from Foraoise's hand, landing with a dull thunk on the deck.

Ally slowly approached Pasha from behind. Laying a hand on her shoulder, she felt the already taut muscles quiver beneath her palm.

"Let her go, Pasha," Ally said, sounding infinitely calmer than she felt. "She can't hurt anyone now."

As soon as Pasha released the captain, Foraoise sank onto her knees. Unable to speak, she clutched at her throat and gurgled around the endless flow of water that bubbled up from inside her own body.

Ally looked away, watching instead as the tentacle retracted back into Pasha's arm. She could have sworn she saw it continue to roll up beneath the mermaid's skin until it reached her shoulder joint. The wound sealed shut, leaving a line of jagged pink flesh that would need time to heal. Ally heard when the captain's body fell and looked up as Ga-Seung approached. He was holding the trove knife from her boot.

The bosun tried to find Dare's pulse. "She's dead."

"What do we do about them?" Anya, dry-eyed and clutching a pistol in each hand, nodded at the pirates, all too afraid to do much except stare at their captain's body. "And the rest of the ships; surely they can tell something has gone wrong for them on this one. We can't sail them all back to Kingsport, and we might only have moments before they attack."

Lady Kingfisher put herself between Ally, Pasha, and the rest of their small band. Though she swayed a little on her feet, she held her head high and demanded their attention. "Before that decision is made, I need you to listen. The sailors with a tattoo of the heart and dagger from their flag are loyal to Dare. The ones with only a broken heart on their arms were conscripted from other ships. Char-range, Utollmir, the Birde Isles, Nuvwaan, each ship you see that was taken from a different nation likely has conscripted sailors aboard."

Kamharida grunted as she eased Maher off her back and helped him lean against a large spool of rope. "How do you know this, my lady?"

"They kept me in the captain's cabin the whole time. I've been paying attention. Most of the conscripted sailors worked the dirty jobs below decks or were forced to climb the rigging. She didn't care if they collapsed, or became ill, or fell from the mast. Only the loyal ones were allowed to operate the guns or board another ship."

"Why are you telling us this?" Anya demanded.

"So you know not everyone in Captain Dare's fleet is your enemy."

"What do you need?" Ally asked Pasha while her mother was briefing Kamharida on what else she'd learned about Dare's fleet. "Do you need to leave the ship? Just tell me, and I'll do whatever I can to help."

"I should get in the water," she cradled her arm to her chest.

"What about the others who were supposed to follow you?"

"Most of them are here. When I dropped the spear, it should have signaled them to wait."

Ally saw no movement in the waves around the ship, but of course that meant nothing.

"When I go down, I'll tell them what to do." Pasha shot a nervous look over Ally's shoulder, "I can't speak to anyone else, Ally, not right now."

"I understand, you don't have to."

"I'm sorry I took so long to get here," she grimaced and held her arm tighter. "If I'd known you were in danger..."

"Don't worry about that. You're here now and you saved my life. Again." Ally smoothed some of Pasha's hair back. "It's probably good we're not keeping a tally."

"You know what to do?"

"I've got everything under control, now stop stalling and get in the water. Tonight, when everything has settled, I'll open the window in the captain's cabin for you."

Nodding, Pasha let Ally usher her to the rail. She had to help Pasha swing her shaking legs over the edge.

"I'll see you soon," said Pasha.

"Yes, you will." Ally watched as she dropped into the sea.

After allowing herself time to give her mother and Maher each a brief hug, Ally spoke privately with Kamharida and Ga-Seung. Before they attempted to negotiate with the pirates, who were still, thankfully, too superstitious to get near Ally, she needed them to know about the leverage waiting beneath the ship. It took some convincing, but Pasha's appearance had instilled more belief than they might have had before. When they were ready, Kamharida walked to the helm and used her booming first mate's voice to address the *Maiden's Revenge*.

"Listen up. We're giving anyone who wants it the chance to leave and, unlike your former captain, you have my solemn word you will actually be free to go. One of us will accompany your flag signaler to begin relaying the message." She scanned the ships surrounding them. In the time since Captain Dare died, only two of the smaller vessels had put more distance between themselves and the *Maiden's Revenge*. Kamharida pointed at the two largest ships, "We will form a chain of longboats for those who want to make the voyage back to the Birde Isles using the *Maiden's Revenge* and these ships here. Any conscripted sailors will be returned to their homelands as soon as possible. Those who were loyal to Dare who choose to surrender and assist in sailing these vessels back will be recommended for leniency."

Next to Ally, Anya scowled at that last part of the offer. She knew what grief the girl must be feeling. Grant was indeed her brother, and he'd been slaughtered before her eyes. But Anya also knew they were far outnumbered, with nowhere to run if the other ships decided sinking the *Maiden's Revenge* was worth it as a means of escape. They needed to use the shock of Dare's death while it was fresh.

"We know there won't be enough volunteers to sail the entire fleet back to Kingsport, but know this, the nations the rest of these ships were stolen from will likely hunt them down. I can promise no clemency there."

There was shouting from the nearest ship, a Saprean vessel if Ally was any judge. Signal flags were waving, and cannons were being rolled across the deck to face them.

Grumbles and sharp gestures wove through those gathered in front of them. Ally counted too many heart and dagger tattoos for her comfort. Before any argument could spread against Kamharida's offer, Ally climbed atop the capstan.

The pirates watched her warily. They'd seen her go overboard and reappear unharmed several days later, bringing the creature that killed their captain with her. Many of them probably already thought Ally was a sea witch, so she'd be a sea witch. Ally'd seen many street musicians perform as a child, the movements they used to gather a crowd. She lifted her hands as if she wore a sweeping robe instead of her ripped, salt-crusted clothes, raising her voice so the nearest ship might also hear the message. "Take this warning, leave while you can. Those of you who wish to fight might soon regret it. My new friends are *hungry*."

The deck shuddered beneath their feet. Ally knew Euphonia had barely brushed her eel-like body against the hull. To their side, the ship that was threatening to turn their cannons on them rocked like a child's toy in a fountain, the sea roiling from beneath. Loose cannons rolled, a handful of the pirates moving them lost their balance and pitched overboard. Euphonia burst through the surface; the bodies of the unlucky ones caught in her open maw.

Pasha had sent the sharks and whales far away. She didn't want them to get hurt, not when there were other things in the water. Things like the red-eyed snapjaws with tougher hides and bigger teeth, who wouldn't care what they were eating as long as it was made of flesh and bone. The blood of the pirates clouded the water, drawing them in. They banged against the sides of the smaller ships, never showing themselves above the surface. The sleek line of ridges along their spines sliced through the water as they moved in to feed on the unfortunates who landed in their paths. Further down, an Utollmir vessel lurched as its hull was lifted clear out of the sea. Four tentacles as thick as tree trunks crept up the sides, pausing only when the tapered ends curled over the railings. The sailors on board crawled over each other to reach the masts in the center of the ship. A longer tentacle wrapped over the prow, dipping it downwards and sending the crew still on deck sliding, screaming for mercy.

"WAIT!" Ally called out, knowing Pasha would relay the message to the rest. She'd warned Ally the snapjaws might not listen once they had prey in their grasp, but they would take that risk if it meant avoiding an even bigger bloodbath on the sea. And knowing now how many of the sailors on those ships had been pressed into service? Ally wanted more than ever to get them free of Dare's fleet.

Ally breathed a small sigh of relief when the snapjaws dipped beneath the waves. Euphonia continued to slither between the ships, opaque eyes trained on the humans still on board. The enormous squid holding the ship aloft paused, tentacles ready to squeeze the wooden hull open like a mollusk.

All around her, pirates cowered. Some became sick as soon as the attack ceased. A handful of sailors who'd come up from the lowest decks looked hopeful. Ally felt a slight thrill, though she wasn't the one bidding the creatures to do anything. The pirates didn't have to know that.

"First Mate?" Ally turned to Kamharida. Her russet eyes were wide, and she was breathing rapidly, but she'd held her position by the helm. Seeing Pasha with her own eyes still hadn't prepared Kamharida for what else was waiting beneath the ship. "Please repeat your offer to those who might not have heard, and have the signalers relay the message. I'll have my friends stay with us until we get each ship's reply."

PASHA

CHAPTER TWENTY-ONE

Pasha and Ally stood alone beneath the forecastle of the *Maiden's Revenge*. A few lamps on the walls provided the only light. Side-by-side, they took in the machine Captain Dare planned to use to conquer the seas.

Six massive cylinders were clustered together on a platform, wrapped in coils of copper wire and sealed with metal caps that connected to each other through thin rods. They were easily as tall as Kamharida or Maher, and Pasha was sure if she wrapped her arms around one of them her hands wouldn't meet. On either side of the group of cylinders were iron mounts that held a structure of gears and levers, the longest ends of the levers connected to a spoked wheel set up in its own frame like a ship's helm. More cogs and wires connected to things neither of them could identify, even after an explanation given by a sailor who'd known more than the rest.

"It's called a turbine, but it wasn't made to stay out on the sea for so long." A Fraollish officer had come forward once the last of the pirates were off the ship. Taken from the machine's original transport craft, she was one of only three left alive from that crew. Six years she'd been on Dare's ship, her life only spared because the Kharaboans who built the turbine had taught her how each piece fit together, even if she didn't fully understand how it worked. Her pale skin was ruddy and rough, hands calloused and cracked as she tried to pull her sleeve down over the broken heart the pirates had tattooed on her arm. "They weren't cleaning it often enough, and it's meant to be kept in a dry environment. Once the rust got inside?" she'd shrugged.

"What would have happened?" Ally asked.

"Not much at first, maybe the charges would have become more erratic. Most likely, it would have eventually locked up or exploded. Those crossbolts and connecting wires were Dare's own design, but no one on her crew really knew what they were doing. A lot of sailors died, trying to figure out how to connect the electric currents to the crossbows. This thing wasn't meant to be a weapon."

Ally's mother was present as well. "What's it for, if not that?"

"It was supposed to be a gift from Kharabo to Fraolland, to seal a new trade agreement. They've had some success using larger turbines to produce heat."

"And Fraolland invests a great deal of money on importing goods during the winter, the whole country spends nearly half the year covered in snow," Lady Kingfisher mused.

"Yes, milady. The scientists assigned to maintain it were to follow on another ship or travel north by land and cross the Split Sea. Since we never arrived, I don't know what happened from there."

"If the Fraollish ambassador to the Isles knew about their missing ship, she never let on," Ally said to Pasha later, when they were together in the cabin. "It's possible she hadn't known about Kharabo giving Fraolland the turbine, but surely she'd have gotten word of a pirate attack on one of their ships."

"Will your father be able to find out?"

"We'll see. After we learned of Mama's capture, the ambassador's first advice was to send their warships after Dare's ship. Maybe she was trying to get it back before anyone else learned what had happened."

"Are you ready?" Ally wore a set of protective leather gloves and boots left behind by the pirates. She'd asked everyone else on board to take the longboats to the other ships until they were sure it was safe.

Pasha nodded. She'd spent the last two days in the sea, building up her energy after depleting most of it to call the old creatures and lead them to the pirates. The ships taken by Kamharida and what remained of her crew sat in the water, waiting until Pasha could assess what kind of charges were stored inside the turbine, if they were like those she pulled from the sea or something wholly different.

This thing might not have been intended to be a weapon, but Dare had figured out how to make it one.

Pasha could feel the residual charges stuck in the copper coils. How they fed through the rest of it was beyond her knowledge, but she knew what it felt like to pull too much energy from the sea too fast. Practicing on her own, not long after the others had left, Pasha took in a burst strong enough to knock herself unconscious.

Stepping up to the machine, Pasha rubbed her hands together, already feeling her own energy's curiosity at the new source.

"Please, be careful," Ally implored.

"Yes ma'am." Pasha gathered all the tiny charges dancing over her skin and formed a ring similar to the one she used to call the sharks and whales. "Step back!" She glanced over her shoulder long enough to see that Ally was back at the edge of the platform. Something inside the machine pulled at Pasha's energy, trying to add it to its own. Threads danced up her arms, and she felt the force of whatever was inside of those coils responding. Stretching it out until it was as wide as her arms could go, Pasha slammed the ring between the two closest cylinders.

An explosion of sparks rained down over her. Bits of metal shot out of the fittings, pinging off the walls and skittering across the deck boards. Behind her, Ally yelped and cursed. Pasha wanted to check on her but couldn't let go of the charge conducting between herself and the machine. A stray iron bolt popped free from the base of the nearest mount and Pasha winced. It felt like a jellyfish had stung her thigh.

Just when Pasha thought they weren't going to break, the top of one cylinder erupted in a bright flash. An arc of lightning bounced to the next cylinder and the next until the last one gave a final pop and sizzle. The charge in the turbine guttered out, the coils blackened beyond repair. Pasha stumbled back as curls of smoke rose out of the charred machinery and even from her own skin.

"Pasha! Are you hurt?" Ally put a gloved hand on each of her shoulders and steered her away.

"I'm fine." Pasha caught a line of red running down Ally's sleeve as she removed the elbow-length gloves. "What about you?"

"A piece of metal caught me in the arm, but it's not bad." The back of Ally's hand ghosted over Pasha's forehead. "I'm glad we asked the others to leave the ship; who knows how it sounded from the outside? Are you sure you're alright?"

"Yes, why?" Pasha noticed the shallow cut on her own leg, where the electrified bolt had skimmed across her flesh.

"You seem far away." Both of Ally's hands turned Pasha's head towards her. "Do you need to go back into the sea?"

"Not yet." Pasha tried to find the words to explain what she was feeling, the buzz of pure energy thrumming beneath her skin. She wanted to test it, to grab the mermaid spear from its hiding place beneath the ship and channel the energy through the green stone. Or see if she could raise the remnants of the *Pike* from the seafloor. But this wasn't like her own energy, the well she gradually replenished with charges that formed naturally in the water. This was harsher and more demanding. It felt completely foreign in her body, and it was burning out quickly. Her heart was beating too fast.

Instead of going for the spear or trying to make some mermaid myth a reality, Pasha wrapped her arms around Ally. Holding her as tightly as she dared, Pasha allowed herself the liberty of pressing her face into the soft curls that hung over Ally's shoulder. She breathed deeply, focusing on Ally's scent rather than the power blazing through her veins. Ally's hands slipped from between them and circled her waist. She rested her cheek against Pasha's head.

"The energy from the turbine feels... strange," Pasha admitted, her voice muffled by Ally's hair. "I don't like it."

"What can I do to help?"

"This. If we could just stay like this for a little while."

Without hesitation, Ally widened her stance and hugged Pasha closer. One hand came up to comb through Pasha's hair, and Ally gently swayed them from side to side.

Pasha's chest heaved. Her heart finally slowed down; the unnatural energy continued to fade. Even once it was gone, Pasha didn't think she wanted the embrace to end.

As if reading her mind, Ally murmured, "We can stay like this as long as you want."

The voyage back to the Isles was slow, with three ships trying to keep pace with one another. Pasha would follow beneath the *Maiden's Revenge* during the day, sometimes swimming, but more often than not, she caught a ride from Euphonia. The creature still refused to let Ally out of her sight for long. Pasha had tried to communicate that Ally was safe now, but she insisted on traveling with them. Truth be told, Pasha was glad not to have to swim the entire way; she was still recovering from breaking the turbine. Staying on the ship the whole journey wasn't a good idea, either. Pasha knew any obvious signs of her presence on board would only unsettle the crew trying to get them home.

Only once did Pasha steal into one of the ship's cabins in the daylight. It was the first day they were underway when Ally begged her to help Maher. The wound in his shoulder was much worse than Ally had realized, and the residual effects of lightning coursing through his body were beginning to show. He was confused for random periods of time, unable to remember anything that had happened between jumping from the *Pike* and waking strapped to Kamharida's back. Headaches plagued him, and he complained of his heart racing or that Ally was moving around too much when she was standing still in front of him.

"I don't know what else to do," Ally said once Pasha made it into the cabin that was set aside for Maher to rest in private. "Mama and I checked the stores, there was nothing strong enough to completely clean the flesh where the metal went through. I'm afraid it will become infected before we make it home." She fought back a wave of tears, and Pasha brushed away the few that escaped to slide down her cheek.

"Let me see him."

Maher's eyes cracked open when Pasha approached his bedside. "So, it's you," his words were slurred. "Come to give me the kiss of death?"

"It doesn't work that way." Kneeling beside him, Pasha glanced at Ally.

"Maher, darling, Pasha is here to help you." She sat next to his uninjured side and took his hand. "Please let her."

"I s'pose nothing worse can happen." His head lolled to one side, eyes wavering over Ally's face. "But you owe me a new suit, Al. I've ruined this one, you know."

He wasn't even wearing a suit; someone had dressed him in a clean shirt and breeches.

"It's a good trade." Ally kissed the top of his hand and nodded at Pasha.

Pasha was unsure how long it would take her to conjure up the precious tear that was needed now. It was rare for mermaids to cry, and she'd spent decades teaching herself to hold her tears in, even when she felt the need to weep. Now she looked at Ally, at the way she stroked Maher's hand and told him everything would soon be fine. Pasha could feel the ghost of Ally's arms around her, slender fingers running through her hair. They'd stayed like that for a long time, even after the machine's energy was finally gone. Ally held Pasha until she was ready to let go.

Throat burning, Pasha uncovered the wound in his shoulder. It didn't *look* infected, but Pasha's sense of smell was stronger than a human's, and she could already detect the faint notes of disease. Ally laid a hand on Maher's cheek, keeping his face turned away from Pasha as she leaned over him. The red lines that branched out from the hole in his flesh were beginning to fade, but the skin around it looked as if it had just happened.

Maher was the only friend Ally'd had for many years. Pasha wouldn't let her lose him now. Eyes welling up, Pasha hovered closer even as the scent of dying flesh assaulted her nose. She focused on the sound of Ally's voice and shut her eyes as two fat tears dropped into the wound.

Pasha sat back on her heels; eyes closed as she listened for the fizz of infection burning away. Her nose twitched as the foul smell was wiped out by the bubbles foaming over where the wound had been. When Pasha looked again, only a thick starburst of scar tissue was left on his brown skin. Maher's eyes fluttered closed, dark lashes stark against his cheeks as his face smoothed and his breathing evened.

"Thank you, Pasha," Ally whispered, still holding Maher's hand.

"I'll see you tonight." Leaving Ally to explain everything to Maher when he woke, Pasha slipped out the cabin window. Euphonia was following along beneath the ship, and Pasha fell asleep as soon as she settled onto her back.

CHAPTER TWENTY-TWO

Every night after that, Pasha would climb through an open window into the captain's cabin. Ally's mother refused to stay there another moment, moving instead to the former quartermaster's cabin. That coward was the first to take advantage of Kamharida's offer to leave.

Pasha didn't blame Lady Kingfisher, not after hearing everything Dare had put her through. She wasn't entirely sure why Ally chose to stay there, except maybe to prove to herself Dare was truly gone. Still, they'd laid out a scrap of sail to hide the red stains on the floorboards. Knowing it wasn't blood wasn't enough. And as much as she wanted to be close to Ally, Pasha chose to sleep on a pallet on the floor, leaving Ally to use the bunk.

Ally and her mother spent the first two days at sea combing through everything they could find in Dare's quarters, trying to uncover the rest of the captain's plans. But a piece of the puzzle was eluding them. Pasha could see in the tense set of Ally's face. The answer to how the captain was always able to stay one step ahead, how she'd gotten hold of the official trade documents and shipping routes they'd found in the desk. Ally admitted to Pasha that she didn't want to say who she thought was to blame until they knew for sure. No matter who it was, the betrayal would cut deep. Perhaps deeper than the knowledge that Foraoise Dare had been Ally's aunt. Before tossing her water-bloated body overboard, the first mate from the *Pike* had ripped something off her hand. A large gold ring with the Kingfisher family crest set in its center. Ally left it in one of the captain's desk drawers with the shipping papers; she wouldn't even touch it if she had to reach inside for something else.

They were halfway home when Pasha found the secret compartment beneath the bunk. From the moment she first set foot in the captain's cabin, she felt the prickle at the edges of her mind that meant some kind of jewel was very near. Once she found them, the feeling would cease, but after searching each nook and cranny, Pasha still couldn't see any jewelry lying around. Finally, she'd had enough. The prickle was turning into a buzz stuck deep inside her ears. There had to be *something* in the cabin.

"Have you found any jewels on board?" she asked Ally.

"Not as much as I would have thought, on a pirate ship, mostly odds and ends left behind by the crew in their bunks. Why?"

"There's something in this room, I can feel it." Pasha started in the middle of the floor and worked her way outwards, pausing every few steps to listen. When she stopped close to the bunk, the tingling made the tiniest spike. Kneeling, Pasha searched beneath it and found nothing. Feeling along the underside, she sent out a tiny current of energy and felt it bounce back against the middle board running across the frame. "It's here!" Pasha was ready to pry the board out when the pads of her fingers found a latch nearly flush with the rest of the panels. She tried manipulating it a few different ways, until the latch gave, and a small compartment popped open.

"That's a neat trick." Ally crouched next to her. "What could Dare have needed a place like that for?"

"You'd be surprised at how many secret hiding places are built into ships. This has to be it," Pasha lifted out a velvet box, popping the lid open to reveal a collection of rings nestled inside. As soon as she picked up the only jewel-studded ring, the prickling stopped.

"Let's see what else is in here," Ally examined a stack of letters tied together with a black ribbon. The paper was quite old, the writing on the top envelope was elegant. "That's Trader's Tongue, but this was penned by someone taught by a writing tutor." Ally laid them on top of the bunk and reached for a small, leatherbound book at the back of the compartment. She wiped a layer of dust off the cover and her eyes widened. "Pasha?"

"Hmm?" Pasha was still picking through the ring box. One had an elaborate seal with flowers and fruit engraved on its face, perhaps Ally would know what it meant.

"Look at this," Ally held the book out. "It's a journal."

Pasha looked at the book gripped tightly in Ally's hands. There was a faded name embossed on the cover: *Aithne.*

Two evenings later, Pasha found herself stuck outside the cabin window, waiting for Lady Kingfisher to leave the room. Thankfully, there was a ledge wide enough to rest her feet on and she wasn't left dangling by the windowsill. After finding the journal, Ally and Pasha had stayed up until dawn reading every entry. Some pages had been saved with bits of ribbon, while others had notes written in the margins in a hand that was not Priestess Aithne's.

Pasha wondered if her brief encounter with Aithne, more than twenty years ago, would be included in the book's pages. They knew now it was that last impersonation of the Birde Isles' sea goddess that prompted the priestess to convince Ally's parents to keep her away from the shore until she was grown. But Aithne never recorded their conversation on the beach, she only noted that the goddess had given her a vision concerning Lady Alphonsine's safety.

By morning, there were some questions that had been answered and many more that remained unclear. Ally gave the book to her mother as soon as Pasha left the ship and then to Maher after that. The three of them spent the next two days comparing its contents to other papers found in Dare's cabin. Pasha always waited until Ally was alone to come aboard, and then Ally would relay any new details.

Pasha's toes were beginning to go numb when she heard Lady Kingfisher say, "If your friend would like to come inside now, I'd like to meet her."

Pasha nearly let go of the ship. Not once had she entertained the idea that any of Ally's family would want to meet her, regardless of the role she'd played in Captain Dare's death. There was still a small, shame-filled part of her that felt responsible for everything that had befallen them since that night she met Gaius I on the beach.

Ally pushed the window open and peered down at her, looking nearly as shocked as Pasha felt. "I know you heard that. Would you like to come in and meet Mama? You don't have to if you're not comfortable."

"No. I mean, I will." Pasha climbed through the window, keeping back in the shadows despite knowing that Lady Kingfisher had already seen her in broad daylight.

Cleaned up and dressed in clothes that had been left behind by the ship's officer closest to her in size, Ally's mother still managed to look as regal as if she were sitting on a throne. Pasha saw the resemblance between them, much stronger than her memories of what the other

Kingfishers she'd encountered looked like. She kept her head down, shifting from foot to foot.

"It's Pasha, isn't it?" Lady Kingfisher approached. Only Ally's hand on her elbow kept Pasha from backing up.

"Yes, Lady Kingfisher." Pasha straightened. Ally's mother wasn't angry or afraid of her, in fact, she looked as if she were about to cry.

"Please, call me Rochelle." She held out her hands and smiled warmly. Pasha carefully extended her own, feeling something tight unwind in her chest as Rochelle clasped them together. "I want to thank you, Pasha, for coming to my aid. But more importantly, for what you've done for Ally."

"There's no need, really." Pasha looked to Ally for help, unsure of what she meant.

"I've told Mama about our swimming lessons," Ally supplied. "And everything else you've done for me, even when I gave you trouble."

"My daughter is more stubborn than she appears," Rochelle's eyes twinkled.

"I... that is..."

"She's well aware, Mama, thank you."

Pasha shook her head. "I think I have an idea where she got it from," popped out of her mouth.

To Pasha's relief, Rochelle laughed and squeezed her hands before letting go. "I'll leave you now." She kissed Ally on the cheek. "Goodnight."

"Goodnight, Mama." Ally turned to Pasha after her mother was gone, smiling wide. "I think she liked you."

CHAPTER TWENTY-THREE

"Why do you think so few of them wanted to become mermaids? The girls that were brought to the sea?"

Pasha glanced up, clearly startled by her question. They hadn't spoken of the daughters brought as sacrifices by the early Birde Islanders since before they departed Kingsport. The mermaid's lips pressed together as she considered her answer.

They were sitting together on the cabin floor, leaning against the bunk. Close, but not quite touching. Papers were spread around, Aithne's diary lay open between them. Ally's hair was draped over her shoulders in wet tendrils; she'd washed up again as best she could in preparation for their arrival home. Tomorrow morning they'd reach Trader's Bay, hopefully by noon they'd be docked, and Mama would be home at last.

There were still so many things Ally wanted to ask Pasha, to tell Pasha, before they arrived and everyone was swept up in the commotion that would surely greet them. She couldn't imagine how her father and brothers would react when they landed in Kingsport. Or when they learned everything that had been discovered during the voyage.

Pasha sighed, "It's not a decision to be made lightly, but if the ones who made the change were..."

"Sea Kissed," Ally said softly.

"Right. If they were Sea Kissed, then it might have been the best choice for them. What other option would they have had?"

"None, really. Live close to the shore and risk drowning if they stayed in the sea too long?"

Ally'd finally confessed her suspicions the night Pasha officially met her mother. How the constant pull she'd felt towards the sea, a thing that had terrified her, finally made sense after hearing Esa's accounts of the Sea Kissed people. What eventually happened to them when they couldn't stay away from the shore. And how Ally was sure now, beyond a shadow of a doubt, that the energy Pasha infused into the shark tooth was the thing that had kept her from losing herself like the others. It had been a difficult conversation, Pasha still felt so ashamed about Ally's dependence on the tooth. At least she knew now how much Ally needed it, needed the energy it provided. But Ally could tell Pasha had trouble wrapping her mind around the concept.

Pasha studied one of the entries in the journal but couldn't seem to hold the book still. "Then I'm sure it's very possible the ones who changed were Sea Kissed."

"I think so too." Ally fiddled with her necklace. "If any of the others before me experienced the pain I felt that night we met, when I was so angry I threw the tooth away? I can't imagine why they wouldn't want to become mermaids."

"Perhaps, but it's not as simple as deciding to make the change and then it's done. It's one thing to be born a mermaid, it's another to be made into a mermaid. There has to be an anchor."

"What kind of anchor?"

"Well, for example, if I were to make you into a mermaid?"

"Just as an example, of course." Ally watched Pasha from the corner of her eye. They'd danced around this discussion for days. Pasha had seemed reluctant to tell her what was required.

"If I were to change you into a mermaid, assuming everything I've heard about what's involved is true, I'd be your anchor. We'd be connected. If you were in the sea, I'd always be able to find you."

"Like with the shark tooth?"

"It's different. The tooth has limits; if you weren't wearing it, I wouldn't know where you were. But I can always feel the energy in it, even from a distance, because I put it there. If I were your anchor, we'd be linked in a different way. I'd always be able to find you if I needed to, but it wouldn't be a constant beacon."

"Would you be able to control where I went?"

"What? No, nothing like that. I don't think I'm explaining this well." Pasha put the journal down. "It wouldn't work just one way like the necklace does. We'd be able to find each other, but it would take a deliberate effort."

"I see." Thinking about the best way to frame her next question, Ally picked up an old shipping plan. She tried to read it, but the words and numbers swam across the page. "Were any of the made mermaids still in your shoal when you were young?"

Drumming her fingers on her knee, one of Pasha's nails glanced off a stray scale. It sounded like she was tapping on glass. "I don't think so. In the stories, they'd all left for other communities long before my sister and I were born. If any were still around, I would think we'd have been able to tell they were made. Only a few of the elders were old enough to have witnessed it, and centuries had passed since the last one was changed."

Ally let the subject drop after that. She couldn't tell if Pasha was unwilling to say more, or if she simply didn't have any other information. Apparently, the carvings and tapestries Ally had seen in the caverns beneath Kingsport were only a fraction of the knowledge the mermaids once kept there. Anything that could be brought with them was taken, leaving Pasha very little to educate herself with, even about her own people. Most of what she remembered was gleaned from the stories told by her older sister.

The idea kept rolling through Ally's head, even as they finished going over the documents for the hundredth time and stored them back in the desk. Pasha had mentioned it when she first told Ally about the mermaids, the ability of the strongest elders to change a human into one of them. At the time, it seemed like an offhand detail Pasha included only because it was what she'd heard, implying the secret of how it was done was lost. But what if it wasn't?

Later, when the lamps were out, and Pasha was sleeping on the floor nearby, Ally lay awake and listened to the waves breaking against the hull of the ship. Ally was fortunate, she knew, compared to the other Sea Kissed. The shark tooth, however accidental, had saved her from the pain, the unendurable call that drove others before her to give up their lives to the sea. Now she had a better understanding of what made the tooth so special. Imbued with Pasha's own energy, it gave her enough of a connection to the sea to keep her from being overcome. It was no wonder Ally felt compelled to always keep the fossil close. Her body had responded to it, the attachment growing stronger as she aged.

Rolling over, Ally found Pasha sleeping just a few feet away. She'd moved her pallet a little closer tonight. Ally nearly suggested Pasha could share the bunk with her, it was marginally more comfortable than the floor. Yet she didn't want to make Pasha uneasy, and the mermaid had seemed more fragile in recent days. They'd played their parts well, tricking Dare into securing her own death. It had made Ally's stomach heave to see the captain kissing her, but Pasha assured Ally over and over it wouldn't have to last long.

Her own limited contact with humans aside, Pasha had told Ally the story of one mermaid who'd used the ability before. She was caught unaware by a fisherman, in the early days of the humans' arrival on the Isles. He'd forced a kiss on her, thinking it would grant him some kind of luck, and she'd watched him drown where he stood. Just as they'd always been taught would happen. When the mermaids began impersonating the sea goddess, they used that knowledge to their advantage.

Still, the moment Dare released Pasha, Ally felt such a dizzying swell of relief. Then she witnessed the fate awaiting her long-lost aunt, and fully understood Pasha's warning when she first gave Ally her gift. Try to take a kiss from a mermaid and find yourself drowning on dry land.

Ally was already reaching for Pasha when she stopped, her palm hovering in the space over the mermaid's arm.

Drown on dry land.

Foraoise Dare had indeed drowned on the deck of her ship, but Ally...

"Ally? What is it?"

The sleepy question startled Ally enough that her hand finally landed on Pasha's cool skin. "I didn't mean to wake you," she whispered.

"It's alright, did you need something?" Pasha's fingers trailed over hers and Ally bit her lip.

"No, I'm fine. Only promise you won't leave in the morning without waking me."

"Of course." Pasha was already dozing off again. "I'll wake you."

Resting her cheek against the hard edge of the bunk, Ally left her hand curled around Pasha's bicep. The rock of the ship and Pasha's steady breathing eventually lulled her to sleep.

PASHA

CHAPTER TWENTY-FOUR

*P*asha woke and found herself alone. It wasn't unusual for Pallagia to get up before her, but it was still night, judging by the dim glow of the corals by the doorway.

She worried Pallagia had gone to see her human. When she met Ealasaid during the day, Pasha was usually able to signal the corals not to shine too brightly for her sister. Sometimes they even put on a sudden light display in the great chamber, distracting and confusing the others while Pallagia left. They'd been doing this all summer. She suspected they were enjoying being part of a secret, there wasn't much else for them to do. Pasha wasn't sure why the corals tended to listen to her. They were living creatures after all, not bones. But, if she asked nicely enough, they'd often do small favors for Pasha.

Stretching and rolling off the seaweed-covered bed they shared, Pasha swam to the corals and spoke softly. "Where did she go?"

A line of corals woke up to her right, pulsing lights beckoning her to follow. Pasha slipped out and stayed close to the tunnel wall. Hopefully no one else was awake; she didn't want to have to explain what she was doing up so late.

The corals led her past the great chamber and down another tunnel that held all of the tapestries and art that belonged to their shoal.

"Why are we here?" she whispered.

Blinking in answer, the lights trailed off and went dark outside of the largest cave in the tunnel. Pasha used the carved ropes set into the wall to pull herself forwards, whoever was down there might hear if she swished her tail too hard.

As she drew closer, a stern voice floated out of the cave. "It's out of the question, Pallagia."

Pasha froze. Elder Nerys.

"You've made that clear," Pallagia answered. "But you haven't said why."

"It's too dangerous. The humans have finally stopped dragging their own children to be sacrificed to the sea. Now you want to draw their attention again?"

"I want you to teach me how to perform the ritual. Please, Nerys, just once more –"

"Absolutely not!" Elder Nerys snapped. "Never mind that you have deliberately disobeyed us and put the entire shoal in danger by revealing yourself to this human. But you can't even guarantee she wants to give up her life on land."

Pasha adjusted her grip, her fingers were going numb from holding the wall.

"She will. I didn't want to ask before I was sure I could change her, but she will. I swear it."

"You don't know that. She could be using you, Pallagia, waiting until your defenses are down..."

"She wouldn't do that!" Pallagia hissed. The water crackled with electricity. Pasha flinched; She ought to leave, but she had to know what the elder would say next.

Nerys sighed heavily, sounding every bit of her advanced age. "My dear, I'm thinking of your own good."

"You mean the good of the shoal."

"Your well-being is the well-being of the shoal. They are one and the same."

"But –"

"I'm sorry, Pallagia. I may not be able to convince you of the foolishness of this choice you've made, but I will not teach you how to change your lover. That is my final word."

"It may be yours, but it isn't mine."

Before Pasha could react, her sister shot into the tunnel. Pallagia gasped, the unspent energy she'd been collecting arced around her hands as she raised them in defense. When she saw Pasha curled against the wall, Pallagia's arms dropped to her sides. The energy fizzled out.

Elder Nerys appeared behind her. The white crop of hair on her head was held back by the circlet she wore as a sign of her rank in the shoal.

"Pasha. Why am I not surprised to find you here?"

PASHA

CHAPTER TWENTY-FIVE

Cold, gray early morning light seeped into the cabin. The chilly air brushed across Pasha's skin as she stretched on the hard floorboards. Summer was well and truly over.

To her left, she found Ally twisted up in her blanket, one hand dangling on the floor. Pasha had a brief flash of late-night whispers and a promise to wake her. Climbing to her feet, Pasha winced at the twinge in her back. She'd never spent so many nights out of the sea and would not recommend it to anyone. Pasha gently lifted Ally's arm, tucking it in next to her and brushing a stray lock of hair out of her face. There was still time before Pasha ought to leave the ship; she could let Ally sleep a little longer.

The bones in Pasha's feet creaked as she crossed to one of the cabin windows. Changing back to her tail was going to be uncomfortable, even with the time spent in the sea during this journey. There was a small table with a half-full jug of drinking water and a set of cups. Pasha didn't usually have to worry about thirst, but all the nights spent on the ship had left her feeling dried out. She filled and drank two cupfuls; even that small amount of water eased some of the ache in her body.

Wiping her mouth with the back of her hand, Pasha's ears caught the sharp note of a whistle. She could see the outline of the big island through the glass, a thin, dark line in the distance. They were already at the mouth of the bay.

Pasha filled another cup and carried it to the bunk. Perching on the edge, she gave Ally's shoulder a gentle shake. "Ally, it's time to wake up. We're nearly there."

Grumbling under her breath, Ally tried to pull the blanket over her head.

"You'd really rather stay on this ship than go home?"

"What... No?" Ally's face reappeared, her cheeks made ruddy by the sun and sea. Her curls were tousled and puffed into odd angles from sleeping on them while they were damp. Pasha pressed her lips together, trying not to smile too broadly at the sight.

"We're in the bay." She offered Ally the water.

"Already?" She thanked Pasha and took a few sips before handing the cup back.

Pasha stood and gave Ally room to get up. She scrubbed her hands over her face and yawned wide.

"I almost can't believe we made it back." Ally's stocking-covered feet thumped faintly on the floorboards as she followed Pasha back to the window. When she saw the island in the distance, Ally pressed a hand to her chest. "There it is; I never thought I'd be so happy to see it."

"I know what you mean." But Pasha wasn't paying attention to the island, she was watching Ally. She wanted to reach out and push back the errant curls Ally was holding out of her eyes. But her hands stayed where they were. "There will be much for you to deal with, when you're back on land, but don't let them keep you from taking care of your own needs as well."

Ally looked at her, and Pasha realized too late she'd drifted awfully close.

"Which needs would those be?" Ally's lips quirked as she pulled her hair over one shoulder to work at a knot.

Pasha's nostrils flared and she turned her head before Ally could see the heat spreading up her neck. "You know perfectly well what I mean. Everyone on this ship needs more than one decent meal, and I suspect you'll need to sleep for several days."

"Several days holed up in the house? I'll go mad. And what will you be doing?"

"The same, I'm sure. You won't even know how tired you are until you can lay down in your own bed, neither will I. We both need the rest." When Ally looked as if she would argue, Pasha held the water out for her again. "Why don't we agree to rest for five days, and on the evening of the fifth day, I'll meet you on the shore."

Ally eyed her over the rim of the cup, her throat bobbed as she drank the rest of the water in one gulp. Pasha told herself she wasn't staring.

"Two days." She set the empty cup down.

"You're negotiating rest time?"

"Yes. We'll rest for two days and meet on the second evening."

"Four days."

Ally propped her hands on her hips. "Three days."

"I can already tell I'm not going to win. Three days it is," Pasha sighed in mock defeat. The sounds of the crew calling out the morning's tasks reached them. She moved around Ally and unlatched the window. "I should leave. I'll see you then."

"Wait," Ally grabbed her wrist. "I have to ask you something before you go. I won't be able to sleep at all if I don't."

"What is it?" Pasha turned back. Ally's slender fingers, pressed lightly against the pulse point on Pasha's wrist, anchored her to the spot.

"We tricked Dare into kissing you,"

"As was the plan," Pasha nodded.

"And then she died. Drowned."

"Which is what was supposed to happen."

"I know, but there's something about it I don't understand." Ally inhaled quickly as if she were steadying her nerves. "I kissed you before, in the mermaid trove."

"I'm aware." The corner of her mouth twitched.

"But nothing bad happened to me. I didn't die. I'm perfectly fine. Aren't I?"

"You are, indeed." Pasha stepped a little closer. "That time was different."

"Why?"

Pasha glanced at the closed cabin door, knowing Lady Kingfisher or Maher could come knocking at any moment. She leaned in and whispered into Ally's ear. "Because I wanted you to kiss me."

"Oh." Ally's breath tickled her cheek. "*Oh*. That makes sense, I suppose."

Pasha drew back until her lips hovered over Ally's. "May I kiss you again?"

Wide hazel eyes stared, unblinking into hers, and Pasha wondered if she might have overstepped. Then the fingers wrapped around her wrist shifted into her hand.

"Yes," Ally nodded, her nose brushing against Pasha's.

Curling her free hand against Ally's jaw, Pasha traced the sharp point of her thumbnail over Ally's lower lip. "That was my first kiss, you know, the one you gave me in the trove."

"I thought it might have been," she breathed.

"I'm sure it wasn't your first." Pasha chuckled low in her throat, and the flutter of Ally's pulse quickened beneath her fingertips. "But I'm glad mine was from you."

Ally's other hand slid up Pasha's arm and settled onto her shoulder. Her thumb swept over the hollow in Pasha's throat. "So am I."

As much as she wished to, Pasha didn't bring them any closer together. She was aware of herself enough to remember that Ally was clothed, and she was not. Asking Ally to hold her after her body's unsettling reaction to forcing energy through the turbine was one thing. This was something else entirely. Instead, Pasha grazed her knuckles over Ally's cheek before sliding her hand behind her neck. Loose, feather-soft curls wound around her fingers. She tried to copy the way Ally had slanted her head during their kiss in the cave and brushed their mouths together. It was the slightest touch, even lighter than the first kiss Ally had given her, but still enough to feel the shape of Ally's lips. The distinct bow's dip at the top and the soft, full lower lip beneath it.

Watching Ally's face for any sign that she'd done something wrong, Pasha's next kiss was a little surer, a little longer. Ally's eyes drifted closed, and she angled her chin to capture Pasha before she could pull back again. This was so different from a kiss in the sea, with the water all around and between them, traces of salt flavoring everything. Pasha could feel every curve and line, could taste the subtle difference between Ally's lips and the skin just around them. Ally cupped the back of Pasha's head, guiding them into a rhythm that sent heat rushing over her skin like a summer wave. She could hear her own heartbeat thundering in her ears, and every muscle not involved in kissing was strained with the effort of staying put.

Without letting go, Ally moved their joined hands behind Pasha's lower back, urging her forward. That Ally wanted her closer was almost enough to make Pasha abandon her earlier resolution. She reminded herself they were on a ship with a large number of people just outside this room. When tugging on Pasha didn't yield any results, Ally took a step towards her instead. Pasha's resolve was now hanging on by a thread.

Ally murmured her name between kisses. Pasha released her hand to circle an arm around Ally's waist, the coarse material harsh against her overheated skin. The tip of Ally's tongue traced the seam of her upper lip. There was a brief flare of concern about the sharpness of her teeth before Ally did it again, and the heat from Pasha's skin rushed into her chest. It hovered there for a moment before dripping down to pool in the pit of her stomach and... There was a sharp knock on the door, and they sprang apart.

"Al? You awake? We have to meet with your mother and First Mate Kamharida to discuss the plan for getting all of the ships docked into port."

With a short huff at Maher's uncanny timing, Pasha pressed a kiss to Ally's forehead and breathed in her scent one more time. "I'll see you in three days."

Maher knocked again. "Come on, Al. Once we get back on land, you can spend the rest of the week sleeping in your own bed!"

Dragging herself away before she gave in to the urge to shout something about rude interruptions through the door, Pasha shoved the window open and hopped onto the sill. At least none of the other ships were close enough for someone to see her diving off the side.

"Pasha," Ally's husky voice made Pasha look over her shoulder. A new kind of smile tugged at Ally's lips, one that nearly made Pasha forget all about leaving and climb back into the ship. "See you in three days."

# MAHER

CHAPTER TWENTY-SIX

Docking the *Maiden's Revenge* into Kingsport harbor was one of the most chaotic moments of Maher's life. The destruction and bloodshed that had taken place on the *Pike* still felt like it hadn't really happened. He often caught himself thinking it was a dream, a nightmare brought on by the stress of the last few months.

Time was limited, even as the ship crawled through the harbor. Everything had to be managed very carefully if the plan he'd gone over with Ally and Rochelle was going to work. Word would have already traveled that the three large ships sailing into the harbor were friendly, despite being armed to the gunwales, and all under the command of the first mate of the *Pike*. Maher prayed Rochelle and Ally would be able to hold their composure and play their roles once they touched land. It would be difficult for them, he knew well enough, but it was the only way they could fool the person who betrayed them all to Captain Dare.

The ramshackle crew of *Pike* survivors and conscripted sailors liberated from the pirate fleet prepared to drop anchor. His left shoulder ached, and Maher rubbed the heel of his right hand against the scar beneath his shirt. It would likely always trouble him, even with the healing he'd received from Pasha. He still hadn't been able to thank the mermaid. She'd saved his arm, indeed probably his life, when she had no obligation to do so. It was done for Ally's sake more than anything, but he still hoped to find a way to express his gratitude. For all his distrust of Pasha and her intentions, she'd still come through for Ally when he'd been left in a wretched state, hardly able to remember his own name.

Tucked into the inside pocket of the jacket given to him by one of the crew, was the heavy gold ring with the Kingfisher seal. Well, it wasn't quite the Kingfisher seal Maher knew. This bird was holding two fish instead of one. He had to retrieve it from Dare's desk himself. Ally still wouldn't touch it, as if Foraoise's bitterness and rage were a curse that would latch onto her if she did. Ally, who'd never believed in tales or superstitions, even when they were children listening to Priestess Esa's stories. Her perceptions of the world had been much altered in the span of a season. So had Maher's, really, after witnessing a woman drown from within and the appearance of honest-to-gods sea monsters that Ally insisted were on their side. He could still see the pirates caught in one of the larger creature's jaws when he closed his eyes.

A great crowd had gathered at the wharf by the time a gangplank was rolled up to their ship. Murmurs and questions wove through the people before Ally stepped into view, helping her mother disembark. Someone shouted that Lady Kingfisher and Lady Alphonsine had returned, and many of the murmurs turned into cheers.

Maher descended with Kamharida's assistance, still not completely steady on his feet. They stayed close to the two women in front of them. People rushed aside as the sound of horse hooves thundered into the wharf. Lord Kingfisher, his three sons, and a squadron of manor guards, all on horseback, raced down the long dock where they'd moored the *Maiden's Revenge*. The guards formed a loose perimeter around the family. Lord Gaius Kingfisher was off his horse before the animal had come to a complete stop. Tears shone in his eyes as he swept his wife and daughter into a tight embrace. Soon Ally and Rochelle were crying as well. Gaius kept pulling back to reassure himself they were really home before dragging them back into his arms. They were all talking over one another and, while Maher couldn't make out what was being said, the joy on their faces was enough to guess.

The three brothers reached them as Gaius released Ally. He kissed Rochelle soundly before holding her again, one large hand smoothing tenderly over her shorn head. As if knowing their father and stepmother would need a moment, the brothers went straight for Ally. She stiffened slightly when Luthais wrapped an arm around her shoulders. The tense moment didn't last long, and she threw herself into a hug with both Gai and Cal. Turning to where Maher and Kamharida stood, Luthais approached and clasped the first mate's hand.

"I'm glad to see you well, First Mate." He scanned the harbor behind them. "I take it you couldn't bring my ship home with you."

"The *Pike* was lost, Lord Luthais, along with most of the crew." She bowed her head. Maher knew she was still quietly mourning their loss. "But if it weren't for Maher, every soul on board would have perished."

Luthais took him in, the weather-worn lines around his mouth deepening when he noted how Maher leaned on Kamharida. "I won't ask right now how you managed to stowaway on my ship. Obviously you were meant to be there."

Maher took the hand offered and had to bite back a grimace at how hard Luthais gripped him. When they let go, the bones running down into his wrist throbbed. "I believe so. We've learned a great deal about Captain Dare and her plans."

"Have you?" He glanced back at the rest of his family. "And will you be imparting this knowledge to the rest of us?"

Maher slipped into an expression of neutrality good enough to rival his father's unaffected ambassador visage. "We most definitely will."

The mantle clock chimed midnight as Maher lay in bed, staring at the ceiling. In the silence of the sleeping house, the dinging bell was the only noticeable sound. Not that he'd been able to sleep for a minute since they'd docked that morning. There were greetings to be made, missives to be dispatched, reports to be given and received. A private audience with Lord and Lady Kingfisher that only happened because of Rochelle's refusal to rest until it did.

Somewhere among all that, he'd made time for a meal, a bath, and a shave. Then a trip to Ally's room to ensure she was still coping with it all. Mrs. Thorley, the housekeeper, had been so happy to have them back, she'd arranged for everything they could ask for. Even going so far as to ask Ally if she would perhaps, this once, want to soak in a larger bath to ease the stiffness in her muscles. Ally politely refused and waved away the look Maher gave her.

"It might sound silly to you," she said once they were alone, "but while I may be able to swim in the sea without any trouble, I still don't think I'll ever like that bathtub."

"Doesn't sound silly to me." Maher understood. The memory of Ally's first panic attack, resulting in a maid dropping her against the side of a copper tub, was still strong. He kissed her cheek and promised to come back once everything was settled. "You can still come if you want. No one would stop you."

Ally shook her head, weary but clear-eyed. "I know, but I don't want to be there. Let me know when it's over, I don't care what time it is."

Now Maher swung his legs over the edge of his bed. Rotating his shoulders, noting how the left couldn't go as far anymore, he gathered what he needed. He'd been lying fully clothed down to his boots, one less thing to stop for. It wasn't a guarantee this would happen so soon, the first fucking night after their return. But his friends and contacts in the Lantern district, Pimm, Mama Bear, the Madam, and Marielle, had all been hard at work in his absence. Word reached him just before dinner, tonight was the night to act. Their best hope now was that they hadn't been misled.

To any deities who might be listening, Maher prayed that wasn't the case.

Taking no light and trusting his memory to navigate the manor, Maher slipped out of his room. Having his pistol back in its place behind his back was both a comfort and an unfortunate reminder. He took the long way, winding past the dignitary quarters, unoccupied at the moment except for his father.

Khafra Villaon had made exactly one appearance since Maher's return to the house, to confirm with his own eyes the rumor that his son was still alive. He'd taken a long look at Maher, then left the room without a word. There was a light shining beneath his door, even at this hour. Maher would deal with him later, whatever that might entail.

His chosen path took Maher through the kitchen and out the garden door. Hardly anyone other than the servants came this way, so it was usually a safe place to leave unobserved. Relaying this plan only to those who needed to know was tricky. There were more moving parts than Maher had worked with in the past. All it would take was for one person to slip up, and the whole thing could fall apart.

"You're certain about this?" Cal asked when Maher met with him, Gai, and Lord Kingfisher earlier in the evening. Luthais had gone down to check on the remaining members of his crew, or so he'd said.

"Absolutely. Captain Dare wasn't as careful as she likely thought. Many of the sailors who defected would pick up on things that didn't make sense at the time. Even Lady Kingfisher was able to learn a great deal from being housed in the captain's cabin."

"I don't want Rochelle bothered with any of this," said Lord Kingfisher. The fire burning in the study hearth streaked his blonde hair and mustache with gold. "Not until she's recovered and able to face it."

Gai nodded, smoothing his own mustache. "Agreed. She has been through enough."

"Of course," Cal rubbed a freckled hand over his rounded chin. "I just wish we had something more solid to back this up."

"We will. Once we get the officers from Dare's flagship who chose to join us talking, we'll have plenty." Reaching into his jacket, Maher withdrew the gold ring and placed it on the table. "And we'll find out how she got this, as well. Dare told Lady Kingfisher it was a gift."

Lord Kingfisher picked it up, the diving bird flashed at them in the firelight. "This belonged to my grandfather, or someone before him."

"How do you know that?" asked Maher.

"The kingfisher bird is holding two fish in its beak. It was meant to signify prosperity. After the near-ruin of the Isles and the rebuilding, the crest was changed to the single fish we have now. As a sign of humility to the sea goddess."

"Too bad it didn't work," said Cal.

There was a horse saddled and waiting for Maher behind the stables. The black and white piebald's hooves had been wrapped in cloth to help muffle their sound on the city streets. Maher hauled himself into the saddle, with only a minor twinge in his shoulder. The horse whickered and shifted but stayed calm while he got comfortable.

"Get me through this night, friend, and I promise you a whole bushel of apples."

Maher rode through the quiet streets of Kingsport. Though there had been excitement at Rochelle and Ally's safe arrival, an official celebration would be held when they were both well enough to attend. Still, he occasionally heard late-night singing and laughter drifting from one building or another. Some of the tension that still gripped the city had eased with the news of Lady Kingfisher's rescue. Perhaps the Birde Isles' fortunes weren't as dire as they'd seemed. That didn't mean they were out of danger yet. There was still the inexplicable funding behind the street crews that grew bolder with each passing day. Even though Maher had a suspect in mind now, nothing was proven. And the depleted fishing catches. Ally said Pasha could bring them back again, but was it really sustainable? Perhaps the people of the Isles needed to adjust their expectations of the sea.

Maher checked his pocket watch as he neared the northernmost end of Kingsport. This was one of the oldest sections of the city, another reason the northern wharf was rarely used anymore. Some of the buildings dated back to before Gaius I's time and were in desperate need of repair yet hadn't been included in the rebuilding of the Isles.

Crumbling patches of plaster and cloudy windows outnumbered the flower boxes and cheap, brightly colored curtains meant to brighten their surroundings. The solid, stone foundations were all that kept many of the structures standing. Supposedly they all had expansive basements that were once connected by tunnels, intentionally collapsed some time ago to prevent people from getting caught in falling debris. Maher couldn't decide why this area hadn't been touched unless its residents hadn't allowed such a thing. People in this district kept to themselves and weren't likely to interact with outsiders, as if the north of Kingsport were its own separate city. For tonight, though, Maher was glad to know he'd be left alone. This was where Pimm rented their rooms.

Half of an entire floor belonged to Pimm, in a squat, four-story structure that bordered the wharf. Mama Bear had tried to convince them to move to the Lantern. If not into the Bear's Den, then close by. Maher wondered at their reluctance to leave, but this was where Pimm had lived as long as he'd known them. Who was he to be any judge? He'd turned an entire guest room at the Kingfisher house into a closet.

Tying the horse to a post in the small patch of dirt that served as the building's courtyard, Maher used Pimm's keys to unlock the main door. Up three flights of stairs that creaked if he breathed too hard, Maher let himself into Pimm's home. He'd only been there once or twice, and never for long. Pimm valued their privacy. So much that Maher didn't feel comfortable looking around too much. He locked the door and crossed the sitting room to a row of windows. The room was clean, but the air was stale from its occupant having been gone for several weeks, healing from a few broken ribs. Pulling back the curtains revealed a mostly unobstructed view of the wharf; enough to see the masts of the ships sitting just beyond the wharf proper.

After consulting his watch again, Maher took out a candle and matches from the bag he'd brought. Sitting the candle on the windowsill, he selected the match he wanted and struck it. A bright green flame burst to life, and he quickly lit the wick before the color burned out. Maher held his breath, afraid of blowing the candle out. Down below, near the place where the cobblestones ended and the old wharf platform began, an answering green flame danced in the darkness like a firefly.

Exhaling slowly, Maher put out the candle and closed the curtain.

Back on the street, Maher left the horse concealed in the courtyard and continued on foot. His immediate problem, whether he could reach the ship first, would only be solved if he paced himself. The wound in his shoulder might have been healed, but the rest of his body had barely begun to recuperate. It had taken an act of sheer will to pull himself out of bed when the clock struck midnight. Huffing and puffing his way through the wharf would only signal his location to anyone nearby. And tip them off to how weak he was at the moment.

When Maher stepped onto the dock, there was no one else in sight, but that didn't mean he was alone. This stretch of dock was nearly as ancient as the rest of the district, the edges of some boards broken off from decay. No crates or equipment to hide behind either. Maher pulled the collar of his black coat up and walked as quickly as he dared. There was a short gangplank already rolled up to the side of the ship, with just enough space underneath to conceal one exhausted Maher. He ducked beneath it and found a fresh lantern waiting for him. The tautness in his chest eased ever so slightly. Now, to wait and see if everything else fell into place.

Maher braced a hand against the boards above him and adjusted his position. He needed to start choosing better hiding places. Or pay someone to do the hiding for him.

Footsteps echoed down the dock. Someone was hurrying in his direction. Maher waited, both hands on the gangplank to keep himself as still as possible. The new arrival turned down towards the ship, drawing closer until they came to a stop. Something heavy thumped onto the rotting planks. Maher thought it might have gone straight through if they'd dropped it any harder.

There was more shuffling, then a gruff voice spoke, "Where the fuck are they?"

In one breath, Maher grabbed the unlit lantern and stepped out into the open. A shadowed figure stood not two yards away, back turned and peering at the small office building at the top of the wharf.

"You're a little late," Maher drawled. "My leg was going to sleep."

The man whirled around. "Who's there?" The outline of an arm reached back.

"Whatever weapon you're going for, I'd leave it where it is."

"Who the fuck are you? What do you want?"

"You're asking a lot of questions for someone who tried to have his own family murdered."

His voice switched to a calmer, more patient tone. "I don't know what you're talking about."

"I think you do. In fact, I know you do." Maher struck a match and lamplight cut through the darkness, shining on the face of Calder Kingfisher.

PASHA

CHAPTER TWENTY-SEVEN

Pasha made it as far as the great chamber beneath the island before exhaustion pulled her down to the sandy floor. She dropped the spear beside her, arms splayed out by her sides. The raw stone of the ceiling seemed to shift and flow, as if it too were part of the current moving through the caves and tunnels.

Closing her eyes, Pasha relished the sensation of the water lifting her limp fins, the soft sand cushioning her scales. She stretched her arms overhead, letting the sea fill her up. It felt so good to be fully back in the water, back in her home. What would have made this perfect was to have Ally sitting next to her.

Ally is safe, she's right above you. Pasha chided herself, reaching out for the faint, reassuring pulse of the shark tooth. *You're the one who convinced her to go rest for a while.*

Which needs would those be?

Pasha's face warmed and she pressed her fingers to her lips. Each time she thought about kissing Ally, the memory became more vivid. Until she could practically feel it happening all over again.

If Ally could make her feel like that from only a few kisses, then...

Rolling onto her stomach, a small cloud of sand puffing up beneath her, Pasha rested her head on her arms and told herself not to dwell on it right now. She'd watched Ally become so worn down, even after they'd set sail for the islands with her mother and Maher in tow. Often during the voyage, Pasha would look up to find Ally burrowed deep into her own mind. The struggles facing her family, all of the humans on the islands, were far from over. But Ally needed to take care of herself first. That's why Pasha insisted she go to her house for a few days. Ally wouldn't have rested as well down here, even with the gift Pasha had given her.

There were other things that had to happen before she could imagine anything more developing between herself and Ally. As they'd gone over everything found in Dare's cabin a final time, Ally went through every detail of Maher's plan. It made Pasha queasy to think of Ally getting close to the brother they hoped to catch. It wasn't smart to swim too near to the place where all the ships were docked, but Pasha had to see Ally make it safely onto land with her own eyes. When that brother pulled Ally into a hug, Pasha's lip had curled back into a snarl. It was only sheer exhaustion that stopped Pasha from hurling a good-sized electric charge at his head. She wanted to take the man herself and drag him to the depths for all that he'd put Ally through. But Ally assured Pasha that she'd never be alone with him, not for a moment, and planned to stay in the house once Maher's scheme went into motion.

Still, Pasha would worry, though she felt some small comfort knowing the shark tooth would tell her if Ally was in any kind of distress. For now, she'd wait and stay alert for any change in the beacon connecting her to Ally. And hope Maher would make his move sooner, rather than later.

MAHER

CHAPTER TWENTY-EIGHT

"Evening, Cal."

"Maher." Sharp green eyes regarded him through the lamplight. A large duffle bag, the kind often used by sailors, sat at his feet. "What are you doing out here? Strange time of night to be about, especially in your condition."

"You know me, a man of constant action if there ever was one." Maher leaned against the gangplank, hoping he looked relaxed and unbothered. Not like he needed help to hold himself upright. "I'd rather like to know what you're doing in this part of the city. Planning a voyage?" He raised the lantern, glancing back at the ship. The *Wave Skipper* name had been hastily painted over, but the outline of the carved letters was still visible.

"You've always been smart, Maher, use that intellect now and walk away. If you can walk, that is. I'm almost impressed you made it up here."

"Sadly, I can't do that," he shrugged. "You've caused a lot of destruction, Cal, people have died because of your actions. Do you honestly think I would let you take off without answering for that?"

There was a clatter somewhere above Maher's head and he stiffened. Cal's eyes darted to the ship behind him, a slow smile spread across his face.

"If you really wanted to prevent me from taking my leave, you shouldn't have come alone." Cal withdrew a small, single-shot pistol from his pocket. "I certainly didn't make that mistake."

"Who said I was alone?"

Maher waved the lantern in an arc above his head. More lights glowed at the top of the wharf, and at least a dozen booted feet pounded toward them on the aged boards. Cal spun in a frantic circle, wild-eyed and searching for a way out. Facing Maher again, he lifted the pistol.

"Get out of the way, Maher. I'm getting on my ship."

"Are you sure you want to do that?" Maher kept the light trained on Cal.

Ignoring him, Cal shouted at the still darkened vessel. "What are you halfwits waiting for?"

In answer, a shot rang out. Sparks flew from Cal's hand as the bullet caught the barrel of his weapon. There was a hiss of black powder going up and the smell of burnt skin.

"Fuck!" Cal tossed the ruined pistol away, dropping to one knee and holding his injured hand against his chest.

A string of lamps came to life along the main deck of the *Wave Skipper*. Marielle, resident gunfighter for the Madam of the black lantern, appeared at the rail with a smoking revolver in her hand. She was flanked by two men in the Madam's employ that Maher recognized, and several others he did not.

"Nice to see you again, Maher." She grinned down at him, a few gold-capped teeth winking in the lamplight. A long coat flapped open behind her, and Maher glimpsed two more guns holstered beneath her arms.

"Always a pleasure, Marielle. I very much appreciate not being shot."

"We do what we can to help." Marielle winked and turned to the others with her. "Let's bring our new friends tied in the cargo hold up for some air. You alright from here, Maher?"

"Fine," he waved her off. "Feel free to clear out whenever you want. I know you won't feel like chatting with Kingsport guards tonight."

"Much appreciated." Marielle and the rest of her crew disappeared below decks.

Cal staggered to his feet as Lord Kingfisher, Gai, and Luthais reached them. A mix of manor and Kingsport guards were spaced out behind them, waiting for their lord's instruction.

"I hoped Maher was wrong," Lord Kingfisher stood ahead of his other two sons. "Calder, what possessed you to do this?"

Before Maher's eyes, Cal's freckled face shifted into the portrait of innocence. He turned wide eyes to his father. "I didn't want to help Dare, Father, I swear it! During one of my trips to Meredia on your behalf, she found out who I was and threatened to kill our entire family if I didn't do as she said. I believed she only wanted to build her fleet, her status as a pirate, so I gave her information on trade routes and cargo. I never thought she'd kidnap Rochelle." Cal's voice wobbled, and Maher snorted. The man belonged on the stage. "I didn't tell you, because I thought I could fix it, make everything right again if I went to retrieve her myself."

"That's not exactly how it happened, was it?" Maher set his lantern down. "You may have seen Foraoise Dare in Meredia by chance and realized who she was, but you never actually met her face-to-face, did you?"

"How could that be possible?" he cried. Cal took a step towards his father, both Gai and Luthais bristled. "How could I have known she was a Kingfisher?"

"You found the priestess' records." Gai held up Aithne's journal. "And you sent her this."

The blood drained from Cal's face as soon as he saw the book.

"Didn't think we found that, did you?" said Maher.

"Your handwriting is all over the pages, Cal!" Gai spat. "Every note and detail added from the other temple records you stole. The Head Priestess finally discovered how many were missing when Ally went to her for help after Rochelle was taken."

"What would you have done with the diary if you hadn't run into Dare? Used it to prove the real heir to the Kingfisher title was out there somewhere, find her, and convince her to raise your rank?" Maher asked.

"What?" Lord Kingfisher's gaze swung to Maher.

That was the one theory he hadn't shared with any of them yet. The idea would have seemed too far-fetched to a close-knit family like the Kingfishers, but such things were often attempted in Saprea and other neighboring nations on the continent. One branch of a family trying to usurp the power or wealth from another. Maher hadn't really considered it to be a possibility, until he learned Captain Dare was a lost Kingfisher. In that moment he'd felt even more confident than ever that Luthais was involved. Then Pasha found the diary.

Cal's head was lowered, his hair fallen into his face to obscure his eyes. The pain on Lord Kingfisher's face was easy to read. "Son, how could you do this to the people who rely on us here? To your family?"

"Family?" The venom dripping off Cal's tongue made the hair on Maher's arms stand on end. When he lifted his head, gone was any trace of warmth or sincerity. Cal's boyish face twisted into something dark, bitter. "Did you call it family when you married a new woman, a stranger, when our mother's body was barely cold?"

Luthais spoke for the first time. "Cal, we were all upset when our mother died, but that's not how it was."

"No? How was it, then? Rochelle gave Father what he didn't have, a daughter. The first daughter in generations, they still say. Precious Ally, so special the Head Priestess herself says she must be protected at all costs. More valuable than a third son."

Gai said, "Cal, that's enough, we never –"

"Shut up! I expected to be overshadowed by my older brothers, to the firstborn goes the finest. There are only so many titles to go around. But to be passed over for a younger sibling? A younger sister, not even fully our blood, birthed by the bitch who thought to take our mother's place?"

"You were never passed over," Gaius tried to reason with him. "I have striven to give all of my children the same opportunities in life. Yes, Gai is the oldest and so he inherits the title. Yes, Luthais was chosen to become Lord of Trade. But when were you ever unloved? When did Rochelle ever not treat you like her own son? Tell me if there was any instance, any slight at all, and I would readily apologize."

Maher knew nothing about Lady Glenna Kingfisher, though he'd seen the portrait that still hung in the gallery. Rochelle had insisted it stay in a prominent place, to honor her memory. Where was Cal getting this idea that he'd been treated as a spare child?

Cal laughed, a strangled sound that made Maher question how long this resentment had been festering inside him. "I should have done what I planned years ago. Every time Ally begged to go out on the water with us, I thought I could do it. I should have taken her out and tossed her overboard. People drown all the time, right?"

Maher's pistol was in his hand, though he had no memory of reaching for it.

"When I saw her sneak out that night to go to the shore, I thought she might take care of one of my problems for me."

"You saw Ally leave the house, the night she nearly drowned?" Luthais' brow furrowed as he and Gai shared a look.

"I did, and I should have followed," Cal snarled. "Turned out she couldn't even drown herself right."

Maher pulled the trigger, right side aching from the kick of the gun. His head swam, and black powder stung his nose. Gai and Luthais shielded their father. Many of the guards dropped into a defensive stance, except for the one who decided to jump off the dock. And Cal. Cal was crouched down, arms thrown over his head. Maher had fired into the dock. Had he wanted to aim right at the back of Cal's head? Yes. But Maher was no executioner. Cal was surrounded, he would be punished by the laws of the Birde Isles.

That would have to be enough.

"Cal," Maher waited for him to look up. "I didn't put a bullet through your skull because your family has the right to deal with you. But you will *never* threaten Ally, or anyone else, again."

It probably should have occurred to Maher, when Cal charged at him, that his reflexes weren't in top shape. There was just enough time to send the pistol skidding toward Lord Kingfisher before Cal tackled him. The back of Maher's head hit the dock, waterlogged fibers buckling under the impact. Cal only got one punch in before Luthais and two guards pulled him off. Maher stared at the night sky and tasted blood on his tongue. His mind wandered to the last time someone had disagreed with his face, as Ally put it. A small chuckle escaped him before Luthais' frown blocked out the sky.

"Maher, are you alright?"

"Fine, fine." Maher flapped a hand at him, it was the best he could manage. "I was just thinking of what your sister will say when I come back with another busted lip."

Luthais blinked at him, then huffed out what might have been a laugh. "Let's get you up."

When Maher reached the solid ground of the wharf, relying heavily on Luthais to get him there, the guards had already taken Cal away. Gai had gone with them, but Gaius Kingfisher was waiting with the captain of the manor guard. Any grief he might have felt over his own son's betrayal was carefully hidden by then.

"Words can't express how much we owe to you, Maher, truly. After you've recovered, I'd like to have a proper talk."

"Of course, Lord Kingfisher." Maher shook his hand.

"My lord," another guard approached from the direction of the *Wave Skipper*. "We've found a dozen sailors on board, all gagged and bound to the mainmast, but there's no sign of who could have done it."

Maher cleared his throat, and Lord Kingfisher glanced at him. "Sea sprites?" he offered.

"Must have been." The lord of the Birde Isles raised a brow. "Luthais will help you back to the house."

MAHER

CHAPTER TWENTY-NINE

"I have a horse tethered nearby," Maher protested when Luthais steered them towards his own mount waiting up on the street. The sturdy dappled gray watched their slow progress with mild interest.

"We still need to get you to it, and I'd rather not carry you the whole way." Luthais rubbed the horse's nose. "Can you climb up?"

"We'll see." Maher took his arm from around Luthais' shoulders. Being shorter than Maher had made him an excellent walking stick. Wrapping one hand around the saddle horn, Maher tried to lift a foot into the stirrup. He made it about halfway before his leg began to tremble.

"Why don't I give you a hand?"

Sighing, Maher dropped his foot. "I'm afraid you'll have to."

The admission barely left him before Luthais bent and hooked an arm around his knees. Maher's ass hit his shoulder, and Luthais lifted him as easily as if he were a sack of grain. The ground rushed away and Maher's sense of balance all but abandoned him. He grabbed the first thing he could reach, the long braid hanging down Luthais' back.

"This isn't undignified at all," Maher muttered.

"Could be worse," Luthais eased one of Maher's legs over the horse and helped slide him onto the saddle. "If you'd been knocked out, I'd've had to truss you across like a deer."

Did Luthais Kingfisher just make a joke? Maher was too tired to tell.

"Let's try to avoid that." He gave directions to Pimm's building and Luthais led the horse along. After passing down one deserted block in silence, Maher kneaded his shoulder and sighed. "I owe you an apology."

"For what?" Luthais guided the horse around a wide, weed-filled crack in the cobblestone.

"I thought you were the one working with Dare, at first."

Luthais' head tilted, but he didn't respond.

"After Rochelle was captured, I saw you in the Lantern at the door with the purple lamp outside. The pleasure district was the last place I ever expected to find you. I assumed if you went to such lengths to hide whatever it was you were doing, you must have been involved. I believed you were guilty without any real proof. I'm sorry."

Another block passed before Luthais spoke. His voice was so low Maher had to lean forward to catch everything he said. "I suspected Cal was making his own trade deals, particularly in Meredia. Making promises that would be impossible to keep and open the door for other nations to accuse us of playing sides. I had a group of guards and sailors I trusted trying to get close to Cal's crew. When Rochelle was taken, I was sure it was retaliation for Cal's doings abroad." He shook his head. "I never imagined Cal hated his own family so much."

"No one knew," Maher said carefully. "He hid it so well, all those years."

Luthais grunted in answer. Maher decided not to push him to speak any more about his younger brother.

"And the foxglove given to Cal's crew so they couldn't sail? Was that your doing? I have to know."

"That was me," Luthais admitted. "It was only enough to make them ill for a short time."

"So you knew the tainted ale was safe to taste in front of your father. How cunning of you, Luthais. I like it."

Luthais glanced over his shoulder. It could have been a trick of the fading nighttime shadows, but Maher thought he saw a smile.

Maher's horse snorted in greeting when they reached the courtyard. "Hello friend; I shall deliver your apples as soon as I can walk unaided." The horse beneath him swung its head. "Alright, apples for you too."

"Instead of moving you, I'll ride your horse back." Luthais let the piebald smell his palm before untying the reins. Maher had never before thought of any of the Kingfishers as being particularly good with land animals. Luthais hitched the gray to the other horse and swung into the saddle. "We should be back around dawn."

"I'll try to stay awake. Actually, could you help me to Ally's room when we get there? She wanted to know when it was over, no matter the time."

"Sounds like Ally."

Maher chose not to ask how Luthais would know that, and they rode on in silence. As Luthais predicted, they were getting close to the manor when the sky really began to lighten.

Luthais patted the neck of the horse he rode. "Did you choose this horse on purpose? A piebald?"

"Huh?" Maher started awake; he'd begun to doze in the saddle. "Why would I have done that?"

"Piebald coloring is named after a magpie. They call you the Magpie in Kingsport, don't they?"

Maher nearly slid off the gray's back and grabbed the saddle horn with both hands. He groaned, "Not again."

"Is that a no?"

"Not all of us feel the need to have modes of transport named after ourselves," he snapped, thinking of the moniker the middle Kingfisher brother had used to name his ship. The *Pike*.

A row of white teeth flashed at him, and Luthais shrugged. "I just thought that might have been the reason."

Two jokes in one night, Maher thought. *Lucky me.*

They made it to the stables without further incident. Two grooms took the horses, and Luthais helped Maher into the house. The few servants they passed stared openly. Whether at himself, or Luthais, or both, Maher didn't have the energy to guess.

"There's still one thing I'm curious about," Luthais said when they reached the second-floor landing.

"What's that?" Maher wheezed. Even with the other man's assistance, he felt ready to collapse right then and there.

"How did you get onto my ship with no one noticing?"

"Um." They were almost to Ally's room. Maher did his best to grin with a split lip. "Sea sprites?"

Luthais snorted. "I'll have to meet these sea sprites one day."

Maher stumbled, but the muscled arm around his waist kept him from falling. "Yes, well, like all magical folk, they do enjoy presents."

"I'll keep that in mind."

Change the subject, Maher. You're so tired you'll say something you shouldn't. Change the subject!

"Personally, I want to know how Cal got his hands on those Saprean coins. I'd appreciate if you could tell me when you plan to ask him; I have a few questions of my own."

Luthais stopped in the middle of the hall, just one door down from Ally's. He turned under Maher's arm enough to look him in the eye. "*What* coins?"

CHAPTER THIRTY

Maher knocked on Ally's door just after dawn. She found him braced against the doorframe, as though it were the only thing keeping him standing.

"Morning Al," he panted. "I very much need to sit down."

"Dear goddess! Of course, come inside." She helped him to her bed and took his coat. When he was seated comfortably, she poured a glass of water from the pitcher on her bedside table. While he drank, she grabbed a handkerchief to wipe the dried blood from his chin. "Darling, why does this keep happening to your face?"

The water seemed to help; he sounded less hoarse, at least. "You know how jealous people can be when you're this handsome."

Ally sat next to him and dabbed the handkerchief against the corner of his mouth. "Perhaps you should grow a longer beard, to help protect this glorious face." Maher snorted but held still while she checked the split in his lower lip.

"Have you been up all night?" he asked.

"Is it that obvious?"

"You're still in your clothes, and the bed is made."

"Not much gets past you, does it?"

"Not much," Maher shook his head, "But some things do."

Ally exhaled slowly. "So, it's done?"

"It's done."

"Good." She took his face between her hands, turned it this way and that to check for other injuries. "This one doesn't look nearly as bad as the last time."

"Well, Luthais came to my rescue pretty early on in the disagreement." Maher swayed, his eyelids drooping.

"Luthais?" Ally took the glass before Maher could drop it and returned it to the table.

"Yes, we had quite the adventure tonight. He even told a joke. Twice."

"Twice? Goddess below, it must have been all the excitement. Lie down." Ally got Maher settled on one of the pillows and removed his boots. Moving around the room, she put out the lamp on her dressing table and pulled the curtains to block the morning sun peeking through the window. He was already asleep by the time she finished.

Not bothering to change out of her own clothes, Ally crawled into bed and snuggled up to Maher's uninjured side. When Ally's head touched his shoulder, his arm fell open and wrapped around her, his hand coming to rest on her curls. Falling easily into the napping position from their childhood. Ally laid a hand on Maher's chest, listening to his heartbeat, so thankful he was there with her.

Maher's head rolled, and his cheek rested in the spot just above Ally's hairline, his shallow breaths occasionally rustling a curl or two. She was just drifting off herself when he spoke, voice thick with sleep. "Love you, Al."

"Love you, too."

They both slept for the first time since they made it home. Though Ally dreamed of the sea, there was no fear or unease when she saw the azure water rising to meet her place on the grass. Because this time, unlike all the other dreams she'd had before, Pasha was waiting for her in the waves.

Ally and Maher slept in her room the entire day, barely stirring when dear Mrs. Thorley made occasional appearances with more water, juice, and the kinds of food that could be easily eaten between naps. The housekeeper must have informed Ally's family she was finally resting since no one else came to disturb them.

When night fell, Maher dragged himself to his own room to bathe and change out of the clothes he'd been in since the night before. Ally did the same, and they met in her mother's private second-floor sitting room to share the dinner Mrs. Thorley had sent up. It was cozy, done in shades of blue and white, with just enough room for a squat bookshelf and a plump sofa covered with Rochelle's favorite patterned fabric: a herd of Balahn deer running through a thick copse of trees. An elegant silver clock sat on the mantlepiece, also engraved with two leaping stags. Beneath the window sat a miniature version of the Balahn altar Mama kept in her bedroom.

A small table was brought in and set just for the two of them. As they worked their way through courses of pastry-wrapped salmon, lentil soup, and roast lamb with potatoes, a bright fire burning in the hearth, Ally felt almost content. Almost. Her mind kept wandering to where Pasha waited beneath the island. If she was also resting, as she'd promised, and if she'd had the energy to eat today with no one else to bring her food. Ally wished she could have brought Pasha to the house with her, but knew the mermaid needed the sea to heal more than anything else. One more day and she'd see her again.

"Are you alright, Al?" Maher asked after their empty plates were taken away and an apple tart was placed on the table.

"Yes, only I'm a little worried about Pasha. She has no one to take care of her right now."

"Why don't you go check on her tomorrow?" He served them each a helping of dessert.

Ally sighed, "We agreed to rest for a few days before we meet on the shore again. But at the time, I didn't think about how she'd have to do everything on her own."

"From what you've told me about her, it sounds like Pasha is used to taking care of herself."

"She shouldn't have to; that's the point."

Maher poured two cups of tea from the fresh pot that was brought in with the tart. "I agree, but I'd wager she won't be pleased to think you weren't taking care of yourself for worry over her."

Ally studied him, stirring milk into her tea. "That's very astute of you, Maher."

"What can I say? I'm gifted with a remarkable intuition."

She smiled, some of the tightness in her chest easing, "Is that what you call it?"

When dinner was finished, they moved to the sofa that faced the fireplace. Ally tucked her feet beneath her and waited for Maher to get his long legs situated on a footstool.

"Have you spoken to your father since we returned?" She'd been debating on when to bring the subject up. They hadn't spoken of Khafra Villaon since their argument aboard the *Pike*. That night seemed like an age ago.

"He came to my room yesterday, to confirm I was really alive, I suppose. But we didn't speak."

"You're saying he just looked at you for a minute and then walked away?" Her brows knit together. "He said absolutely nothing?"

"Absolutely nothing. Neither did I."

"I'm sorry, Maher." Ally took his hand in hers. "Maybe he needs time to take it all in. You didn't exactly part well last time, and for all he knew you could have died out there. You almost did."

"I'd say not," he snorted. "He'll have to face me soon, one way or another, once I get this Lord of Trade nonsense cleared up. He can't possibly expect to get away with it now that you and Rochelle are both home safely."

"You think he'll still try to push for that? Mama was furious when I told her of Khafra's plans to oust Luthais of his title. The disloyalty to Luthais aside, his actions could have jeopardized her rescue more than I think even he knows. Her affection for you is the only thing standing between Khafra and his dismissal. She'll step in if it comes to that."

"I'm sure she will, Al, and I'll ask for her help if I need it, but I have some conditions of my own to set with my father."

"I'm sure you do."

They sat in comfortable silence for some time. The warmth of the fire soaked into Ally's skin, and she let her head fall onto Maher's shoulder. His head tilted back against the sofa, and he very quickly fell asleep. His soft snores soon drowned out the ticking clock. Ally sighed, and breathed in the pine and cardamom scent of his cologne. Tucked beneath the neckline of Ally's dress, the shark tooth beat a steady pulse of energy that seemed to match her heartbeat. She'd just dozed off when Maher snorted awake and dislodged her.

"All the gods and their grandmothers, I can't believe I forgot!"

"What is it?" Ally groaned, rubbing where his shoulder had knocked against the side of her head.

He turned to her, chestnut eyes wide in the firelight. "The sea monsters, Al, what happened to the sea monsters? Where did they go after we left with Dare's ship?"

Ally blinked. She and Pasha had convinced Euphonia to stay out in the deeper water, far enough away from any land that she could hunt in peace and not be noticed by humans. It had taken a great deal of cajoling and a promise from Ally to visit as soon as possible, but Euphonia finally agreed not to follow the *Maiden's Revenge* back to the Birde Isles.

But there had been so much else on her mind at the time, Ally had quite forgotten about the others. She wasn't so worried about the massive squid, but the snapjaws?

"Al?" Maher prompted.

"Um..."

"*Um*? That's not an answer that inspires confidence, Ally."

"I mean, Euphonia, my creature, the one that helped me find Pasha, she's gone back out to sea. It would have caused a mass panic if she'd followed us home."

"Followed you home? It's not a stray puppy, Al, it's a... it's a... Fuck I don't know what it is! But you're sure she'll stay put?"

Ally nodded. "Positive. She listens to me."

"We'll circle back to my questions about that later. What about the rest?"

"The squid went home, I'm sure; we'd woken it up from a fairly long nap."

The look on Maher's face told her exactly how comforted he was about the words *squid* and *nap* used in the same sentence. "And the others? That pack of nightmare crocodiles?"

"I don't know," she admitted. "They didn't cross my mind again after the pirates surrendered."

"How is that possible?"

"Well, let's see, I'd just learned the woman who kidnapped my mother was my long-lost aunt. Then I had to watch her murder half of Luthais' crew and force a kiss on my... Pasha, and then witness said aunt drowning *outside* of the water. I'd only just learned you'd survived the sinking of the *Pike* but were still on death's door. We still had to sail home and confront my own brother who betrayed us," Ally knew she was talking too fast, breathing too hard, but couldn't seem to stop. "I had a lot on my mind, Maher!"

"Al, hey, I know. I'm sorry." He pulled her into a hug and rubbed her back until her breaths smoothed into an even rhythm.

"I thought I'd lost you," she hiccupped into his shoulder. "It still comes over me, out of nowhere. I thought you were *dead*."

"I'm here," Maher soothed. "Thanks to you, and to Pasha, and a monster squid, I'm right here and I'm not going anywhere," he chuckled. "It'll take more than an exploding ship and being struck by lightning to get rid of me."

Ally sat up, her smile wobbly. "It had better. Who else will I embroider all those clothes for?"

"Certainly not Pasha," He flashed a cheeky grin when Ally flushed and pushed him away. "Seriously, though, when you see Pasha, you should ask about those monster crocodiles." Maher shuddered. "My memory is, admittedly, a little hazy, but from what I've heard from Kamharida, they seemed far worse than the other two for some reason."

Chewing her bottom lip, Ally looked back into the dying fire. The memory of a cold, rasping voice and glowing red eyes raised the hair on the back of her neck.

We accept.

"You're right. They were worse."

PASHA

CHAPTER THIRTY-ONE

"*Pallagia, please, you have to eat something.*" Pasha brought the hunk of fish wrapped in seaweed to her sister's lips. She'd been trying to coax Pallagia to eat for days. At first just leaving the food by their bed, but when Pallagia only ignored it, Pasha started giving her small bursts of energy.

Now she needed to build her own well back up before attempting that again.

"*Just one bite,*" Pasha tried again. Pallagia's emerald eyes stared unfocused at the ceiling. Her mouth stayed closed. The silvery shine of her skin had faded to a stony gray. Her fern green hair hung limp around her face. The knot that had settled deep in Pasha's chest tightened painfully. Setting the food on the floor by the bed, Pasha gently pushed Pallagia's hair back and kissed her forehead. "*I'll be right back. Please try to eat something while I'm gone.*"

Every day Pasha made the same request, and every day Pallagia grew weaker. Fighting back the tears that burned behind her eyes, Pasha left their chamber and went in search of Elder Nerys.

Something had to be done. Pallagia couldn't go on like this, blaming herself for what happened. No one could have expected... Pasha shook *the thought away. Her sister had been careless, she knew that, but Pasha couldn't help thinking this wouldn't have happened if Nerys had helped Pallagia from the start. Instead, her refusal only made Pallagia desperate. Reckless. Enough to pull the girl into the sea with her without changing her, or even giving her the ability to breathe in the water.*

And maybe Ealasaid would still be alive.

The great chamber was a flurry of activity. It had been since Pallagia was spotted by the humans. Most of the mermaids swimming by ignored Pasha, but the others? Pasha knew they blamed her just as much as her sister for the danger they were all in now. She felt the weight of their gazes as she crossed the cavern and slipped down the tunnel to the tapestry-filled cave. The elders had been studying each woven piece for some time. What they were looking for, Pasha didn't know.

The corals in the tunnel flashed at her. Pasha paused, uncertain of what they wanted. There was no time to guess, a mermaid carrying a small carving pushed through the doorway and slammed into Pasha.

"Watch where you're going!"

Righting herself, Pasha came face-to-face with her cousin Hama. One of the few in their shoal with a direct familial link to Pallagia and Pasha. Something the older mermaid was not currently happy about.

"Sorry, Hama." Pasha ducked her head.

"I'm sure you are," she sneered, showing a row of sharp teeth. "What are you doing down here?"

"I - I was looking for Elder Nerys."

"She has no time for you."

"I will be the judge of that, Hama." Nerys said from inside the cave. "Let her through and take that carving to the great chamber."

"Yes, Elder Nerys." Hama looked down her nose at Pasha as the small mermaid tried to squeeze by. Before Pasha reached the doorway, Hama

leaned down and hissed, "This is as much your fault as it is Pallagia's. You should have stopped her. What, were you too busy playing with your dead things?"

Pasha shrank back and darted into the cave. The elder was floating by the far wall, studying a smaller tapestry that laid out the last known mermaid shoals throughout the seas.

"Elder Nerys?" Her voice trembled, still shaken by the venom in Hama's words.

"Yes, child. Come here."

Pasha joined her at the tapestry. "I need help, Elder Nerys. Pallagia won't eat, she won't move, she just stares at nothing all day and all night."

"Your sister is heartsick." Nerys traced a dark gray fingertip across the glass encasing the map. "There is not much we can do for her if she will not help herself."

A heavy tear slid down Pasha's cheek, and she scrubbed it away. The magic fizzled into the water, wasted. What about Pallagia's well-being being the same as the shoal's? Did that not matter anymore because Pallagia made a mistake?

The elder mermaid finally looked at her. Leaning down, she took Pasha's hands. Warmth flowed up her arms as Nerys gave some of her own energy to Pasha. She breathed deeply, and the knot in her chest loosened ever so slightly.

"Pasha, there is something important we must discuss."

"What?" Pasha tried to pull her hands back, but Nerys held them fast.

"We are concerned, not just for our shoal but for the others scattered across the seas. It has been many years since we've received a visitor or even a message from the others. We must ensure they are all safe and well." Deep azure eyes bore into Pasha's. "Right now, it is no longer safe for all of us to

remain here. We will go and search for the rest of the shoals and give the humans in this place time to forget again."

A trickle of dread crept up Pasha's back, making her dorsal fin flare. "We're leaving our home? Everyone?"

"Not everyone." Nerys' grip on her hands bordered on painful. "Someone must remain, to guard these caverns until the shoal returns."

"You... you're going to make Pallagia stay behind, aren't you?" This wasn't right, Pallagia was sick. She needed care, not to be abandoned. Pasha wanted to scream, to rip the map from the wall and smash it against the stone.

"No, Pallagia is too ill to take on this task."

Relief flooded through Pasha, until Nerys spoke again.

"We have chosen you, Pasha. You will stay behind."

CHAPTER THIRTY-TWO

The evening Ally and Pasha had agreed to meet finally arrived. True to her word, Ally did nothing for the last three days but sleep, eat, and spend time with her family and Maher. Both she and Maher came downstairs for dinner that night with her parents, Gai, and Luthais. Khafra Villaon had yet to appear again. Ally thought he would have been overjoyed to know his son was alive and well. Or mostly well. She could see Maher's shoulder bothered him if he tried to use it beyond his new limits. The damage had been far worse than anything she'd imagined. That Pasha was able to heal him as much as she did was a miracle, as close a thing to magic as Ally had ever witnessed.

Ally's fingers drummed restlessly against her leg throughout the meal. Though the conversation was pleasant, and this was the first dinner with everyone together since Ally and Rochelle's return, there was still a somber note in the air. No one acknowledged the empty chair that had always been Cal's place at the table. It would take some time, Ally felt, before they'd be able to discuss his absence.

After fidgeting through the first two courses, Ally started when Maher leaned over and whispered, "You'll see her soon, Al. Just be patient."

When Ally finally bade everyone goodnight, she raced to her room to change out of the gown she'd worn to the dining room. The small tapestry she'd taken from Pasha's home was safely stored in the linen trunk at the foot of her bed, and it was almost ready. Not the least of Ally's regrets after their fight aboard the *Pike* was that Pasha had trusted her with one of the few pieces of her family she had left, and Ally might never have had the chance to return it to her.

Though some of the discolored portion down the middle had been impossible to restore, she had a plan that would hopefully reduce the chances of further damage. Maher had even contributed to the idea, a sign of his changed feelings towards Pasha, if there ever was one. Still, Ally was eager to show Pasha the progress she'd made before the final step. She carefully rolled the map up and tucked it into a satchel to bring with her to the shore.

Crisp evening air filled Ally's lungs as she made herself walk at a normal pace through the grounds, tamping down on the urge to run full tilt to Pasha. But it was like a fishhook was stuck through her ribs, reeling her faster and faster down to the shore. She pulled her cloak snugly around her shoulders and raised her lantern higher as she neared the old seawall. A lithe figure waited by the water's edge, and Ally's heart lifted.

Finally. She kept her eyes on the uneven stone steps until her feet touched sand, then looked to where Pasha stood.

"Ally!" Pasha waved, and the scales on her arm glistened in the faint moonlight.

Ally broke into a run, her feet eating up the distance between them. She scarcely remembered to put the lantern and satchel down, and then she was throwing her arms around Pasha's neck.

Relief, sweet and clear, filled Ally up until tears burned behind her eyes. The cool scent of the sea filled her nose, and she felt Pasha's crackling store of energy thrumming beneath the mermaid's skin. Pasha's arms slipped beneath her cloak, and she held Ally close. Her face found its way into Ally's hair, and Pasha's deep breaths ghosted beneath the collar of Ally's shirt. A sharp gust of wind blew in off the waves; Ally shifted and pulled her cloak tighter around both of them.

"And you wanted to wait for five days," Ally sniffled.

"I don't know what I was thinking," Pasha said, lips brushing the crook of Ally's neck.

Combing one hand through Pasha's damp, dark blue hair, Ally coaxed her to look up. She ran her other hand over the smooth ridge of Pasha's brow and settled on her cheek. "I missed you." Ally planted a kiss at the corner of her mouth.

Pasha's arms, still buried beneath Ally's woolen cloak, nearly squeezed the breath out of her. "I've missed you too."

"I should hope so," Ally closed her eyes as Pasha tilted up to kiss her forehead, "since it was your idea to stay apart for so long."

Extracting one arm from her waist, Pasha gently grasped Ally's chin and turned her head. She kissed her temple, then just barely grazed her mouth over the healing bruise on Ally's cheekbone. "As you've said already."

"Just reminding you." Ally lost whatever she meant to say next when Pasha's impossibly soft lips touched the spot beneath her ear, then skimmed over her jawline. Her fingers wound tighter into Pasha's hair. "For – for someone who had their first kiss such a short time ago, you're awfully good at this."

"I didn't have much to do in the last three days." Pasha tilted Ally's head the other way. Sharp teeth grazed her skin as Pasha spoke. "If I wasn't dreaming of you, I was thinking of what I wanted to do when we finally met again."

"A very good use of time." Ally thought Pasha was going to kiss her properly then, but the mermaid brushed past Ally's mouth and traced over her nose instead. She breathed in sharply at the unfamiliar, featherlight touch on the crooked bridge, going still to see if Pasha was going to stay there. Immediately, Pasha drew back. The hand holding Ally's chin slid to cup her cheek.

Ally opened her eyes to find Pasha studying her, brow creased with concern. Her black eyes reflected the lamplight as they searched Ally's face. "Was that alright?"

Ally's lips parted. Was it? Once, the thought of someone touching or, goddess forbid, *kissing* her nose would have left her feeling exposed and self-conscious. She'd instinctively tilted her head away the last time a woman tried to do something like that. The whole evening ended soon after when the woman had taken offense.

It took her by surprise, the tenderness Pasha was showing, the care she was taking to learn what would and wouldn't make Ally happy. She hadn't disliked anything Pasha had done so far. Far from it. Ally wanted to do the same for her, but there was no need to rush. Ally's face still tingled where Pasha's lips had been. Almost the same way it felt when Pasha gave her the gift of breathing underwater. She wondered if Pasha realized she was giving tiny sparks of her power with each kiss. Had their kisses on the ship been like that?

Ally realized she hadn't answered Pasha yet and could feel her body tensing with each second that passed. Smoothing both hands over Pasha's hair and down her shoulders, Ally pressed a quick peck to her lips. "It's fine, I promise. I was surprised, that's all."

Pasha relaxed under Ally's touch. "Surprised by what I did?"

"More because of how much I enjoyed it." She grinned before pulling Pasha in for a proper kiss. The hand still around Ally's waist shifted to her hip, Pasha's nails pinpricked into the fabric of her trousers. Ally rested her hands above Pasha's shoulders, relishing the silken texture of the silvery-gray skin beneath her fingertips. The glistening, slick scales scattered across her cheek and down her neck made Ally want to follow the jeweled trail wherever it led. Before her imagination carried that thought any further, Ally gave Pasha a last kiss and pulled away. Pasha tried to follow, but Ally pressed a finger to her lips and felt the huff of frustration as Pasha halted. It was so endearing that Ally nearly let Pasha have her way, but there were things they needed to discuss.

"I have something to show you," Ally whispered.

MAHER

CHAPTER THIRTY-THREE

After seeing Ally off to meet Pasha, Maher hobbled back to his own room. For the first time, having quarters on the far side of the manor seemed like a bad idea.

He was glad Ally and Pasha would have this time alone together. The mermaid hadn't been mentioned at dinner, but he knew Rochelle had met her. And he was perfectly happy to let her ladyship ease the rest of the Kingfishers into the idea that Pasha and Ally had formed an attachment. Besides, it was hard to still be wary of someone who'd saved your life. In fact, all of his suspicions had been proven to be entirely wrong.

Pasha. Luthais. Maher shook his head.

A fire was already burning in the hearth when he reached his rooms. Maher lit the lamps by the door and on his dressing table. Shrugging carefully out of his jacket, he laid it over the foot of his bed and sank onto the stool in front of his mirror. The last three days of rest and good food had helped immensely. But he still looked, and felt, like shit.

His boots really ought to come off next, but the thought of bending that far was not appealing. He'd forgotten, Ally had helped him dress to join the family for dinner.

Maher was working up the energy to ring for a servant when there was a soft knock at his door. Stifling a groan, Maher pushed himself up and crossed the room.

"Luthais?" He blinked at the other man standing in the doorway. Had he forgotten some meeting with Lord Kingfisher? If Luthais said they were due in his lordship's study on the other side of the manor, Maher might actually cry. "What can I do for you?"

"We haven't really spoken since returning to Kingsport,"

"You mean since you propped me up outside Ally's room?"

"Right," he snorted. "And then the two of you were recovering together, I didn't want to intrude." Shrewd green eyes traveled down Maher's frame and back up again. "But you looked like you could hardly keep yourself upright during dinner. I wanted to check in on you."

"Oh. Oh, well, thank you, but I'm fine. Really –" Maher's balance chose that moment to fuck off and he listed to the side. Luthais caught Maher under his good arm and steered him back into the room.

"Well, this is familiar," Maher deadpanned. "At least you didn't have to pick me up again."

"Sit down." Luthais deposited him on the edge of the bed. "What else do you need?"

"Nothing, I..." Maher glanced at the pull cord hanging in the far corner and sighed. "I was about to ring for a servant. Al helped me dress earlier, but she's gone to meet her... friend." Luthais' head tilted, but he didn't ask him to elaborate. "If you could just pull the cord?"

"It will take some time for one of the staff to come." Luthais' arms crossed over his broad chest. "What do you need?"

Any embarrassment Maher might have otherwise felt evaporated. All he wanted was to lie down and sleep until spring. "I can't get my boots off."

There was a brief pause, and then Luthais Kingfisher, Lord of Trade of the Birde Isles, was kneeling on Maher's floor. One big hand wrapped around the back of Maher's heel while the other gripped the boot's sole. "Can you lift your leg?"

Mumbling something that was close enough to 'yes,' Maher braced a hand on his shoulder and together they wrestled the boot off. "This is ridiculous. I'm going back to Saprean style shoes; they just slip right on and off."

Luthais gave Maher a moment to rest, then made quick work of the other boot.

"I appreciate the help, really. You can just leave them by the door." It took entirely too long for Maher to unbutton his waistcoat. A task he could usually accomplish without thinking about it. When he looked back up, Luthais was examining a painting on the opposite wall.

It was one of the last large scale paintings Maher had finished, before his father's demands took more and more of his time. He'd gone down to the wharf early one morning to observe the crew of a Char-range trade ship preparing to make way. Half of the vessel was still wrapped in shadow, while the rest was bathed in the soft orange light of a new day. The hull and railings were stained a brilliant shade of amber. Sailors moved nimbly across the deck and in the rigging, others mingled with Birde Isles workers on the dock. A lone gull perched atop the prow, watching the activity below.

"This is one of yours, isn't it?"

"It is." Maher eased out of his waistcoat, deciding that was good enough for the night. He certainly wasn't going to ask Luthais Kingfisher to help him off with his trousers. Blood rushed to Maher's face and he searched desperately for something else to say before his mouth caught up with that particular thought.

He was learning quickly just how much fatigue loosened his tongue.

Luthais turned around. "Have you had any further word about the Saprean silver?"

"Not since we returned," He said carefully. Those godsbedamned coins had been at the forefront of his mind since he first let that knowledge slip to Luthais. "What about you? Has Cal said anything?"

"Nothing."

Maher didn't push any further. The Kingfishers were having a hard enough time where Cal was concerned. Though he hadn't been to visit himself, Maher had heard more than enough to gather that Cal had dropped his loving-son-and-brother mask altogether.

"When you do, I hope you'll tell me. An influx of coin like that could have drastic effects on our own currency, but you already know that. Or, if there's a way for us to find the source together," He trailed off, stopping in the center of the room. "Why does your rug smell like a perfumer's workroom?"

"It's pine. My father spilled an entire bottle of scent all over the floor. And me." Maher shrugged. "It's how your first mate caught me aboard your ship."

"Of course it is," Luthais gave him a searching look. "You still haven't said how you got onto my ship in the first place."

"That's right."

He moved closer. "You're not going to tell me, are you?"

"Not at the moment." Maher tried to shift more of his weight onto his good arm. "Perhaps another time."

"We'll see," Luthais bent to his eye level. Close enough to see the rough, blonde stubble shadowing his jaw. "Anything else you need, while I'm here?"

If anyone else had posed that question, Maher would've come up with a smart response. Quite possibly a bawdy response, if it were one of his Lantern district friends doing the asking. But in that moment, all Maher could do was try to swallow past the growing lump in his throat.

Luthais raised a brow, clearly waiting for an answer.

Maher cleared his throat, "Be a lamb, would you, and put out the lamps?"

He straightened, and Maher breathed a little easier. "Of course. It's always been my goal in life to be a lamb."

A short laugh burst out before Maher could stop it. Surely he was hallucinating this entire conversation. This was not the serious man he'd known for nearly thirteen years. Or had their relationship changed so drastically in the last few days that Maher was now seeing the real Luthais?

When all the lamps were out, and only the glow of the hearth illuminated the room, Luthais paused at the door. Firelight cast long shadows down his face and turned his sun-bleached hair to gold. "I'll ask Mrs. Thorley to ensure you have help in the morning, should you need it."

"Thank you, Luthais." Maher nodded. "Goodnight."

"Goodnight, Maher."

As soon as the door snapped shut, Maher collapsed back onto the pillows, his long legs still dangled over the edge of the bed.

"I suppose that's three jokes now," he said to himself. "Maybe I should keep count, otherwise Al might not believe me."

CHAPTER THIRTY-FOUR

Pasha burned with the need to pull Ally close again.

Panic had spiked when Ally stilled after Pasha kissed her nose. She hadn't specifically planned on doing that, it just felt like the next natural spot on Ally's face to touch. But then Ally was smiling and pulling her in for another and Pasha let herself sink into it as long as she could.

Now that they were farther up the beach, out of reach of the tide, Ally placed a satchel Pasha hadn't noticed before on the rocks next to the lamp. Whatever Ally wanted to show her, Pasha hoped it was worth letting Ally out of her arms. On the walk up the beach, she told Pasha that Maher's plan had worked. Her brother Cal had been arrested, trying to flee the islands. From the satchel, Ally produced a roll of cloth and spread it out.

"The map..." Even in the scant lamplight, Pasha could see the brighter shades of red, blue, and green woven into the tapestry. "I can't believe how clear it is."

"I couldn't save this part," Ally traced the darkened line dividing the map down the middle, "but I have an idea to help protect it from any future damage. I'll need to keep it a little longer, but I wanted you to see what I'd done so far."

Ally sounded so proud of her work, and it was incredible how well she'd done. Sliding her hands beneath the tapestry, Pasha lifted it closer and scanned the mermaid shoal markers she hadn't seen clearly in over a century. An unsettling weight landed on her chest. Before they'd left to rescue Ally's mother, when she tried to let Ally out of their bargain, Pasha had been so sure she'd know what to do if Ally could restore the map. Loneliness, no matter how great, was never a good reason to force someone to do something against their will. If they made it back and Ally returned the map, Pasha had made up her mind to leave. To find the others. Now the thought of leaving Ally made her sick. Heartsick.

"Pasha? Is there something wrong?"

"I don't know what to say." And it was true. "Thank you."

Ally rubbed the edge of her cloak between her palms. "Will you try to find them, when it's finished?"

There was no need to consider her options, Pasha already knew the answer. "No. It will be useful if any of the other mermaids do return, but I won't go looking for them."

"Because they left you here?"

Pasha shook her head. "Because I don't want to leave *you*, Ally."

The smile Ally gave her was a little sad, and yet it eased some of the dread building in Pasha's chest. When Ally first unrolled the tapestry, Pasha was afraid she would want her to go. That somehow Ally would feel the family that abandoned Pasha was more important than what they had together.

Glancing at the map still in Pasha's hands, Ally's teeth sank into her lower lip. "We could still go if you ever change your mind."

"*We* could go?" Yes, Ally could swim fairly well and breathe underwater, thanks to Pasha, but to spend weeks or months in the sea? Her human body couldn't handle such a thing.

"I know what you're thinking, and I *could* go with you, if you changed me."

Pasha fumbled the map, barely catching it before it hit the sand. "Ally, you don't know what you're asking."

"I think I've learned enough from you these last months to know what I'm asking."

"Then you should also remember that I don't know how to perform the ritual. I've never even seen it done."

"But if you did, would you consider it? Would you consider making me a mermaid?"

"What if... what if something went wrong?" Pasha held the map against her chest, like some kind of woven shield. "It would be a huge risk even if I'd successfully changed someone before."

"And it will be a huge risk the longer I stay on land," Ally countered. "The necklace you gave me has bought me more time, much more than I might have had. But what if it becomes lost? Or stolen? What if whatever it is inside me that makes me Sea Kissed becomes stronger than the shark tooth, no matter how much energy you put into it?" She took the tapestry from Pasha and draped it back on the rocks. Then Ally held out her hands, waiting for Pasha to take them.

Pasha's heart raced as she slid her palms over Ally's and let her draw them together. Choosing to stay on the islands for Ally would only affect the two of them, but if Ally gave up her life on land? Even if Pasha already knew how the ritual worked, she would have never dreamed Ally would want this. Sea Kissed or not, it was too much to hope for.

Ally said, "I'm not trying to guilt or frighten you into agreeing. I'm thinking about how my being Sea Kissed could affect us in the future, whether we find the steps to the ritual or not."

Pasha was running out of excuses to deny how happy it made her for Ally to even suggest this. "If I make you like me, then you will be tied to the sea. You wouldn't be able to go far from it, I don't think you could leave it at all for some time after the change. What if you're needed here?"

Ally looked over her shoulder, into the darkness. "Would I be able to make it to the manor again?"

"Not at first. But after a while, as you became stronger, you might be able to."

"Alright," she held Pasha's hands against her heart. "The shop I need to bring the tapestry to said it could take a few weeks before it's ready. Let's use that time to learn as much as we can about the ritual. If we can determine how it's done, then we'll decide together."

Pulling Ally into her arms, Pasha trailed a line of kisses down her face, to her lips. She lingered there, Ally's breath mixing with hers as this future she hadn't allowed herself to want before was suddenly within reach. But at what cost to Ally? That was the one question that kept her hope in check. Ally nestled her face into the crook of Pasha's neck, lips brushing over skin and scales alike with equal care.

Pasha's mouth met Ally's ear. "We'll see what we can find."

CHAPTER THIRTY-FIVE

S wain leaned heavily against the helm of the small, Nuvwaan-made ship. The sails barely stirred as a faint breeze swept past them. Nothing but inky black water as far as the eye could see. A handful of stars, still visible at this time of night, told him they were headed north. But towards what?

A sailor shuffled up behind him. "Quartermaster?" When he didn't answer, she tried again. "Sir?"

Swain blinked slowly. "What is it, Smith?"

"We're down to the last barrel of freshwater in the hold sir, weren't much to start with when we took to the ship. Same with food. We've only got enough to feed all on board for another day or two. Maybe three."

"And?"

"And… when will we make port for more supplies? We've passed at least a dozen by now."

Swain pointed at the tattered map weighed down on the boards by his feet. "Every single one was an ally of the Birde Isles. Can you tell me which would have allowed us to dock with no flag and no documents? Which would have let us be long enough to do our business and leave? Well?"

"Of course, I can't say for sure,"

"Neither can I." He pulled roughly on his long mustache. "We keep sailing until we hit a smaller port that's less likely to ask questions."

"But, the supplies –"

"Then we go to half rations."

"Quartermaster,"

"Quartermaster of what?" Swain snapped. "Of this fucking moldering pile of wood? The *Maiden's Revenge* is gone! Everything's gone."

Smith's jaw clenched. "Quartermaster of what's left of our crew! We jumped ship with *you* rather than take our chances with a witch what calls sea monsters to do her bidding. We trust *you*, Swain; you were the only one what could keep Dare in check. She signed all our death warrants the moment she set her sights on the Isles –"

Swain loomed over the sailor, voice low. "One disrespectful word from you about Captain Dare, and you can swim to the nearest port. Understood?"

"Aye, sir." She backed away. "I'll just go secure the rations, shall I?"

"Go." he turned back to the helm. When her footsteps faded, Swain gripped the wheel on either side and leaned his forehead against the worn wood.

Everything was gone. She was gone. His last link to Jon was gone. Bitter grief laced with a deep, simmering rage tore at his stomach.

A sound reached him then, over the creak of the ship and hiss of the sea. Something soft, almost familiar. It made Swain think of the lullaby his mother sang when he was just a lad. But it was so faint, he wanted to hear it better.

Swain had left the helm and crossed to the railing before he'd made up his mind to do so. The lullaby was stronger now, floating across the waves and wrapping around him like a warm embrace.

Maybe, if he went out into the water, he'd hear it even better. Maybe the singer was waiting for him to find her. Maybe...

Lurching back from the rail, Swain shook his head and slapped himself across the face.

"Fuck," he groaned, staggering back to the helm. What in the gods' names was that? When had he last slept? Swain grabbed the map and squinted at the inked lines of the nearest coast. They needed to make port before starvation or delirium took hold.

ALLY

CHAPTER THIRTY-SIX

A few days later, Ally was sitting in the parlor with her mother, a half-finished embroidery project resting in her lap. Lady Kingfisher was reading aloud, her Balahn accent making the words rise in odd places and fall in others. It was all Ally could do to keep her eyes open, let alone concentrate on the threaded needle that had gone lax in her hand. During the day, her mind was often foggy, thoughts slipping away before she could catch them. Only when she was down at the shore did her thoughts sharpen enough to sort through them properly. On land Ally felt so stiff, so slow, the lingering soreness in her muscles only truly easing when she was in the sea.

The irony did not escape her. If anyone had told Ally at the start of the year that she'd soon be *longing* to step into the waves, she'd have been sure they'd gone daft.

Things weren't all bad on land, there were quite a few improvements. She could freely speak of Pasha to her family. Mama asked after Pasha's well-being, and it was nice to have someone else to talk to about their friendship. No one questioned her nightly walks to the shore; a supply of lanterns, oil, and wicks had been left in the small alcove by the front door. They were all aware of her condition, if being Sea Kissed could truly be called a condition. There were days Ally thought it more of a curse. And others she didn't.

What's more, the three weeks requested by the shopkeeper who was working on the tapestry would be up before long, and Pasha hadn't found anything that specifically referenced the ritual. Perhaps it would take longer than estimated. When Ally made the trip into town to drop off the tapestry with the shopkeeper, she'd left strict instructions on the age and delicacy of the piece.

Ally spent many evenings swimming through the tunnels with Pasha, into deeper parts beneath the island than they'd gone before. There were carved murals all over the walls and tucked into corners of caves. Ally'd learned so much more about mermaid culture from them. How different tasks were divided up amongst the shoal, based on each mermaid's innate talents. Pasha's sister was always the one to search shipwrecks for usable metals. How the mermaids had cultivated relationships with other sea creatures, like Pasha's whales and sharks, or the corals that made their home in the caves. They'd even found a brief mention of how rarely mermaids produced offspring, how difficult it was for an egg to reach maturity. Pasha remembered everything from moments just after she'd hatched, over 300 years of her life so far. Ally almost couldn't fathom it. Her earliest memories were of toddling after Priestess Esa through the manor library, but nothing before that. They'd learned all of this, and more, but still hadn't found the information they were looking for.

Picking up her neglected hoop, Ally tried to concentrate on the floral pattern. A wreath of double-headed tulips woven with foxglove, for Maher. She only seemed to have the patience for handkerchiefs at the moment, with a growing pile of folded squares sitting next to her on the sofa. At this rate, everyone Ally knew was going to end up with a brand-new set.

There was a knock on the double doors and Maher's head popped into the room. "Good morning Lady Kingfisher, Ally."

"Good morning?" Ally wondered at the formal tone he was using.

"Maher," Rochelle smiled, lowering her book. "Come to join us?"

"I'm afraid I can't at this time, thank you, but I wanted to ask if you were both free to talk?"

"Of course," Ally set her hoop aside as he stepped into the parlor. Maher was looking much better now, with his injuries healing and back into his usual, eye-catching clothing. Today's suit was in a shade of dark cinnamon, the orange and yellow leaves embroidered on the waistcoat a nod to the approaching season.

"I wouldn't have disturbed you, only it concerns our recent troubles."

"Is this about Cal?" Rochelle asked, and her lips thinned into a grave line when he nodded.

"There's something new that's come to light, and I felt you both ought to hear it before the knowledge becomes public. It will only be a matter of time."

"What is it?" Ally made to offer him a seat, but he chose to remain standing. She took a few steadying breaths; Maher wouldn't have brought this to them if it wasn't important. He'd been working closely with Lord Kingfisher and the trade guild leaders since his health improved.

"You will remember the many trade documents and route maps we found in Dare's cabin. How we weren't sure how she could have obtained so many, with such detail, even with someone feeding her information from the inside?"

Ally and her mother both remembered; it had been a frequent topic of conversation between the three of them.

"Now that things have become a bit more stable, I've been investigating the origins of those papers myself." Maher cast a sidelong look at Ally, and she suspected the friends who helped him stowaway on the *Pike* were involved. "There was someone else bringing sensitive information to Cal before he passed bits and pieces of it along to the pirates. She's been brought here, to explain herself to Lord Kingfisher before it's decided if she'll go to trial, and she's asked to speak to you."

"She?" Ally glanced at Mama, her elegant hands were clenched in her lap.

"I told her you both had to agree," said Maher.

"Maybe now isn't the best time,"

"Bring her in." Lady Kingfisher's back went straight and she draped her hands over the arms of her chair. A queen sitting on a throne. "If Alphonsine also agrees."

Ally gave Maher a questioning look. His brows raised in return, and he said quietly, "I think you'll want to know, Al."

"Fine." Ally crossed her ankles and tried to adopt Mama's aloof appearance. Though she felt nothing like a princess, let alone a queen. More like a barnacle clinging to the sofa.

Maher went back to the doors and spoke to someone waiting outside. That explained the formality, there were others listening. Both doors were opened wide. Gai walked in, followed by two guards. Standing between the guards were Mister Tapper and his daughter.

"Beitris!" Ally lost any attempt at copying her mother's cool demeanor and jumped to her feet. She hadn't come across anyone in the Tapper family in some time. Now she was standing across from the girl who'd made her childhood a misery, in the same place where Maher finally put a stop to Beitris' bullying. The room seemed to shrink for a moment, and

Ally slowly sat back down. The guards posted themselves by each of the doors leading out of the parlor, swords sheathed at their sides.

Beitris Tapper's pale skin was splotchy and streaked, her eyes red and puffy from crying. Her father didn't look much better, his face haggard and fine clothes rumpled as if he hadn't slept in days. The bright red hair he'd passed on to Beitris had thinned a great deal since Ally last saw him. He kept running a shaky hand over the balding crown of his head.

Gai folded his arms and regarded the Tappers. "Well? You wanted an audience with Lady Kingfisher and Lady Alphonsine, and they've granted it. Say your piece."

When Beitris turned to them, no doubt taking in how gaunt Lady Kingfisher still looked and the silk scarf tied around her head to cover the places where her hair was still growing back. When she saw the obvious disbelief on Ally's still-bruised face, the red-headed young woman burst into fresh tears.

"I'm... I'm so sorry, Your Ladyship, Lady Alphonsine. I... I took copies of the trade maps and shipping manifests from my father's study, and I gave them to Cal." Beitris hiccupped. "He promised we would be married, as soon as he proved to his family he could be trusted to manage his own trade charter. He... he said we had to keep it a secret, because of what happened between Lady Alphonsine and I when we were young, that is, how I treated her. If he wasn't able to support us on his own, he said you'd never agree to our engagement. I swear, I didn't know he was giving them to the pirates w-who..." Beitris sobbed into her father's shoulder until he patted her back and gently lifted her off.

Mister Tapper placed a hand over his heart and bowed deeply to Lady Kingfisher. "My lady, I offer no excuse for my daughter's actions and can only offer my deepest apologies on behalf of our family. Everything we have built was the direct result of the generosity of the Kingfisher family and their care of the Isles. I will take my share of the responsibility for not securing the files kept in my home, and we will respect whatever punishment you or the courts feel is appropriate. I only ask for a small consideration of mercy, since I truly believe my daughter was deceived of the reasons she took them."

Lady Kingfisher looked down her nose at the Tappers, considering how to answer. "As a parent, I can appreciate your love and concern for your daughter. It does sound as though our son was not honest with Beitris. We never had any knowledge of a desired engagement."

Beitris wailed, and her father rubbed her back until she quieted again.

"The law will require some form of punishment, to be sure, for it wasn't only my life that was endangered by Captain Dare obtaining that information. Not to mention the sailors' lives that were lost." Lady Kingfisher's eyes softened slightly. "But I will speak to his lordship with regards to your request. We were all deceived in who Cal was, and there may be more who come forward."

How many others had Cal tricked into believing he cared for them? And Mama had still called him son just now, which might have only been for the Tappers' benefit. Was Cal even capable of real love for anyone?

"Thank you, your ladyship." Mister Tapper bowed again. Beside him, Beitris was trembling like a leaf clinging to a branch. Her sobs had subsided, but she fumbled through the pockets of her gown but came up empty-handed.

Rising from her seat, Ally took one of the finished handkerchiefs from the pile and crossed the room. Beitris was trying desperately to wipe her eyes with her sleeve. She placed the handkerchief in Beitris' hand, closing her trembling fingers around it. Her bloodshot blue eyes locked on Ally as she clutched the embroidered cloth.

Ally returned to her place next to her mother.

MAHER

CHAPTER THIRTY-SEVEN

Maher followed the familiar route through Kingsport to the Lantern district. It had only been a few weeks since Pimm arranged to sneak Maher aboard Luthais' ship. Actually, it was the Madam of the black lantern who got Maher onto the *Pike*, Pimm was more of a facilitator.

His as-yet unpaid debt to the Madam was something Maher would have to deal with sooner or later. Preferably later. He wasn't naive or stupid enough to hope for never.

It was still early in the evening, and he passed several lamplighters finishing their rounds through the city. As the streets narrowed and he crossed the invisible boundary into the Lantern, something tight in Maher's chest eased.

Khafra's threats to destroy all that Maher had built and imprison everyone he'd ever had contact with in the district held no weight now. But it was still a relief to see with his own eyes that everything was as he'd left it. For the most part. One of the orange lantern establishments he frequented, the Whistle and Bells, was boarded up. The apricot panes of its lantern were smashed. Even the lacquered sign with the club's carved tongue-in-cheek name was off its hinges, leaning sadly against the side of the building. Nailed to the chained door was a large sheet of parchment. Maher let himself through the short front gate and peered at the sign in the fading daylight.

Closed for repair. All employees have moved to temporary establishments. Inquiries must be made and vetted at the Bear's Den. A reward is offered for any information leading to the identification or capture of those responsible for the damage to the Whistle and Bells.

"At the Den?" Maher questioned under his breath. The other Lantern owners must have come together to help. But what in all the gods' names had happened here? Beneath the top message was another in bold print.

UNTIL FURTHER NOTICE, ESTABLISHMENTS WITHIN THE LANTERN WILL NO LONGER ACCEPT SAPREAN CURRENCY.

At the bottom of the page was a sketch of both sides of a standard Saprean silver coin. Maher's hand immediately went to his trouser pocket. The coin he'd been carrying on and off for weeks was solid against his palm. He'd found it still miraculously on his person after the downing of the *Pike*, the pirates hadn't bothered to search him. Since then, he'd taken it everywhere, like some maudlin good luck charm. Like Ally with her shark tooth, he'd realized. Except Ally's charm brought her warmth and comfort. Maher's filled him with a mercurial sense of dread. It was proof that, though the pirates had been thwarted, there was still something sinister at work in the Isles.

Backing away from the door, Maher dropped the coin back into his pocket and continued down the street. Now that he was paying attention, he saw similar notices about the Saprean coins posted on every door. He could only hope this meant someone had located the illusive origins of the coins that had been flooding Kingsport since the spring. As he reached the square in the center of the district, Maher noted several people stationed around the edges, hardly moving as the patrons of the Lantern milled about. Though they were dressed in plainclothes, it was obvious they weren't the bruisers typically employed by the owners. They were too clean-cut, practically standing at attention. One woman on Maher's side of the square kept a hand on her belt as if she were used to carrying a weapon there. Maher would have bet his best suit they were Kingsport guards sent to keep watch. What exactly had happened in his absence? He didn't see any other signs of damage in the square, but that didn't mean there wasn't more trouble down the side streets.

Finally, he reached Bear's Den. It didn't appear any different on the outside but, being one of the few after-hours clubs that required membership tokens, they were more selective in their clientele. Pushing open the wide door with its bear head knocker, Maher was enveloped by the warm colors and soft-spoken voices waiting inside. He turned to greet whoever must be standing in as door guard and found a pair of startled gray eyes waiting for him.

"Maher!" A wide grin spread across Pimm's narrow face. Instead of their regular barstool, they were seated on one of the plush, red-cushioned chairs from the Den's lounge area. Pillows propping them up on either side made Pimm look like a young royal on a throne.

"Pimm!" Maher surged forward when they tried to stand. "Don't get up! What are you doing down here?"

"I'm not made of glass," they huffed, slapping Maher's hands off their shoulders. "And I was going mad, bored out of my skull stuck upstairs in bed all day."

"Might be the first time someone has ever said that about one of the beds here." Maher gave Pimm space as they carefully stood up. Only a slight grimace passed over Pimm's face as they straightened; their cracked ribs must be on the mend. "You do look much better, Pimm."

"Thank you, friend. You look like a whale swallowed you whole and spat you back out again."

"Thanks, I try." Maher smiled, opening his arms to accept the hug Pimm offered.

"I'm not made of glass, but be gentle." Pimm grunted when Maher squeezed too tightly.

"Sorry." He eased up. Seeing Pimm in their usual place wasn't what he'd expected at all. They'd been so badly hurt when they were jumped by one of the street crews spreading the Saprean coins. Maher had shot one of the bastards where he stood, then carried an unconscious Pimm all the way back to the Den. Even when he needed access to Pimm's rooms to track Cal, he'd sent word to Mama Bear through one of Luthais' most trusted guards. And she, in turn, had contacted Marielle. This was the first he'd seen of Pimm since his return. Maher carefully let them go. "I'm glad to see you, Pimm."

"You as well." Pimm's hand ghosted over his left arm. "How's the shoulder?"

"How did you know about that?" Maher looked down, checking that he had, in fact, remembered to dress the top half of his body and his new spiderwebbed scar wasn't on display.

Pimm raised one sandy brow. "You're really asking? A different version of the story has made its way to every corner of the city. You were struck by lightning and survived; you were touched by the goddess and given her mark; you were drowned but brought back to life by the collective sting of a smack of jellyfish," they snorted. "That's not even the most ridiculous of them. I admit, I'm curious to hear the real tale."

"Fantastic." Maher ran a hand over his face. "At least none of them could possibly involve magpies."

"Well..."

A sudden shriek cut them off. Maher spun around; Mama Bear was frozen on one of the staircases built on either side of the Den. Her red-painted lips were frozen in a perfect little 'o'.

"Don't try to stop her," Pimm whispered hurriedly. "When we learned you were back, it was all we could do to keep her from charging into Kingfisher Manor to check on you for herself."

"Don't stop her from doing what?" He barely got the question out before he was swept up into a bone-crushing, perfume-scented embrace.

"Maher! We were so worried about you!" Mama Bear sobbed into his jacket. Her loose, fawn brown hair obscured his vision. "Don't you *ever* scare me like that again."

"Yes, dear," he wheezed, acutely aware of all the eyes that must be on them. Mama Bear was not a woman who cried easily, least of all in front of her patrons.

Pimm cleared their throat. "Ma'am? You're blocking the door."

Seeming to realize what she was doing, Mama Bear released Maher, only to take hold of his arm and tow him farther into the room.

"Wait." He looked back at Pimm. The door guard gave him a wry smile and tipped their flat cap in a way that said they'd continue their conversation later. Then they turned to greet the stunned guests waiting on the threshold.

BEAR'S DEN

PIMM

Chapter Thirty-eight

Pimm chuckled to themself as Mama Bear herded Maher into the lounge, shooed two patrons from a sofa, then pulled him down onto the cushions with her. They knew how worried she'd been these last weeks. If they hadn't already been injured, Mama Bear might have been harder on them when she learned Pimm was the one who snuck Maher on board the *Pike*, with her mother's help. Mama Bear had most definitely had words with the Madam about leaving her in the dark. Pimm hadn't wanted to indebt Maher to the owner of the black lantern in order to do it, not after he'd barely squeaked out of her establishment without owing her anything the last time. But they hadn't seen any other way by that point, and Marielle had given her word she'd look out for Maher's interests with the Madam. Still, Maher didn't know half of what had transpired in the city after the *Pike* set sail and word spread that Luthais Kingfisher had jumped from his own ship. He was sure to have seen the damage done to the Whistle and Bells on his way into the Lantern, and all the signs warning patrons against paying with Saprean coin.

Pimm had never felt more useless, confined to bed rest while Maher sailed unaware into whatever dangers awaited them. The first thing

Pimm wanted to know, was what really happened to Maher on the *Pike*. Then they wanted to learn what Lady Alphonsine had truly done to make a burgeoning pirate fleet surrender without a fight. And lastly, they wanted to hear the truth of what had befallen Captain Foraoise Dare. The rumors had spread throughout Kingsport like wildfire, growing larger and more fantastical with each new telling. Maher had told Pimm once Sapreans believed retelling a story over and over only gave it more power.

Of course, Pimm knew the most ridiculous of the tales, like Maher's glorious resurrection by jellyfish, were nothing but idle twaddle. But, they reasoned, the truth had to be as astounding as the least imaginative gossip.

Mama Bear called for drinks. Pimm's attention drifted to the bar, where one of the displaced Whistle and Bells employees was following Barkeep around the small space like a bewildered duckling. Kit had to be around Pimm's age, with wide blue eyes and a crop of tawny curls on top of his head. He'd already become quite popular around the Den. The kitchen maid, Olga, was positively smitten. Pimm didn't have the heart to tell her that coming from an orange lantern establishment likely meant Kit's interests would not tend her way. Let her enjoy a pretty face while she could, Pimm supposed. Barkeep said something over his broad shoulder, and Kit nodded quickly, curls flying before he disappeared back into the kitchen. Another glimpse for sweet Olga.

The Bear's Den was probably much quieter than he was used to, at least downstairs. That was by design, though, something Pimm appreciated many a time. A patron at a nearby table lit up a pipe, and Pimm's nostrils flared.

Dear gods, I want a smoke. Their fingers itched to just *hold* a cigarette again. Mama Bear had confiscated their tobacco pouch and papers after the incident that had left them with a split skull and broken ribs.

Smoking is what got you into that trouble in the first place.

Pimm hated it when their brain used its own logic on themself.

After checking the door once more, Pimm eased back into their chair. They'd let Mama Bear fuss over Maher for a while. She was as tough as anyone Pimm had ever met, but they knew well the soft spot she had for her little magpie. Soon she'd have other matters to attend to, and the crowd in the Den would thin out. Then, when things quieted down, the two of them would talk.

ALLY

CHAPTER THIRTY-NINE

*A*lly didn't know how long she'd been standing at the manor library window. She'd been on her way to grab another text for Esa and then...

Whatever had led her from the towering stacks of books to this back window facing the sea just wouldn't come to mind.

At first, Ally thought maybe it was the view of her brothers preparing to take the new Saprean ambassador's son out into Trader's Bay. But she couldn't have seen that from across the library. Still, she'd watched as the gangly boy, somewhere between herself and Cal in age, trudged after the three blonde Kingfisher brothers to board the sloop tied at the small manor dock. He didn't appear to be enjoying himself very much, and Ally couldn't blame him.

She hated the sea.

She hated the constant rushing of the waves against the cliffs and shoreline running just behind their home. Hated the ever-present taste of salt on the air, how it coated and corroded everything it touched. But what Ally hated most of all, was how much she feared the sea. The nightmares that still plagued her, reliving the night she nearly drowned. The memory of being pulled by the undertow, the suffocating press of water on every side.

Ally's vision swam, and she gripped the freshly polished wood of the windowsill. Breathing deeply, she fished around inside the pocket of her dress until her fingers wrapped around the shark tooth. Its strange warmth had become so comforting to her recently. So much that Ally started carrying it with her, even at home.

"Alphonsine?" Esa's gentle voice floated through the library.

Dropping the tooth back into her pocket, Ally turned just as the priestess rounded the nearest row of bookshelves. "Yes, Esa?"

"I asked for the next volume of the History of Kingsport *over half an hour ago. What kept you, child?"*

"Oh, I was," Ally pointed out the window. "Gai, Luthais, and Cal were taking Maher Villaon sailing again. I stopped to watch."

Esa peered out the window, sharp brown eyes scanning the water before returning to her. "The boys are long gone. Was there something else?"

Ally shook her head. Esa knew better than to ask if Ally had wanted to join them. The priestess was Ally's only real friend, and privier to her fears than even some of her family.

"Shall we finish our lesson so you can meet your sewing instructor on time?"

"Of course." Ally followed her back to their usual table. If Esa still wanted that other book, she made no mention of it.

Biting her lip, Ally looked back once more at the strip of blue still visible through the window. She still hated that water. So why did she feel the need to see it?

BEAR'S DEN

PIMM

CHAPTER FORTY

Maher stayed through the night, allowing Mama Bear to fret and fuss over him until business pulled her away.

Finally free, he pulled a chair over to join Pimm by the door. With only a few hours until dawn, they didn't expect many more patrons to arrive.

"So, she finally released you?"

"Barely." Maher sank heavily into his seat, rolling his left shoulder.

Pimm handed him a handkerchief. "Here, you might want to clean the lip paint off your cheeks."

Sighing, he scrubbed at the rosy color staining his face. "I hate she was so worried."

"You're a part of this place as much as anyone else."

"I'll replace this," Maher tucked the ruined handkerchief into his pocket. "How are you, Pimm, really?"

"Really? I want a cigarette more than anything else I've wanted in my life. That's how I am."

"Ah, right, no smoking allowed while your ribs heal," he smirked.

"Jackass," they muttered.

"I missed you too, Pimm."

"Um, begging your pardon," Kit appeared before them, two stoneware mugs in hand.

Pimm blinked, they hadn't even heard the lad approaching. "Yes, what is it?"

"Barkeep sent these over, and wants to know if you'd like anything from the kitchen?"

The scent of cinnamon and cloves hit Pimm's nose as they accepted the mug of spiced cider. "I'm fine, thank you. Maher?"

"Nothing for me. This will hit the spot, though." He gave Kit a full Maher Villaon smile, and the lad looked as if he'd swallow his own tongue.

"Where are my manners? Kit, may I present Maher Villaon. Maher, this is Kit..." Pimm's head tilted in question.

"Na-Naumenko," he stammered.

"Kit came to us from the Whistle and Bells," Pimm added.

"Naumenko? Your family is from Zavatleo, then?" Maher sipped his cider.

Curls fell into his eyes as Kit nodded quickly. "On one side. Father is Zavatleon, Pa's from Gull Isle."

"And you didn't fancy it all the way up north?"

"Too many cows." Kit made a face, then caught himself. "Sorry, not that cows aren't important."

Pimm chuckled. "You've not offended anyone here. Neither of us is fit for a farm."

"Kit!" Barkeep called from across the lounge.

"Yessir!" Kit dipped his head. "Pleasure to meet you, Mister Villaon."

"Just Maher, please."

Crimson stained his cheeks before Kit hurried back to help at the bar.

"Well, that was adorable."

"How do you do that?" Pimm asked.

"Do what?" Maher raised a brow over the rim of his mug.

"You learned more about that lad in one conversation than I've had out of him in a week."

"It's a gift."

They snorted. "Right."

"I don't remember him from the Whistle and Bells last time I was there."

"I think he'd only been in their employ for a short time before the attack on the establishment." They drank, the cider warming them from the inside.

"It's good of the Den to take him in." Maher's expression shifted. "It seems we have much to tell each other, my friend. Where do you want to start?"

"Most of the attacks started right after you left," Pimm spoke low, so the few remaining patrons wouldn't hear them. "The street crews grew even bolder, sometimes harassing the district patrons during the day."

"But they still only stayed in the Lantern?"

"So far. One crew tried something on the wharf, and got their clocks cleaned by a group of sailors."

"Not surprised. They'll not try that again soon, I'll wager."

"I'd say not. Shortly afterward though, they destroyed the Whistle and Bells." Pimm shifted into a marginally more comfortable position. "That's when the Lantern owners went to the Kingsport guard for help."

Maher helped straighten the pillow behind their back. "All of them? Even the black lantern?"

"Marielle went in the Madam's place."

"Impressive," Maher whistled. "She'll make herself indispensable at this rate. But those guards blend in about as well as a snapjaw in a garden fountain."

"A what?"

"Never mind. Are they making a difference?"

"At first, but the crews learned the times they'd trade off and would strike then." Pimm tapped their fingers against the arm of their chair. "Then word spread that Lady Kingfisher and Lady Alphonsine were returned safely home and everything suddenly dropped off. Like it took them by surprise."

"What do you mean?"

"I mean, that it appears that wasn't the news they were expecting."

MAHER

CHAPTER FORTY-ONE

Maher and Pimm talked well into the morning, when all the Den's patrons had cleared out and the door was locked for the day.

At some point, Olga came for their empty mugs. She welcomed Maher back and even planted a kiss on his cheek. He tugged on the white mop cap covering her wheat-blonde hair and sent her on her way.

Pimm listened intently as Maher described the trap Dare had laid for them, nearly falling from their chair when he revealed Dare's connection to the Kingfishers. At the mention of the turbine, Pimm questioned if the Kharaboans were still making them. There'd been no news of a machine of that scale on the Isles.

"What about the coins?" Maher asked. "Any word there, besides the Lantern establishments not accepting Saprean currency anymore?"

"Nothing," Pimm's brow pinched. "And they've only been banned in this district, the crews can still spend them all over the Isles. If anything, it's made it harder to track them. Nobody is jumping to give up good silver."

Maher stretched, winced at the pull in his shoulder, and rubbed his jaw. "Maybe it's time to bring in more help?"

"Who else could be trusted with this?"

"Well, I think Marielle has proven she can be trusted and has displayed a talent for infiltrating places we can't."

"You want to go into even deeper debt with the Madam?"

"Do we have to go through her for Marielle's aid?"

Pimm reached into their vest pocket, then sighed when no tobacco pouch was found. "Damnit."

Maher thought for a moment. "There's also Luthais Kingfisher. He all but offered his help after we stopped Cal from escaping Kingsport."

"Now you want to involve the Lord of Trade? I know he's freed himself from suspicion, but do you really trust him that much?"

"I think so, yes." Maher surprised himself with how quickly the answer came. He also wondered if Luthais was involved with the street crew skirmish on the wharf but kept that question to himself.

"So our choice comes down to the Madam of the black lantern or Luthais Kingfisher, Lord of Trade?" Pimm groaned. "Gods, I need a smoke."

"You know Mama Bear won't allow that."

"Fine. Distract me by finally telling what happened when Lady Alphonsine rescued you all from Dare's ship."

Maher licked his lips. He'd spent most of their conversation trying to work out in his mind the best way to tell them. Despite his being there, Maher's memory was hazy, winking in and out as he'd gained and lost consciousness. Never would Maher have thought he'd see Kamharida Anyanwu, first mate of the *Pike*, look as haunted as when she'd recounted the nightmares Ally and Pasha brought with them to face Captain Dare.

"Pimm, I swear, I thought it was a fever dream until Kamharida and Ally told me all that I'd missed."

"Tell me the truth, did Dare really drown on the deck of her own ship?"

"You truly want to know?"

"The rumors have been spectacular, it's hard to know what to believe."

"It happened. A drawn out, excruciating way to die."

"Gods above and below." Pimm made the Saprean sign against ill fortune, a gesture Maher'd rarely seen them use. Apparently, even practical Pimm was shaken by recent events. "And after she was dead?"

"I saw a squid large enough to lift an entire ship out of the sea like a child's toy."

Chapter Forty-two

Ally slipped out of the house and into the cool, predawn mist hanging over the island.

Walking the path she'd taken countless times before, Ally hardly felt the twigs and pebbles strewn through the grass that pressed into the soles of her slippers. The shawl around her shoulders slid down into the crooks of her arms, but she couldn't be bothered to block the chill.

That same sensation she'd felt on the shore with Pasha had returned, a fishhook caught between her ribs, pulling just enough to coax her forward. Burning just enough beneath her skin that it couldn't be ignored any longer.

Reaching the top of the slope, Ally passed the grassy spot where she usually stopped and kept going until she reached the stony edge. A gust of wind swept up from the sea below and whipped her hair around her face. The tugging beneath her rib cage eased, and Ally took a deep breath of salt air.

Blinking slowly, as if waking from a trance, Ally looked down to find herself a mere step away from the edge.

With a sharp gasp, Ally lurched back until her feet found the grass. She sank down and gripped handfuls of the dry blades, heart hammering in her chest.

"Why am I up here?" Her voice felt small and frail, carried away by the wind. Ally squeezed her eyes shut, freeing one hand to hold the shark tooth hanging outside her nightgown. Heat seeped into her palm, but unlike every other time she'd held it, that's where it stayed. No warmth or comfort traveled up her arm or spread through her chest.

What if Pasha's energy is running out?

A sense of clarity hit Ally like a rogue wave. That was why Mama and Maher both seemed to be improving, while Ally only felt worse as time passed. Her bones and joints ached, the very air around her felt heavy. Just yesterday, she'd tried to repair a rip in Gai's coat and couldn't keep hold of the needle.

The only relief came when she was in the water with Pasha. The small doses of energy that came with each kiss. How the waves lifted the weight from her body.

At first, Ally thought it was the relief of being home. Of having those she cared about most back safe and sound. But if that were so, she should be feeling better. Ally opened her eyes, squinting against the glare of the sun rising over the sea.

Long pushed-aside memories came back to her then. Pausing at windows or wandering through the grounds until she could glimpse the sea, with no recollection of how she'd gotten there, or even of deciding to do those things. And the nightmares.

All of that stopped when she started wearing the shark tooth and climbing up to the cliff each morning. Now, she was in the sea itself nearly every day, and still, this had happened again.

I have to tell Pasha, she cupped both hands around the tooth. *Maybe she can put more energy into this, or...*

But Pasha put so much pressure on herself to find the secret that would allow them to change Ally into a mermaid. Wouldn't this only make it worse?

I did promise not to keep things like this from her anymore, Ally chewed on her lower lip. *I'll give it a few more days. If we don't find anything by then, I'll tell her.* The tooth pulsed once, and she frowned at it. *I swear it, I will tell her.*

MAHER

CHAPTER FORTY-THREE

Maher made his way through the manor to Lord Kingfisher's study. The note he'd received that morning, requesting his presence at 1 o'clock sharp, burned a hole in his jacket pocket.

There was no other information given, other than Lord Gaius Kingfisher wished to meet with him. The gears in his mind had been turning ever since. If his lordship wanted to revisit just how Maher was able to capture Cal's crew the night of his arrest, Maher was in deep trouble. The last thing he wanted was to lie to Ally's father, but neither could he tell him the truth.

Sweat trickled down the back of his neck when he reached the second floor. His shoulder twinged as each step brought him closer. The study door was shut, and he was a little early, so Maher leaned against the opposite wall and tried to convince himself this meeting was about something other than his connections at the black lantern.

The hour hand on his pocket watch hit one just as the study door opened. Several advisors and trade ambassadors filed out, most giving him some form of greeting. Then Khafra Villaon stepped into the hall. Seeing his son standing just across the way, he froze.

They still hadn't spoken since Maher's return. He honestly wasn't used to this kind of silence from his father, Khafra usually had no compunction about speaking his mind.

"Father," Maher inclined his head.

"Maher." He moved stiffly. "Were you looking for me?"

"Not at all, I have a meeting with Lord Kingfisher."

That piece of news was enough to earn him a frown. "On what business?"

Maher pushed off the wall. "That's for his lordship to decide, don't you think? If you'll excuse me."

Not wanting to keep Gaius waiting, Maher breezed past Khafra. The look on his face was almost worth the churning in Maher's stomach. They couldn't go on like this forever. Maher wanted nothing to do with Khafra's schemes or whatever future he'd envisioned for his son, but Maher still cared about his father's well-being.

Lord Kingfisher was standing at the head of the long table that took up most of the room. "Maher, thank you for coming. Please have a seat."

He took the offered chair to Gaius' right. "Of course. What can I do for you, my lord?"

Gaius sat, crossing one knee over the other, and regarded him. "Your health seems much improved since your return to Kingsport with Rochelle and Ally."

He'd been asked here to discuss his health? "It has, your lordship. A little trouble from my shoulder now and then, but I suspect it will always give a little trouble from now on."

"And there is nothing else you require for your comfort?"

"The manor staff have taken excellent care of me. Mrs. Thorley has made it her personal mission."

"I'm sure she did," he chuckled. "She is grateful, as we all are, for everything you've done for the Isles. And my family."

"I'm not sure how much I really did, my lord. Being unconscious for a large portion of the journey. It was really Ally who pulled everyone together to save Lady Kingfisher."

"Don't mistake me, I am not diminishing my daughter's bravery in all of this. And Ally herself is the one who informed me of how important your role was, albeit largely below the surface. All of this to say, I have a request to make of you, Maher, but I want it understood that you are in no way required to accept. Indeed, I really have no right to ask this of you." A flash of weariness passed over his face.

"My lord?" Maher waited while Gaius appeared to collect his thoughts.

"Maher, I would like to offer you a position on my council."

None of this came close to the conversation Maher thought he would have this afternoon. "What position is that?"

"Intelligencer of the Birde Isles."

Ally is never going to believe this. Maher blinked, then refocused on Lord Kingfisher as he continued speaking.

"I know it is unusual for someone of your age to hold such a position, but you've displayed a particular aptitude that makes you the best candidate."

"Aptitude?" He cleared his throat.

"Exactly. You have built relationships throughout Kingsport. You are able to move freely through different groups from all walks of life, no matter their station. It's easy to see how well others trust your word. And while I don't know how it was accomplished, nor do I wish to, you have been in possession of crucial information concerning the Isles before anyone else." Gaius paused. "Almost as if a little bird was collecting secrets for you from around the city."

Maher held back a groan. If Lord Gaius Kingfisher III called him the Magpie, he would eat his best pair of shoes. "And what exactly would be required of me, should I accept?"

"You will continue to do as you have been the last few years, except you will also hold this position on my council and may be required to travel for trade talks. There is no point in hiding your title, something like that never stays a secret for long. Any and all information you collect that pertains to the health and safety of the Birde Isles, you will report directly to me."

Maher laced his fingers together. Here was the kind of opportunity he'd been searching for, a guarantee that Khafra couldn't force him back to Saprea. But did he really want to be Gaius' personal spy? It was one thing to build the relationships he'd cultivated throughout the city, but he refused to use those connections for one ruler's gain. He'd ship himself back to the continent before he'd let that happen.

"I will accept, but only under certain conditions." Maher watched, but Gaius' expression remained neutral. "I will only report information critical to, as you said, the health and safety of the Isles and the people who have made their homes here. I will not be your personal watchdog. I will not spy on others for anyone's personal or political gain. And I must be free to conduct my business as I see fit, none of my sources will be forced to reveal themselves, else no one would trust me again." His shoulder burned, he needed to stand but forced himself to remain seated. "If those terms are acceptable, I would be honored to take on this responsibility."

With a slow nod of approval, Gaius stood and held out a hand. "It's a good trade."

Maher rose gratefully and clasped Lord Kingfisher's hand, the pain in his shoulder eased. "Thank you, my lord."

"Congratulations, Intelligencer. We'll settle the details of your contract and pay tomorrow," Someone knocked on the study door. "Enter."

Gai and Luthais stepped into the room.

"Did he accept?" Gai's blonde mustache lifted with his lopsided smile.

"He did, may I present our new Intelligencer of the Birde Isles." Lord Kingfisher placed a hand on Maher's good shoulder.

An unexpected bubble of emotion lodged in his chest. He'd never gotten half as much approval from Khafra.

"Congratulations," Gai was shaking his hand then and Maher thanked him.

Gaius went on, "You'll work directly with Gai and Luthais, anything you need will be provided through them."

Maher turned to Luthais, as they clasped hands he grinned. "Looking forward to working with you, my Lord of Trade."

Luthais' grip tightened, his voice almost too low for Maher to catch. "Don't start with titles now unless you want me to use yours, Magpie."

PASHA

CHAPTER FORTY-FOUR

Moving restlessly through the shallows, Pasha waited for Ally to descend the ancient stone steps connecting the lands around her home to the shore. Late afternoon sunshine warmed her shoulders. She'd considered going onto land, the more she left the sea the easier it was to split her tail into legs, but a growing sense of unease kept the mermaid where she was.

Even knowing next to nothing about humans and how they should appear when healthy, Pasha could see Ally wasn't well. She moved slowly down the steps, one hand touching the blocky stones that made up the wall. As if she wasn't steady enough to make it down on her own.

What if all this extra time searching through the caves is accelerating her Sea Kissed state?

And Pasha had no good news for Ally that day. She'd spent the morning searching the last open chamber and come no closer to learning how to change Ally.

Giving Pasha a small wave, Ally toed off her leather slippers and laid her blue jacket over a large rock. In a loose shirt and breeches, she waded into the surf. The tight lines around her eyes and mouth smoothed out as she adjusted to the cold and swam to Pasha.

Their hands met and Pasha towed Ally beyond the place where the waves crested. Feeling much like the first time Ally joined her in the sea, Pasha buoyed them above the swells. Here was a calm, gently swaying current that belied the damage those waves could do once they met the shore.

"Well?" Ally asked, a last glimmer of hope in her eyes.

Pasha shook her head, not quite trusting that the words wouldn't come out stilted.

Ally slumped against her, face falling into the deep hollow of Pasha's collar bones. "What do we do now?"

Pressing her lips to Ally's forehead, Pasha searched for a way to comfort her. When Pasha was a hatchling, Pallagia would calm her using mermaid language. Ally wouldn't be able to understand, but maybe she could *feel* the intent behind what Pasha said.

Even before the shoal left, Pallagia was the only one who willingly used their innate language with Pasha. It wasn't the same as giving energy to one another, or feeding it into an object like the shark tooth. This was deeper, this opened up one mermaid's true thoughts and emotions to another. There was no lying, no hiding of the truth, you were laid completely bare.

Tapping into that part of herself was harder than Pasha remembered, it really had been centuries since she'd last tried. But Ally only sank further into her, unaware of what Pasha was trying to do, but also with no clear intention of pulling away.

Pasha cupped the back of Ally's head, lips still touching her skin. Finally that long unused place inside of her cracked open, and Pasha let herself tell Ally everything she'd never said aloud.

I am so happy to have found you.

I am so sorry this is happening to you.

I am so afraid you being Sea Kissed is somehow my fault and I promise, I will do all I can to help.

I want all the good and wonderful things in the world for you.

I worry I'm unworthy to be your friend, let alone... anything else.

I never want to lose you, but I never want to hold you back.

I will be forever grateful we met. I care so much for you. I –

Pulling back with a gasp, Pasha scrambled to stop the tidal wave of thoughts rushing out of her mind. Only then did she feel how tightly Ally was clutching her shoulders. When her head lifted, tears were streaming down Ally's face.

Wide eyes blinking in shock, Ally whispered, "Goddess save me. What was *that*?"

"It's... I was..." Pasha finally beat back the wave, her own senses clearing. "That was mermaid language."

"But how? I thought you couldn't use it with me."

"I said you wouldn't be able to hear it. You didn't, did you?"

Ally gave a small shake of her head. "No, I couldn't, but it felt so," she grasped for the right word. "Intense. What did you say?"

"Everything."

Ally seemed genuinely improved after Pasha's unexpected use of her own language.

At least, she seemed less tired and some color had returned to her cheeks. And, to Pasha's relief, Ally didn't press her when Pasha admitted she wasn't sure she could accurately translate everything she'd said into Trader's Tongue.

Was that completely true? Perhaps not, but Pasha had startled herself with some of the things she'd said. She needed more time to parse through them on her own before explaining anything to Ally.

Now they were swimming through one of the tunnels leading to the caves. Corals lit up in a welcoming display as they passed. They'd come to like Ally since her first visit.

Pasha considered their options as they reached the caves. Ally'd asked what they could do next, and Pasha had an idea.

"We haven't searched everywhere," she'd said as they left the land behind and dove beneath the surface.

"Between the two of us, we've been down every open tunnel. What else is there?"

"The sealed caves."

They floated together in the center of the great cavern. Ally was looking up at the giant mural on the back wall, the one showing all the different mermaids who'd lived there over the centuries.

"Why would the other mermaids have sealed some tunnels, but left others open?"

"Good question. There are rooms and tunnels in this place I haven't seen in ages. Some that I've never seen. They never explained their decisions to me."

Ally muttered something too low for Pasha to catch. Her impression of Pasha's family was not improving. "Where do we start?"

"Let's map out where all of the sealed tunnels are first, then decide."

"How do you know where they are? I haven't seen anything resembling a walled up doorway."

"They blend in really well," Pasha led her to the far end of the cavern, where the closest one was tucked behind a protruding shelf of stone. Various objects rescued from the seafloor, and even scavenged ship parts, had been wedged in with the rocks covering the entrance. Over the years, sand had piled up nearly to Pasha's waist, but if she tilted her head just right, she could make out the outline of the curved doorway. "This is the one I know best."

"Should we just begin here, then?"

"I don't think we need to look there. Not yet, at least."

"Why not? What's down there?"

"The tombs."

SWAIN

CHAPTER FORTY-FIVE

Swain didn't know how much longer he could keep himself and what remained of the *Maiden's Revenge* crew alive.

They'd briefly made port at one of the small islands off the coast of Myrre, but Swain hadn't wanted to stay any longer than was necessary. Even in that small town gossip was spreading about Lady Alphonsine Kingfisher of the Birde Isles and her power over the sea.

The sight of Foraoise drowning from within was burned into his brain. Every time he closed his eyes to try to sleep, the gruesome memory appeared.

And that mermaid, or witch, or whatever the fuck she was, circling the captain with those shark teeth bared. The writhing tentacle she'd pulled out of nowhere to stop Foraoise from defending herself... his stomach turned every time he thought about it.

What had he done to help her? Nothing. He'd allowed fear to take hold and did nothing but watch.

Perhaps it was the guilt eating away at his mind, but since they'd left Myrre he kept hearing the same haunting, oddly familiar song on the wind. Twice more Swain had found himself standing at the ship's rail in the dead of night, with no recollection of how he'd gotten there. None of the others seemed to have heard it so far, which only convinced Swain further this was all in his head. Or maybe Captain Dare had come back to haunt him. She'd have every right. And there'd been no last stitch given to her before they rolled her body into the depths.

It was his time to keep watch, not far from two bells. His breath fogged in the air as he drew his thin coat tighter around his frame. Winter would be upon them before long. If they were going to sail for warmer climes, it would have to be soon. But they'd need another supply run to make it as far as Nuvwaan. There were plenty of places to hide there between the Bridge of Islands.

Blowing a puff of warm air into his cupped hands, Swain squinted at the stars above them. When dawn arrived, he'd tell the crew his plan, they'd need at least...

The eerie lullaby reached him then, louder than he'd heard it before. This time it was like a lover whispering into his ear. He was crossing the deck, boots dragging over the boards.

"Godsbedamned," Swain tried to stop, but his feet had a mind of their own. They all but threw him against the side of the ship. Gripping the rail, Swain glared out at the endless stretch of black water. "If you're going to haunt me, Foraoise, either show yourself or leave me be!"

"Fora-shuh?" A soft voice hummed from the sea, stretching the name out like a tune. "Who is Foraoise?"

"What the..." An icy finger of dread trailed down his spine. "What is this trickery? Who's out there?"

"Down here,"

Swain's neck craned over the edge of the deck, and his breath caught. The most beautiful woman he'd ever seen in his life was clinging to the hull of the ship. Moonlight danced across skin the color of fresh cream.

Long, sunset-red hair trailed behind her in the water. A pair of bright green eyes winked up at him like two emeralds.

And she wasn't wearing a stitch of clothing.

Snapping out of his trance, Swain called down to her. "Hold on, lass!"

Without pausing to question how the woman had ended up out at sea in the first place, he scrambled for a rope. Racing back to portside, Swain tied the long coil to the rail and threw the line over.

"Grab on! I'll pull you up."

"I can't, I'm too cold." She reached a hand up to him. "Please, come and get me."

Swain had his coat off and one leg over the rail before he stopped to think about what he was doing. He peered down at her again. Despite the freezing waters and pleas for help, her cheeks were rosy, and her eyes were alert. Not at all how she should look after spending even a few minutes in water that cold.

"How did you end up here?"

"My family's boat sank, everyone else drowned," her voice cracked. "Please, please help me."

Again, Swain's body started to act of its own accord. What crossed his mind then was not that a beautiful, naked woman needed his aid. Instead, it was the memory of how the mermaid first appeared much the same way on the *Maiden's Revenge*. It took everything he had, but Swain managed to pull himself back until both feet were planted on the deck again.

Breathing hard from the effort, he shouted, "What the fuck are you?"

Startled for the briefest moment, the woman let go of the hull and floated easily next to the ship. Those stunning eyes hardened, and a wicked smile spread far too wide across her face.

"You are smarter than you look," she hissed.

"What are you?" he said again.

"We've been looking for you, for this ship." She ignored the question. "The trail is faint, but the energy called to us in our prison."

"What prison?" Swain edged one hand towards the rope. One good pull and he could free the knot before this *creature* noticed.

"Swain?" A pair of sailors climbed up from belowdecks. "What's all the shouting about, sir?"

"*Swain*, is it?" She savored his name. Faster than he could track, she snatched up the rope. "Don't move, Swain."

"Stay back!" Swain snapped at the sailors. He thrashed against the invisible bindings holding him fast to the rail. "Wake the others, arm yourselves!"

The crewmates ducked belowdecks, shouting the alarm.

"That will do you no good,"

He looked back down, the creature pulled herself out of the sea. Her beauty, as stunning as it was, ended right around her rib cage. Bile rose in this throat when Swain saw the rest of her emerge from the depths. This wasn't one of the monsters that had attacked the *Maiden's Revenge*, but she was every bit as much of a nightmare.

"What do you want?" he whispered.

"We want the source," she drew closer. "We want to know where you found the energy that gave us the way out."

"I don't understand."

"It clings to you; it follows this ship like blood in the water."

Swain's small crew came bursting onto the main deck. He couldn't turn to see them, but he could hear the click of pistols being loaded and the clang of blades.

"Tell them to stand down," she was just below him now. Close enough to snatch him overboard. "They stand no chance against my *friends*."

A harsh, ear-splitting note left her throat. Around the ship, the sea began to roil. Slowly, a dozen or more bodies rose to the surface. Some floated face down, others stared up at him with milky eyes. Another high-pitched tone, and the corpses rolled until they were bobbing rightside up. The nearest one began climbing the side of the ship like a spider on a wall.

Swain's heart beat so wildly, he thought it might stop there and then.

One of his crew came up behind him, brandishing a sword. When she saw the creature and the corpses, she screamed. "Goddess save us!"

"There's no goddess here, pet." The corpse had nearly reached the railing when she halted it. Now that he could get a closer look, Swain realized the man, or what was left of him, appeared to have a tiny green gem embedded into his forehead. It pulsed with an eerie glow. An answering flicker drew his attention back to the creature. The same gem was on the inside of her wrist. Was that how she was controlling them?

"Tell me, Swain," she grabbed his chin. Her skin was like marble against his. "Where is the source of the energy?"

Looking into her eyes, Swain found he wanted nothing more than to make her happy. Even as he wracked his brain for what she could possibly mean, the desire to please her was so strong it almost made him sick.

"I knew it," a sailor babbled from behind him. "I knew we was cursed. We should've never taken all those ships, should've never crossed the sea witch, should've never let Dare bring that great bleedin' spinner onboard–"

"Turbine!" Swain rasped.

"What?" her hold tightened painfully.

Swain felt so relieved to have an answer for her, the words left him in a rush. "The turbine. It was a machine, it could make electricity with sea water. That has to be the source you need."

"Where is it now?"

"Gone." His legs trembled from staying in place so long. "But, but I know where we can find another!"

"Where?" Her hands framed his face and he completely forgot how monstrous she was from the waist down.

"In Kharabo, on the continent, they make them –"

"On land?" she hissed, nails digging into his skin. The pain brought Swain back to himself. And he noticed then how ragged her breathing had become.

She can't leave the sea for long!

The corpses below moved again; the one that had nearly reached the deck looked to the creature for direction, but she was too angry at Swain's answer to notice. The green stone on his forehead flashed, and Swain made a last bid for mercy.

"Let's make a bargain." He winced as a few of her nails drew blood. "Spare us, and we'll get another turbine for you. I know exactly what you need to retrieve it."

"And what is that, Swain?" The creature drew his name out into a moan, and something in his gut twisted.

"You're going to need a much larger ship." He eyed the corpses still awaiting orders. "And a captain."

CHAPTER FORTY-SIX

Cal was being held at the Kingsport guard headquarters rather than the prison sitting just outside the city limits. With a rotating assignment of both city and manor guards on duty at all times. Both Gai and Luthais had been to see him several times, tried to question him about all that he'd done and what else he might have planned. Their success seemed to be entirely dependent on what kind of mood Cal was in that day, his demeanor was completely changed from the brother they'd known for twenty-nine years. One day he tearfully pleaded his innocence, begging his brothers to let him out. The next he openly bragged the blue and silver cloak the brothers had given Rochelle for her birthday, the one he'd pushed for until they agreed, was used by Captain Dare to identify her on the *Swan Song*.

Their father had only gone once, and whatever was said between them was enough that Lord Kingfisher hadn't been back yet. Ally found she wasn't remotely curious about what Cal revealed, unless it was something that could help the Birde Isles recover. She didn't know if she would ever be able to look at him again. Her whole life, Cal had been the brother who'd seemed to care the most for her, had looked out for her when Gai and Luthais only thought of her as a nuisance. Was all of it a lie? A mask put in place so no one would know how much hatred he had for Ally and her mother? For their father? Ally couldn't see his face now without questioning every conversation, every encouragement, every embrace. It made her skin feel too tight to think about it, brought back the remnants of her old panic attacks to stir in her chest.

Only one question had refused to leave the back of Ally's mind. Were any of Cal's crew involved in his plans from the very start? And, if so, did they know Cal's true motives? Or, like Beitris and so many others, did they only know whatever lies Cal told them? There were a dozen sailors found on the *Wave Skipper* the night Cal was arrested. It eased her mind to learn neither Weams nor Olebile had been among them. But some of the others who'd assisted Cal with their sailing lessons were there. Those whom Cal had kept in the dark were offered a place on Luthais' crew when they were ready to sail again, under Kamharida's watchful eye.

With only a few days left before the tapestry would be ready, Ally ventured into town early one morning. She walked as slowly as needed, stopping once to rest just as the sun finished its climb above the waterline to her left. The extra dose of energy Pasha had accidentally given her was starting to dwindle. Ally'd tried and tried to recall each sensation that had washed over her when Pasha used mermaid language with her. It was no use, her memories were faint shadows compared to what she'd felt then.

At least she now understood why, when they'd first met, Pasha had insisted Ally wouldn't understand the mermaids' language. It wasn't something spoken aloud or written down. It wasn't communicated with pictures or the way hand-languages were used by deaf folk. It wasn't something she could *learn*. She truly had to be a mermaid to comprehend what was said.

If Pasha can change me, then I'll be able to use mermaid language. A shiver traveled up Ally's spine. *As overwhelming as it was to experience as a human, what would it be like then?*

After making a quick stop at an artist's shop recommended by Maher, Ally found herself skirting the edge of the crowded market and heading towards the docks. As warm as her welcome home had been, people were still unsure of how to act around her. She'd particularly tried to give the wharf a wide berth when she came into town. It wasn't Ally's old fears that kept her away now, it was others' fear of her. Why distract the people there with her presence when the tales flying about were disturbing enough?

But today Ally had a special reason for visiting the district spanning Kingsport Harbor. The *Maiden's Revenge* was being dismantled, by order of Lord Kingfisher but also at the request of the sailors who'd been conscripted into Dare's burgeoning fleet. That ship represented something malevolent to them, just retiring the vessel and letting it rot in the northern wharf wasn't enough.

Kamharida Anyanwu was supervising the disassembling of the ship. Ally found her at the top of the wharf, going over records of everything that had been confiscated from the *Maiden's Revenge* upon their return to Kingsport. The remaining pieces of the turbine had been removed first, locked in an undisclosed location until Kharabo could send a team from the university to assess the situation.

They hadn't really seen each other since their return to the Isles. After taking her own recovery time, Kamharida had been granted authority to oversee many of the daily port responsibilities that usually fell to Luthais. One of the ships brought back from the pirate fleet, a well-built Utollmir vessel that had gone missing a few years ago, was offered to Luthais by their ambassador as thanks for the safe return of the remaining crew who'd been captured. He'd immediately turned over the restoration and refitting of the as-yet unnamed vessel to his first mate. Kamharida had been quite busy indeed.

Ally stood next to the other woman and clasped her hands behind her back. "Good morning, Kamharida."

"My lady, good morning." The first mate gave her a half-smile before returning her attention to the long section of mainmast being lowered over the side of the main deck.

"Please, call me Ally, I insist." She gazed up at the ship, now a skeleton of what it was before. The crew were working their way from the top of the masts down to the hull. It put Ally in mind of a giant ship in a bottle. Sitting on a makeshift bench at the top of the dock was one of the sea temple priestesses. The pearls woven through her hair marked her as a newly confirmed initiate. Every so often, a sailor would stop next to her and receive a brief blessing before continuing with their work. "What is a sea priestess doing here? They're not usually present at ship retirements, are they?"

"Not usually, no. It was the only way we could get some of the crew to assist with dismantling the ship. Her presence makes them feel protected."

"Protected from what?"

"Captain Dare."

"The Captain Dare who has been dead for weeks?"

The enamel cuffs secured to the ends of Kamharida's long braids clicked together when she inclined her head. "The very same. There's been some talk among those who witnessed her death, and the story is spreading from ship to ship like wildfire."

"The story of how she died?" Ally twisted her fingers together.

"The most widely accepted story has become one that claims you summoned an unnamed sea creature of legend to kill Captain Dare, my la– Ally. But more troubling for them, there was no stitch put through Foraoise's nose before her body was tossed into the sea."

Ally relaxed a little. If no one was saying Pasha was a mermaid, that Ally had only summoned some type of creature, then there wouldn't be much speculation on who Pasha was for now. But what was that about a stitch? Where had Ally heard that before? "And that's why the priestess is here?"

"Their hope is that enough goodwill will be created with the goddess that she'll be pleased and keep Dare where she lies."

"Was it really so bad, not stitching her body up?"

Two crewmates who were pushing a cannon up the dock saw Ally standing with the first mate and changed course to the far side. Ally's reputation among the sailors of the Birde Isles had grown into something of mythic proportions.

Lady Alphonsine was a tamer of sea monsters; no, she'd made a deal with the goddess for power over the tides; no, she'd betrothed herself to a sea witch in exchange for Lady Kingfisher's safe return; no, Lady Alphonsine was herself a sea witch and all Kingfisher daughters were cursed. That's why the Kingfishers hadn't produced a daughter in generations.

The last one was actually the closest to the truth.

Kamharida sighed. "Well, you know how superstitious sailors can be."

ALLY

CHAPTER FORTY-SEVEN

Ally stayed long enough to watch the last of the mainmast come down. Something about knowing the *Maiden's Revenge* would never catch the wind again gave her some measure of comfort. Too many had suffered and died on that vessel.

Bidding Kamharida goodbye, Ally started the walk back home. She badly wanted to sit down, but the sailors and dock workers were already made skittish by how long she'd lingered. When she made it out of town, she'd rest a spell on the sea wall. Then she'd nap until it was time to join her family for dinner and meet Pasha afterwards.

Their search of the sealed caves and tunnels beneath Kingfisher island was going slowly. It required considerable time and strength on Pasha's part to break the stones apart. The first took her an entire day and she was utterly exhausted by the time Ally arrived to help search. Thank the goddess Pasha discovered she could channel her energy through the spear she'd found in the mermaid trove. Digging the point of the black spearhead into the seams between the stones, Pasha could push enough power through it until the blocked doorways cracked open. It still took some time, but at least Pasha wasn't completely drained by the end.

Lost in thought, Ally didn't realize someone was speaking to her until two shadows crossed her path.

"Milady?"

Ally looked up into a sailor's pale freckled face, a few orange curls stuck out from beneath his knit cap. "Weams!" she gasped, then focused on the Kharaboan sailor standing next to him. "Olebile! What are you doing here?"

"First Mate Kamharida was good enough to take us on Lord Luthais' crew. It's good to see you, my lady." Olebile smiled warmly, then elbowed Weams in the ribs. "I told him to leave you be, but he never listens."

"I was just so glad to see you out and about," Weams grinned, not the least bit put off by the jibe from his shipmate and lover. "We worried you wouldn't want to come down to the wharf after... well, all that's happened."

"It isn't that. I don't want to make the folk who work here uncomfortable."

"Don't let that wild scuttlebutt stop you from going where you wish." Olebile glared at a dock worker who'd stopped to stare at them speaking together. She scurried back to her post.

Weams pulled off his cap and held it meekly in both hands. "We are so sorry, milady, for everything. We had no idea the captain, that is, your brother," he floundered.

Olebile laid a hand on his shoulder. "If we'd known what Cal had planned, we would have done everything we could to stop him."

"I know you would," Ally offered a hand to each of them, feeling a little unsteady on her feet. "And I appreciate everything you've done. Including teaching me to sail, as little as I can, anyway. I know I wasn't the easiest student."

from leaning into the smoke. "Saw a right tall fella who had yer keys some days back, let himself into your rooms."

"Ah, yes, he's a friend."

"Figured so, since it didn't look like he took anything. And that young miss who's been stoppin' by said he was alright."

They chuckled. Only Bernhard would describe the gun-toting Marielle as a young miss.

Pimm made it to their door without any further encounters. They'd known the other residents of the building were concerned, especially when Pimm stayed at the Bear's Den to heal. But Marielle had diligently delivered notes back and forth with updates on Pimm's recovery.

After locking the door behind them, Pimm collapsed into a chair. Everything was just as they'd left it, not that they had much here to begin with. Soaking up the silence, Pimm's head fell back and their eyes drifted closed.

There was a soft click from the window overlooking the wharf below and the barest puff of air as it was quietly opened and shut.

"You could have used the door," Pimm didn't even bother to look at their visitor.

"Got to keep my skills sharp," Marielle's husky voice answered. "And this place is nearly impossible to tuck up without making some kind of noise."

"I know."

"How are you, Pimm?"

With a slight grunt, Pimm raised their head and stood up. "Better than before. Were you able to bring everything?"

"Of course," she moved to the far corner and lifted the floorboard against the wall. Pimm scanned the supplies hidden beneath the floor.

Enough to keep his neighbors and others in the district supplemented through the start of winter.

Pimm was the only resident of the building under sixty years old. They'd been helping the other tenants with necessities for years. Then, about two years after Maher got them the job as door guard at the Den, they were able to buy the whole building. Some of the neighbors, like Ms. Orel, insisted on still paying rent, but the money went right back into their own pockets. Medicine for Ms. Orel's bad knee, new blankets and bedding for the married couple on the floor below, even the tobacco in Bernhard's pipe.

"Do the old folks in this place realize how much you do for them?"

"If they do, I suspect they pretend not to," Pimm sighed. "Otherwise some wouldn't accept it. Besides, I get back more from them than they realize. It's a good trade."

"They missed you something awful, I was no substitute. Ms. Orel told me so the last time I came by." Marielle replaced the board. "We have three guests leaving the black lantern soon, you'll be able to house them for a few days?"

Pimm nodded. "They can stay in the rooms next to mine. I'll make sure everything is well stocked."

"The Madam appreciates it." Marielle shook their hand and started to leave, then turned on her heel. "I meant to ask, what's your friend Maher Villaon make of these ghost ships they're finding in the Southern Strait?"

"Ghost ships?"

"Aye, the ships they've found out at sea with no crew aboard."

"What are you talking about? They were abandoned?"

Her dark brows knit together. "I thought surely he would have known. They began to appear not long after he returned to Kingsport."

Chapter Forty-nine

Maher was being summoned left and right these days.

A short, extremely vague letter arrived from Pimm just before dinner. He'd only just been sworn in as Intelligencer that morning and already mysterious notes were showing up at the house.

Khafra was noticeably absent, not that Maher was surprised. It wasn't lost on him that this was just the sort of post his father had coveted for himself. Had been willing to use Maher's friendship with Ally to manipulate himself out of his ambassadorship and into a position of real power. What he'd truly wanted was Luthais' title, Lord of Trade. That would have never come about, Maher was sure. But just because Khafra was silent on the matter now, didn't mean he was backing down. Not in the slightest. He was too much of a strategist to give up so easily.

Maher was grateful for the small, private ceremony held in Lord Kingfisher's study. It would have felt silly to include all the pomp and circumstance that came with most official appointments. Especially for a position that relied on discretion. Besides that, Ally wasn't looking at all well lately and he didn't want her to have to deal with a large crowd.

It wasn't that she was slow to improve, she truly looked worse than she had when they arrived home. But how? Was Ally spending too much time in the sea with Pasha? When they'd hugged after the ceremony, Maher could feel how unsteady she was. He'd nearly written back to Pimm that he'd come the next night, but Ally had insisted he check in with them.

She'd tried to assuage his worry. "It's your first day as Intelligencer, Maher. You can't afford to laze about here with me."

After securing a promise that she'd rest and let her mother call for the physician if she didn't improve by the next morning, Maher changed into a black suit and left the manor.

The Bear's Den was crowded that evening. Maher squeezed past a group of patrons milling about the lounge, waiting for a table or crimson-cushioned sofa to become available. Kit hurried by with a tray of drinks, bobbed his head in greeting, and disappeared into the crowd before Maher could return the gesture.

The lad is fast. Maher observed as he turned to where Pimm usually sat by the door. But the chair was empty. Instead, a rather large man with long, red hair stood guard. One look was enough to know this had to be Barkeep's elusive brother. Changing course, Maher wove through the patrons until he reached the bar.

"Where's Pimm?" He raised his voice over the noise.

Barkeep jerked a thumb upwards. "Fourth floor. Takin' care of some business for Mama Bear."

Maher waved in thanks, and soon he was on the blissfully quieter top floor of the Den. Knocking on the door of the room Pimm had used before, Maher straightened his clothes and took Pimm's note from his breast pocket.

When the door opened, he held the paper up with two fingers. "What's this about then?"

"What does it look like?" Pimm huffed and waved him inside.

"How am I to know? You couldn't have been vaguer if you'd tried."

"Jackass" they said and led him to the long map table against the back wall. "Come look at this."

Instead of the map of Kingsport that Maher expected, a long illustration of the lower half of the continent, the Strait, and the Southern Icewilds was laid out in its place. A handful of carved ships were spread throughout the Strait. Two were close to land, but the rest were scattered with no rhyme or reason, none resting on known trade routes.

"Alright, what in all the gods' names am I looking at?"

Pimm tore off their cap and dragged a hand through their sandy hair. "Something bad, I think. Very, very bad."

Maher gently placed a hand on their thin shoulder. He'd never seen Pimm this agitated. "What's wrong, Pimm?"

"All of these ships were found in or near the Southern Strait. Their crews were all gone, not a soul on board."

"Pirates?"

"With all the cargo still accounted for? Not even a coil of rope missing?"

"What about wreckers?"

"They were found at sea, not run aground. And again, no cargo missing. Wreckers take everything of value."

Maher struggled for what else this could mean. "Sickness?"

"That caused every sailor on board to jump ship?" Pimm shook their head. "Without the longboats?"

A nagging feeling that he was forgetting something itched at the back of Maher's mind.

"There's one more thing." Pimm put the cap back on with trembling hands. "They started appearing *after* you returned with Lady Kingfisher and Lady Alphonsine."

All the air left Maher's lungs. He looked at Pimm, then back at the map. "You don't think..."

"The sea monsters."

"I don't have any other explanation. I've gone over everything, talked to every source I have. Nothing else fits."

"How did we not hear of this before now?" Maher paced the small room. "This kind of news usually arrives faster than the ships bringing it."

"I have no way to account for that. When Marielle told me three days ago, I thought she was playing the woodpecker with me." Pimm sank into a chair. "Turned out she was serious. And Marielle had only just had it from the captain who'll be ferrying some of the black lantern guests soon. *She* saw one of these so-called ghost ships with her own eyes when it was pulled into port in Myrre."

"What if," he walked back to the map, "what if they're choosing ships farther from the Birde Isles intentionally?"

They considered the idea. "Possibly. But are sea monsters that calculating?"

"They were smart enough to execute a coordinated attack with Pasha, and smart enough to listen to Ally when – Oh, fuck me."

"What?" Pimm reached reflexively for one of their knives. "What is it?"

"I have to tell Ally, that's what."

They relaxed, nodding slowly. "You definitely have to tell her."

"I have to tell her, and what if Pasha decides to go after them? What if Ally goes with her?"

"Doesn't matter, not now. You still have to tell her."

Maher pressed his palms over his eyes. "Ally isn't... she's not getting better, Pimm. Whatever else happened to her out in the sea, she's getting weaker by the day." He jerked his hands down. "She *can't* go with Pasha, not in that condition. She might not make it back."

Silence stretched out between them. Pimm picked up one of the model ships, rolling it nimbly between their fingers. "Five ships they've found so far, with an average of fifty sailors in a small crew, a hundred or more in a large crew. That's hundreds of souls, Maher. All gone without a trace. And who knows how many others haven't been found yet?"

The ache in Maher's shoulder spread through his chest and down into his stomach until he felt hollowed out inside. "We just got Ally back; I can't lose her again."

"You *have* to tell her. She and Pasha might be the only ones who can stop this."

"I know."

CHAPTER FIFTY

"Are you sure I should call on her?"

Pasha nodded, her tail swishing beneath her in broad strokes. "Euphonia can search those parts of the sea faster than we can, even faster than the whales."

Maher had come to Ally early that morning with the news of the ghost ships. The idea would have seemed impossible to her a year ago, but now? Before Maher had even finished telling her, the snapjaws filled her mind. She could see how worried he was, knew without asking that he was afraid she'd try to go after them herself. Even if she'd wanted to, Ally didn't think she'd make it one day's swim away from the Isles. At the same time, she didn't want Pasha venturing out alone either. It was a relief, after she proposed they enlist the whales' help again, that Pasha agreed and then suggested Euphonia could handle the task alone.

Ally turned slowly, hair billowing around her face. They'd come a fair distance from Kingfisher Island, indeed this was the farthest they'd been out at sea since returning with her mother and Maher. Looking out at the endless stretch of shadowy blue, Ally didn't feel any of the anxiety that used to plague her at the mere thought of being in the open ocean. Now it was like the water was wrapped around her in a snug embrace.

Soothing the ever-present ache in her bones. *You are safe*, it seemed to say.

"Ally?" Pasha swam up behind her. "I can call her if you'd rather not."

"No, I can do this." Lifting the shark tooth out of her shirt, Ally held the sharp point against the pad of her thumb and tried to picture Euphonia in her mind. Pasha said it would be easier that way. When she had a solid vision of the sea creature, with her long, powerful body and curved teeth, Ally pierced her skin. A trickle of blood floated in front of her face. "Euphonia. We need your help again, please."

"Good." Pasha took Ally's hand. "If she doesn't answer by the time we have to return to shore, I'll leave a beacon for her."

"I hope she can find what's going on, Maher seemed convinced the sea monsters had to be involved." Ally's breath hitched when Pasha drew her thumb into her mouth and licked the tiny wound. The points of Pasha's teeth just barely grazed her skin. Pasha was so careful about her teeth; they'd kissed countless times by now, and the mermaid never let them deepen too much. She was still amazed by Pasha's control.

"Don't you dare bite down."

Slipping Ally's thumb from her mouth, Pasha smirked. "Wouldn't dream of it."

Ignoring the fact that she'd need both arms to stay afloat, Ally grabbed the back of Pasha's neck and pulled her into a kiss. Pasha locked her arms around Ally's waist, her tail kept them both from drifting.

Ally wasn't sure how much time had passed, part of her wished they were already back in Pasha's home beneath the island. There was no rush, Ally could wait as long as Pasha needed to make love. But that didn't stop her from fantasizing about what it would be like when they did. She'd know what to do to give Pasha pleasure if they were on land when the time came, but she'd yet to learn exactly how lovemaking worked for mermaids in the sea. Ally wanted to know. She wanted to lay Pasha down on the soft sands of the great cavern. Wanted Pasha to tell her everything she needed. She wanted to give Pasha everything she'd been denied when she was left alone.

A low croon rang through her ears, and Ally pulled away enough to see the hazy outline of Euphonia in the distance. The ball of light attached to her head bobbled on its flexible appendage. When she looked back at Pasha, Ally nearly groaned at the sight of her. The mermaid's pitch-black irises had expanded to twice their size. Her lips were kiss-swollen, and her chest heaved with each breath.

"Euphonia's here," Ally licked her lips, tasting the salt of the sea. Pasha's blacked-out eyes followed the motion. "She must not have been that far away."

"Apparently not." Pasha stole one more kiss and reluctantly put some distance between them.

Ally took Pasha's hand and laced their fingers together. "Let's see if she can hunt down whoever or whatever is creating those ghost ships."

BEAR'S DEN

PIMM

Chapter Fifty-one

Pimm started carrying a pistol shortly after their first trip back to the Northern district.

It wasn't that they'd never carried a pistol before, in fact there was usually one tucked in a hidden wall panel by their post inside the Den. But over time, blades had become their preference, easier to hide than a pistol for one. Even in a bustling city like Kingsport, in a district like the Lantern, a well-placed knife or dagger offered more options. But after seeing how far they still had to go to recover, Pimm decided to err on the side of caution. Even while moving through the Den, they kept the small pistol close.

As winter slowly worked its way towards the Isles, they noticed a significant drop in the street crew activity around the city. A small mercy, though it did little to ease Pimm's mind. They weren't gone, they'd just fallen back and for who knew how long. It made it even harder to track the path of the silver coins. All they knew for sure was they were as real as any coin minted in Saprea, but Pimm was beginning to question whether they'd actually come from Maher's homeland. The Sapreans were too careful, too guarded with their wealth to let a fortune in newly minted silver disappear across the Eastern Sea without a trace.

Pimm came to a halt at the bottom of the Den's left staircase. *What if those coins weren't made in Saprea at all*? Their mind latched onto the idea. *But if that were the case, someone would first need to get their hands on an exact replica of a recent currency plate. And that still doesn't explain where they're sourcing all the silver from, not this great of an amount.*

Mama Bear rounded the corner of the landing above them. "Pimm?"

They jumped, turned too fast, and caught their heel on the bottom step. She grabbed Pimm's elbow and steadied them. "Are you alright, dear?"

"Yes, ma'am, of course."

"What were you doing?"

"Only thinking." Pimm followed her into the lounge. It was time to prepare the Den for opening. "We're no closer to finding the source of the silver coins flooding the city."

Mama Bear fluffed a few red velvet pillows and pursed her lips. "My offer still stands; I can ask Mother to see what she can uncover."

Pimm sighed. "Thank you, ma'am. We may have to accept sooner or later. I should talk to Maher first."

"I understand. But do assure my little Magpie, he wouldn't owe Mother another debt for her help in this. Whatever or whoever is behind those coins and the crews spreading them, it's in all of our best interest that they be stopped."

Pimm hid a smile, helping her to move one of the sofas closer to the hearth. It only pulled at their ribs a little, that was an improvement. Maher never was going to escape being the Magpie of Kingsport. They wondered if Mama Bear knew just how much she'd changed Maher's life with that little moniker.

Later that night, Pimm was still mulling over the Saprean coins. If they could find some clue as to where they'd originated, if it was indeed outside of Saprea, maybe they could pick up the trail again.

Around midnight, Kit appeared at Pimm's side with a cup of tea.

"What's this for?"

"Barkeep thought you could use it." Kit set the saucer down on the little table that had taken the place of Pimm's bear paw ashtray.

"Thank you," Pimm took a sip. Instead of hurrying back to the bar, Kit edged closer to their chair.

"I wondered if I could ask," he started, then stopped when Pimm gave him their full attention.

"Yes?" They gestured for the lad to go on.

"I was coming downstairs earlier to help stock the bar, and I couldn't help overhearing what you said to Mama Bear."

"About what?" Pimm kept their expression neutral. They hadn't even heard Kit moving on the steps above them.

Letting out a deep breath, he asked, "Do you really think the same ones spending those Saprean coins around town are also helping the street crews?" When they made no move to answer, he soldiered on. "I'm only asking because I want to help."

Pimm's brows rose, not the request they'd expected. "Help with what?"

Kit shoved his fists into his pockets. "I want to help catch them that destroyed the Whistle and Bells. Archie, the owner, didn't deserve that. He was a good employer." He gave a short laugh. "I know I fit in better here, the Den's where I'd rather stay, but Archie gave me my first job in Kingsport. I want to give him some justice, if I can."

"How exactly do you propose to help, Kit?"

"I'm not sure, but there must be something I can do."

Though Pimm was reluctant to bring anyone else into this, they had to give Kit credit for having the bottle to approach them.

"I appreciate your reasons for offering. Let me think on it, and I'll give you an answer in a few days."

"Alright, thank you, Pimm."

"Kit!" Barkeep bellowed. "I said deliver the damn tea, not sail to Char-range to harvest new leaves."

"Right!" Kit called back.

"And Kit?" Pimm said softly.

"Yeah?" He stopped mid-turn, glancing back at the bar.

"Don't let me catch you eavesdropping on me again. You won't like it if I do."

Caught on whether to shake his head or nod, Kit settled for a short bow instead and hightailed it across the lounge.

"I'm going to let Kit help us with the Saprean coins." Pimm and Maher were walking through the Lantern square, weak afternoon sunlight filtered through clouds hanging low in the sky, promising rain.

"Kit? How does he even know we're looking into that?"

"The lad's very light on his feet."

"Oh?" Maher's chestnut eyes widened. "Oh! Pulled a sneak on you, did he?"

"So it would seem," Pimm snorted.

"Impressive. But how exactly can Kit help us with these damn coins if we don't even know where they're coming from?"

"No one will recognize Kit outside the Lantern; he can move through the other districts without much notice. Unlike you, Intelligencer of the Birde Isles."

"That's Mister Intelligencer to you," he sniffed, brushing an imaginary smudge from his sleeve.

"And besides," Pimm ignored him. "I still can't move very quickly, even if I'm not as well-known as you. I won't send him anywhere dangerous, but he could make inquiries at the businesses that are still accepting the coins as payment.

"True enough," Maher smoothed a hand over his beard. It was longer than he usually kept it. "I certainly don't have time to run all over the city like that. Who knew I'd have to sit in on so many blasted meetings?"

"I could have told you that." They smirked. "You're not working for yourself anymore, Maher."

"Oh, shut it."

They reached the front gate of the Bear's Den. Pimm leaned on the cold iron railing. "It's decided. I'll start Kit in one of the closer districts, and he can branch out from there."

"You haven't said why Kit is so eager to aid us in this."

They shrugged, pulled their coat a little tighter. "He wants to catch the crew that attacked the Whistle and Bells. Archie was good to him."

Maher's expression softened. "Can't fault him for that."

ALLY

CHAPTER FIFTY-TWO

Ally and Pasha had broken into two sealed tunnels and searched five new caves. For the most part, they appeared to be unused storerooms, their contents taken when the shoal left.

But why seal them up if there was nothing inside? Not all of them had carvings on the walls, but those that did were simple, even mundane. It was difficult to not be discouraged. Ally knew Pasha was reluctant to search the tunnel that led to the shoal's tombs, but they'd have no choice if none of the other caverns offered anything useful. It made sense to Ally, humans kept important documents and artifacts in temples and shrines. There were entire libraries on the continent maintained by the servants of different faiths. Why wouldn't the mermaids do something similar?

Ally swam through the main tunnel connecting the great cavern to the outside world. The corals lit her way, some of their lights blinking rapidly in greeting, as Pasha had explained. Ally was glad Pasha trusted her to find her own way beneath the island, at least during the daylight. The last week had been especially draining. Tension ran like a snarled thread through the Kingfisher household. Her family increasingly frustrated with Cal's refusal to admit what all he'd done to undermine the Birde

Isles during his travels. At this rate, they would have to send delegates to every nation that might have been tainted by Cal's schemes.

What's more, the infusion of energy she'd gotten from Pasha was draining fast. The relief Ally felt when she reached the sea each day was enough to make her weep. Pasha could see it, Ally was sure, but she couldn't steal what little energy Pasha had left these days.

Reaching the great cavern, Ally expected to find Pasha waiting for her, but the mermaid was nowhere in sight.

"Pasha?"

A row of corals to her right woke, light bouncing from one to the next before disappearing down the tunnel that led to the tapestry chamber.

"I can't believe I'm taking directions from a colony of corals." Ally swam down the tunnel, using the braided ropes carved into the side for balance. A pop of light spiraled through the corals by her head; Ally could've sworn they were laughing at her.

They took her farther down that passage than she'd been before, past the last open cave they'd searched and around a wide turn to what she'd thought was a dead end. Rounding the curve, Ally found Pasha.

Both hands gripping the long, green spear shaft, she wedged the black blade between two stones in the middle of the wall. Pasha's eyes were closed, her sharp teeth clenched as she concentrated. White hot arcs of electricity gathered around her arms like shining bangles. They collected at her wrists, then fed into the spear. The water around them crackled, stinging inside Ally's nose.

Pasha's silvery-gray fins fanned out wide, muscles in her shoulders flexed as the last thread reached the spearhead. With a low hiss, Pasha jammed the blade further into the wall and white light spiderwebbed through the cracks in the stone. Twisting the spear, Pasha wrenched it from the wall and moved back as hunks of rock began to crumble and fall to the floor of the tunnel.

Ally gawked at the mermaid. She'd never actually seen Pasha do this before, it was always finished by the time Ally joined her.

The corals nearest to Pasha lit up. Breathing heavily, she turned and caught Ally staring.

"If you keep your mouth open like that, something's going to swim in there." She panted.

Ally didn't give a barnacle's backside, but shut her mouth anyway. Closing the distance between them, Ally trailed her fingers up Pasha's arm. Tiny shocks followed in their wake.

"That," her other hand hooked beneath Pasha's jaw. "Was very impressive."

"Was it?" Still a little breathless, Pasha leaned the spear against the side of the tunnel. "I'll have to remember that." She pushed Ally's hair away from her face, black eyes studying her with an intensity that still caught Ally off guard. "Are you alright?"

"Of course," Ally stole a kiss. Her lips tingled with the last wisps of excess energy leaving Pasha's skin. "Now, what room is this?"

"I have no idea." Pasha shrugged, then brushed her lips over Ally's cheek. "This one was sealed before I was born."

"Let's see what's inside then," Reluctantly, Ally released Pasha. "Before we become too distracted."

The cavern was pitch dark and smelled of decay. Any corals that were left inside when the entrance was sealed had long since fossilized. Pasha formed a ball of energy between her palms and sent it floating up to the cavern ceiling.

"It's bigger than I expected." Ally followed Pasha inside. "What was this used for?"

"I don't know. I suspect no one has been here for quite some time."

They picked their way around several massive slabs of stone arranged into a circle at the center of the chamber. Pasha sent two more lights into either side of the oblong space. Every inch of space on the walls, from floor to ceiling, was covered with carvings.

"You're very good at that now," Ally remarked as she tried to find the natural start of the mural. All of the others they'd found told a story, this room had figures spanning the entire space with no discernible beginning.

"Here," Pasha beckoned her over to the wall to the right of the doorway, "these look slightly older than the rest."

Ally squinted at the mottled stone. "I can't see very well."

Pasha summoned a smaller light and held it close to the wall.

"What *are* those?"

"I'm not sure," Pasha shook her head. "I've never seen anything like that before."

"Neither have I." Ally brushed a hand over one of the dozens of creatures carved into this first scene. From the waist up they were human women. Particular care had gone into crafting the beauty of each face. Long, flowing hair streamed behind them like capes. But from the waist down, they were birds of prey. Like eagles or osprey. Massive, feathered wings sprouted from their backs, fully extended as if they were in mid-flight.

"They're pretty, but something about them feels unsettling," she trailed off as Pasha's light illuminated the bottom half of the wall.

A group of more crudely carved figures was running away from the bird-women, their mouths open in silent screams. Humans. They were chasing humans. Hunting humans.

The next panel showed some of the bird-women carrying humans off in their taloned feet. Another had three of them circling the masts of a ship, their mouths opened inhumanly wide. Long, winding lines were carved from their lips down to the deck of the ship, where the sailors' arms were thrown over their heads. More ships followed, with dozens of bodies falling overboard or clinging to the sides of the vessels. But something was off about their faces. Instead of the terror Ally would have thought they'd have been enduring, many of their expressions were just... blank. Ally drew so close her nose nearly touched the stone. Their eyes were different, too. They had no pupils carved in like the humans running from the bird-women. Instead, the stone had been left smooth, as if they had no eyes at all.

"Do you understand this?" Ally glanced at Pasha, but she was frowning at the mural. The tip of her tongue rested against the points of her teeth as if she were puzzling something out. Ally moved around the curved corner to the cavern's side wall, where one of the orbs floating along the ceiling gave enough light to see by. "Pasha, look!"

Pasha was by her side in an instant. Her black eyes roamed over another scene that took up the entire height of the wall. Mermaids of every shape and size were fighting against the bird-women. Some wielded spears like the one Pasha found in the trove, others were slinging weighted nets. A few were even throwing what had to be concentrated electric charges into the air, a lone bird-woman appeared to have been struck by one and was plummeting into the sea. At the bottom, a mermaid warrior with a boned crest on her head was tangled with a bird-woman, a tentacle sprouted from one arm to wrap around the shrieking, feathered creature's neck. Pasha rubbed the scar on her forearm, this was the first evidence they'd found of another mermaid with the same affliction.

Silently, they moved through each panel. More battles between the merfolk and the bird-women. More humans being slaughtered. There was one image of a group of mermaids who'd gone on land to speak to the humans. Just below it was a large gathering of mermaids arranged into a circle. Some wore trouble expressions, while others were clearly arguing with one another.

"It looks like a council." Pasha waved one of the lights closer. "But this isn't our shoal, it's too large."

This was the longest, most detailed record they'd found so far. But there was no such story she could think of in the human world, not even an old fairytale. The style of the human ships were somewhat familiar, but they had to be far older than anything Ally'd seen before. Ally moved around Pasha to view the next scene, brushing a hand against the small of her back.

At first, she couldn't comprehend what she was seeing. The same mermaids from the council were speaking to a new group of humans with more defined features than any of the others. Several of them had long hair hanging loose down their backs or bound with multiple strips of fabric. They all had noticeably missing teeth, which was odd in itself, except it seemed like they'd all lost the same ones.

Then, the new humans were trying to keep the bird-women away from a low structure of wood and stone. It appeared they had no hope, until dozens upon dozens of mermaids emerged from the sea. Jagged lines of energy connected between them, expanding up until it surrounded the bird-women.

One by one, their wings melted away, their taloned feet fused together and elongated into tapered, serpentine tails. Gaping wounds appeared on their sides as they dropped from the sky into the water around the land occupied by the humans.

"I thought you said mermaid energy wasn't magic, what else could this be?" Ally traced the curling tail of one of the creatures.

"This makes no sense," Pasha whispered. "None of our stories ever mentioned anything like this. No creatures from the air, only those that came from the sea."

"But, they *changed* them from one thing to another." Ally's pulse raced. "This has to be similar to how they changed those Sea Kissed girls into mermaids."

Turning to the last wall, Ally hoped to find something that explained this mass transformation. Instead, all she saw was the humans bidding the mermaids farewell and some kind of pattern drawn around the place that now held the bird— no, the serpent-women. Ally's heart sank. Was this truly all of it?

"I don't understand," her gaze drifted down. "Why go through the trouble to record all of this and not... Pasha! She can speak to bones!"

"What?" Pasha nearly collided with Ally. "Where?"

She pointed at a lone carving, almost hidden at the base of the wall. It was the same mermaid warrior who'd used a tentacle against the bird-women. Her arm was free now, but she held one of their long spears pointed above her head. At first, Ally'd thought the tiny bones arranged around her were just fossils left in the stone. But they'd been intentionally embedded there by the artist. The warrior was calling them out of the sand and sending them up to join the pattern winding around the top of the panel.

Pasha traced a pointed nail over the crest fanned out down the center of the mermaid's head. "Everyone in my shoal, they always acted as if I was the only one who could do this."

"Maybe they didn't know," Ally glanced back at the human ships at the start of the mural. "I may have gotten a late start with sailing as a Birde Islander, but even I know those ship designs are very old. This place has been sealed off for so long, I can't believe we've searched all this time and this is the only evidence of the mermaids using this kind of power." She leaned in for a closer look. "Haven't we seen her before?"

"What do you mean? Where?"

"Pasha, she's the same warrior in the great cavern mural."

PASHA

CHAPTER FIFTY-THREE

Ally was right. This was the same mermaid warrior whose visage Pasha'd slept beneath for most of her life. It was maddening enough that Pasha had no recollection of the events depicted in this room. But to find the mermaid she'd thought of as a kind of guardian could also speak to bones? Pasha *ached* to know more, and yet couldn't wait to get out of that chamber.

"I think we've searched enough for tonight." Pasha flexed her aching fins. "Let's go back."

"I'm not ready." Ally's eyes were locked on the mural, as if the stone figures were going to whisper the answers at any moment. She'd sounded so pained when they found the panel of those bird creatures being changed by the mermaids, and then nothing to explain how it was done.

Pasha laid a hand on her shoulder, "It's getting late –"

"I said, I'm not ready!" Ally jerked away, her back hitting the wall. Scrabbling at her chest, Ally found the shark tooth and clutched it tight.

"Ally, what's wrong?"

"I *don't* want to go back on land yet. It *hurts*."

"It hurts you to go on land?" Pasha eased closer, palms held down by her tail. "When did that start? Does it hurt all the time?"

She shook her head, brown curls whirling around in the water and tangling together. "Not always, but, after we've been out in the sea for a while, and if I stay away too long."

"You come down to the shore every day,"

"I know that! Please, can't I just stay the night? I won't drown, you know I won't."

Pasha tried to choose her next words carefully. "No, you won't drown, but you're still human, Ally. Your body isn't made to stay underwater, it's not safe."

"It would be if you could change me," Ally hissed, wide eyes rolling over where the mural started on the opposite wall. "We've been searching and searching and found *nothing* of use. For the goddess' sake, what if we unseal every tunnel and chamber and still find nothing? What if your shoal took the secret with them? What if you can never change me?"

Pasha felt like they'd been here before. Ally was having a panic attack. She hadn't seen Ally have one since their argument onboard the *Pike*, though at the time hadn't realized what was happening. "Ally, listen to me, it's going to be alright. We'll find the answer somehow."

"You don't know that –" Ally broke off with a shuddering gasp.

Pasha pulled Ally into her arms. Swishing her tail for balance, she rocked from side to side, much like Ally had done for Pasha the day she destroyed the turbine on the pirates' ship. "Everything is going to be fine, I promise. We'll find a way to change you. And if the solution isn't here, we'll track down the other merfolk until one of them gives us the answer. You aren't in this alone."

Slowly the tension melted out of Ally's body. With trembling hands, she wrapped her arms around Pasha's waist. "It's been getting worse. And the dreams are back, only now the waves try to pull me under"

"Ally, why didn't you tell me sooner?"

"I thought we'd have found the answer by now, or at least a clue. *Something.*"

Pressing a kiss into her hair, Pasha drew back enough to search Ally's face. The wave of panic appeared to have passed, for now. But how much longer could Ally last? How long before her own body betrayed her?

Pasha didn't know what caused some humans to be Sea Kissed. Some cruel joke by their goddess or random stroke of fate. Whatever it was, she was going to do everything in her power to save Ally from the suffering that came with it.

Taking one of her hands, Pasha pressed Ally's palm against her chest, over the place where her heart beat a slow and steady rhythm. "I swear, we'll find the answer."

Ally's eyes were clear as she nodded. "Until the sea runs dry?"

"Until the sea runs dry." Pasha repeated. "I thought we were finished with you hiding things like this from me when I can help, Ally."

"You've already put so much energy into this thing, I didn't want to take anymore."

"You didn't take it in the first place, I gave it freely. And I can always make more." Pushing away the memory of the nightmares she'd had in the trove, of the tooth giving out and Ally's body freezing before her eyes, Pasha reached out. White arcs gathered along her fingers. "I don't want to wait until you're truly in distress to feed more energy into the tooth. Please?"

When Ally gave a shaky nod, Pasha cupped the shark tooth in both hands. Through the open collar of her shirt, Pasha glimpsed the triangular scar that marked Ally's chest. Was that sudden flare of power, that night on the *Pike,* the cause of the energy draining from the necklace now? Or was Ally's body pulling it faster than before because her symptoms were worsening? A steady trickle of energy flowed out of the seawater, through Pasha, and into the tooth. Even knowing it had gotten low enough for Ally to feel the call, Pasha was startled by just how little was left. She tried not to dwell on what could have happened to Ally if Pasha had never given her the tooth. Or if the energy stored within it were to have run out before Pasha gave her the mermaid's gift. Her hands tightened reflexively, and a surge of energy jumped through her. Ally gasped, flinching as if she'd been shocked.

"Sorry!" Pasha slowed the charges down again before cutting off the flow completely. "That should help."

Ally's hands closed over hers. "Thank you, Pasha."

They took their time returning to land, with Pasha stopping every so often to check in with Ally. But the tooth was holding up and Ally assured Pasha she wasn't feeling nearly as uncomfortable as she'd been the last few nights. Still, Pasha went onto the beach and walked Ally all the way to the stone steps at the top of the shore.

"I think we should rest tomorrow." She removed a wet lock of hair from Ally's cheek. "You can still come down here whenever you wish, but let's do something to relax."

Ally gave her a tired smile. "That's a good idea. You need to take care of yourself too, you know."

"I know." Pasha gave her a quick peck on the lips and gently nudged her towards home. "Go ahead, I'll wait here until you reach the top."

Rolling her eyes, Ally carefully climbed the stairs. When she reached the landing, Ally turned and blew her a kiss.

Pasha stayed until the energy from the shark tooth faded into a pinpoint in the distance, only returning to the sea when she was sure Ally had made it safely home.

CHAPTER FIFTY-FOUR

Maher was waiting for Ally in Lady Kingfisher's parlor. Her sea monster had returned already, much faster than Maher would have guessed. It had been, what, only ten days? They'd agreed to meet there so she could share what Euphonia had found in the Strait.

Euphonia, he snorted. *Trust Ally to name a sea monster something like that.*

He lifted the lid of her embroidery basket. She'd hardly used any of her supplies since their return. Too busy searching beneath the island with Pasha. When he'd asked what they were looking for, all Ally said was that it was something that would help her with her Sea Kissed symptoms. Despite everything they'd encountered over the past year, Maher was still having trouble wrapping his head around Ally being Sea Kissed. He'd even gone to Head Priestess Esa for her advice. Hearing in detail what had happened to past Sea Kissed people on the island, he found himself blessing Pasha for giving Ally the shark tooth, the one thing that had kept her from losing herself.

What truly puzzled him was how this had happened to Ally in the first place. Why her out of the hundreds of children born in the Birde Isles each year? Not even the head priestess had an answer for that question.

At least now her declining health made sense, somewhat, but what would happen if they couldn't find this mysterious thing Pasha claimed would help? His chest ached at the thought. The parlor doors slid open and Ally greeted him with a wide smile.

Forcing his own smile to cover his dark thoughts, Maher opened his arms and squeezed her tight. "Hey Al," he held her a bit longer before letting go. "What's the news?"

They sat together on the sofa. "There's news, but I don't know what to make of it. Euphonia didn't find any trace of the snapjaws or Pasha's squid friend in the areas where the ghost ships were found."

"Well, that's good, isn't it?"

"But she didn't find *anything*. No trace of what creatures could have done this. Not a scent or even a trail of energy like Pasha leaves behind her."

Maher stored that bit of information away; Ally rarely gave many details on the mermaid. "What in all the gods' names and their grandmothers does that mean?"

"We're not sure. It's one thing to know the other creatures who were there when we took the *Maiden's Revenge* aren't involved. It's something else altogether when there's simply *nothing*."

"You're right, that makes no sense." Maher rubbed his shoulder. Ally noticed and slid her hand beneath his, her strong fingers massaged the stiff joint. "Thank you, really. Say," he took a closer look at her and perked up, "you're looking a little better, less drained. Did you find what you were looking for?"

"Not yet, unfortunately. Pasha fed more of her energy into the shark tooth; it's helping, but I'm not sure how long it will last."

He didn't like the sound of that. "Is there anything I can do to help?"

Ally shook her head. "Not right now. Pasha will know it when she sees it, and you're busy enough as it is. Euphonia is going to continue searching as well. Pasha and I might eventually need to go with her, but it will have to wait until…" she trailed off.

Maher tensed, any relief he'd gotten in his shoulder vanished. "Until what, Al?"

"Until we get my Sea Kissed symptoms under control."

He didn't question her, but Maher started to worry that Ally's condition was more complicated than she'd let on.

ALLY

CHAPTER FIFTY-FIVE

A faint knocking roused Ally from a fitful sleep. She hardly slept at all these days. Vivid, often disturbing, dreams filled her mind's eye the moment her head touched the pillow. Outside it was still pitch black; the fire in the hearth had burned low.

The knocking started up again, this time in a jaunty rhythm, and Ally suspected she knew who her late-night visitor would turn out to be. Fumbling for her robe and slippers, Ally felt her way through the dark and cracked her door open.

"Surprise!" Maher stood there, dressed for a party in wine-red trousers and a waistcoat that she'd embroidered with ivory thread. Pearl cufflinks held the sleeves of his white shirt closed. Light from the lamp in his hand bounced off the silver hoops in his ears.

"Maher?" She yawned, pushing a handful of curls from her face. "What time is it, and whatever the answer is, why in the goddess' name are you here at this hour?"

Grinning, he pointed to the small clock ticking on her mantle. "It's five minutes after midnight, which means it's officially your coming-of-age day."

"And we're celebrating now?"

"Exactly! Let me in before one of your brothers wakes and tries to join the party." He passed her the light.

Ally stepped aside as Maher retrieved a large basket from the hall. Shutting the door quietly, she went around the room, lighting the lamps and stoking the fire in the hearth. When she turned around, Maher had set the basket in the middle of the room and was spreading a blanket over the rug.

"What is all this?" she laughed softly.

"First things first," He took her hands and kissed her on each cheek. "Happy birthday, Al."

"Thank you, darling. I feel like I'm underdressed." She straightened his lapels.

"I'm glad you brought that up." Turning back to the basket, Maher withdrew a dress in the same shade of red as his clothes and presented it with a flourish. "We may not mark this day the same way in Saprea, but I thought you could share the traditional colors we wear for coming-of-age."

"It's lovely." Ally took the edges of the skirt and spread it out to catch the light. It was a silken, looser garment with belled sleeves trimmed with white and a violet sash meant to be tied in an intricate knot. "The colors are for good health, right?"

"Health, wealth, and the blessing of the gods." Maher gave her a little nudge. "Now, you change while I finish setting up here."

"Yes, sir," she snorted, stepping behind the dressing screen in the back corner of her room. Draping her robe and nightgown over the screen, Ally slipped the new gown over her head. The fabric was cool against her skin and fit her full figure perfectly. She tucked her necklace beneath the high neckline, then fastened the knot and loop closure at the back. The shark tooth blended in well beneath the draped silk. Had Maher only been asking for ideas of what present to get for her seventeenth so she wouldn't guess

what he really had planned? She couldn't imagine how much it cost him to have this made, especially if it was sent from Saprea.

"You'll have to help me with the sash." She emerged to find a picnic set out in the middle of her bedroom. Ally bounced on her toes, trying to keep her voice low. "This is wonderful! When did you have time to arrange all of this?"

"I had more than a little help from Mrs. Thorley," Maher took the sash. Looping it around her waist, he tied a small knot before bringing both ends over her shoulders, crossed them around her back, and ended with a more complex bow at her right hip. His hand lingered on the tails of the sash, a rare trace of nostalgia softened his features. "You're lucky I remember helping my mother tie one of these."

Ally nodded, knowing he didn't need a response. Maher didn't talk about his mother often; all Ally knew was that she'd died when he was a boy. Then Maher's father took his first ambassadorship in Meredia, and they hadn't been back. She wondered if that was Khafra's way of dealing with grief; it couldn't have been easy on Maher.

Sensing the shift in his mood, Ally held out her arms and twirled around. "How do I look?"

"Like you're ready to celebrate."

They sat together on Ally's floor, dressed in their finest, eating and talking until sunlight began to creep in through the closed curtains. Maher poured the last of the small bottle of wine and raised his glass.

"To Ally Kingfisher on your seventeenth birthday. May you always receive back the joy you bring to others tenfold."

They clinked glasses, and Ally sighed, content. There was a huge celebration planned for that evening, a Birde Isles tradition for all of the Kingfisher children when they came of age, but it wouldn't compare to this. She'd been somewhat nervous about the size of the guest list, and Maher knew that.

"This small party was the best gift you could have given me."

"Oh? Does that mean you don't want your actual gift?" He reached into the basket.

"This wasn't my gift?" She looked down at the Saprean dress, then at the remains of the picnic spread around them. "What else could you have possibly fit in there?"

"Don't tempt me to make a crude joke on your birthday, Al."

Ally clapped a hand over her mouth and snorted into her palm. Maher had recently been sharing stories about his ventures into the Lantern. Ally'd never blushed so much in her entire life.

Muffling his own laugh in the crook of his arm, Maher took out a slim parcel and laid it in her lap. "This is the last thing, I promise. Happy birthday."

"You really didn't have to do this," Ally composed herself and untied the red ribbon holding the package together. When the paper dropped away, she gasped; it was a painting no larger than one of her embroidery hoops. Maher's initials were visible in the bottom right corner.

Holding it up to the light, Ally took in a scene that she knew by heart. A group of selkies together on the dock, already stripped down to their loincloths and breast bands, preparing to dive for oysters. They ranged in age, the older ones showing the younger how to secure their nets. One selkie in particular caught Ally's eye. She could easily be Ally's age, full figured, all bronze skin and coal black hair cut at a blunt angle beneath her chin. Her eyes were staring out of the painting, a dark, rich brown that made it seem like she was going to come to life any moment. A crescent-shaped scar curved around the back of her shoulder. Gooseflesh raced up Ally's arms.

"I'd been at the docks sketching on and off for days." Maher had moved to sit beside her. "It's hard to get a clear look at the selkies, they're always on the move. You'll notice the others' faces are turned away or have vague features. But one morning, she saw me drawing and paused, as if she was giving me a chance to see her."

"When was this?"

"Towards the end of last oyster season. I've been helping my father so much lately, I wasn't sure I'd have it finished in time for your birthday. That's why I kept pestering you about what else I could give you as a gift."

"I love it," Ally rested her head on his shoulder and held the painting out so they could both see it. "And I love you, Maher. Thank you, for everything."

Maher's chin found its way onto her hair. "Love you too, Al."

BEAR'S DEN

PIMM

Chapter Fifty-six

"**S**omething feels off here."

Pimm couldn't say exactly what, but standing there in their sitting room, they felt it deep in their gut.

It was as if they'd forgotten something important. Nothing was out of place, there was nothing visibly missing, and still... The very air they were breathing wasn't right.

Pimm had made the trip to the Northern district early that morning, to ensure everything was alright at their building and prepare for the black lantern guests currently staying on the fourth floor to depart. Marielle arrived shortly before noon, and together they escorted the three former Lantern workers to the northern wharf.

This group was quiet, as most of the Madam's guests tended to be. Pimm never asked what circumstances brought them to seek her help. Whatever it was, whatever their stories might be, all that mattered to Pimm was that they were now safe. The healing would come later, in its own time.

Marielle and Pimm waited on the aging dock until they'd boarded the ship that would take them to Swan Island. From there, they could either stay with another acquaintance of the Madam's or book passage to the continent. The black lantern covered every expense. The last one to board, a young girl with auburn hair and a wispy frame, turned back at the last moment and threw her arms around Marielle. Without hesitation, the gunfighter hugged the girl back.

"Thank you, Miss," she whispered into Marielle's shoulder.

"Don't forget to write and tell me how you're getting on."

Sniffling a bit, she nodded and scurried up the short gangplank.

Waiting until the ship had weighed anchor, Pimm asked, "Do any of them ever write to you?"

"Once in a while, but usually not." She sighed and rolled her neck. "I understand though. They want to move on, writing to anyone here would only keep the pain alive. The point is they know they can write, if they want to."

They'd parted ways at the wharf. Now the afternoon sun streamed in through the windows, warming the sparsely furnished room. It was time to make their way back to the Den, yet Pimm still couldn't shake that nagging sense of wrongness.

If I really have forgotten something, perhaps it will come to me on the walk back. They locked up the fourth floor and started down the stairs. Catching a whiff of Bernhard's pipe, Pimm forced their feet to keep moving. *Just a few more weeks, and maybe Doctor Tambara will give me leave to smoke again.*

Out in the courtyard, Pimm tugged their cap down and buttoned their coat up to the neck. Ms. Orel was sitting on a wooden stool just beyond the main door, with nothing but a thin shawl over her shoulders, peeling potatoes.

"Ms. Orel, you really should bundle up. Where's the scarf I gave you for your birthday?"

"I'll not wear something so nice to do kitchen work," she tutted, as if the answer were obvious to anyone but Pimm. "This is not cold," she added, brandishing her short peeling knife. "I know cold. This weather could pass for springtime in Zavatleo."

Holding back a sigh, knowing arguments were futile when Ms. Orel started reminiscing about her homeland, Pimm tried a new tack. "Shall I help you, then? We could continue our comparison of Birde Isles and Zavatleo weather."

"Bah, away with you, cheeky child." Ms. Orel muttered something else in Zavat that Pimm was fairly certain was both an insult and a term of endearment, depending on her mood.

"I'll be back in a few days, but send word if you need anything before then." Pimm kissed the top of her snow white hair. Then said goodbye in, what she often informed them was horrendously accented, Zavat.

Ms. Orel swore and stabbed her knife into a potato.

"What is it?" Pimm halted.

"I can't believe I forgot. You had a visitor while you were away at the wharf with the Madam's girl. I tried to get him to wait for you, but he asked that you meet him at the market square instead. What was his name?"

"Was he tall? With a black beard?" Pimm asked, thinking Maher must be looking for them.

"No, no, not that one." She wiped her hands on her apron. "He was a small lad; had the loveliest face I've seen in a bull's age. We had a nice chat in Zavat."

"Kit?" They frowned. How did Kit even know where Pimm lived?

"Aye, that's him!"

"Thank you, Ms. Orel, I'd better go find him." Discreetly ensuring all their weapons were in place, Pimm walked as quickly as they could out of the courtyard. They'd figure out how Kit knew about their rooms later. As they neared the end of the district, that same feeling of wrongness they'd pushed down bloomed back to life.

Pimm was panting hard by the time they reached the outer edge of the Kingsport Market. They were so distracted by what Kit could have discovered, the thought of hiring a carriage didn't even occur to Pimm until they'd crossed into the damned district.

"This had better be good," they puffed, slowing as the market square came into view. It was particularly quiet this time of day, with the sun already low in the sky. Long shadows crept across the colorful mosaics set into the streets. Pimm hadn't allowed themself to dwell too long on the fact that the fantastical creatures depicted in the tiles were actually real. But standing in the middle of the square now, Pimm almost felt the nearest mermaid's eyes watching from between the cobblestones.

Where was Kit? Surely he would have stayed close to the square so Pimm could find him. There were a few shops still open, maybe if they described Kit one of the shopkeepers would remember seeing him.

Making their way down one side of the square, Pimm was about to step into the first shop when they caught a flash of movement across the way. Kit appeared in an empty storefront, banging on the glass paned door with both fists. Pimm couldn't hear him, but the lad was clearly trying to get out. A pair of hands came from behind Kit and yanked him back into the shop.

Pimm dashed across the square. Stealth be damned, they wanted to draw attention. With any luck, one of the shopkeepers would alert the Kingsport guard. Grabbing the door latch and pulling hard, Pimm confirmed what they'd already suspected. The bolt was locked into place.

They cupped their hands around their eyes and peered through the fogged glass. The shop appeared abandoned inside, but a faint strip of light glowed beneath the door leading to the back rooms.

Stealing around to the side street, Pimm drew their pistol and weighed the options before them. They had no idea how many people were in there with Kit or how they were armed. Was it one of the street crews keeping him captive, or someone else entirely? And why did they target Kit in the first place?

Rounding the corner into the back alley, Pimm counted down the row until they reached the right shop. There were no windows here, only a plain wooden door. Pimm held their breath as they tried this latch. *Unlocked.*

They eased it open; the waning daylight revealed a bare storage room and a short hallway beyond. A curtain was drawn across the only doorway. Muffled voices reached Pimm then, at least three and none were Kit's. For the first time in many years, Pimm felt unsure of what to do next. The memory of their own attack was still fresh in their mind. Not even Maher knew how much that night had rattled Pimm.

An icy hand of indecision gripped the back of Pimm's neck, holding them frozen in place. They counted their own heartbeats as the seconds ticket by.

There was movement behind the curtain.

"I told you, I don't know what you're talking about!" Kit shouted.

"We'll see about that," a shrill voice replied. Then there was a distinct sound of something hard hitting skin and Kit cried out.

Pimm stumbled into motion, moving silently across the room and pressing their back against the wall. Transferring the pistol to their left hand, Pimm flicked their right wrist and a thin blade slid into their palm. Using the tip of the blade, Pimm lifted the edge of the curtain just enough to peek inside.

This room was stacked with old crates and empty liquor bottles. Kit kneeled in the far corner, his right cheek was an angry shade of red and blood dripped from the corner of his mouth. A woman in a long gown in a sickly shade of green stood over him, a blackjack resting on her shoulder. Her gray streaked, mouse brown hair was pulled into a tight bun. They couldn't see her face, but Pimm had a terrible feeling they knew her from somewhere. Two others that had the look of sailors about them watched from behind her. One swayed on his feet, possibly drunk. The oily smile on his face made Pimm's stomach turn. The other, noticeably bigger, sailor leaned on the closed door leading to the front of the shop. Neither were holding weapons, but that meant nothing. Pimm couldn't tell if there was anyone else in the room.

"I'll ask again," the woman grabbed Kit by the hair and jerked him upright. "Why were you following me?"

"I wasn't," Kit ground out.

"You know," she held the blackjack against his chin. "It would be a shame to ruin such a pretty face. I could get a nice bit of coin for it."

Kit's blue eyes widened, but his mouth stayed shut.

Blood roared through Pimm's ears, drowning out whatever else she said. On the floor they found a bottle that had rolled out of the other room. Pimm kicked hard, shattering it against the opposite wall, then crouched down.

"What was that?" the woman demanded. "Don't just stand there you idiot, go check the back!"

The drunk sailor lurched through the curtain. Pimm waited until the thin fabric had swung shut, then brought their blade up to slice through the artery in his groin. As soon as he tilted to the side, Pimm wrapped a hand over his mouth and pulled him to the floor with no more than a slight scuffle. A few breaths later, he sank into unconsciousness.

"Well, what was it?" That nerve-grating voice cut through the silence.

Pimm eased out from behind the sailor, leaving his body slumped against the wall. The odds of successfully completing that move again were low. Instead, Pimm stood in the center of the room and pointed their pistol at the doorway.

"Godsbedamned drunkard," the other sailor whipped the curtain open and came face-to-muzzle with Pimm's revolver.

"Hello," Pimm said coolly, choosing to overlook the way their heart raced. "I believe you have a friend of mine there. I'll be collecting him now."

Hands held palm up, the sailor backed into the room. "We got company, Ez."

Pimm finally got a look at the woman's gaunt face. *Fuck.*

"Well now," her orange painted lips stretched into a tight smile. "I might have known. Hello Pimm."

"Ezmira." Pimm stopped in the doorway, checked to either side for any others and found the rest of the room empty. "You were supposed to leave Kingsport, or did you forget?"

"How could I, when that cow you work for ruined my business?"

Pimm ignored the insult to Mama Bear. They jerked their chin at Kit. "Get up. We're leaving."

"This pretty one belongs to the Den, does he?" Ezmira sneered as Kit staggered to his feet and rushed to Pimm's side. "Venturing outside your lamp color aren't you, Pimm?"

"He belongs to no one but himself." Pimm handed Kit their blade and pushed the lad behind them.

"How sweet," her pale blue eyes darted behind them. "Where's my other man?"

"If he's still alive, you can collect what's left of him after we're gone."

"The fuck did you say?" The bigger sailor stomped forward. Pimm fired a warning shot into the floor, just missing his boots.

"Stay," Ezmira snapped. "If your shipmate was stupid enough to get himself killed, he's not going anywhere."

"That's right, stay like a good dog." Pimm backed up. Kit held the back of their coat in a tight grip. "I suggest you leave the city, Ezmira. The Madam won't be pleased to learn you're still skulking around."

Ezmira had the sense to look worried for a moment, then her scowl snapped back into place. "You can tell the old hag from me, to enjoy her position while it lasts. Her little reign over the Lantern won't last forever."

Keeping the pistol level, Pimm steered Kit through the storage room and out into the darkened street. When the door blocked Ezmira and the sailor from view, Pimm took a short, wide dagger from their boot and jammed it into the door latch. It wouldn't hold for long, but it would give them a bit more time.

"Come on," Pimm took Kit by the arm and towed him down the back street.

After a few steps, Kit found his voice again. "Shouldn't we –"

"Quiet."

Kit's mouth snapped shut with an audible click of teeth.

Together they moved deeper into the city, skirting around the few lamps that had already been lit by the shopkeepers. When they reached the next alley, Pimm took a sharp turn leading away from the market. Blood pounded against Pimm's temples and a burning pain was spreading through their rib cage. They needed to put as much distance as possible between the two of them and Ezmira before Pimm could stop to take stock of anything.

Pimm knew most of Kingsport's streets by heart, easily navigating through the dark back streets and alleyways. Kit stumbled along behind them, Pimm's knife still clutched in his free hand. His quick breaths and occasional grunts of surprise when Pimm changed course were the only sounds he made.

When they crossed into the Lantern, Pimm finally slowed their pace. Relief bloomed in their chest when the back entrance to the Den was in sight.

Olga was outside, dumping out a pan of wash water into the drain that ran beneath the street. She squealed and nearly dropped the pan when they appeared out of the shadows.

"Pimm! Kit! You gave me such a fright," Olga's cornflower blue eyes widened when she saw Kit's face and the weapons in their hands. "Oh goddess, what happened?"

"Everything is fine," Pimm managed to get out. "But do me a favor and call for Doctor Tambara. It's not urgent, but we need her to come tonight. And tell Mama Bear we'll be upstairs for a while."

Nodding quickly, Olga dashed back inside. They followed, but instead of heading for the lounge Pimm took Kit's arm again and pulled him into the pantry.

"What are..." Kit trailed off when Pimm pushed a panel and the entire back wall gave way to a narrow set of stairs. "A hidden staircase? Really?"

"They're leftover from before the Lantern owners formed the guild." Pimm braced themself and started climbing. "The old owners would call the Kingsport guard on each other, sometimes the employees needed a quick way out."

The wall swung shut, plunging them into darkness. Kit grabbed Pimm's coat again, following the whole way in silence. On the fourth floor, the passage split in two directions. Pimm turned and soon they exited through another panel in the room Pimm had been using for several months. The wall lamps were already lit.

Laying the pistol on the map table, Pimm shrugged out of their coat and moved to stoke the coals in the little stove. When they turned around, they found Kit unmoving, staring at the bloodied knife in his hand.

"Kit," Pimm gently took his wrist. "You can let go now."

Slowly, his white knuckled grip loosened and Pimm took the blade. The lad's face was ashen around the injury on his cheek. A line of dried blood still ran down his chin.

"Sit down," Pimm guided him to a chair. Grabbing the pitcher and washbasin from the bedside table, Pimm poured half the water into the basin and the other half into the iron kettle on the stove. Then they pulled a handkerchief from their vest pocket and sat across from Kit.

Dipping a corner of the cloth into the water, Pimm tried to hand it to Kit. When he made no move to take it, Pimm sighed and scooted closer.

"I'm going to clean this cut on your lip, alright?"

Kit nodded. So Pimm held his chin with one hand and wiped carefully at the blood. Kit winced at first but held still. In that moment he looked so much younger than Pimm had originally thought.

"How old are you?"

Kit blinked, confused, but the question seemed to snap him out of wherever he'd gone to in his mind. "Twenty-one."

Pimm hummed in answer. They'd just assumed the lad was closer to their own age.

"What about you?"

Pimm dipped a clean corner into the bowl. The water was turning pink from Kit's blood. "I'm twenty-seven." They never talked about themself, even saying that much felt strange.

"Really?" Kit looked them up and down, as if he'd find Pimm's real age hidden in one of their pockets.

"Is that a problem?"

"What? No, no, I just, you look younger."

"I know." Pimm wiped his chin once more and examined the welt left by the blackjack. Their stomach turned sour and they couldn't help but think this could have been prevented if they hadn't frozen outside the shop. Pimm laid the red stained cloth aside and leaned back in their chair. "Tell me what happened."

BEAR'S DEN

PIMM

CHAPTER FIFTY-SEVEN

K it fidgeted in his seat. "It's not what you think,"

"Kit, you know you were only supposed to be visiting the shops on the list I gave you, not trailing street crews through the city."

"I wasn't! I swear, Pimm, I was doing what you asked. But that woman," he cringed.

"Ezmira."

"Right. She was also visiting several of those shops, at least the last five or six. She met the same man at a few of them. I realized what was happening right about the time she did."

"And she had her gonys snatch you off the street." Pimm scrubbed a hand over their mouth. It was bad enough that Ezmira was back in Kingsport, but if they hadn't seen Kit in that window?

"Who is she?" Kit asked. "I've never heard anyone talk about Mama Bear that way."

Pimm signed. *Might as well be honest with the lad.*

"Mama Bear and the Madam of the black lantern shut down Ezmira's so-called business nearly five years ago. She would lure people from the continent to the Isles with offers of daywork and then bring them to the Lantern instead. Her place was on the outskirts, none of the owners in the guild knew what was happening until one of her victims escaped and came straight here."

Kit shook his head. "How did they know to come to the Den?"

"I'm not sure. Even locked up in a strange city, I suppose word still reached them of a safe place to go." Pimm remembered that day well. They'd only been working there for about six months. Walked into the Den to find a nineteen year-old Balahn hiding behind the bar, refusing to leave the safety of Barkeep's side. "Mama Bear was livid, she made sure every victim of Ezmira's was found and even tracked down most of her... customers." Maher had stepped in then, using his position as an ambassador's son to get the Kingsport guard involved. Ezmira should have been thrown in prison for the rest of her miserable life, but she managed to escape. The Madam put the word out that she'd better not show her face in Kingsport again. Yet, here she was, and up to some new scheme.

The kettle on the stove whistled. Pimm rose stiffly and crossed the small room.

"I'm sorry," Kit said softly. "I should have been more careful. Maybe I can –"

Pimm lifted the iron handle and pain shot through their sides. "Fuck!" The kettle slipped from their grasp, landing with a loud clang and spilling boiling water across the floor.

"Pimm!" Kit dashed to them and ducked beneath Pimm's arm as they stumbled sideways.

Vision going gray, Pimm tried to tell him to help them to the bed. Then the door flew open and Doctor Tambara swept into the room. "What in the great Mother's name is going on here?"

"Good evening, Doctor." Pimm waved at her, then they passed out.

When Pimm came to they were propped up in their bed, pillows stacked on either side.

This is familiar, they thought with a groan.

"What were you thinking?" Tambara's stern face came into view. Before they could answer, she turned on Kit. "Do you realize they could have broken their ribs again because of your foolishness?"

Kit hovered by the foot of the bed. Mama Bear was just behind him. "I know, I'm so sorry."

"Stop." Pimm coughed, a fresh wave of pain circled their rib cage. "It wasn't his fault." They caught Mama Bear's eye. "Ezmira's back."

Mama Bear's finely arched brows snapped together, and her lips thinned. "You're sure."

"Have you seen the lad's face?"

Nodding grimly, she placed a hand on Kit's shoulder. "Why don't you go have a rest, dear?"

"I'd rather stay here," he looked up at her. "In case Pimm needs anything."

The doctor huffed. "Come, let me see to your face first." Tambara drew him back to the table, where her medical bag lay open.

Mama Bear came to Pimm's side. "Tambara says you didn't break anything this time, but it was a near thing. Why didn't you call for help?"

"There was no time," Glancing to where Tambara was examining the welt on Kit's cheek, Pimm lowered their voice and quickly told her what had transpired in the shop. By the time they finished, Mama Bear's fists were clenched into her skirts.

"That loathsome bitch," she spat. "I have to warn Mother, and I'll send word to Maher as well."

"I think that's best. With his new position, he may be able to track her down faster than we can."

Mama Bear placed a kiss on Pimm's forehead. When she pulled back, the lines on her face smoothed out, but Pimm knew how angry she was underneath. "I'll come check on you later, send Kit down if you need anything." Bidding the doctor goodbye and squeezing Kit's shoulder once more, Mama Bear left the room.

"This should heal with time, apply this ointment twice a day." Tambara gave Kit a small jar from her bag. Her dark eyes cut to Pimm. "As for you..."

"I know, rest."

"And?"

"And don't do anything stupid."

"Good. I'll leave a packet of willow bark tea. I want you to drink it tonight and tomorrow. No arguments."

"Yes ma'am." Pimm gave her a weak salute.

When they were alone again, Kit pulled a chair closer. "Is there anything I can get for you?"

"Not right now. You don't have to mother hen me, Kit. I'll ask for something when I need it."

Kit bit his lip, looking as if he wanted to argue, then nodded.

Closing their eyes, Pimm tried to sort their thoughts and recall everything that'd happened before they passed out. There was a question they'd meant to ask Kit after the tea was ready. What was it?

Pimm's head snapped up. "Kit?"

"What?" Kit jerked awake. The lad had already started to doze in his chair.

"You said Ezmira met the same man in some of those shops. It wasn't one of the sailors that were with her tonight?"

"No, actually, I noticed him before I realized she was there. I thought it was Mister Villaon at first."

"Maher?"

"But he was much older. From a distance, I swear they could be related."

They leaned forward, ignoring the pull in their sides. "This is very important: did you hear his name?"

Kit thought for a second. "Just once. I remember he got angry with her for being so familiar as to call him by his given name. I think she called him Khafir, or something similar."

Pimm felt the blood drain from their face. "Khafra?"

"Right. Khafra."

"When he arrives, I'm going to need you to tell Maher and me about each time you saw them together. Everything."

ALLY

CHAPTER FIFTY-EIGHT

Pasha and Ally were lying back against a sand dune, listening to the tide roll in. With her cloak draped over both of them, Ally leaned her head against Pasha's shoulder. An open book was propped against Ally's bent knees. She'd been reading one of her favorite stories to Pasha, until the lull of the waves made her eyelids grow heavy.

The day of rest was more needed than either of them realized. After sleeping through most of the day, Ally suggested they take breaks between exploring the remaining sealed caves. Allowing Pasha more time to rebuild her stores. Ally didn't know what else to call the place inside of Pasha that pulled energy directly from the sea.

It helped Ally as well, there were still the occasional twinges and aches – she could still feel that damned fishhook lodged beneath her ribs – but she hadn't recognized how much stress the daily searching was putting on her body. The worries about what would happen if Pasha couldn't change her were ever-present in her mind, but the time spent like this soothed Ally in a way that she'd missed.

And, for right now at least, just being next to the sea was enough to quiet that need. She could finally distinguish between her own anxiety and the *pull* of being Sea Kissed.

Ally took Pasha's arm, the one with the healed-over scar, in her hands. Running her fingers over smooth skin and counting the scales that curved over Pasha's elbow. There was still nothing else, no fine material or silken ribbon, which could adequately compare. Pasha's other hand was behind Ally's head, sharp nails scraping lightly against her scalp as she played with Ally's curls. Taking care not to tangle her fingers in the loose tendrils. The more time they spent together, the more Pasha couldn't seem to stop herself from touching Ally's hair.

Examining the scar more closely in the bright afternoon sunlight, Ally swept her thumb over the thick, jagged line. "Why didn't you tell me what was hidden beneath here?"

"I try not to think about it."

"I'm sure, but I still don't understand the purpose."

"It's a reminder, or a punishment if you'd rather call it that. It was likely meant for Pallagia, but since she died..."

"They gave it to you instead."

"If any other mermaids were to arrive in their absence, they'd recognize the scar and know what it meant," said Pasha.

"What would happen?"

She moved to another section of Ally's hair. "I don't think they'd be unkind, but they wouldn't do anything to help me remove it either."

Ally frowned, massaging the tight skin on either side of the scar. "So you have this thing in your arm forever? And it rips the wound open each time you use it?"

"It's also a weapon more of us used to have, warriors, like in the mural we found. But I don't know why or how it started. That one tentacle is physically stronger than I am, but to use it is to be in constant pain. And if I were to wield it often, the more reliant on it I'd become. I don't want that." Her voice dropped an octave. "I've only used it three times."

"Three times, in all these years?"

"The first, when it was given to me, I couldn't stop myself from letting it out. After that I kept seaweed and whatever else I could find wrapped around it until I was used to how it felt. The second time, as I made the bargain with your great-grandfather, I used it to help convince him I was the goddess." Pasha's arm flexed. "And the third,"

Ally paused her ministrations, "When you used it to help me."

Quickly, Pasha took Ally's hand and kissed her palm. "I made the choice to use it in that moment, you don't have anything to worry about."

"But won't it bother you more now that you've released it again?"

"There's pressure there, it's irritating but it's fading every day." Another kiss was placed on the inside of Ally's wrist. "Tell me more about the investigation into your brother. Has Maher found anyone else who helped him, besides that girl?"

"You're trying to change the subject."

"Is it working?" Sharp teeth nipped her skin.

Ally sighed, "No one who gave him so much information, not in the Birde Isles at least."

"And she really stole those documents from her own father?"

"She did." Ally settled back against her shoulder and Pasha traced a nail over Ally's palm. Watching the black point dip from one line to another was almost hypnotic. "Beitris really was horrible to me when we were children. My family didn't learn the extent of it until we were older and we rarely saw each other by then." There was a low growl beneath her ear, but Pasha didn't interrupt. "And she always had her eye on Cal, it must have been easy for him to convince her the family wouldn't approve of their so-called engagement unless he could make his own fortune."

"Was her father supposed to keep those documents in their home?"

"I don't know for sure, but he must have thought they were safe. Cal would have been able to get a lot of information during his travels, but Mr. Tapper is one of the damned trade guild leaders. Cal had Beitris taking whatever else he needed right from the source."

"Right from the source," Pasha echoed, absently threading their fingers together. They were quiet for a while after that, only occasionally whispering a thought or question to each other. Talking about nothing and everything. Ally could easily fall asleep right there.

"I meant to tell you, the map will be ready tomorrow." Ally yawned. "And Esa's done her best to find everything the priestesses have written about mermaids, but mostly their records are the same myths I know now are untrue. I suppose I should leave them as they are, I daresay the more mystery we keep about your people the better–"

"From the source!" Pasha shot up, sending Ally rolling face-first into the sand.

"What?" Ally felt grit on her tongue and spat it out. "What was that about?"

"I'm sorry!" Pasha gripped Ally's elbows and hauled her up. She dusted sand from Ally's hair and off her cheeks. "I'm so sorry, I didn't mean to do that, but I think that could be it!"

"*What* could be what?" Ally's hands wrapped over Pasha's to hold them still and tiny threads of energy zipped against her skin.

Pasha's eyes were bright. "When you don't want to know something second-hand, where do you go to get it?"

"The source?"

"Exactly!" Pasha hugged Ally so tight her feet lifted off the ground, and her spine cracked. It still amazed her how much stronger Pasha was than she let on.

"Pasha," Ally gasped. "Please, put me down, slow down, and be more specific."

When Ally was set back on her feet, Pasha took a deep breath and held her hands again. "We've been searching beneath the island for how the ritual is done and have found nothing. Not even a mention of it. What if that's because the ritual was never *performed* in our home?"

"Where else would it have been done?"

"The hatching grounds!"

"What are you talking about?"

"It's the place where all mermaids in our shoal were born, hatched, there are only a few in all the seas. Ours isn't far from here. What if they kept the knowledge of how to change a human into a mermaid there?"

Ally's eyes went wide as Pasha's words sank in. "Why haven't you ever mentioned this place before?"

"I haven't been there since I hatched myself, only the elders were allowed."

Ally couldn't help seeing the similarity between Pasha's family and her own. Forbidding certain actions and never explaining why. She checked the sun's position above them. "How far away is it? We still have quite a bit of daylight, let's look there now!" Ally started for the water, but Pasha pulled her back.

"Ally, I think I should go there by myself first." Pasha looked as solemn as she'd been the first day she took Ally into the ocean. "It's been empty for centuries, we don't know what state it was left in or if any damage happened while I slept. I'll go first thing tomorrow morning and, if it's safe, I'll bring you there afterwards. Alright?"

Ally didn't like the idea of Pasha exploring this place, wherever it was, alone. She was right though; it would be foolish for them both to go barging in. Pasha would know what to look for to ensure nothing was wrong.

A tiny bud of hope bloomed in Ally's chest. What if the answers they'd been searching for all this time were right within their reach?

"Yes, alright, but please be careful."

"Of course," Pasha smiled, her expression turning thoughtful. "I'm looking forward to finally seeing the place where I was born."

MAHER

CHAPTER FIFTY-NINE

Maher sat by Pimm's bedside in the Bear's Den. The note from Mama Bear had arrived early that morning, but he couldn't get away from his Intelligencer duties until late in the afternoon. Thank the gods she'd included that Pimm wasn't seriously injured this time. After recounting everything he could remember, Kit had gone downstairs to prepare the willow bark tea left by Doctor Tambara.

"I'm not pleased that we're doing this again so soon, Pimm."

"We've already been over that," they waved him off. "What do you think about this business with Khafra?"

"I'm not sure, there are too many new details coming to light that don't seem to have anything to do with one another. The Saprean coins. Ghost ships. Ezmira is back in Kingsport. And now Khafra? The idea that he'd lower himself to associate with someone like Ezmira is more troubling at the moment than what they might be plotting together."

"Why is that?" Pimm shifted higher on the pillows, gray eyes narrowing in question.

Maher rested his elbows on his knees. "It means, regardless of whatever else Khafra's been planning this whole time, he's become desperate."

A soft knock broke the thread of tension building between them. Kit pushed the door open with his shoulder, carrying a tray laden with two pots of tea, snifters of brandy, and a small jug of water. A rounded market basket hung from his elbow, stuffed to bursting with an assortment of foods. "Everyone downstairs may have gone a tad overboard," he admitted sheepishly.

Pimm chuckled, then winced and held their side. Taking pity on the lad, Maher rose and relieved him of the tray.

"I can do that, Mister Villaon,"

"It's alright, looks like you have quite a bit to unpack there." Maher slid the tray onto the end of the table that had been cleared of maps and model ships.

No doubt, most of this was due to Pimm, but Maher could also see how well Kit had fit into the Den. And godsbedamned if his own heart didn't sink when he first saw the raised mark on Kit's fair skin.

Fucking Ezmira. Even without Khafra's involvement, that woman's presence in Kingsport is bad news.

Maher poured a cup of willow bark tea and brought it to Pimm. He waited until his friend had taken a healthy sip. While he understood Pimm's aversion to pain-relieving medicines of any kind, the tea was the weakest option the doctor could have prescribed.

Taking a brandy for himself, Maher watched as Kit laid out the small feast that was no doubt sent up by the Den's cook and Olga.

Pimm drained the last of their tea, made a face, and showed the empty cup to Maher as proof. "Any more thoughts on what you'll do about Khafra?"

"I don't even know what he's planning yet," Maher poured Pimm a fresh cup from the other pot. A rich black tea, their favorite. "It's not like I can knock on his door tonight and ask him. 'Good evening, Father.

Could we have a quick chat about the new scheme you're plotting with one of the most repulsive creatures to walk the streets of Kingsport?' That would go over famously."

Kit muttered something under his breath in Zavat and Pimm choked on their drink.

"What was that?" Maher smirked.

Face flushing red as a ripe tomato, Kit cleared his throat. "Sorry, it's just I could never imagine my father or pa doing harm to anyone. Let alone working with someone like *her*."

"I understand." Maher's smile dropped. "It's not something I'm proud of, but Khafra isn't going to hurt anyone else. Not while I breathe air." He patted a still-coughing Pimm's back.

"Maher's right." Pimm finally caught their breath. "And don't ever let Ms. Orel hear you talking like that."

"I won't," Kit laughed a little and tucked the empty basket under the table.

They all ate an early dinner, with plenty of food still left afterward. As Kit was clearing the table, politely but firmly refusing any help, Maher sat next to Pimm again.

"Last of the willow tea," he waited for Pimm to finish before continuing. "I think I know how I can get more information on Khafra's movements."

"How?" They passed their cup to Kit.

"After I leave here, I'll stop by the black lantern and speak to Marielle."

Kit sucked in a breath at his casual mention of the black lantern, but then the lad didn't know yet what really went on there, only the dark rumors the Madam circulated.

Pimm nodded. "I was thinking the same thing."

"It's the only option, really. Besides, Marielle and I need to get our accounts in order."

CHAPTER SIXTY

The dour door guard of the black lantern looked down his nose at Maher.

"Evening, friend." He offered his most winning smile, knowing it wouldn't help his case in the slightest. "I wish to speak to Marielle."

A deeper frown on the man's pale face was all the reply he received. The effect was not unlike negotiating with an old hound dog.

"I have no invitation this time, it's true, but it concerns a matter of particular interest to the Madam."

"Wait here." The guard closed the black-painted door hard enough to rattle the hinges.

"Lovely man," Maher said under his breath. "I really should come here more often."

Time passed, and while Maher didn't expect to see another soul down this dead-end alley, he wasn't anxious to spend the entire night there either. Finally, the door creaked open again. If it were possible, the guard looked even more displeased.

"Come in." He grudgingly held the door wide enough for Maher to pass through.

"Many thanks," The entryway was better lit than the last time Maher set foot inside this place. The darkness and secrecy was a show only for those who didn't know the black lantern's true purpose of offering aid to those with nowhere else to go, among other things. They walked down the short hall in silence, then the guard unlocked the inner door.

"She will meet you in the lounge. You may wait there and only there."

Maher gave him a sharp nod and crossed into the ground floor. As expected, it was completely empty. A chill hung in the air, and Maher moved closer to the fire burning in the brick hearth. This place had none of the welcoming touches of the Bear's Den, but he supposed that was rather the point.

Turning his left shoulder closer to the heat, Maher checked his pocket watch. He was relying on the timepiece more than he'd expected. It would be well after midnight by the time he returned to the manor. Perhaps it wouldn't hurt to take on a small set of rooms in the city. At least that would cut down on how often he had to sneak into the Kingfisher house.

"Maher," Marielle descended the wide staircase. A hefty pistol hung from each hip, and he spotted a third beneath her jacket. "Good to see you."

"And you," they clasped hands.

"Please sit," she indicated a pair of chairs close to the hearth. "What can I do for you? Eustace was quite put out that you arrived without invitation."

"Eustace?"

"Our door guard." Marielle grinned; four gold-capped teeth winked at him in the firelight.

He snorted. "That knowledge just made this visit worth whatever else I'll owe you after tonight."

"You need another favor so soon?"

"I'm afraid so."

She sighed, running a palm across her shorn black hair. "You already owe the Madam for getting you onboard the *Pike* and then for our help catching Calder Kingfisher. Are you sure you want to add to your account with her?"

"It's actually with you I'd like to make a trade, if you're open to the idea."

Her head tilted, dark brown eyes assessing. "What sort of trade?"

Maher shifted, trying to get comfortable on the hard wooden seat. Even their chairs didn't invite one to spend much time there. "I learned something very troubling this evening. I'm sure you're already aware that Ezmira has returned to Kingsport."

Marielle nodded and crossed her arms, her expression hardening.

"In addition to that, she's been seen more than once in town in the company of Ambassador Khafra Villaon. My father."

"My soul and body," she leaned forward. "What would an ambassador be doing with the likes of her?"

Maher appreciated that this was Marielle's concern, rather than the fact it was his own father consorting with Ezmira. "I don't know, but after his plans to take the title of Lord of Trade from Luthais Kingfisher failed, he must have become desperate. He wouldn't have touched her with a bargepole before now."

Marielle's smile was grim. "You want me to uncover whatever it is those two are plotting."

"That's right. In exchange, you'll have an open-ended favor from me. My influence is considerably greater than it was before I was made Intelligencer."

She stood and paced slowly by the hearth, hands resting on her wide gunbelt. "Do you think this is connected to those Saprean coins? We've not heard of any progress from Pimm on that front."

"Even with his position in Saprea, I don't see how Khafra could be involved, especially with access to that much silver. Why bother using it to gain a position on the Birde Isles when that much wealth could buy him a title in most countries?" He shifted again. "But, if I've learned anything this year, it's that nothing is impossible."

Propping her fists on her broad hips, Marielle pursed her lips and then nodded. "It's a good trade. I'll see what I can learn."

"Thank you," Maher stood, and they sealed the agreement. "If I hear of anything else connected to this, or the coins, I'll send word."

"Good. If you'll excuse me, I have guests to attend to."

"Of course." Maher followed her back to the front door. She knocked four times, with a slight pause after the first two. "You don't have a key?"

"It's not my floor." She gave him the same cryptic answer as the first time they'd met. Perhaps Maher wasn't privy to everything in the black lantern after all.

The lock turned, and the door guard appeared, looking as happy to see Maher as ever.

"We're finished. Please see Mister Villaon out." Marielle clapped Maher on the back. "Until next time, Maher."

"Until then," Following the guard, Maher wondered if he'd have time for one more stop that night. It would put him getting home even later, but it might be worth the time taken.

The door to the street opened and Maher was waved through. Once he was safely on the cobblestones, Maher turned back and gave a short bow. "Much obliged, Eustace!"

He was halfway down the alley before old Eustace recovered and slammed the door shut.

Sure enough, it was morning when Maher dragged himself into the house. The servants were already up and going about their tasks, so he simply let himself in through the front door. They hardly noticed his odd hours anymore.

Trudging through the foyer, Maher was mentally preparing to climb all those stairs to his room, when a wide body blocked his path.

"Maher," Luthais deep voice cut through his foggy thoughts. "I was calling your name outside; did you not hear me?"

"What? Apologies," he yawned. "I've been awake for more than a day; my faculties aren't in the best shape."

"What were you doing that you haven't rested since yesterday?"

Maher fluttered his fingers through the air. "Intelligencer responsibilities."

Luthais snorted. "That makes about as much sense as the sea sprites."

Maher chuckled, despite himself. They stepped aside so a maid could pass with a mop and bucket. "What are you doing up and about so early?"

"I have a meeting at noon with the trade guild and the harbormaster, but there are dock inspections to be done first."

A meeting? Maher hadn't heard of any meeting involving both the guild and the harbormaster's office. "What about?"

Luthais looked away and cleared his throat, almost as if he was reluctant to tell Maher. "We have no idea how much damage Cal has done abroad, and we've learned nothing from trying to speak with him."

Maher didn't dare interrupt; this was the first time he'd heard either of the elder Kingfisher brothers mention Cal directly in weeks.

"As Lord of Trade, it's my responsibility to ensure none of our allies were caught up in Cal's web. Today's meeting is to discuss which nations will require the most attention. And our fishing trade agreements will all eventually have to be renegotiated, now that the Isles aren't benefiting from the presence of Ally's, uh, friend."

Maher hummed in agreement. Personally, he was glad Pasha would no longer be draining herself to bring an unnatural number of fish to the waters around the Birde Isles. It was the final thread cut between her and old Gaius Kingfisher I, and good riddance.

"Does that mean you'll have to send delegates to each country where Cal was supposed to be acting in our interest?"

Luthais tugged on the single braid hanging over his shoulder and blew out a rough breath. "It means I have to go to each of our allies myself. Possibly even the few nations where we have little to no trade agreements."

"Because you don't know if Cal stuck to the routes he claimed to have taken."

"Right. Kamharida is preparing the new ship as we speak."

Maher wasn't exactly surprised by the news; it made sense given Luthais' position and the potential fucking mess Cal had made. As Lord of Trade, he made annual trips to the continent. Sometimes for as long as a month or two at a time. And still, Maher felt a strange twisting in his stomach as he asked the next question. "How long will you be gone?"

Luthais' moss green eyes finally met his. "It could be up to a year. Maybe longer."

"A *year*?" The twisting suddenly let go as Maher's stomach turned to lead.

He nodded. "A year."

"Fuck."

"Mhm, that's about the right word for it."

SWAIN

CHAPTER SIXTY-ONE

A ship crewed by the dead.

Swain stood on the quarterdeck near the helm, surveying their new vessel. The creature had kept her end of their agreement so far. He and the dozen-odd sailors under his charge had been spared the same fate as the corpse puppets. They now had a new ship, a Fraollish trader by the look of it, even larger than the *Maiden's Revenge*. They'd abandoned the dilapidated Nuvwaan ship. Left it floating out at sea as it slowly shrank into the horizon.

What Swain hadn't anticipated was that the ship would arrive with a crew made entirely of the dead. He'd thought surely the creature would keep some of them alive. There were sailors of all ranks and most ports of call. Some still wearing the uniforms they'd died in, others who might have once been pirates themselves. Each with one of those green jewels placed somewhere on their faces. He was certain now that's how they were controlled. They were possibly even what was keeping the bodies in motion. He wanted to pry one off to see what happened; if the twisted spell would be broken.

"I don't like this, sir." Smith hovered by his shoulder. "It ain't right."

The living sailors all huddled together at the stern of the ship, watching the corpse crew pull in lines and climb the rigging with stilted, unnatural movements. Never tiring, never stopping.

"I know," he murmured, still unsure if any of the dead could understand or even hear them. "Hold fast. We're doing what we need to survive."

The creature lurked somewhere beneath the hull, searching for the trail that would lead them back to the last place the turbine was used. Everything hinged on how quickly she could find it. Swain didn't know how many more there were like her, or what they wanted.

And neither do I care. He gripped the helm. *Not if it means they'll bring her back.*

A corpse shuffled by, and Smith dodged out of the way. The crew refused to go belowdecks. They'd elected Smith to tell him as much, and that they intended on sleeping out in the open.

Swain couldn't blame them. He'd only gone into the empty captains' quarters long enough to find a decent map and a compass. They had to gauge their position at sea to plot how long it would take to reach Utollmir, which had the closest port to landlocked Kharabo.

"Swainnn," the creature called from the waves below.

Teeth clenched, he crossed the main deck to the starboard side. She was waiting there, only her head and shoulders visible. Every time Swain saw her anew he was struck by how perfect she seemed. Then he'd remember exactly what she was hiding beneath the surface.

"Come here, Swain."

The hull of this ship was much deeper than the last had been. If Swain needed to speak to her, his crew would have to lower him in a longboat.

Smith voiced her apprehension again, but in the end helped the others send Swain down. When the little boat touched the water, the creature draped her arms over the side, chin resting on her hands.

"Hello, Swain." Knowing his name had given her some kind of power over him. No matter how repulsed he was in his heart and mind, his traitorous body was ready and willing to do anything she asked. He'd forbidden the rest of the crew from saying their names aloud.

"What is it?" His gruff response only made her smile widen.

"Is that the thanks you show for this lovely ship I've brought you? Why, I even included some of the original crew."

Swain's mouth went dry, and he tried to not think about the truth behind her words. "I thank you. There's more than enough room for what's needed."

"Wonderful," she leaned closer, tilting the longboat towards the water. Full, pink lips brushed against his ear; her breath carried the sickly-sweet scent of rotting fruit. Swain braced himself. "You'd do well to have your course set, Swain. It won't be long now."

PASHA

CHAPTER SIXTY-TWO

Pasha felt the subtle shift in the water long before she saw the faint outline of the solitary island in the distance.

She'd swam past this place countless times, always aware of its presence but never curious enough to explore it for herself. Perhaps it was foolish, after all this time, to still feel reverence for this place. For the air of secrecy and power that shrouded the sacred space from prying eyes. Often putting its very existence out of her mind. But Pasha felt it, the aura of deep-rooted energy that recognized her own and at the same time tried to warn her away.

What, are the elders going to suddenly appear the moment you cross the threshold?

Pasha snorted, startling a school of fish that had been mirroring her path since she reached the open water. "If I'd known that was all it took to get their attention, I might have done this a century ago."

Would you have, though? Really?

Pasha didn't have an answer for that.

Shafts of sunlight broke through the surface, reflecting off the scales and skins of the creatures going about their lives around her. Far below,

Pasha glimpsed a pair of smaller sharks making their yearly journey to warmer waters.

The closer she got to the hunk of rock spiraling down into the ocean floor, the more the energy around it tried to redirect her. It was a gentle nudge at first, then more insistent, as if it were growing cross with her. The water grew thick and heavy, forcing Pasha to use her arms as well as her tail to keep moving.

"Let me through," she built a ring of energy between her palms, much like what she used to call the sharks or whales. Just a little closer, then she'd let it go. "Please, I'm the only one left." The ring sailed towards the island and, all at once, it stopped fighting her.

Breathing a sigh of relief, Pasha swam the rest of the way with ease. The light from above quickly dimmed as she dove beneath the wider upper edge of the island.

"Where is it?" Pasha laid her hands against the craggy surface. The sheer power contained within overwhelmed her senses and nearly sent her reeling back. Pasha sank into the sensation, letting the energy inspect her own until it was satisfied that she belonged to the shoal. "I'd think you would recognize me. You helped to make me, after all."

There was a low hum beneath her palms, and then something tugged her over and down, towards the place where the rocky mass started to narrow.

Pasha was tempted to ask how far it intended to pull her. She opened her mouth to do just that, when everything suddenly tilted and Pasha tumbled straight through.

"Tides protect me," Pasha gasped when her head broke through the surface of the pool contained within the island.

The hatching place was perfect. Completely untouched by the years that had passed since the others left. Not a single stone was out of place. The corals lining the edge of the pool lit up in a dazzling display of greens and blues, welcoming Pasha back to the place where she'd first entered the world.

The clear water hardly stirred as she drifted closer to the strip of sand hugging the curve of the domed space. Bright white grains shifted beneath her fingers, the fine texture dotted with spots of brilliant color. Reds, blues, and greens. Purples and pinks. Silver and gold. And everything in between. They looked like jewels scattered through the sand, but one touch and Pasha knew what they truly were. Eggshells. These sands had cradled and warmed generations of mermaids, fed her own egg energy drawn from the wellspring of the shoal's power until Pasha was ready to emerge.

It took so long for a mermaid to hatch, Pallagia had said. Decades. Maybe even a century. And it took a very special set of circumstances for an egg to even be laid. The fact that Pasha and Pallagia were from the same laying made them special. But Pallagia had hatched nearly two centuries earlier than Pasha. Many in the shoal thought Pasha might never hatch. It had been too long and layings with multiple eggs rarely yielded more than one mermaid. Those that didn't hatch would eventually drain of all color and join the row of stone eggs resting against the cave wall.

Tearing herself away from the sand, Pasha splashed a handful of water on her face. "Remember why you're here."

Climbing out of the pool, Pasha's tail split into legs with hardly a thought and no discomfort at all. She pushed aside the new questions that raised and focused on the walls. The murals in this place were *immaculate*. As if they'd been freshly carved that very morning. The details far surpassed anything in Pasha's home. Every scale on each mermaid was defined, the unique lines and patterns polished until they shined like the real thing. Faces were so expressive, Pasha half expected them to begin speaking to her.

There were so many things recorded here that Pasha didn't understand. Things that would take days or weeks to decipher. If she could figure them out at all. But nothing about humans.

The awe Pasha felt at being in the hatching grounds dulled with the prospect that, even here, she wouldn't find what Ally needed.

"It has to be here." Pasha doubled back, determined to start again in case she'd missed something.

The first mural showed an egg nestled in the sands beneath Pasha's feet. Swirled waves of energy were carved around it, feeding the mermaid inside and dipping down behind the stone eggs propped against the wall. Each one came up to Pasha's knees, narrowed tops widening out into rounded bases. Kneeling down, Pasha carefully rolled the first egg back to get a look at the bottom of the mural. Her fingers smoothed over the pebbled surface and curved around the back to keep it from falling. Not that she expected a stone egg would break easily, but...

"Wait," Pasha's hand brushed against a place on the egg that was unlike the rest of it. Gripping the sides, she turned it until she could see the backside. There, hidden from view, was a small carving of a human woman wading into the surf. On the shore more humans looked as if they were calling out to her, but she only had eyes for the sea.

Moving quickly, Pasha turned the rest of the eggs. Her arms were shaking and her heart pounding by the time she finished, but there it was. Scattered across a dozen mermaid eggs that would never hatch. The ritual that would change Ally into a mermaid.

PASHA

CHAPTER SIXTY-THREE

Ally was already waiting on the shore when Pasha left the sea. Her mind was still spinning with everything she'd found, she didn't even know what to tell Ally first.

As her tail split and legs formed, Pasha gathered her thoughts. Ally was pacing at the water's edge. If it wasn't so cold she'd probably be swimming out to meet Pasha halfway. Finally she was able to stand, wading through the last of the waves until she reached Ally.

"Pasha!" Apparently not caring that Pasha was soaking wet, Ally wrapped her into a hug the moment she touched dry sand. Pasha didn't mind, she welcomed every embrace, every touch, every time Ally's curious fingers wanted to compare what her scales felt like to her skin. She let her face rest in the crook of Ally's neck; it had quickly become a favorite spot. "I know we agreed you'd go on your own, but I spent the whole day thinking about what you might find. I embroidered a fabulous knot into one of Maher's handkerchiefs!"

Pasha hid a smile in Ally's hair. She didn't want Ally to worry about her all the time, but it still felt good to know someone was thinking of her.

When they pulled apart, Ally kept hold of Pasha's hand. "How was it? Was there anything left behind?"

Her lips parted, but the words lodged in Pasha's throat. Ally was waiting for her to speak, to learn what Pasha had seen. Still, Pasha hesitated.

Sitting in the middle of that space, absorbing the centuries of history, the countless lives tied to this one spot in the vastness of the seas, Pasha felt so incredibly small. She'd never felt so connected to her own kind, and yet more far away than ever. Ally said she wanted this, and in her mind Pasha knew there was nothing or no one coercing Ally into that decision. She'd seen exactly what Pasha was, every flaw and crack running beneath the surface. She'd witnessed what a lifetime of loneliness had done to Pasha's heart and mind, the lengths she'd gone to escape it, and Ally had forgiven her. Ally *wanted* to be with Pasha, she wouldn't have said so if she didn't mean it. Pasha knew that.

But that voice deep inside of Pasha that had plagued her for so long, it whispered lies into her ear. It told her Ally only wanted the change to save herself from the fate of the other Sea Kissed humans. That once she was free of the burden, she'd leave too.

Why would she want to spend a nearly immortal life with you?

Pasha hoped the ritual would take the pain of being Sea Kissed away from Ally, and if it did then that alone would make the change worth it. And Pasha was sure enough of herself to know she wouldn't make the same mistakes as Pallagia. She wouldn't try to make Ally's decisions for her. It would rip what was left of her heart into pieces if Ally decided to leave, but never again would she try to force someone into her life.

"Pasha? What's wrong?" Ally touched her face. "You can tell me. Whatever it is, we'll figure it out together."

Throat burning, Pasha cradled the back of Ally's neck and kissed her once, twice. She kissed her until the chill of the sea and that nagging voice both melted away. When she trusted herself to speak again, Pasha drew back far enough to see her face. "I found it."

Ally's half-lidded eyes flew open. "You found the hatching place?"

"And the ritual."

"You... you found it?" she whispered.

Pasha's hand drifted to her shoulder. "I *found* it, Ally."

"You found it!" Ally flung her arms around Pasha's neck, nearly knocking them both onto the wet sand. "I can't believe you found the way to change me, I thought we'd never, I –" A soft sob was muffled into Pasha's shoulder.

Pasha could feel Ally's heart hammering against her chest. Holding her close, Pasha murmured into her ear, "It's so beautiful there. Everything is just as the elders left it, all the carvings were perfectly intact."

Sniffling, Ally pulled back and used her sleeve to dry her tears. "How is that possible?"

"The entire place is imbued with a power like I've never felt before. It wasn't left there by mermaids in the past, it's a part of the hatching grounds itself."

"I want to see it," Ally's eyes darted towards the sea. "Can you take me there now? What do we have to do?"

"It's farther away than I remembered and the ritual is a little difficult to explain. I think we should wait, until we've chosen the day to make the change, to go there again. It will be easier to show you then and, once you've seen everything, you can decide once and for all if you still want to do it."

"Of course I do, this is what we've been looking for." She paused for a moment. "Do *you* still want to do this? Would it harm you to perform the ritual? Because if this will put you in danger—"

"It's nothing like that. I need to study the carvings more closely, but I think I'm strong enough to do this for you." Pasha's voice grew hoarse. "Ally, I will change you if it's truly what you want, but I..."

Ally brushed her thumb over the back of Pasha's hand. "What is it?"

"I don't want you to think I'm trying to trap you, that you have to stay with me because I'll be your anchor or because I was alone for so long and you're the first friend I've had... the first everything, really, and I've never..." Pasha growled at herself, *Stop babbling!* Ally waited for her to continue. "I'm hundreds of years old, but I feel like I just hatched yesterday. I don't know what I'm doing; I don't know what kind of life I could give you after the change is done."

Ally laced their fingers together. "Pasha, I don't feel like you're trapping me, and this is what I want, no matter what kind of relationship we have. There will always be something we can learn from each other," The corner of her mouth tipped up. "You taught me how to swim and to love the sea. I can teach you other things. We can build whatever kind of life we want."

Heat spread across Pasha's face. "There's something I want you to do before we make any plans. I want you to spend some time with your friends and family."

"But that's –"

Pasha kissed Ally before she could build an argument. "Please, do this for me. I want you to be absolutely sure and to understand what you'd be giving up."

"I'm already sure, and I don't think there's much I'm giving up if I'll be able to eventually come back onto land."

"Still, you should build as many memories as you can with your family and with Maher. With anyone else you want to say goodbye to, because there *are* some people you might not see again. It wouldn't be safe if the entire island learned you've become a mermaid. Besides," Pasha tilted Ally's face up until she was looking at the place where the outline of the moon was beginning to appear, "we can only perform the ritual during a full moon, and there won't be one for another five days or so."

"Five days?" Ally breathed deeply and nodded. "I can handle that."

CHAPTER SIXTY-FOUR

Five more days on land.

Five days to spend with her friends and family, to see her favorite places one more time, until she could return again.

Five more days as a human.

Pasha was so concerned Ally would regret her decision, she wasn't allowing herself to feel the excitement of her discovery. It seemed to calm her once Ally agreed to take the time with her family and friends. She'd take advantage of every moment she could, including the evenings they usually spent together on the shore or beneath Kingfisher Island. Pasha was smiling by the time they arranged when and where to meet when the five days came to an end.

Before it was time for her to return to the house, Ally led Pasha up to the rocks. A bundle was waiting there, the long shape covered in thick fabric.

"It's finally done," Ally unwrapped the fabric to reveal a canvas-bound tube with a strap attached at each end. This was Maher's suggestion, similar to the cases used to transport maps, but also used to protect artwork painted onto more delicate materials like calfskin. The sail canvas around the outside was treated with the same weather-proofing technique as the tapestry stored inside. She showed Pasha how to unlatch the top and pulled out the rolled map. "Cal really did find a new water-resisting method from Meredia, that part wasn't a lie." Ally stopped herself from saying anything else about Cal, she didn't want to travel that road just yet.

Pasha ran her hands over the map. It was, Ally had to admit, a little stiff now. The shopkeeper had been wary of its age, unsure how the linseed oil compound would take to the fibers.

"Between the sealant and the case, it should stay fairly dry. We should try to only open it above the surface if we can."

"Thank you so much, Ally." Pasha rolled the map up and locked it back inside the case. "You've outdone yourself."

"It's my masterpiece. The closetful of clothes I've embroidered for Maher can't hold a candle to this."

Pasha laughed. "Don't tell him that, or you might spend the next five days making even more clothing."

"Maybe something out of silver, or gold perhaps?"

"That would be impressive," Pasha reached for her, and they settled down on the sand, leaning against the rocks. Ally spread her wool cloak over them again.

When they'd taken their friendship to this new intimate place, Ally wondered if she'd become more attuned to Pasha's constant nakedness. She was even more mindful of where she placed her hands but, other than that, not much had changed. This was how Pasha had always been and Ally had appreciated her beauty long before now. Pasha's body was sleeker and more angular than her own, built for slicing through currents and gliding over waves. But the first time Ally really saw her, the first time she helped Ally walk into the sea, all she could focus on were Pasha's scales. The rich colors and ornate patterns. Ally sometimes felt drab by comparison, but she was more aware now of Pasha's eyes on her when she stripped down to her breeches and shift for a swim. How they lingered over the rise of her breasts and the curve of her hips. When her arms were around Ally, she could feel Pasha tentatively exploring the soft dip of her waist and the plump flesh stretched across her abdomen.

They sat together the rest of the night, sometimes talking, sometimes dozing, sharing kisses and brief touches in between. Even though Pasha didn't generate much body heat, Ally hardly felt the cold. She stayed until the pink light of dawn was breaking over the waves.

When it was time to go, Pasha helped Ally to her feet. Ally stretched a crick out of her neck. "No more laying on rocks, I think."

"Agreed," Pasha winced as several joints in her legs and feet popped.

Wrapping her cloak around her shoulders, Ally picked up the map case and walked Pasha to the water's edge. Pasha sighed when the first wavelet washed over her feet. The scales on her legs glittered. Ally knew she ought to let Pasha go, so she could have her tail again.

"Five days?" Ally confirmed one last time.

"That's right, the first night of the full moon." She held out her hands for the case.

"You're not going to disappear on me, are you?" Ally smiled, but her heart raced. She knew Pasha wouldn't go back on her promise, so why did she not want to let go of the map?

You know why.

Because deep down, in the place where her fear of the sea used to reside, Ally was terrified Pasha wouldn't be waiting for her when she returned.

"Of course not," Pasha slung the strap across her chest and kissed Ally goodbye. "Enjoy your time with your family. I'll see you soon."

ALLY

CHAPTER SIXTY-FIVE

After a few hours of sleep and a change of clothes, Ally found her parents lingering over breakfast in the family dining room.

"Good morning, dearest," Mama said as Ally kissed her cheek. "Lately we haven't seen you this early in the day."

"I know, but I wanted to talk to both of you."

"What about?" Lord Kingfisher rang the bell for a plate to be brought for Ally and poured her a cup of tea.

"I'd like the three of us to do something together today." She stirred milk into her tea and took a sip to give herself a moment to choose what to say next. "And I want to tell you about a decision I've made. It will mean I'll be away for a while, but I think it's the right choice for me."

Her parents looked at each other, sharing something unspoken. Mama smiled, even though tears were gathering in her eyes. "You know all we want is your happiness, Alphonsine."

Gaius took Rochelle's hand. "We're ready to listen to what you have to say, and we'll support your decision as best we can."

Rochelle Kingfisher had picked up on more than Ally realized, especially after being introduced to Pasha, and had shared as much with her husband in the weeks since they arrived back home. Still, Ally told her parents all she thought they needed to hear. How Pasha was the one to pull Ally from the sea the night she nearly drowned. The research she'd done with Esa on what it meant to be Sea Kissed, and how the shark tooth Pasha gave her had held off the effects. And she told them there might be a way to free her from being Sea Kissed altogether, but it would require certain sacrifices. Ally was long past the age of needing their permission, but she wanted to know that they respected her choices. Or at least tried to understand them.

They talked until Lord Kingfisher's steward came looking for him. He promised to clear his schedule for the afternoon so they could go somewhere together, as Ally requested. Mama suggested the two of them continue their conversation in the parlor.

There were some things Ally could only say to her mother. Things she'd held in for a long time about how the family had handled her fears. How horrified Ally'd been when Mama was taken and how much she was going to miss them. How nervous and excited she was to join Pasha in the sea. What she was going to become.

Rochelle listened to it all, seated with Ally on the sofa, not minding at all when her daughter began running the brocade fabric of her mother's skirt through her hands. It was such a weight off Ally's mind to get out everything she needed to say.

When Ally finished, Rochelle sighed deeply and kissed the top of her head. "Thank you for telling me, dearest. I only wish you'd felt you could come to me with all of this much sooner. I'm so sorry if I ever made you feel you couldn't confide in me."

"It's not that I felt I couldn't come to you with how I was feeling," Ally smoothed her mother's skirt, trying to memorize the sensation of the raised flowers beneath her palms. Touching Mama's clothes had always been comforting, as far back as she could remember. "But, when *no one* would talk about it, when it seemed the entire household was pretending like it had never happened and my fears were only in my mind..." Ally touched the raised knot on the bridge of her nose. The result of her first panic attack after nearly drowning and a daily reminder that her fears hadn't come out of nowhere. "It was easier to push specific thoughts and feelings down."

"Until you met Pasha?"

"Yes, until I met Pasha. I didn't realize it then but standing there with her on the shore that night we met, shouting at each other over that ridiculous bargain great-grandfather Gaius had made," Ally chuckled, "It felt so good, so freeing to finally let it all out. I admit I was looking for someone to blame, after I was too afraid to join you on the *Swan Song* and you were all alone when Dare attacked the ship."

"None of that was your fault, Ally."

"I know, Mama, I know. But at the time? I felt so helpless. It's strange how all of our fates have been intertwined by the decisions of others, but those were their choices, not ours. Pasha helped me see that, too."

"I'm so glad you've found someone who cares for you so much. That you can be there for one another and help each other, even if it means... losing you for a time." Rochelle's voice wavered. "Ally, do you remember the stories I told you, about the deities we worship in Balah?"

"Of course," she glanced over at the small altar Mama had added to the parlor since their return. That made three altars to the Trio in their house. The largest was in her parents' bedroom and a tiny version resided in Lady Kingfisher's private sitting room. "What about them?"

"I've been thinking, since learning you are Sea Kissed and all of the pain this has caused you, and I worry. What if I'm to blame?"

"What do you mean, Mama?"

A tear slid down Rochelle's cheek. "What if you are Sea Kissed, because of something I've done?"

"How could you possibly think that?"

"The night you were born, I watched the moon the entire time."

"People look at the moon every night,"

"Remember the story." Rochelle looked at the altar. "The Moon and the Sun share the sky, but they do not always agree. The Moon controls the seas, the rivers, the rain. When she is angry with the Sun, she sends fierce storms to ruin crops, floods to wash away landscapes, she is constantly striking the waves against the shores. The Sun is master of all the land, the plants, every rock and grain of sand. He needs the Moon, needs the rain to nourish the earth, but he also tries to steal from her. He shines down so hot, until the water rises out of the lakes and pools, and the cycle begins anew. You know the rest."

"Mama," Ally tried again.

"Please, Alphonsine, finish the story."

Ally held her mother's hand. "The In-Between is the essence of what connects us to one another, and it waits to welcome us when we leave this world. Souls can only cross over into the next life during the In-between's time at dawn and dusk."

"We should each of us have all three forces guiding our lives, the Sun, the Moon, the In-Between. I know you don't believe in them, dearest, but what if... what if I prayed so hard to the Moon that you belong only to her? What if I deprived you of the others and now the Moon is calling you away?"

"Mama, nothing you did has caused this. Esa told me, there were Sea Kissed people long before anyone who believed in the Trio ever settled on the Isles. I know you're trying to find an explanation, but it is absolutely not your fault. No one knows why this happened, not Pasha, not Esa, or the priestesses who came before her. Maybe it was pure dumb luck. Or maybe it's because, despite everything that happened to drive me away from the sea, this is the path I was meant to find."

"You're right, darling." She smiled sadly. "This is all very philosophical of you, Alphonsine. I didn't think you were one to believe in fate."

"I'm not sure that I do, but what I do believe is it doesn't matter if it's fate or the gods or whoever else that puts options before me in my life. I'm the one who will decide which to take, or none at all."

Ally couldn't remember the last time she'd walked through the manor grounds with both her parents. They started in Rochelle's garden and found the path up the sloping hill behind the house.

Gaius had arranged for them to have a picnic late that afternoon. Blankets and cushions were already spread out on the dried grass, with extra shawls to wrap up against the chill. Mrs. Thorley arranged a simple fare of bread, cheese, fruit, and cold chicken. A covered dish of bite-sized Balahn pastries soaked in syrup waited for dessert. Ally desperately wanted to say goodbye to the housekeeper who'd been a comforting presence in her childhood and a steadfast friend to her as an adult. But, while Mrs. Thorley had probably heard that Ally was Sea Kissed – there really were no secrets in a household full of servants and staff – she wasn't sure the older woman would fully understand why becoming a mermaid and leaving their home was what Ally needed to do.

As they were finishing, Gaius took Ally's hand in both of his. The wide band of his onyx ring was warm against her skin. Another little thing she wanted to remember.

"I hope, Ally, that you will accept my sincerest apology for not trusting you to make your own decisions, and for not addressing your fears with the respect you deserved. I'm not expecting forgiveness right now, or ever. I just wanted you to know, before you leave, how sorry I am."

Slowly taking her hand back, Ally caught the resigned look that passed over her father's face. He really was leaving it to Ally whether she forgave him or not. Ally rose onto her knees and wrapped him into a tight hug.

Gaius' big arms enveloped her, squeezing so hard Ally let out a squeak. His mustache tickled her face and she felt like a little girl again. When her father had always seemed larger than life, until he scooped her into his arms.

"You two are going to make me cry again," Rochelle sniffed, dabbing the corners of her eyes with a napkin.

Pulling away, Ally straightened the lapels of her father's coat, lingering over the kingfisher bird embroidered on the breast pocket. "I can't tell you how much that means to me, Father, thank you. I do forgive you, and I love you both very much."

It was one of the most peaceful afternoons she'd ever spent with her mother and father. Seeing them relaxed and teasing each other. Knowing they were still so much in love made leaving a little easier. Ally showed them where she'd sat nearly every morning to watch the sun rise over the sea. She half-hoped to see Pasha in the waves below, but knew the mermaid was giving Ally space to be with her loved ones.

It was dark by the time they made their way down the hill. Ally hugged them tight before they went inside, grateful they'd accepted the choices she'd made for herself, even though it would be hard to say goodbye.

MAHER

Chapter Sixty-six

Lamplight flickered above Maher's head, casting everything around him in an orange haze.

He was waiting just across the way from the headquarters of the Kingsport guard. It was quite late, or incredibly early, depending on how one viewed it. Maher checked his pocket watch for the tenth time, half past three in the morning. Slipping the watch back into his charcoal waistcoat, Maher pulled up the collar of his overcoat to block some of the chill.

The Saprean silver coin he'd been carrying for months sat heavy in his pocket. Maher palmed the coin, feeling the sharp ridges around the edge and the face of the Saprean queen stamped into one side. His thumb grazed the tulips on the opposite side as his attention stayed on the tall, imposing building across the street.

Marielle had come to him at the Den earlier in the evening. She had no real lead on Ezmira or her dealings with his father. The viper appeared to have left the city for now. No doubt she was still lurking somewhere on Kingfisher Island.

No, what Marielle had found involved Khafra alone. And Maher still didn't know what to make of it.

Apparently, Ambassador Khafra Villaon was paying regular visits to Calder Kingfisher in his holding cell with the Kingsport guard. Only at times when no one but the guards would be there. Before Maher could ask why this wasn't reported to the Kingfishers, Marielle confirmed that Khafra had one of the night guards on account and only went on the nights they were on duty. According to the guard roster she'd somehow obtained, that guard would be on tonight. Maher had arrived around two o'clock and relieved Marielle of her post. Khafra had shown up as expected, not ten minutes before. All Maher could do now was wait.

Leaning his good shoulder against the lamp post, Maher considered the possible reasons for these secret meetings. Was Khafra hoping to break Cal's silence himself, to earn a place of trust with the Kingfishers another way? Or, the more likely and unsettling choice, Khafra was attempting to use Cal's betrayal for his own benefit, regardless of what it did to the Isles. What else had Cal learned from the records he'd stolen from the sea temple? They'd found no trace of them in his rooms at the house or on board the *Wave Skipper*.

Maher's stomach rumbled. When was the last time he'd eaten? As soon as he returned home, he'd pay the manor kitchens a visit.

The heavy bolt securing the door drew back with a loud clank. Maher withdrew back the shadows, out of the halo cast by the lamp. A guard's head poked out to scan the street.

Ah, they're Saprean. Maher's brows rose. This didn't really answer any questions, but he could easily see Khafra using their shared heritage to convince the guard to accept a bribe. The guard disappeared, and soon Khafra walked out, buttoning the toggles on his long coat.

Shoving his hands into his pockets, Maher waited for Khafra to cross the street before emerging back into the lamplight.

"Good evening, Father."

Khafra jumped and clutched his chest, eyes wide as if he'd just seen a ghost. The sight cheered Maher to no end.

"Maher!" he hissed, closing the distance between them. "What in the gods' names are you doing here?"

"I was going to ask you the same question."

The corners of his mouth jerked down before Khafra smoothed his features. "Using your newfound power to spy on your own flesh and blood?"

The barb stung, but Maher pushed past it. "Why are you visiting Cal so often?"

"Hasn't whatever little bird you've employed to follow me already told you?"

"I don't have time for games."

Khafra scoffed, "Of course not, you've secured yourself a position of your own and no longer have to feign any sort of regard for me."

Maher's jaw clenched. The longest conversation they'd had in weeks, months even, and his father's only instinct was to mock him. "If that's what you truly think, Khafra, then there's no point in arguing."

"How disappointing," he sighed.

"Just answer the question, and we can both get on with our nights."

His father paused, clearly considering his reply. "I'm here to see if perhaps there is something Calder will confide to me that he is withholding from his father and brothers."

"Why would Call tell you anything?"

"Not everyone dislikes me as much as you do, Maher. Young Calder and I have always had a cordial relationship. One could even say we were close for a time, but you'd know that if you hadn't made it your life's calling to avoid your own father."

Maher sucked in a deep breath of cold night air. Rationally, he knew Khafra was trying to goad him into reacting or giving his own motives away. He'd never once seen Khafra and Cal speak on their own. That did nothing to ease the burn in Maher's stomach. Why, why in all the gods' names did he still care what this man thought of him?

Squeezing the coin in his pocket until his knuckles creaked, Maher feigned a look of boredom. "And did your adopted son tell you anything of note tonight?"

"Sadly, not as of yet. Calder has become a deeply troubled young man. I doubt anything he says can be fully believed."

Every word of that was a lie. It was one of Khafra's only tells, faking sympathy for another person.

"Well, if you do learn anything important, I trust you'll tell the Kingfishers."

"Just as I trust you'll be informing them of our conversation tonight." Khafra inclined his head. "Are you returning to the manor?"

"Not quite yet. You?"

"Oh no, not at this hour. I've taken rooms in the city for those times when business requires a late night. You should consider doing the same. Perhaps in one of the brothels you frequent."

Maher smiled tightly. "I think I'll keep to the manor, just the same. After all," he leaned into Khafra's space. "*I'm* always welcome there."

Khafra turned on his heel and walked away. Maher stayed beneath the lamp and watched until his father was out of sight.

CHAPTER SIXTY-SEVEN

On the second day, Ally rose early and walked into town. She browsed through her favorite shops and warmly greeted the owners. There were a few who'd become more wary of her than they'd been before, and she understood why. What stories would they spin when she disappeared from the Isles altogether?

At Su's Perfumery she found the owner's daughter Su-Minn chatting with a boy about her age, the oyster man's son. Ally smiled to herself and bought a new set of altar oils for Mama. Saving the oyster stall for another day, she stopped by Mrs. Ekmekci's bakery instead. The elderly woman was in her usual form, and far more curious about Maher's absence than any rumors she might have heard about Ally. After leaving the bakery, a twine-tied box of toasty pastries in hand, Ally walked to the wharf.

She found Gai in the private room he often used at the harbormaster's office. He was, understandably, rather surprised to see her. Ally had never set foot in his workspace before.

She presented him with the bakery box. "I was hoping you'd join me for a noonday cup of tea."

"I, well certainly, Ally." Gai blinked for a second before sending his clerk to fetch some tea and plates.

They ate and drank and conversed about nothing in particular. The unusually cold autumn weather, some repairs that were needed on the docks, their father's upcoming birthday. Gai had pastry crumbs in his mustache and Ally howled with laughter when he dislodged them with a twitch of his lip.

"Tell me," Ally poured the last of the tea into their cups. "What do you want to do next?"

"After tea?" He divided the last walnut pastry and placed a serving on each of their plates.

"Not just after tea," she chided. "What do you want to do, Gai? Sure, you're helping Father and Luthais to bring our trade operations back in order, but what about after that? Father is going to live a long and healthy life, goddess willing, what do you want to do until you become Lord of the Birde Isles? What will make you happy?"

Gai looked at her as if she'd asked him to take up a career on the stage or run off with a company of acrobats. "I don't know. I hadn't thought about it."

"Well, think about it! You've studied at Father's side since you were a boy, you will make a wonderful Lord of the Isles someday, but there must be something else you want for yourself. Some unfulfilled dream, a place you've always wanted to visit?"

"Ally, our father is not going to sit idly by while I run off on some adventure or suddenly decide to take up the piano."

"Do you want to play the piano?"

"That's not the point! I want to be Lord of the Birde Isles. I had the option, by law, to pass the title to Luthais when he came of age, but I knew that would be the wrong choice for both of us."

"Because Luthais would have tied you to the yardarm if you had." She smirked.

"You're probably right," he grumbled. "Still, there is no way Father would allow me to shirk my responsibilities as his heir, even for a short time. So there's no point in considering what will never happen."

"Yes, he would! I've already spoken to him about it."

Gai choked on his last bite of pastry. "By the goddess, Ally! You've done what?"

"Not about you specifically, but about listening to his children and letting them make their own decisions. If you explain everything to him, assure him you still want to inherit the title, I'm sure he'll agree." Ally leaned closer and lowered her voice. "He's also feeling particularly remorseful after everything that came to light about Gaius I and how it affected our family. He'd probably let you hold a public piano concert in front of our house if it fulfilled some pushed-aside dream."

Her eldest brother snorted and shook his head. "When did you become so devious?"

Ally imitated Pasha's wide, shark-like grin. "Spending time with a certain mermaid has had an effect on me."

"I'm glad to see it."

"Seriously, though, promise me you'll give this some thought and talk to Father. And Mama, you know she'll be on your side."

"Ally," Gai sighed.

"Or, if you don't want to become a great pianist, what about love? Is there someone who's caught your fancy?"

"I was joking about the piano." Face flushed, Gai scrubbed a hand over his mustache. "Alright, you win, I promise I'll give it some thought and be honest with both of them."

"Thank you," Ally drained her teacup. "It nearly took the whole teatime, but you finally arrived at the point."

Suspicion lined his face. "Why are you so set on this, Ally?"

"I want to know that you'll be happy, while I'm gone."

After all the tea and pastries were gone, Ally helped clear Gai's desk off. "I'll let you get back to your day, brother. This was lovely."

"It really was." He cleared his throat, still a little stunned by Ally's news. "Let's do this again. Preferably before you leave, but if not, as soon as you return."

"Absolutely. Next time, you can buy the treats."

Gai wrapped an arm around her shoulders and walked her to the door. "It's a good trade."

Chapter Sixty-eight

Ally stood at the entrance to the Kingsport guard headquarters. The heavy brick structure took up an entire block, with an open courtyard in the center used as a training space. She'd only been inside a few times, usually for some official ceremony or another, and honestly hadn't expected to find herself there now. Since the night Cal was arrested, one thing Ally was sure of was that she didn't care what his motives were.

But now, on the precipice of starting an entirely new life with Pasha, she felt her heart breaking around the edges. Ally was mourning the brother she thought she had. The Cal she'd known and loved had been swept out to sea, and in his place was this stranger. She hadn't told anyone she might come here, except Pasha, hadn't known for sure she'd go through with it until she was standing at the door. But Ally woke up that morning knowing she'd never fully heal if she didn't at least try to talk to him before she left. After today, she doubted she'd ever see Cal again.

The time spent with Gai had given her the lift she needed to walk inside with her head held high. The guard stationed at the entryway desk was quite startled when Ally Kingfisher came through the door.

"I'd like to speak to Calder."

The guard jumped up and gave a belated bow. "I, um, are you sure, my lady?"

"Yes, I'm sure. Take me to him, please."

After wavering for another moment, he took a ring of keys from the wall and unlocked one of the gates flanking the desk. "Follow me, my lady."

Down one long side of the building and up a flight of stairs, they arrived in a sparse corridor. There were several closed doors lining the inner wall, but only one of them was secured with a manor guard on one side and a Kingsport guard on the other.

"Lady Alphonsine?" The manor guard on the left blurted out. "What are you doing here?"

"She wants to speak to the prisoner," said Ally's guide.

The other Kingsport guard watching the cell took a different key from her belt. "As you wish, milady, we can open the first door but request you stay well away from the second. If he threatens you in any way, we will be forced to cut your visit short. Otherwise, call for us when you're finished."

Ally nodded and the guard unlocked the thick door banded with iron. Inside was a narrow space and another door made entirely of metal bars. There was a small window, also barred, set at the top of one wall. That and the lamps by the first door provided the only light. They wouldn't have been able to trust him with a lantern or candles within reach.

"Someone is here to see you." The manor guard said curtly. Looking at his face, Ally saw yet another person who'd been deceived by someone they'd once trusted. The guards moved out and down the corridor, giving some semblance of privacy but staying close enough to step in if needed.

Cal was sitting on a cot pushed against the far wall, head down and elbows resting on his knees. His hair was shaggy and a patch of stubble was visible on his boyish face. His clothes were rumpled and simple, but the room was clean and warm enough. She hadn't thought their father would keep Cal in cruel conditions, but it was good to know she was right.

He hadn't looked up yet. Did he even know who was standing outside of his cell? Ally supposed Gai and Luthais would just start speaking and see if Cal responded.

"Was any of it ever real?"

His head lifted, "Hello to you too, Ally."

The casual way he said her name made Ally's skin crawl. "Was any of it ever real?"

"What do you mean?"

"Don't toy with me, I don't have the time."

Cal's hands covered his face and his shoulders hunched. "I don't know what you're talking about. I don't know why I'm here." He pulled in a shuddering breath. "Did Father send you? Ally, did he tell you to help me?"

"Cut it out, Cal," she snapped.

The sobs halted. His hands dropped and he sat up straight, his expression unbothered and eyes dry. "Little sister has gotten tougher than I remembered."

"Are you going to talk to me, or continue to lark about?"

"Right, you don't have the time." Cal stood and stretched his arms overhead. "Somewhere to be, squirt?"

"As a matter of fact," she crossed her arms, bristling at the use of the childhood nickname.

He stalked closer. "Answer my question and I'll answer yours."

"What question is that?"

"How did you do it? How did *you* convince a mermaid to give you her powers?"

"I didn't convince her to do anything. She offered."

"Why?" His fingers wrapped around the bars. Ally knew she was out of reach, but the urge to back up was a knife pressing against her chest. She pushed it down.

"That's two questions. You made the rules, it's your turn. Was any of it ever real, Cal? Did you ever care about me, about any of us, at all?"

"I think you already know the answer to that."

She shook her head. "I don't understand you."

His green eyes hardened. "You never have."

"You never gave me a chance!"

Cal's upper lip curled into a sneer. "I wanted you gone the day you were born. Is that what you wanted to hear? While everyone else was celebrating your arrival, I was already thinking of ways to get rid of you."

Ally let her arms drop, feeling something in her heart fall away with them. The brother she'd lived with, grown up with, and loved with all her heart was truly gone. He'd never really been there to begin with, and this person deserved no more of her time.

"Thank you," she backed away, feeling a little lighter with each step "that's what I wanted to hear."

The grin that had stretched across his face at her silence faltered. "Oh? Don't you want to know why?"

"Not particularly," Ally shrugged.

"What?" Cal's knuckles whitened against the bars.

"You told me what I wanted to know. I'm done wasting any more of my time here." She turned to leave.

"Ally!" Cal snarled, shaking the door hard enough to rattle the bars in their foundations. "We're not finished!"

"That's where you're wrong." Ally called for the guards and looked at Cal one last time. Whatever he saw in her eyes made him recoil back into his cell. "I'm done."

PASHA

CHAPTER SIXTY-NINE

The rest of the shoal left the islands the day Pallagia was laid to rest.

It was as if the elders had known Pasha's sister wouldn't survive much longer. That soon her spark would go out and the unique energy that made Pallagia who she was would become part of the sea once again.

Pasha knew the time was near long before Elder Nerys came to sit by her side. Pallagia didn't know her anymore and had started speaking as if Ealasaid was there in the room. Maybe she was.

She supposed Nerys meant for her presence to be comforting, but Pasha felt the elder was only there to satisfy her own conscience. They'd already abandoned Pallagia, and now they were going to do the same to Pasha.

A few mermaids closer to Pallagia's age showed real grief as her body was prepared and interred in the deepest level of their home. One even helped Pasha seal her sister into her resting place, lending the strength that one so young didn't yet possess.

Pasha drifted through it all, silent and dry-eyed. She knew what was coming next. The only surprise came when some of the younger mermaids stacked large stones over the entrance to the catacombs and Nerys sealed it with her own energy. But Pasha was too exhausted by then to ask why.

Now she floated at the edge of the great cavern, watching the rest of her shoal split off into the tunnels leading out to sea. The fresh scar on her forearm burned like she'd been stung by a hundred jellyfish, but Pasha refused to look at it, refused to acknowledge the punishment Nerys and the other elders had bestowed onto her before departing. Pasha'd told herself she wouldn't give them the satisfaction of seeing how much this hurt her, but as the last of them left she couldn't help herself.

"Don't go. Please, don't go."

Some spared a last glance her way, a few may even had held sympathy for the little mermaid they were leaving behind. But none of them stayed.

Nerys waited until everyone was gone to face Pasha. "You know what you must do until we return?"

"Yes." Pasha's dull words echoed in the empty chamber. "Stay put. Stay out of sight. Guard our home."

"Good. If any of the other shoals are faring as badly as we fear, we'll send them here for shelter. Make them welcome."

"I will."

Nerys reached out, as if to rest a hand on Pasha's shoulder, but stopped short of touching her. "This is an important task given to you, Pasha. You are young, but I know you will not fail us. Remember, a mermaid must always remain beneath this island."

When Pasha said nothing else, the elder turned and swam towards the nearest tunnel.

Alone for the first time in her life, Pasha slowly sank down to the sandy floor. Her fingers dipped into the packed grains, the urge to call the bones strong in her veins.

No. That was probably one of the reasons they chose her to stay behind. Not just because of what Pallagia had done. They were always repulsed when Pasha spoke to the bones.

Light shifted through the corals as time passed. The creatures closest to her brightened even more, trying to get her attention. Turning stiffly, Pasha's gaze traveled over the mural taking up the entire back wall of the chamber. Mermaids from all across the seas, of every shape and size, but still none that were like her.

Directly above her towered a great mermaid warrior. A bony ridge sprouted down the middle of her bare head. Chin held high, she brandished a spear with a blade nearly as long as Pasha's tail. Something about the warrior drew her closer, and Pasha curled up against the wall, beneath her carved fluke.

"They'll come back." Wrapping her arms around herself, Pasha imagined it was Pallagia holding her close. "They have to come back."

ALLY

CHAPTER SEVENTY

Ally spent most of the third day searching the manor grounds and then the Kingsport wharf for Luthais. His schedule was never as easy to predict as Gai's, and now with the preparations to visit each and every trade partner underway, he was damn near impossible to find. Always one step ahead of her, like some burly sprite giving her the slip before she could catch a glimpse of him.

By midafternoon, Ally was exhausted. Enough so that she hired a carriage to take her back to the house. She'd pushed herself too hard and could feel it in the pronounced soreness that settled into her muscles and joints.

Depositing her cloak and dusty boots in the front hall, Ally grudgingly accepted that she'd have to speak to Luthais when he returned home. There was no plan in place for when she found him but, then again, Ally had never quite known what to say to her middle brother. It would just have to come to her in the moment.

What she really wanted was a quick nap before dinner, but first she'd ask Mama if they expected Luthais for dinner. Her hand was on the parlor door handle when she heard movement inside.

"Mama?" She walked in. "Do you know if..."

Ally stopped short. Mama wasn't in the parlor, but Luthais was. Her sewing basket was open. She'd walked in on him replacing the supplies she'd recently used up on a thousand handkerchiefs.

"Hello," Ally said at last. Seeing Luthais with spools of colorful embroidery thread in his large hands was like seeing a bull with a huge satin bow tied around it's horns.

"Ally," he grunted and dropped the rest of the items into the basket.

"I always thought one of the maids did that. Mrs. Thorley said so, anyway."

"That's what I asked her to say." Luthais shoved his hands into his pockets. He seemed so out of place in this room, with its delicate furniture and charming view of the hedge garden.

Ally left the door open so he wouldn't feel boxed in and meandered to the center of the room. "Why not tell me it was you replacing my supplies? I would have made something for you, as thanks." Every few years, she initialed handkerchiefs or pocket squares for all of her brothers, but never anything specifically for Luthais. He never seemed the type to want anything special embroidered onto his clothes.

He shrugged, focusing on the wall behind her. "I wasn't expecting you to make me anything. I just wanted to do something…" Luthais huffed and finally looked at her. "It was never about you."

Ally didn't need to ask what he meant. "I know that, now. You were all so young when Lady Glenna passed."

"Yeah," he ran a hand over the blonde stubble lining his jaw, "but I'm sorry, I am. And I wanted to do something to make up for it."

"You've certainly supported my hobby," she chuckled. "Maher will be so grateful when he finds out."

To her amazement, Luthais laughed - really laughed - and shook his head. "I'm sure he will."

Ally stepped a little closer. Before she could change her mind, she said to him, "Luthais, I'm going to be going away for a little while."

"Why? Where are you going?"

"I'll explain everything before I leave, but suffice to say, I'm going to live with Pasha. I'll come back eventually, but it will be at least a year before I can. I've already talked to Gai, Mama and Father."

"What about Maher?"

Something clicked in the back of her mind and she smiled slyly. "Don't worry, I'm going to tell him tomorrow. We'll spend the day together, like we used to before he became Intelligencer."

"Good. I didn't think you'd leave him in the dark."

"That was kind of you to ask." Ally fought back a yawn. "I'm sorry, I'm about dead on my feet. I spent the whole day looking for you in town, you know. Can we finish this after dinner?"

"Of course, you should get some rest." Luthais sighed. "I'm... damn it, I'm going to miss you."

"I'll miss you too, Luthais." She grinned when he blushed and looked away. "And I expect my sewing basket to be fully stocked when I return."

For the first time in her entire life, Luthais pulled his sister into a real hug. It was a little rough and he couldn't seem to decide how tightly to hold her, but her heart swelled for her brother who'd been looking out for her in his own quiet way.

Taking pity on him, Ally squeezed Luthais' waist and held on until he matched her. She buried her nose into his shoulder, smelling salt and leather and soap, tucking the memory away for when she was out at sea.

After a few minutes, Luthais cleared his throat and slowly let her go.

"Think that will hold you until I come home?" Ally nudged him with her elbow.

He smiled at her. "I think so."

As Ally got ready for bed that night, she laid out her favorite blue skirt and the shirt with periwinkle flowers around the collar. She'd have to add her cloak and some wool stockings to combat the chill, but this was what she wanted to wear on the fourth day.

Her last full day and night on land, and she wanted to spend them with Maher.

MAHER

CHAPTER SEVENTY-ONE

When Ally knocked on Maher's door, he pulled the blanket over his head and prayed she'd come back later. When she bounced into the room and threw open the curtains instead, he nearly hurled a pillow at her.

"Get up! We're going to the market."

"Al, have some mercy, I just went to bed a little while ago."

"And how many times have you gotten me out of bed or distracted me from my lessons to run off for the day?" She jumped onto the bed, and the motion sent him rolling onto his stomach.

Maher groaned. "Come back at noon, I beg you."

"Maher, it's going to be a beautiful day, and I want to spend it with my dearest friend." She rubbed his back. "Please?"

Something in Ally's tone broke through Maher's fog of sleep. He pushed onto his elbows and fixed an eye on her. "On one condition, you're buying all the food. I mean it, whatever I want, it's coming out of your pocket."

"It's a good trade." Ally planted a kiss on his forehead. "You can sleep all you want tomorrow."

"I'm sure I can." He yawned so wide his jaw creaked. Sitting up as she left his side, Maher checked the clock on the mantle. Seven o'clock in the fucking morning.

"I'm going to get us some breakfast from the kitchen, while you get ready." She opened the door. "By the way, darling, with your hair like that, you bear a remarkable resemblance to a rooster."

"The roosters aren't even up yet," Maher grumbled, but Ally had already left. Trudging to his dressing table, Maher caught a glimpse of what she meant. He'd gone to sleep for those few precious hours buried beneath his pillows, to block out any light. Now most of his coal black hair was stuck up at an awkward angle. The jug next to his wash basin was still half full. Maher leaned his head over the bowl and tipped the frigid water onto his head.

It was a good thing he had no neighbors at the moment. The resulting string of shouts and curses would have woken the entire hallway.

Maher's spirits had greatly improved by the time they reached Kingsport. Bundled up in his coat, one of the manor cook's breakfast buns warming his stomach, Maher hooked his arm through Ally's as they watched the vendors open up for the day.

"Whatchya looking for?"

"Nothing in particular." She tugged him towards the oyster stall. After a few minutes the owner came up front, apologized for the delay in serving them, and grumbled under his breath about his son taking off to the perfumery at all hours. "Su-Minn has a new friend," Ally whispered after the man went to retrieve their order.

"We won't give them away then," Maher said quickly before a tray of oysters was placed in front of them.

Ally was right, it turned out to be a lovely autumn day. The air was crisp, but the sun was shining, and Maher found he needed to unbutton his coat by the time they reached the square in the market proper. Ally took her time looking at everything, stopping at each stall to admire or ask questions. He wasn't fond of the suspicious looks some of the proprietors cast her way, but she simply wished them all a good morning and moved on.

Lack of sleep aside, Maher soon relaxed into the slow pace Ally set for them. He strolled by her side, content to listen as she recounted the picnic she recently shared with her parents and the look on Gai's face when she dropped by the harbormaster's office for tea. When Ally revealed Luthais was the one who'd been replenishing her embroidery supplies all these years, Maher smiled to himself. There really was more to the middle Kingfisher brother than the rest of them knew.

Maher knew he'd been more than a little preoccupied, now that his responsibilities had drastically increased. Between that and the hours she spent with Pasha, he only saw Ally for a few moments each day, usually at breakfast or dinner. It helped to know she was spending more time with her family and Pasha filled much of the rest of that time in his absence. The pair had become near inseparable. Something uncomfortable tugged at Maher's chest, but he brushed it aside. Ally deserved to be happy, and if she'd found that happiness in Pasha, he had no room to complain.

Khafra hadn't spoken to Maher since the ambush outside of the guard headquarters, but he couldn't avoid his son forever. Maher was keeping the secret of Khafra's late night visits to Cal to himself, for now. But

Ambassador Villaon wasn't as protected as he liked to think, and now Maher had the resources to uncover every scheme he might have in place.

Let the residents of the Lantern continue to know him as the Magpie if they wished. It was affording him a level of access throughout the city he hadn't reached before. Just as stories continued to spread of Lady Alphonsine Kingfisher controlling sea monsters and drowning a pirate captain on the deck of her own ship, so too did the tales of Maher Villaon, Magpie of Kingsport and Intelligencer of the Birde Isles, who was struck through the chest by lightning and healed in a matter of days. Though he hoped no one would take it upon themselves to test that last rumor.

Ally kept her promise and bought whatever dishes tickled Maher's fancy throughout the day. He hadn't planned on holding her to it, but Ally gave him a look of mock affront and rather loudly accused him of attempting to sully her good name.

"A trade is a trade," she'd announced, drawing stares from the other marketgoers around them. "And you traded sleep for food."

They walked through more of the city than usual, Ally seemed almost reluctant to turn back. It was late in the day by the time they hit the high street that would take them past the wharf.

At the southern end of the wharf district, they passed the remains of the *Maiden's Revenge*. Only the bones of the hull were left. They didn't linger, there was nothing about that ship that either of them wanted to remember.

"Let's take the seawall road back to the house," Ally suggested.

They left the city, taking the short section of road that split off towards the shore. Soon, the sea rose up on their right, and a swath of farmers' fields stretched to the left. City noises faded away until there was only the crunch of the gravel and broken shells beneath their feet, and waves breaking on the sand. Ally looked out at the water. A small, content smile tugged at her lips.

"I'm sorry, Al," Maher said softly, not wanting to break the spell that had settled over them.

"What for?"

"I've been going over it and over it in my mind and... I'm the reason Dare found out about Pasha. I was upset, that night we fought on the beach. When I ran into your brothers on the way back, I told them she was a mermaid, not a sea witch. Cal must have written to Dare that same night. I'm so sorry, to both of you."

She let the words sink in. "You didn't tell them everything. You didn't tell them Pasha taught me to swim, which worked out in my favor in the end." Ally took a deep breath, held it, then let it out. "Thank you for telling me."

They walked a little farther before Maher asked, "Are you truly not afraid of the sea anymore?"

"No," she said simply. "I'm not afraid."

"Do you think you would have ever overcome it without Pasha's help?"

Ally stopped and looked up at him. The growing evening shadows stole the green from her hazel eyes, leaving only burnt caramel behind. "Honestly, I don't know. There's still so much I don't understand about the sea, but I'm not afraid to learn it now."

"Makes me happy to hear that, Al. You know I never wanted you to stay afraid your whole life, but I didn't know what I could do to help you either."

"You helped me by being the greatest friend I could have asked for." She lifted onto her toes and pecked him on the cheek. "I hope I've been even half as good a friend to you."

"You absolutely have." He kissed the top of her head and wrapped his hand around hers as they started to walk again. But the closer they got to the house, the slower Ally's steps became. She gnawed on her lip, opened her mouth to say something, then closed it again.

"When are you leaving?" Maher asked.

"What do you mean?"

"When are you leaving with Pasha?"

She stopped. "How in the goddess' name did you know?"

"I'm Intelligencer of the Birde Isles, remember?"

"You're not *that* good, Maher."

"But I know *you*, Al. The two of you spent every night together on the trip home. You come down to the shore every day. And I see the look in your eyes when you talk about her. Tell me, honestly, you're going to be with her, aren't you?"

"Yes, I am. I wanted to tell you when we were alone. I wasn't sure where to begin." Ally explained how Pasha had finally found the secret that would ease Ally's Sea Kissed symptoms. That changing her into a mermaid was the only cure.

"And you really have to be gone for so long?"

Ally touched the shark tooth hanging around her neck; she didn't bother trying to hide it beneath her clothes anymore. "Whatever being Sea Kissed really means, or wherever it comes from, there's no other way to stop it. Even with the shark tooth and Pasha's help, it's only going to get worse. This isn't just what I want to do, it's what I need, Maher."

Maher nodded slowly, not trusting himself to speak. He knew, after everything Ally had been through, this was the best option. She would be free. She would be happy. She wouldn't be alone. That knowledge did nothing to alleviate the pain in his heart at the thought of being separated from Ally. "Do you love her?"

"We haven't had much time to figure that out, to be honest. I know I care about Pasha. I care about her very much, and I want to be with her." Her eyes softened, as they always did now when she spoke of the mermaid. "I want the chance to find out if I love her."

They walked in silence the rest of the way to the manor. When they reached the edge of the grounds, Maher asked Ally to come sit with him on the hill one more time. He had to help her make the climb. Even though they'd stopped to rest many times throughout the day, he could see the fatigue settling over her. Ally was right, it would only get worse the longer she waited. The sun was just touching the water when they reached their spot at the top of the cliff.

Sitting close together as the evening breeze plucked at their clothes and wove through Ally's hair, Maher wrapped an arm around her, and they watched the sun sink into the horizon.

"Before I forget," Ally reached inside her skirt pocket, "I have a present for you." She held something up for him to see, a glint of metal winked at him.

"What's this?" Maher squinted in the fading light. Pinched between Ally's fingers was a tiny bird. Its body was shaped with gold; black enamel filled it in from the top of its head down to the end of its long tail feathers. Splashes of white enamel painted its spread wings and belly. A black stone no bigger than a grain of barley was set as its eye.

"It's a lapel pin. I bought it while we were in the square. For an Intelligencer, you weren't paying much attention. You'll want to work on that."

"You bought me a magpie." Maher shook his head; of course she had.

Ally grinned. "If you start wearing it without any explanation, maybe it will add to the mystery of your new position."

She dropped the pin into the palm of his hand and wrapped his fingers over it. The enamel bird was smooth against his skin. Maher reached for something else to say. The reality that Ally was leaving, at least for a time, pressed on his heart. But every time he wore the pin, Maher knew he'd think of her. "You know, I don't think I've ever painted a magpie."

Ally tucked her head into his shoulder. "Now you can, and you'll have something to show me when I come back."

CHAPTER SEVENTY-TWO

For her last morning on land, Ally packed a basket and walked down the private path that led from Kingfisher manor to the temple of the sea.

Esa welcomed her with open arms. The Head Priestess, who'd been a patient teacher and dear friend to Ally all her life, was the only one who needed no explanation when Ally told her she'd be joining Pasha in the sea.

"I will miss you dearly, child, but it is a relief to know you will be spared the fate of other Sea Kissed souls." The lines around her warm, brown eyes deepened as Esa smiled and drew Ally to sit with her on the bench in the temple garden. Ally laid her hand on the cool stone of one of the whale statues that arched up behind them. How many summers had she spent with Esa in this very spot, listening to the priestess' stories of merfolk and other sea creatures of old?

She was sorely tempted to ask Esa if she knew anything of the bird-women. But on the walk to the temple, Ally decided it would be best to wait. Perhaps she and Pasha would uncover more after she was changed.

"I have something for you," Opening her basket, Ally withdrew a white linen kerchief and presented it to Esa. She'd spent the last few evenings embroidering a pair of mermaids on the back edges that would hang over Esa's shoulders when worn. Taking special care with the detail in their tails and giving them the more otherworldly qualities that Pasha and her kin possessed.

"Thank you so much, Ally, I love it." Esa ran a hand over the mermaids, a soft laugh leaving her as she considered the design. "I take it our depictions of the merfolk are not entirely accurate?"

"Not quite." Ally shook her head, thinking of the many different mermaids carved throughout the caves beneath the island. "I hope you'll think of me when you wear it."

"Of course I will, and I will be most eager to see you as a mermaid once you've grown accustomed to your new life." She paused. "If that would be permitted, I would never ask if it's not something you're comfortable doing."

Ally bit her lip, unsure of how she felt about someone from her human life seeing her as a mermaid. "I don't think I would mind, but I should ask Pasha if letting you see me would break some kind of merfolk decree."

"Understood. Do you know what will be required to complete this transformation?"

"Not yet. Pasha's been studying the ritual for several days, I only know that we need a full moon in order to complete the change."

Esa nodded, "Fascinating. I wish you every happiness, Ally."

They sat together the rest of the morning, reminiscing over shared memories of Ally's childhood and discussing a tentative plan to meet when Ally would be able to return to land. Ally's head eventually found its way onto Esa's shoulder and the priestess told her one last story, about the goddess of the sea and how she created her trusted guardians, the mermaids.

ALLY

CHAPTER SEVENTY-THREE

Ally descended the seawall steps for the last time. The ancient stones felt as familiar to her now as the rooms and hallways of the manor. A full moon, so bright she hardly needed the lantern, bathed the shore in silver light. Sand crunched beneath Ally's boots, and her breath steamed as she scanned the beach.

It was empty.

This was the right time, two hours before midnight. She knew Pasha didn't own anything remotely close to a clock, but the mermaid had always been able to tell what time of the day or night it was regardless.

What if she's not coming? What if she's decided what she *thinks is best for* you? Ally pushed down the nausea that rolled through her stomach. *Pasha wouldn't do that, she wouldn't. She'd never try to take my choice from me.*

Time crawled by, and she paced in front of the rock outcropping. Ally didn't dare walk any further, this was where they said they'd meet. Her breaths became quick and uneven. Leaving the lantern on dry land, Ally walked into the sea until she felt the current pulling at her ankles. Freezing water splashed into her boots, and her toes curled. Fumbling for the shark tooth, Ally pressed her thumb against the serrated edge. She took a breath and bared down until she felt the bite of breaking skin. A hot trickle of blood dripped down the side of her chilled wrist. Kneeling in the shallows, Ally thrust her hand into the path of the next wave. The open wound pulsed in the salt water, and the shark tooth grew warmer against her chest.

Please come back, Pasha. Please, please...

"You really thought you needed a blood signal to call me?"

Ally shot up, turning so sharply she nearly lost her footing. Pasha was standing calf-deep in the waves, hands braced on her knees. She was panting hard, as if she'd run up the shore.

"You were late. I was worried you'd changed your mind."

"The sea is quite large, Ally, it does take time to travel."

Ally sloshed through the water to Pasha and pulled her into an embrace. "I may have overreacted."

"Just a little bit." Pasha hugged her back. "You're shaking. Were you really that troubled, or are you cold?"

"Both, I think." She backed up a step and looked down. "My toes are numb."

"Here, this will help." Pasha placed a hand over the shark tooth and concentrated. A rippling band of energy gathered around her arm before it shot into the tooth, and a surge of heat flooded Ally's limbs.

"Thank you," Ally sighed in relief. They walked back up to the rocks, where Ally yanked off her sodden boots and stockings.

"You didn't bring anything else with you? None of your sewing things?"

"No, there's nothing I have that would last long in the sea anyway." Ally got stuck in her damp coat and Pasha helped her escape. "It's alright, Luthais has promised to keep my embroidery supplies in order until I can come back."

She watched Ally bundle her clothes together and put out the light. "And you've said your goodbyes?"

"Yes, to everyone who matters."

One of the ridges above Pasha's eyes rose at Ally's choice of words, but then she nodded. "Then I suppose we're ready to leave. We've already lost some of the moon."

"Because *one* of us was late."

Pasha's teeth flashed in the moonlight, and her hand rested against Ally's lower back. "Let me make it up to you, then."

She left her heavy outer clothes, her boots, and the lantern tucked between the rocks. Maher would come for them tomorrow. Walking into the waves, Ally looked back once at the outline of the old seawall with its crumbling steps. Knowing that just on the other side and down the path were people who loved her, and that she'd see them again soon.

They swam through rippling shades of blue and black, broken by shafts of silver light from above. Ally tried to concentrate on the task ahead and not on the rapid beating of her heart, or how tightly Pasha was holding her hand. To save them some time, Pasha was towing Ally to their destination. The wake created by the powerful beats of Pasha's tail buffeted against Ally's legs. If the ritual was a success, Ally hoped she'd finally be able to keep pace with Pasha in the water, if nothing else.

It wasn't long before Pasha angled them upwards, and they broke through the surface. Ally blinked water from her eyes and found herself looking at a barren hunk of rock.

"That's Snake Island."

"Is it?" Pasha smirked.

"Why are we here? There's nothing on Snake Island but stone."

"Nothing on top, you're right. We're going beneath it."

Ally held on as they dove beneath the waves and broke through the current trying to pull them towards the edge of the island. They swam down and down until the moonlight was all but gone, and the underside of the Snake Island twisted into a catacomb of rock and coral running down to the seafloor. Ally half-expected one of the wide openings below would open into a tunnel like those that led into Pasha's home beneath Kingfisher Island. But Pasha stayed along the rough, unbroken section that made up the middle of the island's underbelly. She was running her free hand over the surface, sweeping it in wide arcs until she brought them to a stop. To Ally, it looked like they were floating in front of a solid wall of rock.

"This is it," Pasha's voice flickered through her mind.

"I don't see anything."

"You're not supposed to." Pasha leaned close enough to lay her ear against the wall, and then her head sank through the rock.

"Pasha!" Ally tugged on her arm, and Pasha's head reappeared.

"Don't worry!" she soothed. Shifting so Ally's back was pressed against her chest, Pasha wrapped an arm around her from behind. "There's an opening, you just have to know how to find it."

Using her tail to propel them closer, Pasha took Ally's hand and pressed it against the rock. Rough edges and shallow dips scraped over her palm as Ally's hand was pushed in and over. Then both of their arms did the same trick as Pasha's head. It *looked* like they'd been sucked into the stone, but Ally could feel open space around her outstretched fingers.

"We'll go together." Pasha's other hand splayed against Ally's stomach. Ally took a deep breath and shut her eyes as Pasha squeezed them through.

When she opened her eyes, they were in a narrow tunnel dotted with the same luminescent corals that lived in Pasha's home. Keeping her arm around Ally, Pasha flipped her tail and they floated through the passage. After turning through a sharp bend, the tunnel shifted straight up. At the top, Ally could make out a bright circle, like the moon was waiting for them at the end. Green and blue lights winked on and off as they passed, Pasha took them the rest of the way and then they were in a shallow pool. The water here was warm, a stark contrast to the chilled sea outside, and perfectly clear. Ally could see everything from the rough pattern of the rock around them to her feet kicking beneath her. Pasha let Ally go, and they surfaced in an underwater cave.

It was a lagoon, the calm water hugging a band of white sand that backed up to the far wall. Spots of brilliant color winked at them from the sand. More of the luminescent corals and other glowing plants, the likes of which Ally had never seen before, clung to the edges of the cave walls, leaving the murals completely visible. In the roof of the cave was a crescent-shaped opening with a view of the sky. The full moon was shining right above the island now, light filtering through the opening to bounce off the pool and fill the cave with silver light.

"This is so beautiful," Ally murmured, not wanting to speak too loudly in such a magical place. She saw the stone eggs Pasha had described, tucked against the wall that curved around the small stretch of beach. Each step of how to change her etched onto their sides. "I can't believe no one from the Isles found the opening in the ceiling."

"That place is set into an overhang, on the steep edge that faces out to sea. There's no way to discover it if you don't know precisely what you're looking for." Pasha swam for the sand and Ally followed.

For the first time, she got a clear view of Pasha's tail splitting into her legs. It looked just as uncomfortable as the reverse process, but Pasha hardly batted an eye this time. Ally stood at the water's edge and waited for her. When she was able to walk, Pasha took Ally's hand and led her to the middle of the beach. Her grip became more viselike with each step. When she released her, all the blood rushed back into Ally's fingers.

"I have to warn you, I don't know what this will feel like."

"I understand." Ally looked over at the eggs again, but the images were indecipherable to her. "Will I look like you?"

"You'll look like yourself, only with a few additions." Pasha couldn't seem to stay still. Her feet shifted in the sand. A hand flitted up to tuck a piece of wet hair behind her ear.

Pasha was nervous.

She stiffened when Ally stroked a thumb across her brow. "I won't lose my eyebrows, will I? Because I don't think that will look as charming on me as it does for you."

Pasha gaped at her before sharp teeth nipped at the heel of Ally's hand. "You are not funny, Ally Kingfisher."

She grinned. "I don't know, Maher thinks I'm hilarious."

Pasha's posture relaxed, but her smile faded. "I know you'll miss him."

Ally took both of Pasha's hands. "Maher isn't going anywhere. He will be plenty busy as Intelligencer until I can return to land next year."

Pasha studied the sand between them. "And you understand you're going to start aging like a mermaid and outlive all of them? Your life won't be tied to mine, but you're going to stay in your twenties for a long time."

"We've already gone over all of this. I understand everything that comes with my decision." When Pasha still wouldn't look up, Ally ducked her head until she caught the mermaid's eye. "I'm here because I want to be here. You've given me every opportunity to change my mind, and I haven't."

"I know, but if you regret it later... there's no undoing it." She blinked hard, a pearlescent tear slid down her cheek.

Ally kissed the tear away. Her entire mouth buzzed for a moment, salt and bubbles and electricity tickled her nose. Lips still tingling, she guessed what Pasha wasn't saying. "You're not Pallagia. No one is forcing me to be here." Ally tugged Pasha to her and let the last of the tear's effervescent magic soak into Pasha's lips. "I'm diving into the water myself."

Pasha's fingers tangled into Ally's hair, nails scraping against her scalp in a way that made Ally's spine fizzle. She pressed a kiss to Ally's forehead, then her nose, then drifted down to brush their lips together. Sighing into the kiss, Ally slid her arms around Pasha's waist, eternally grateful they were nearly the same height. The ends of Pasha's dark blue hair brushed over her arms as she pulled her closer. When Ally took Pasha's lower lip between her teeth the mermaid gasped, lips parting further, and Ally swept her tongue over Pasha's. The hands in her hair clenched so tight her scalp throbbed. She did it again. There was no pain when Ally's tongue grazed one of Pasha's teeth, but she tasted blood.

"Mind the teeth," Pasha whispered between kisses. "For now. After you change, you won't be as *delicate*."

Ally barely registered the words; she was too busy mapping the swirl of scales that decorated Pasha's lower back with her fingertips. She wanted to memorize each one, each color, each stretch of sleek skin between them.

Pasha broke away, panting. "If we don't begin soon, we'll have to wait until the next full moon."

Ally was reluctant to let go, but neither did she want to put this off even one more day. She huffed and nodded as Pasha pulled Ally to sit together on the beach.

"There are a couple more things we need to talk about before we begin." Pasha's tongue rested against her teeth for a few seconds. "While you're changing, you're going to become sort of malleable." She gently ran a finger over the knot in Ally's nose. "Would you like me to do anything to your nose?" When Ally tilted her face away, Pasha rushed to add, "You're beautiful just as you are, sweetheart. I'm only saying, if it still bothers you I can try to reset the bones."

"I know I'm not going to look exactly the same once we're done, but I wouldn't feel like myself if you changed my nose." She paused, then smiled. "Did you just call me sweetheart?"

"You know I did," said Pasha. "Don't let it go to your head."

"I can't promise that." Ally schooled her expression. "What's next?"

"There's a last decision you have to make." Pasha held her arm out, the one without the scar. "Choose a scale."

Ally looked from Pasha's face to the shining scales and back. "Why do I need to choose one?"

"It's going to be the starting point the rest of your scales grow from, so pick the one you like the most." She rested her arm across Ally's lap. "Think of it like a seed."

Ally chewed on her bottom lip. The kaleidoscope of blues, greens, even a silver one here and there, wrapped over Pasha's wrist like a jeweled bracelet. How could she possibly take one?

"It will grow back." Pasha read her mind again. "Don't worry about that. Take your time."

Ally lifted Pasha's arm closer. The glow from the plants around them bounced off each scale. Pasha said to choose the one she liked most, but they were all so lovely. Ally's thumb swept over bright grass, pear, and emerald greens. Sapphire, teal, and robin's egg blues. Turning Pasha's arm over, Ally's eye caught on a small scale resting against the heel of her hand. It was the same deep azure hue as the sea in her recurring dreams.

"This one," Ally murmured, tracing one finger against the edge.

"You're sure?" Pasha asked. The weight of those two words carried more than just Ally's choice of color.

Ally nestled her cheek against Pasha's palm. "Yes, I'm sure. I want that one."

Pasha's fingers curled against her face. She grazed her lips over Ally's temple but pulled away when Ally tried to tilt her head for a real kiss.

"There will be more than enough time for that later." She pointed at the opening in the ceiling. "We only have a few hours before the moon passes over.

"You're right." Ally's heartbeat skipped. "What do I need to do?"

"Wait just a moment, I have to get your scale." Pasha lifted her hand to her mouth and carefully slid one of her pointed teeth beneath the rounded edge. She bit down hard, the sound like an iron nail driving through glass, and pulled it off.

Ally gasped. It left a bare patch of raw skin behind, but she tried to remind herself that it would grow back soon.

"Hold this for me." Pasha dropped the scale into her palm.

Ally cupped her hands around the azure jewel Pasha had given her. It was no bigger than the pad of her little finger. How was this one scale going to sprout enough to make her a mermaid?

"Ally?" Pasha brought her out of her dizzying thoughts. "Are you ready to begin?"

Ally turned; Pasha had brushed some of the sand together into a sloped mound.

"It's best if you lay down, so you don't have to worry about holding yourself up during the change. And you'll want to take the rest of your clothes off. They'd only get in the way."

"I figured as much." Ally said, suddenly nervous for reasons that had nothing to do with the ritual. "I think I've only seen you in some sort of clothing twice. If a bit of sail counts as clothing."

A darker shade of gray bloomed over Pasha's cheeks, and Ally made a mental note of it. There would be time to tease Pasha later, and ideas for how to make that blush happen again would also have to wait. They were losing the moon, Ally didn't want to wait any longer. Passing the scale to Pasha, she quickly shrugged out of her still-damp shirt and breeches, laying them across one of the large rocks that framed their little beach. Then off came the undershirt and bloomers, quickly before she had time to even think of being embarrassed. She could feel Pasha's eyes on her back, taking in every inch of exposed skin. Feeling very much like she did the night Pasha began teaching her to swim, Ally lifted her chin and turned around.

Pasha's onyx eyes glittered in the blended light from the moon and the glowing corals hugging the walls. Ally's own face heated up and, after a solid minute of staring, she cleared her throat, "As you said, there will be plenty of time later for whatever it is you're thinking about, Pasha."

The mermaid quickly shook her head and flashed a wicked grin. "Promise?"

"Absolutely." Ally's hand paused over the shark tooth. Would she have to remove that too?

"You can leave it on," Pasha said. "It might be safest until we're done."

Relieved, Ally left the necklace where it was. "Now what?"

Pasha gestured to the place she'd prepared for Ally. Her voice turned solemn, and Ally knew this was the true start of the ritual. "Lay down here."

Reclining back on the raised pile of sand, Ally felt the sugary powder pressed into every inch of her skin that touched the ground. It was fine and soft, not coarse like the sands around the Isles, conforming around her body as she settled in. Even the shards of eggshell were smooth against her skin, not rough or uncomfortable.

"Are you sure this isn't magic?"

"It might be, for all I know." Pasha knelt beside her. "Remember, I don't know how this will feel to you. I can't promise there won't be some discomfort when your body changes."

"I know, it's alright." Ally rested her hands on her stomach, but Pasha moved them, pressing her palms into the sand. The shark tooth was shifted up against her collar bones. Then she lifted Ally's long hair and draped it around her head. Her nails skimmed across the faded, tooth-shaped mark on the skin above Ally's breastbone.

"Try to stay like that." She breathed deeply and asked one more time, "Ready?"

"Ready." Ally gazed up at Pasha, her beautiful mermaid, knowing it was true.

Pasha leaned down, giving her a brief kiss as she placed the scale on Ally's chest. The tiny scale, which was so light in Ally's hands moments before, pinned her to the ground. Like a length of thread was running straight through her body and buried into the sand. A spark of energy warmed the skin beneath it.

Sitting next to Ally, Pasha tucked her legs beneath her and held one hand above the scale. "Close your eyes, Ally. I'll tell you when you can open them again."

Ally's eyelids fluttered down, blocking out Pasha's face and the moon above.

"Breathe deeply and listen." Pasha's voice filled the cave. Ally smelled the electric spark of her power. "I'm going to ask you a question, but don't answer aloud. Think very carefully about your answer, focus only on that." She paused, and the energy snapped. "What do you feel?"

Ally stopped short of opening her eyes and demanding that Pasha be more specific. What did she feel? Truth be told, she felt so many things. Nervous, yet excited, and even a little frightened. Is that what Pasha meant? Ally's fingers flexed, the sand tickled her palms.

Oh. What did she *feel*?

Ally stretched her fingers again. She felt the fine grit of the sand pressing into her skin, the few tiny grains that had gotten under her nails. She felt the warmth of the cave wrapped around her like a thick blanket. The mist that clung to the rock and dripped onto her from above in fine droplets. She felt the scale weighing her down, a comforting presence like her shark tooth had been, and the heat from Pasha's hand poised just above. Ally breathed deep and felt the cool air fill her lungs.

There was a sharp pinch in her skin, next to the scale, and everything she was feeling faded away. It was a surprise, but not unpleasant.

"What do you hear?" Pasha asked.

Ally understood now what Pasha was doing, she was connecting Ally to their surroundings. The easiest sound to pick out was Pasha's breathing, a little faster now than when they'd started. Beyond that, Ally heard the water lapping against the sides of the cave. The drops of moisture falling from the rocks. She even caught the whistle of the wind moving over the moon opening above.

Another pinch latched onto her skin next to the first.

"What can you taste? Smell?"

Salt. There was salt on her tongue and in her nose from their swim to the rocky island. The bitter tang of Pasha's electric magic hit the roof of her mouth. And Ally could still taste that last kiss from Pasha before they started the ritual.

Two more answers. Two more tiny hooks into her skin.

Pasha's lips brushed against her ear. "Open your eyes. What do you see?"

More easily said than done. Ally felt so at peace, so grounded into the sand, it took a moment for her eyelids to obey.

The first thing Ally saw was the cave opening high above them. Barely a sliver of moon was left at its edge. How long had her eyes been closed? Letting her gaze drift down, over the luminescent plants and bright flecks embedded in the rock, she found Pasha's face off to the side. Her brow was creased into a tight line, lips parted as she breathed heavily.

Ally looked at Pasha's hand. It was trembling, an arcing line of electricity shooting off from her four fingers and into Ally's chest. That explained the sharp pinch after each question. The azure scale glowed bright, casting a cool halo up into Pasha's hand. She watched, mesmerized, as the edges of the scale melted into her skin like hot candle wax. A fifth thread shot off Pasha's thumb, forming a circle with the others.

Lightning crackled through her bones and Ally's back arched off the ground. Things were moving and twisting, shifting in their moorings. Azure light filled her up, spilling out of her eyes and soaking back in through her pores.

It was the moment when she first set foot into the sea all over again. Only now, that feeling of completeness was taking up every possible space. Everything Ally had locked away out of fear and pain, like a clock wound too tight, all let go at once.

Pasha's hands were smoothing her brow, ghosting over her shoulders and down her arms. Ally barely felt them. She knew they were there, but physical touch paled compared to the sparks jumping beneath her skin. She was in her body, and yet it didn't belong to her.

Something warm bloomed deep inside her chest, next to her heart.

Ally sighed, *Finally*.

Pasha's hands slipped away. The blue light cleared from her eyes, and the cave walls exploded into fireworks.

CHAPTER SEVENTY-FOUR

Pasha collapsed onto the ground next to Ally. She could scarcely get one breath out before her body demanded another. Digging into the warm sand, Pasha focused on rubbing the grains between her fingers until the world stopped spinning.

Pasha could have studied those carvings for a year, and it still wouldn't have prepared her for what it would be like to experience this ritual for herself. The sheer amount of energy it had taken to start the transformation... for a moment, Pasha was terrified she wouldn't have enough. Even with the charges pulled from the water and the power contained within the hatching grounds. It also took much longer than she'd planned to coax Ally to tap into all of her available senses. But then, Ally needed the time to come out of her own mind and connect with the wellspring around them. The nearest swath of corals that lined the cave walls were scorched, burnt out from the pull of Ally's change. They would heal and grow back eventually.

Pasha's head lolled to the side, it was all she could manage. She studied the differences already visible on Ally's body, the things that marked her as no longer human.

The scale Ally chose was embedded in the middle of her breastbone, surrounded by the shark tooth scar that was apparently there to stay. Spiraling out from the scale was a dazzling array of new plates in never-ending shades of blue. Here and there, copper scales stood out from the rest like shafts of sunlight hitting the waves. Pasha had no clue where those had come from. Ally was breathing evenly, her face serene, half-lidded eyes fixed on the dark, empty space where the moon once sat.

"Ally?" Pasha's throat was raw. "Can you hear me?" She placed a hand over Ally's, feeling the smooth scales that spread overtop the lines of her bones and capped each knuckle.

Shifting against the sand, Ally's wrist turned and her fingers threaded through Pasha's. She looked at Pasha with expanded hazel irises and pupils that dilated to filter through the soft light. Now she'd be able to see underwater without Pasha's help. Ally would see farther and clearer than she ever did as a human. It would take some getting used to.

"How are you feeling?"

"I'm..." Ally paused, head tilting as if she were analyzing the timbre of her voice. It sounded the same to Pasha, but Ally was probably hearing notes she hadn't picked up on before. "I'm quite amazing, actually."

"Yes, you are." Pasha rubbed her arm. "Was it painful?"

"Not exactly. But I'm not sure how to describe it." She slowly rolled onto her side. "Are you alright?"

Pasha nodded. "I'm pretty drained, feeling a bit like a whale landed on top of me, but it's nothing that time in the sea won't cure."

"The sea!" Ally popped up onto her elbows and looked down at herself. "Oh my..."

Pasha held her breath, desperately hoping Ally liked what she saw.

Ally tilted this way and that, the cave lights reflecting off her new scales. "This is incredible, it's– Wait, where's my tail?" She frowned and wiggled her toes.

Chuckling, Pasha sat up with her. "You have to get in the water, then it will come. We'll go together."

Standing and stretching the cramps out of her own legs first, Pasha helped Ally to her feet and steadied her as she tested her balance.

"I wonder if I can take this off now?" Ally touched the shark tooth.

"Let's get you into the sea first, before we try anything." Pasha dusted a patch of sand from her shoulder, tracing the band of scales that draped across the front like the fold of a cloak.

Ally leaned into the touch, but her eyes strayed to the gently lapping water. She gripped Pasha's arm, trying to anchor herself.

"Are you feeling the pull?"

"I think so, just now." Her voice grew husky, newly altered pupils going wide. "My *bones* felt heavy and for a moment all I could hear was the sea. Is it always like this?"

"Not always, only if we stay on land for too long." It was all Pasha could do not to pick Ally up and carry her into the pool. But, just like when she was facing her fear, Ally needed to take those first steps without Pasha's help.

They moved to the edge of the water. Ally peered at her reflection in the glassy surface, fingers drifting up to touch the spiral of scales that ran over one cheek. "My pattern is different from yours."

"If it helps, you still have your eyebrows."

Ally laughed. "It's probably for the best."

"Come on." Pasha took her hand, and they stepped into the lagoon together. Ally was totally unafraid, tugging Pasha's arm to move faster. She was so proud of Ally; it made her chest ache.

When they were waist-deep, Ally let go of her and dove under. Pasha followed, hardly noticing when her own tail unfurled behind her. She kept her full attention on Ally. Tremors rocked through Ally as her new body tried to figure out what to do. Pasha circled her, ready to move in if it looked like Ally was going to hit the cave wall. When the first spindly thread appeared on Ally's skin, Pasha felt her own energy surge to answer. Something that had been weighed down inside of Pasha for centuries was cut loose, and a wild arc of white-hot energy shot down her arms and out her fingertips before she could even register its presence. The arc blended with the dozens of tiny threads running down Ally's body, pulling them into a thick band that was finally strong enough to bind her legs together.

Ally curled into herself, crying out as a ring of scales sprouted around her waist and enveloped her new tail in sparkling blue armor. Her spine twisted, and another flash left Pasha of its own accord. It formed a bubble around Ally and compressed inward. As the last of it sank into Ally's skin, her fins appeared. The webbing was the same azure shade as her first scale. Like Pasha, Ally had two pelvic fins, but they were longer and reached further down her hips. She had no dorsal fin running the length of her tail, instead there was a set of smaller fins where the backs of her ankles used to be.

And her fluke. Pasha's lips parted at the sight of the ribbonlike fins that dipped up and back down into a curved notch wider than her own. The colors melted from azure at the base to streamers of copper flowing beneath her. She was magnificent.

Ally floated limply in the lagoon, the water going calm around them again. Slowly, her breathing evened out, and she stretched her arms overhead, inadvertently flexing her fins as well. The movement caught her attention, and Ally finally saw her tail. A flurry of bubbles escaped her lips as she twisted and turned, trying to see herself from every angle. She ran her hands over the dip in her waist where her skin ended and the scales began, fingers skimming across sensitive pelvic fins, then back to the body of her tail.

Pasha waited for Ally to finish before she said anything. The urge to close the distance between them was a living thing roaming beneath her skin. She had to bite her lip to keep from spouting every word of adoration that whirled through her brain.

Finally, Ally looked around and found Pasha across the pool. Her voice filled Pasha's head. "Pasha... I never imagined it would be like this."

"Neither did I," she admitted. "But are you happy?"

"Happy?" Ally looked down at herself again and shook her head.

Pasha's heart sank. One of her greatest fears was that Ally would hate her new body. Ally as a mermaid was one of the most beautiful sights Pasha had ever seen, but if Ally didn't feel the same...

With a wild cry, Ally flung her arms overhead and twirled through the water. Her hair swirled about her head while the iridescent ribbons of her fluke danced and fluttered beneath her. When she came to a stop, Pasha felt lightheaded with relief. The pure joy on Ally's face banished any lingering doubts from Pasha's mind.

Unable to stay away any longer, Pasha swam towards Ally just as she was trying to do the same. Ally flipped her tail too hard, fins whipping behind her. They collided together and Pasha caught her around the waist. Ally's longer fluke curled over hers, scales scraping together as they steadied each other.

"I'm going to have to teach you how to swim all over again," Pasha laughed.

"I'm looking forward to it." Ally wrapped one arm around Pasha's shoulders and there was nothing but the water between them. Pasha didn't have much time to think before Ally kissed the streak of scales on her face, then her jaw, then her lips. Something bright thrummed through Pasha's veins and it took her a second to realize Ally's new body was trying to communicate with hers. *Mermaid language.* She hadn't felt that in so long. Pasha grabbed for the sensation again, but Ally returned from her trip down Pasha's neck to capture her mouth, and all other thoughts floated away. She could always teach Ally later; they had all the time in the world.

"That feels so different, I like it." Ally hummed inside her head, caressing Pasha's mind with a thread of raw desire. Pasha's spine went rigid, she was going to have to show Ally how to control that too.

Ally was apparently unaware of the torture she was currently inflicting on Pasha. "After you teach me to swim, again, we can go look for your family. I still hate what they did to you, but we'll go if it's what you really want. We have the map whenever we want to use it."

Gently pushing back the dark brown curls floating around Ally's head, Pasha said, "We might look for them one day, when you can handle a long journey. Or we might not. We could go anywhere we want, or we can stay right here. Wherever we are will be home, if you're there with me."

Ally cradled Pasha's face in her hands. "Until the sea runs dry."

Pasha's eyes burned and she squeezed them shut. Ally was going to make her cry more this year than she had in her entire life. "Until the sea runs dry."

Soft lips traced her eyelids, kissing the burn away. Pasha looked at Ally, she was intently studying Pasha's face. Probably taking note of things she hadn't seen as a human.

Pasha was content to let her look, for a while. When she tried to lean in for another kiss, Ally held her head still.

"What is it?"

"They're blue," Ally whispered.

"What's blue?"

"Your eyes, Pasha. They're *blue*. Dark blue, open ocean blue."

She blinked. "Ally, they've always been blue."

"This whole time I thought... sharks' eyes are blue, too, aren't they?"

Pasha turned her head, pressing her lips to Ally's palm. "You'll see for yourself."

CHAPTER SEVENTY-FIVE

Maher had always loved winter. His birthday fell during winter. There were countless holidays and festivals and warm fires in winter. Saprea didn't have the same kind of winters as most of the continent and the Birde Isles, but he loved those too. The first time Maher saw snow drifting through the sky in fluffy, white clumps, dusting everything it touched until the world was coated in crystalized sugar, only deepened his love of winter.

Unfortunately, winter no longer loved Maher. The frosty air that once exhilarated him now aggravated his shoulder more than any overexertion or late night. He felt the cold deep in the center of the joint like an invisible hand was holding a slab of ice there. Which made no sense, as the socket itself wasn't even hit by the electrified hunk of metal that punched clean through all those months ago.

Still, the cold made him ache from his shoulder up through the side of his neck. Sometimes down into his elbow. He was going to turn into one of those old men who could predict when snow was coming and announce it to anyone who would listen.

Sitting in Lord Kingfisher's study, his last meeting for the day, Maher eased farther back in his chair to take the pressure off. One of the advisors was prattling on about the negotiations taking place to relieve them of their previous fishing export obligations, now that they no longer had the 'miraculous and inexplicable' influx of fish around the Isles.

Maher shifted again, this man could apparently finish one sentence and begin another without a breath in between. He looked up and found Luthais watching him from across the table. One unexpected benefit from these meetings was that Maher was learning to decipher Luthais' minute facial expressions. For instance, the slight head tilt and almost imperceptible quirk of one brow essentially meant "alright?" Or possibly "what's wrong?" Also, in rare circumstances, "what the fuck are you doing?" Maher guessed this example was one of the first two, though he couldn't completely rule out the third. He used the fountain pen dangling from his fingers to point at his shoulder. Luthais did something Maher could only describe as nodding with his eyes.

He'd tried and tried to figure that one out, even practiced it in front of his mirror at night. Which accomplished nothing other than making bizarre faces at himself.

At the other end of the table, Gai finally interrupted the advisor's monologue. "Until we hear back from the rest of our allies, there's no point in speculating on surplus. I doubt we'll have any excess of fish for several seasons. We have to focus on feeding our own people and find other ways to make up for the lost catches."

"I agree," said Lord Kingfisher. "And I think this is a good place to stop for today."

"Thank all the gods and their grandmothers," Maher muttered under his breath as chairs scraped across the floor and papers rustled. He gathered his own things and slipped into the hall. The change in position and chance to rotate his shoulder helped, but Maher wondered if he'd have time to soak in a hot bath before he was due in the Lantern that night to meet Pimm. At least they'd made a full recovery, and celebrated by promptly taking up smoking again.

When Maher teased Pimm about resuming their habit, they'd simply shrugged, "Everyone has their vices."

Pimm and Maher were no closer to identifying the financial backers of the street crews that sprang up over the summer. Though most of them had gone quiet the last few weeks, Pimm suggested it was only a temporary respite. The Saprean coins were still showing up in businesses scattered throughout the city. If they could only find the *source*.

"You don't have to stay seated the whole time, you know," a deep voice said from behind him.

Maher glanced over his good shoulder, Luthais was leaning against the edge of a statuary alcove. For such a solid man, Luthais moved through the world on cat's feet.

"And pacing around the room wouldn't be distracting?"

He snorted. "Not as distracting as your chair creaking every ten minutes."

"Get me a more comfortable chair, then." He threw on the lazy smile that had become a part of his Intelligencer image. "Maybe a tufted piece with a wide back. I'm quite partial to green."

With a shake of his head, Luthais said, "I'm sure you can find your own chair and, if you do, I'm sure Father won't mind. By the way, a package was left for you on my new ship. I delivered it to your room before this meeting."

"A package?"

"Aye, First Mate Kamharida found it this morning." He ran a hand through his hair. "We're preparing to leave soon, for the trade delegation visits on the continent."

Maher didn't know which part of that statement to address first. "How did a package, for me, end up on your ship?"

"Don't know, but there was a trail of water leading from the desk in my cabin to the window." His eyes widened a fraction and Maher caught on.

"I see, well, must have been those pesky sea sprites again."

"Must have been."

"I'll see that they don't bother you on your voyage."

Luthais slid his hands into his pockets. "Think you have that much sway over such things?"

An awkward silence settled over them. Maher found himself unsure of what to say next. Their relationship had changed drastically in such a short time. Now Luthais' duties as Lord of Trade were taking him away for months. Possibly even a year.

And Maher was going to miss him.

"Bring me back something pretty."

"Aye, I'll do that." With a slight smile, Luthais started back down the hall.

"Wait!" Maher called after him. "How in all the gods' names did you get into my bedroom?"

"You left your door unlocked," he said without looking back. "Not a good habit for an Intelligencer to have."

Maher's mouth dropped open. He scanned the hallway, but at least no one else had been around to hear that.

He smirked. *Seven jokes total.*

A small bundle was waiting on Maher's dressing table, just as Luthais had said. Calling it a package was generous, really it was a rolled wad of canvas the size of his fist. Tucked beneath it was a folded piece of paper. His name was scrawled across the top at a sharp angle and there was an ink blot at the end of the last letter, as if the writer hadn't known when to lift the pen.

Maher unfolded the note, the top of the page was stamped with the Kingfisher crest. This came from the stationery aboard Luthais' ship. He held the paper close to the lamp, squinting at markings that barely counted as letters. As the message became clear, he felt a tug around the vicinity of his heart.

Dearest Maher, I've asked Pasha to write to you on my behalf, as I can't yet leave the sea. I've got my fins and I don't need to wear this anymore. It's your good luck charm now. You'd best take care of it, or I'll be cross with you. See you next year, darling. Love, Ally

Tearing the cloth apart, Maher smiled when he saw what was wrapped inside. A large shark tooth, polished black with age and secured onto a metal chain. Maher slipped the chain over his head, letting the tooth rest beneath his shirt. Warmth spread through his chest, sinking into his muscles and even soothing some of the ache in his shoulder. It was like Ally was there with him, her arm looped through his on a walk to town, or her head on his shoulder as they sat before the fire. Tears threatened to slip from his eyes, he blinked them back.

He started to fold the note, intending to keep it somewhere safe, then saw another line scribbled on the back.

If you're ever in trouble, just bring the tooth home. Someone will help.

Bring the shark tooth home? How exactly did one bring a fossilized tooth home?

Resolved to solve that riddle later, Maher decided to make time for that bath after all. There was no telling how late he would be out. Unpinning the magpie from the lapel of his waistcoat, he placed it in a little dish on the dressing table. He wouldn't risk losing it if his jacket were ever stolen again, and Ally had been onto something when she bought it for him.

By embracing the nickname that started as a term of endearment from Mama Bear and grew into a title whispered throughout the streets of the city, Maher had truly reinvented himself. He was no longer just the son of the Saprean ambassador, or the best friend of Lady Alphonsine Kingfisher. He was the Magpie of Kingsport. Intelligencer of the Birde Isles.

And now the real work would begin.

Maher stumbled back into his room at dawn. He blessed both Ally and Pasha for giving him the shark tooth. Whatever magical mermaid spell had been cast on it didn't matter, the necklace had kept the chill of the long night from totally sinking into his bones. Even Pimm had noticed he wasn't as bothered by his shoulder.

"Found a new remedy? Something I don't know about?" Pimm asked, smoke from a cigarette mingling with their breath fogging in the cold. "Or someone?"

Maher declined to respond.

Stripping off his coat and suit jacket, Maher turned to light the fire in his hearth only to find a small flame already burning. On his bedside table was a lit candle, nearly melted to the end. Next to that, was a small jar and a slip of paper.

Maher sank onto the bed and examined the jar. The label was from one of the apothecaries in town, near the wharf. He picked up the note. It wasn't long, and it wasn't signed, but he knew well that blocky hand that not even years of writing tutors could refine.

Liniment. Easier to find than a tufted green chair. You lock your closet and leave your bedroom open. Clearly the clothes are more important. Tell Mrs. Thorley you want a door connecting the two, so you'll remember to lock both rooms.

Cracking the lid, Maher held it beneath his nose and inhaled. The balm was a masterpiece of blended herbs and spices. He caught notes of chamomile and lavender, ginger and rosemary, and... a chuckle started low in his chest, growing until Maher was laughing so hard his sides hurt. They were all the usual ingredients except for the last. Pine.

PASHA

CHAPTER SEVENTY-SIX

Pasha and Ally lay curled together beneath the mural in the great cavern. It had felt odd to Pasha, the idea of them sleeping in the chamber she'd once shared with Pallagia. But Ally had understood and suggested this place until they decided to sleep elsewhere.

So Pasha had built up a nest of sand and seaweed, trying to make it as comfortable as possible. Ally rested on her side, one plump arm tucked beneath her head. Pasha molded herself to Ally's back, their flukes overlapping and fingers intertwined atop Ally's stomach.

It amused Pasha how Ally still breathed like a human while underwater, her chest rising and falling in a steady rhythm. While Pasha's only moved if she was excited or upset. She didn't mind either way; watching Ally sleep peacefully here with her beneath the island reassured Pasha that this was real.

"Pasha," Ally yawned. "Go to sleep. You can stare at me all you want tomorrow."

Laughing softly, Pasha brushed a kiss over her temple. "Yes, sweetheart."

Settling back down, Pasha smiled when Ally's thumb swept lazily over the back of her hand. Totally content for the first time that she could remember, Pasha finally drifted off.

In her mind's eye, Pasha was a part of the caves that ran beneath the big island. She flowed through the rock, between every crevice. Her energy expanded to fill the empty spaces, bringing back memories of every cavern and tunnel, every grain of sand. Each bone trapped inside the stone called out to her.

The tombs were the loudest. Generations of mermaids buried together. Their souls returned to the sea, but their bones remained behind. They'd never heeded her call before, even when Pasha had lost control. Now they were shouting, clamoring for her attention.

It's here. It's here...

Here with us. Keep it safe.

Pasha stretched more of herself down, down, down until she reached the tombs. When she passed through the stones blocking the entrance, the voices crashed over her in a wave. The words ran together until Pasha heard only the droning undercurrent echo. A sharp pang started behind her eyes and wrapped around her head. Still, she pushed through the noise, deeper through the long chamber lined with graves. The further Pasha went, the more pain shot through her skull and down her shoulders.

Finally, Pasha reached the end, a wall of stone that at first appeared to be a natural part of the cave. Until she pulled back and saw the intricate pattern woven into the rock. A pattern filled with bones.

There were bones from many creatures she recognized, and others she didn't. But the middle skeleton she knew as well as her own, a mermaid. Reaching for the delicate bones at the base of her fluke, Pasha had a sudden flash of the carvings she and Ally had found. The bird-women losing their wings and growing those serpentine tails. The lines curving out of their mouths, the humans they'd taken, the mermaids fighting them out of the sky.

The voices pushing in around her hit a fevered pitch. Pasha connected with the wall; the voices all dropped away into a tense silence. Watching. Waiting to see what Pasha would find. One blink and Pasha was on the other side of the wall of bones. Darkness enveloped her, not even the glowing corals grew in this place.

A faint halo of light began to take shape in the middle of the space. This wasn't like any energy she'd felt before. Something about it was deeply, profoundly *wrong*.

The thing that lay within the halo began to take shape. Pasha wanted to leave. It didn't matter that this thing was not, nor had it ever been, alive. Pasha was no good at sensing metals, but the tang of iron hung heavy in the sealed chamber. Whatever this was, it was easily as long as her and twice as wide. Pasha tried to back out through the wall and couldn't. She tried again, pushing with all her might, but the barrier held firm.

The light brightened and the pounding in her head doubled, but she was part of the caves and had no hands to cover her eyes.

Let me out. She demanded, feeling for the bones embedded in the stone. *Let me out, now.*

Designs stamped into the rounded metal caught her eye, and that feeling of wrongness intensified. Pasha threw herself against the wall.

Let me out! This time the bones actually pushed back, propelling her closer to the thing and its sickly glow.

Pasha…

LET ME OUT!

"Pasha!" Ally shouted. "Wake up!"

Pasha's eyes flew open, roaming wildly until she found Ally's face.

"Listen to me, Pasha, you were having a nightmare." Ally ran her palms over Pasha's shoulders and down her arms. "You're alright."

She was awake. Ally was there. She should feel relieved, but something still weighed heavy on Pasha's mind.

"There's something wrong," she whispered. "I can *feel* it."

"Is it like when we were beneath Dare's ship?"

"No, the energy from that machine was unnatural, but this is… old."

"Old?"

"Ancient. And hungry. As if it were asleep for a long time, and now it's waking up." Pasha recounted everything she'd seen in her dream. "I thought it was only here, in the caves, but it's everywhere."

Ally cupped her face. "Do you think it has some connection to the ghost ships?"

"I don't know. Maybe. I can't…" Pasha bit off her own words as pain shot through her skull again.

Helping her sit up, Ally wrapped her arms around Pasha, and soon their energies were mingling together. Warmth flooded Pasha's chest and eased her headache.

"Thank you," She sighed into the soft column of Ally's neck. "What do you think all of this means?"

"I'm not sure, maybe breaking the turbine only solved part of the problem. But like I promised you before, we'll figure out what's causing this and put a stop to it."

Pasha shifted until her lips found Ally's. The kiss was slow and sweet. How had she lived so long without this? And though this new worry had taken root at the back of Pasha's mind, Ally's companionship was a reminder that she wouldn't have to face any of this alone.

EPILOGUE

The closer the creature swam to her quarry, the more the green scale embedded into her forearm throbbed. It recognized the energy surrounding this place, it called to its kin.

She'd given up much to have the scale and the power it provided. All the pain, all the degradation, every moment of torment would be worth it when they were finally free of the cage built by the mermaids.

Sneering at the scale one last time, she whipped her long, tapered tail. Shooting through the water too fast even for the fish to notice. She banked down and the shadow of the ship following in her wake gradually blended with the murkiness of the sea. A small sphere of light lit the way, pulled along by the scale.

At this depth, she encountered creatures that thrived in the dark. Oddly shaped things with reaching appendages, translucent skins, and opaque eyes. But even these creatures were instinctively giving a certain place on the seafloor a wide berth. And something else was lurking nearby, something much older and meaner than the rest, yet they were also keeping their distance. Perhaps it would be helpful to make their acquaintance before leaving the area.

When she reached the boundary of the energy calling to her stolen scale, it was easy to understand why. Here everything was tainted with a delicious blend of bitterness and rage. And the slightest undercurrent of fear.

Sweet, sweet fear. How long had it been since she'd tasted that drought of her own making?

Pushing through the miasma, she grew the sphere until everything within its limits was illuminated. There, suspended in the same posture in which she'd died, was the one they'd been searching for.

Well, died wasn't quite right, because she wasn't quite dead. The humans had forgotten one of their earliest lessons: The sea would not keep the dead with nothing to weigh them down.

And the mermaid that did this must not know the true limits of her power. That was a useful bit of knowledge to have.

Swimming right up to where the body rested, the creature reached into the pouch secured around her neck and withdrew a scale in the same shade of green as the one in her arm. When the scale was against the body's skin, she brought up her arm and pressed both together. White hot agony laced up her arm and down her spine. The energy constricted around them, almost to the point of suffocation.

Just when she felt like her body was going to split apart, the pain vanished. Pulling her arm down, she watched carefully as tremors and twitches rolled through the body. The head lolled forward, then lifted as movement started behind the eyelids.

Slowly, she raised her head and then the creature was looking into eyes a paler shade of green than her own.

She smiled and the scales glowed. "Hello Captain."

ACKNOWLEDGEMENTS

I almost can't believe this is happening. The second book in a series that is so dear to my heart is going out into the world.

To my friends, parents, and family, thank you so much for cheering me on since this journey started. Even those of you who aren't usually fantasy readers have given this series a chance, and I couldn't be more grateful.

To my fabulous beta and sensitivity readers, you know I couldn't do this without your feedback! Thank you so much for your time and for dealing with a much shorter reading period this time around!

To my critique partner and fellow writer, Toni, can you believe we're on book 2 of this series? Seems like just yesterday I was trying to describe the idea to you in a way that made sense and now here we are. I know we don't get to see each other often, but I value our friendship more than you know!

To my editor Rowe, I can't say enough about how much I love working with you. I'm so proud of the books we are creating together.

To Foraoise, Captain Dare's namesake, and my amazing character artist, Celipher, you both are just the best. And I'm holding you to our travel plans!

To my cover artist Sandra at Maldo Designs, I've lost count of the number of people who have said they love the covers for this series! I hope we get to work together on many more.

To my map artist Rachael at Cartographybird, you took probably one of the worst sketches in history and made it into the gorgeous maps that represent this world that only existed in my head for so long. I hope we can work together again!

To Jessie at Book Blurb Magic, I freely admit I wouldn't have been able to write the blurbs for this series without you.

As always, I have to thank my wonderful online community of writers and readers. I'm always so excited to see you reaching for your own writing goals!

Last, but not least, thank you so much to everyone who read and loved and shared *To Kiss the Sea*. Knowing that my characters and their stories resonated with so many of you gave me the confidence to keep going, even when 'Imposter Syndrome' reared its ugly head. Like I said, this book is really for you.

INDEX: PLACES

Index of all places in *To Brave the Deep*

<u>The Known World</u>

The Birde Isles (bird): Capital: Kingsport (kings-port); Symbol: Kingfisher bird holding one fish in its beak; Worship: Henotheism (The Goddess of the Sea and her messengers); A collection of islands off the east coast of the continent, the three main territories are Kingfisher Island, Swan Island, and Gull Island; They are the only stopping point on the Unending Sea crossing, built into a bustling trade hub by Gaius Kingfisher I.

Balah (bah-la): Capital: Ehlafi (Eh-lah-fee); Symbol: Stag; Worship: Polytheistic Trio of Deities (Sun, Moon, & In-Between); Prosperous country on the southeastern end of the Split Sea; Known for cultivating beautiful gardens and home to many world-renowned jewelers; Strong Birde Isles ally.

Saprea (say-pree-ah): Capital: Laleseir (lah-lei-seer); Symbol: Double flower tulip; Worship: Polytheistic pantheon of deities, varied by region; Large, mid-continent nation that relies heavily on trade; Their major export is textiles and they hold a strong influence over fashion trends; Political intrigue runs rampant through much of the country.

Fraolland (fray-oh-lund): Capital: Laivastho (Lah-ee-vahs-thoh); Symbol: Crossed cannons; Worship: Nature based; Located at the northeastern end of the Split Sea; They hold a large territory on the Zavatleo and Saprean borders, a holdover from the old Continental Wars; Powerful naval presence, they hold the highest number of warships on the Eastern Sea.

Meredia (mare-eh-dee-ah): Capital: Pravil (prah-vill); Symbol: Crossed gavel and quill; Worship: Henotheism; Western neighbor to Balah; High level of control at the mouth of the Split Sea; They have a strong, but strictly regimented, arts culture; Generally more concerned with their own affairs over mutual needs; Those raised in the capital tend to call it New Pravil.

Tjordun (sch-ohr-doon): Capital: Midthe (mid-teh); Symbol: A horse with an empty saddle; Worship: Polytheistic pantheon of deities; Shares the inner Split Sea border with Fraolland and Meredia; Strong ally with Balah, they control most land travel from the Eastern Sea coast to the Split Sea coast; Tjordun horses are said to be the finest in the Known World.

Utollmir (oo-toll-meer): Capital: Darajha (dah-rah-ha); Symbol: Circle of waves around the sun; Worship: Ancestral; The largest southern nation on the west side of the Split Sea, they are a major stopping point on the Southern Strait; Utollmir sailors learn to sail through the powerful Strait currents and are often sought after by foreign crews; There is a prominent farming culture throughout the inland portions of the country.

Kharabo (kh-air-ah-boe): Capital: Botsa (boat-sah); Symbol: Crossed scrolls in front of a flowering tree branch; Worship: Ancestral; Landlocked northern neighbor of Utollmir, also their strongest ally; Known for the Great University at Botsa and multiple advancements in modern science; First nation on the continent to implement education for all citizens.

Char-range (ch-ah-r-raynj): Capital: Illsik-yun (ill-si-ck-yoon); Symbol: Mortar & pestle filled with various herbs; Worship: Deism; The largest country on the continent, Char-range takes up the entire west coast and has the strongest naval presence on the Unending Sea; Known historically for alchemy, later channeled those skills into mass herb farming and production of concentrated oils.

Teratsu (teh-rah-tsoo): Capital: Ine (ee-neh); Symbol: Three trees of staggered age framed by a mountain; Worship: Mix of Deism and Non-theism (ethics based); Landlocked country between Char-range and Zavatleo, the country is mountainous and heavily forested; Teratsu controls the largest mining interest on the continent and are known for a specialized type of woodworking that integrates metal throughout each piece.

Nuvwaan (noov-wa-ahn): Capital(s): NuvLunsoh (noov-loo-n-soe) (Left Star) & NuvDamseh (noov-dahm-say) (Right Star); Symbol: A constellation with stars representing each island; Worship: Celestial; A collection of islands, the two largest are connected by a string of smaller land masses called the Bridge of Islands; Their closest neighbors are Utollmir and Char-range; Known for beautiful coastlines, secluded coves, and export of rare fruits.

Agriya (ahg-ree-yah): Capital: Muevat (Moo-eh-vah); Symbol: An ornate metal brazier with high flames; Worship: Nature based; A smaller nation that sits in the middle of Saprea's southern border, they have had tensions in the past over access to the Southern Strait; Primary exports include carmine powder and other paint pigments; Known for elaborate funeral processions that include the use of massive decorative pyres to burn the dead. People will travel to Agriya just to say they've witnessed one of their funerals.

Myrre (meer-ay): Capital: San Aveth (sahn-ah-vett); Symbol: Multiple hands joined together in a circle; Worship: Mixed, largely taken from their surrounding neighbors; Smallest and newest nation on the continent, they broke off from Agriya more than a century ago. They border Saprea and Agriya, and control the western shore of the mouth of the Split Sea; There is a strong culinary culture, many professional cooks will travel to Myrre to study their methods.

Zavatleo (za-vaht-lay-oh): Capital: Straihorn (stray-horn); Symbol: Two bulls locking horns; Worship: Henotheism; Closest ally to Teratsu, they boast the northernmost settlement ranging into the expanse of largely uninhabited northern tundra; Lost their entire territory along the Split Sea to the Fraollish during the Continental Wars; Known for hardy livestock breeding, also their biggest export.

The Riddles: Capital: Unknown; Symbol: Unknown; Worship: Unknown; Volcanic archipelago known for pink sands and clear seas; The Riddles are surrounded by an abnormal water formation, known to most sailors as The Currents, that makes sailing to the islands nearly impossible unless the crew includes someone who has made the passage before; Mostly isolated for centuries, only in the past decade have their uniquely designed ships been making the passage across the Unending Sea to trade at major ports like those in the Birde Isles. But, those who make the crossing remain secretive about their homeland; From a young age, Riddle Islanders will cap a portion of their teeth with gold.

Major Bodies of Water

Eastern Sea, Western Sea, Split Sea, Southern Strait, Unending Sea, the Fraollkin Inlet.

INDEX: CAST OF CHARACTERS

Index of all named characters in *To Brave the Deep*

The Sea

Birde Isles Shoal:

   Pasha (pah-shah): Mermaid; Last member left in the Birde Isles shoal; Location of Pasha's remaining kin: Unknown. (she/her)

   Pallagia (pah-la-gee-ah): Mermaid; Member of the Birde Isles shoal; Pasha's older sister; Deceased. (she/her)

   Nerys (neh-riss): Mermaid; Elder of the Birde Isles shoal; Location unknown. (she/her)

   Hama (ha-mah): Mermaid; Member of the Birde Isles shoal; Cousin to Pallagia and Pasha; Location unknown. (she/her)

The Manor

The Kingfishers:

Gaius Kingfisher I (guy-uhs): Former Lord of the Birde Isles; Ally's great-grandfather; Deceased. (he/him)

Gaius Kingfisher III: Current Lord of the Birde Isles; Father to Gaius IV, Luthais, Calder, and Alphonsine. (he/him)

Glenna Kingfisher (glen-nah) Former Lady of the Birde Isles; Mother to Gaius IV, Luthais, and Calder; Deceased. (she/her)

Rochelle Kingfisher (roh-shel): Current Lady of the Birde Isles; Mother to Alphonsine; Step-mother to Gaius IV, Luthais, and Calder. (she/her)

Gaius "Gai" Kingfisher IV: Eldest Kingfisher child; Heir to the Birde Isles title by birth order; Ship: None. (he/him)

Luthais Kingfisher (loo-tye-iss): Second-eldest Kingfisher child; Lord of Trade by appointment; Ship: the *Pike*. (he/him)

Calder "Cal" Kingfisher (kal-dur): Third-eldest Kingfisher child; Sea captain and Birde Isles trade representative; Ship: the *Wave Skipper*. (he/him)

Alphonsine "Ally" Kingfisher: (ahl-fahn-seen/ahl-lee): Youngest Kingfisher child; Only child to Rochelle and Gaius III; Ship: None; Maher's best friend. (she/her)

The Villaons:

Khafra Villaon (kah-frah : vill-ay-on) : Saprean ambassador to the Birde Isles; Maher's father. (he/him)

Maher Villaon (Ma-hehr): Khafra's only child; Also known as the Magpie of Kingsport; Ally's best friend. (he/him)

Staff:

Mrs. Thorley (thorr-lee): The Kingfishers' housekeeper. (she/her)

Kingsport

The Lantern:

Mama Bear: Owner of the Bear's Den, a private, green lantern afterhours club; Given name unknown; Friend of Maher. (she/her)

Pimm: Door guard at the Bear's Den; Friend of Maher; Origins unknown. (they/them)

"Barkeep": Bartender and general strong-arm at the Bear's Den; Originally from Swan Island. (he/him)

Olga (ol-guh): Kitchen maid at the Bear's Den. (she/her)

Dr. Tambara (tahm-ba-rah): Physician kept on payroll by the Bear's Den. (she/her)

The Madam: Owner of the black lantern establishment; Mama Bear's mother; Given name unknown. (she/her)

Marielle (mar-ee-ell): Gunfighter; Employee at the black lantern; Originally from The Riddles. (she/her)

Eustace (yoo-stuhs): Door guard of the black lantern; Dislikes Maher on principle. (he/him)

Kit Naumenko: Former employee at the Whistle & Bells orange lantern club; Assistant to Barkeep at the Bear's Den; Originally from Zavatleo. (he/him)

Archie (aa-chee): Owner of the Whistle & Bells orange lantern club. (he/him)

Temple of the Sea:

Eschina (eh-schh-ee-nah): Former Head Priestess in the time of Gaius Kingfisher II; Deceased. (she/her)

Aithne (eye-ehth-ne): Former Head Priestess; Studied under Eschina; Deceased. (she/her)

Esa (ee-sah): Current Head Priestess; Ally's former tutor; Studied under Aithne. (she/her)

Citizens:

Ms. Orel (oh-rell): Elderly tenant in Pimm's Northern district building; Originally from Zavatleo. (she/her)

Bernhard (burn-hard): Tenant in Pimm's Northern district building; Indeterminate age; Originally from Tjordun. (he/him)

Parvan Dayal (pah-r-van : duh-yahl): Head of the Birde Isles trade guild. (he/him)

Edgar Dayal: Parvan's husband; They love to wear matching outfits. (he/him)

Su-Yonn (soo-yo-nn): Owner of Su's Perfumery. (she/her)

Su-Minn (soo-min): Su-Yonn's daughter; Helps her mother at the perfumery. (she/her)

Kamharida Anyanwu (kahm-ha-ree-dah : ahn-yahn-woo): First Mate of the *Pike*. (she/her)

Ga-Seung (gah-seh-yung): Bosun of the *Pike*. (he/him)

Anya (ah-n-ya): Barrelman of the *Pike*. (she/her)

Grant (gr-ant): Helmsman of the *Pike*; Deceased. (he/him)

Olebile (oh-leh-bee-leh): Crewmember of the *Wave Skipper*. (they/them)

Weams (weems): Crewmember of the *Wave Skipper*. (he/him)

August Tapper (aw-guhst): Birde Isles Trade Guild member; Has trade connections to Agriya through family. (he/him)

Beitris Tapper (bee-triss): Daughter of August Tapper. (she/her)

Thara (ta-rah): Former Agriyan ambassador to the Birde Isles, now retired; Related by marriage to the Tapper family. (she/her)

Etty (eh-tee): Thara's wife; Younger sister of August Tapper; Originally from Gull Island. (she/her)

Safiye (sah-fee-yeh) & **Latife** (lah-tee-feh): Twin sisters from Saprea who often follow Beitris' lead. (she/her)

Ealasaid (eal-ah-saych): Pallagia's lover; Deceased. (she/her)

The *Maiden's Revenge*

Foraoise Dare (fora-shuh): Captain of the *Maiden's Revenge*; Privateer; Origins unknown. (she/her)

Jon Dare: Former captain and privateer; Foraoise's husband; Deceased. (he/him)

Swain: Quartermaster (first mate) of the *Maiden's Revenge*. (he/him)

Smith: Crewmember of the Maiden's Revenge; Loyal to Swain. (she/her)

Frossard (froh-sah): Crewmember of the *Maiden's Revenge*. (he/him)

About the Author

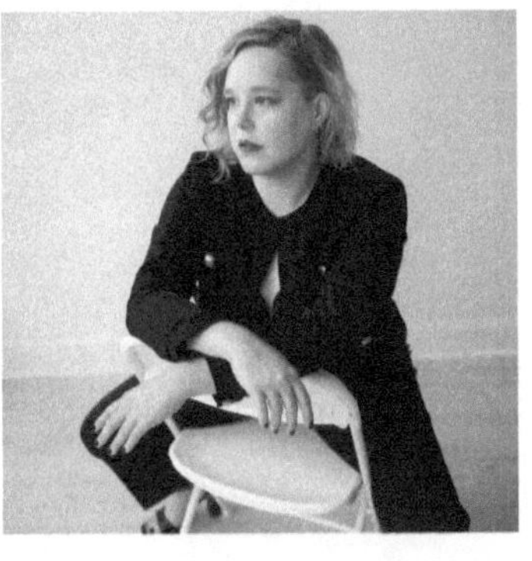

C.H. Carter is a fantasy author with a lifelong love of the genre in all its forms. In middle school, she wrote a fan letter to Tamora Pierce and received the most encouraging reply! That experience cemented her desire to become an author. (She also still holds out the hope they can meet in person one day!)

When not writing, you can find her working on a number of rotating projects (Crochet, anyone?) and obsessing over her two rescue dogs.

The Kingsport Chronicles is Carter's debut series.

THE KINGSPORT CHRONICLES WILL CONCLUDE
WITH BOOK 3: TO FREE THE WAVES

(COMING WINTER 2024/2025)

JOIN MY NEWSLETTER FOR PUBLISHING NEWS,
EVENT UPDATES, AND EARLY COVER REVEALS

WWW.CHCARTERWRITES.COM